# EUROPE
# IN THE BALANCE

STUDIES IN INTERNATIONAL POLITICS

(Editor: F. S. Northedge)

Other books in the series

*International Theory and European Integration*
by Charles Pentland

*Law and Power in International Relations*
by James Fawcett

*The International Political System*
by F. S. Northedge

# EUROPE
# IN THE BALANCE
*The Changing Context of*
*European International Politics*

ROBERT S. JORDAN
WERNER J. FELD

*faber and faber*
LONDON · BOSTON

First published in 1986
by Faber and Faber Limited
3 Queen Square London WC1N 3AU

Photypeset by Wyvern Typesetting Limited, Bristol
Printed in Great Britain by
Redwood Burn Limited, Trowbridge
All rights reserved
© Robert S. Jordan and Werner J. Feld, 1986

*British Library Cataloguing in Publication Data*
Jordan, Robert S.
Europe in the balance: the changing context
of European international politics.——
(Studies in international politics)
1. Europe——Foreign relations——1945–
I. Title   II. Feld, Werner J.   III. Series
327′.094 D1058
ISBN 0–571–13511–0

*This book is dedicated to our wives,*
*Jane Jordan and Betty Feld*

# CONTENTS

# FIGURES

# TABLES

# ACKNOWLEDGEMENTS

This book would not have been possible were it not for the support of Professor F. S. Northedge of the London School of Economics and Political Science, who arranged the initial contract. Persons who provided research assistance for earlier drafts are Thomas Bolle, David Ewing, Stuart Greenberg and J. Kenneth McDonald, all of whom are former colleagues at The George Washington University in Washington, DC. Valuable assistance in manuscript preparation was provided by the Faculty Support Unit of the College of Family, Home and Social Sciences of Brigham Young University, whose facilities were made available by Dean Martin Hickman. Jan Davis assisted also in manuscript preparation, and June Haley, then of the staff of The Atlantic Council of the United States, supplied data on the East–West military balance.

Our thanks must also go to the College of Liberal Arts of the University of New Orleans, and its Dean, Edward Socola, for a grant to cover some of the preparatory expenses; to Dean Donald Hendricks of the Earl K. Long Library at the University of New Orleans; and to the Department of Political Science at the University for making available a graduate student to assist in data research. Special thanks go to Captain Thomas Fitzgerald, USN, of the Department of Strategy, Naval War College, for commenting on portions of the manuscript and to Dr Robert S. Wood, Director of the Center for Naval Warfare Studies, Naval War College, for his general support and encouragement.

Inspiration for this book has come from our longstanding association with colleagues in North America and in Europe who share membership with us on the Committee on Atlantic Studies.

Newport, RI, and New Orleans, La.
July 1985
Robert S. Jordan
*Distinguished Visiting Professor of Strategy,*
*Naval War College (on leave from the University of New Orleans)*
Werner J. Feld
*Distinguished Professor of Political Science,*
*University of New Orleans*

# INTRODUCTION

Many of the books now written dealing with post-World War II European international politics and diplomacy have suffered from a natural tendency to regard the *status quo* of Europe, as defined in 1945–9, as the 'normal' state of affairs. The political evolution of a divided Europe during the course of the 1950s appeared to be sharply circumscribed by the mutual antipathy of the Superpowers. However, appearing in the late 1950s, and extending through the 1960s, the individualistic tendencies of the states of Eastern Europe and the nationalistic reassertion of France in Western Europe, rekindled the fires of nationalism elsewhere in the region. These potential changes in the configuration of Europe that were appearing on the horizon would affect inevitably the practice of European international politics and diplomacy. These changes were shaped during the 1970s and early 1980s by three dimensions of global as well as European politics.

First, we can discern the security dimension, in which the Superpowers, by virtue of their nuclear stand-off, have made it possible in varying degrees for their allies in Eastern and Western Europe respectively to pursue nationalistic policies in relative freedom from the hostile intentions of the opposing Superpower – this hostility being at the base of the motivation which aligned many of them with either Superpower. In the case of Eastern Europe, Soviet military coercion also provided a motivation. In the security dimension, neither Eastern nor Western Europe has been an active determinant of the overall power balance; rather, by withholding or denying occasionally their resources to their 'hegemonic' Superpower, and in the cases of Britain and France, retaining incremental national nuclear forces, they have been more the objects than the determinants of the balance. SALT I and unratified SALT II (leading to START and other nuclear arms testing and/or deployment negotiations), have helped to define the nature of the bilateral Superpower relationship. The Helsinki Accords, resulting from the

Conference on Security and Co-operation in Europe (CSCE), have also contributed to the potential for expanded 'bloc-to-bloc' interactions, even while contributing to bloc-to-bloc recriminations.

By virtue of this situation, a second dimension, whereby the states of Western Europe are still attempting to draw closer together in political and economic affairs, yet not repudiating the presence on the Continent of the United States in political and security affairs, has become more difficult to sustain. Similarly, the states of Eastern Europe, while continuing to acknowledge Soviet control and domination, have at times signalled the desire for a relaxation of the Soviet presence and have become more flexible in political and economic affairs *vis-à-vis* the West, although they remain dependent on the Soviet Union in political and security affairs. A third dimension appeared in the 1970s: the states of both Eastern and Western Europe are beginning to enter in a *mélange* of economic and perhaps political relationships with each other that in the long run could take on some quasi-institutional characteristics.

'Europe', therefore, can be seen and defined according to these three dimensions, which are not mutually exclusive. It cannot be regarded as entirely subservient to the Superpowers, nor obviously can it be regarded as a clearly re-emerging major presence – or 'Third Force' – in world politics. But the degree and nature of its coalescence, whether through Eastern and Western sub-regional groupings, or perhaps in a broader pan-European sense, is likely to alter the relationships of these states, whether in combination or singly, towards one or both of the Superpowers. Nonetheless, it is not yet clear to us what kind of 'Europe' will eventually emerge that would have a distinct and unambiguous self-identity. The special circumstances of what has been called a German 'nation' encompassing two German 'states' – one Eastern European and one Western European – contributes directly to this problem of a 'European' self-identity.

Looked at from an international relations theory perspective, we can also discern Europe as constituting part of a loose bipolar system[1] in which the United States and the Soviet Union constitute the 'poles' of the system, with Western Europe providing the supporting cast for the United States, and most of Eastern Europe playing a similar role for the Soviet Union. Moreover, in systemic terms, Eastern and Western Europe can be viewed as regional sub-systems of their own. Both the overarching bipolar Superpower-dominated system, and the two regional sub-systems have different sets of actors and dynamics. For the bipolar system, the various

states and certain security-enhancing intergovernmental organizations (IGOs), in particular the North Atlantic Treaty Organization
(NATO) and the Warsaw Treaty Organization (WTO), are the chief
actors. By strengthening collectively the military capabilities of their
member-states, these multilateral actors have provided the
dynamics for various bi-lateral as well as multilateral interactions
over the years.

For the two regional sub-systems, the states also, of course, are the
main actors, but a number of IGOs seeking to promote and to increase
the economic welfare of the peoples in their regions play important
roles and inject particular dynamics into the interactions of the two
sub-systems. The European Communities (EC) in Western Europe,
and the Council for Mutual Economic Assistance (CMEA) in Eastern
Europe are the most significant IGOs in this respect. Furthermore,
powerful and influential non-governmental organizations (NGOs),
especially large multinational corporations, may participate in the
interaction process. It is thus necessary in this book for us to pay
attention to the possibility of system transformation, both on the
bipolar and on the regional sub-system levels.

International relations scholars are not quite sure what constitutes
change in a system which eventually results in the transformation of
a particular system into another one. But clearly this implies 'that
something is happening through time and that what was true at one
time point is different at a subsequent time point'.[2] But while this
definition describes the process, it does not offer any clues as to what
magnitude of change is required to produce the transformation of a
system. The answer may well be that the change must be dramatic
and involve either drastic alterations in power distribution,
engendering major modifications in alliance patterns, or the disap-
pearance of system actors and the emergence of new actors. Such
events would restructure fundamentally the existing interaction
process and would have major influences on system dynamics.
System transformations can thus be viewed as comprising resulting
major upheavals produced from historical or short-term discontinuities. In the West, the prospect of the French withdrawal from
the NATO military structure, Brandt's *Ostpolitik*, or Greece's periodic
non-cooperation in NATO, and in the East the Polish Solidarity crisis
and the earlier Czechoslovak Prague 'Spring', were once thought to
harbinger such drastic alterations, but the reality of the Superpower
domination of their respective spheres of influence continues to
overcome such discontinuities.

A stark example of the transformation of the Superpower bipolar systemic relationship and their sub-regional alliances would be nuclear war. The consequences of such a holocaust are likely to be such tremendous casualties and devastation that either one or both Superpowers would cease to function as organized societies. This could spell the end of the existing global bipolar system, but it is unclear what kind of system could replace it. Perhaps some kind of polycentric system would emerge, consisting of various power centres of differing magnitudes, or alternatively a strictly hierarchical system dominated by the Superpower that emerges the most intact from the nuclear holocaust.

Less dramatic may be economic changes in the regional sub-systems. If the hopes of some Europeans were fulfilled, and the European Communities were to develop into a political union with the member-states surrendering much of their sovereign statehood, Western Europe would become a very different sub-system. It would consist of one large, economically and politically very powerful yet pluralistic federated national unit, coexisting alongside a very few, very small economically and politically weak states lining its perimeter, especially along the Eastern boundary of the sub-system. This would mean that not only the political dynamics and interaction processes in the Western Europe regional sub-system would change radically, but also the dynamics and interaction patterns in the bipolar system as a whole would be affected materially. A similar situation might evolve if CMEA were given greatly enhanced authority at the expense of its members, even if the Soviet Union, the dominant member, were to retain a powerful national influence.

Thus we not only seek to describe and assess from a historical perspective Europe's evolution and its relations with the two Superpowers, we also seek to evaluate some of these conditions from a theoretical point of view. This will permit us to draw specific conclusions where appropriate, and perhaps offer tentative projections for the future based on the evidence discovered and on the evaluations flowing from this evidence.

NOTES

1  See Morton Kaplan, *System and Process in International Politics* (New York: John Wiley and Sons, 1957), pp. 36–43.
2  Dina A. Zinnes, 'Prerequisites for the Study of System Transformation', in Ole R. Holsti, Randolph M. Siverson, Alexander L. George, eds., *Change in the International System* (Boulder, Colorado: Westview Press, 1980), pp. 3–22, on pp. 16–17.

# I

# The Changing Political Environment
of Europe

The notion of the balance of power, from the Congress of Vienna in 1815, which ended the Napoleonic wars and led to the creation of the Concert of Europe, to the political demise of Bismarck in 1890, was a constant element of European international politics and is still very much with us today. It has not been an institutionalized system of European political interaction; instead, the balance of power notion recognized that the European state system operated according to the interaction of the *relative* power of its members. Thus, the history of Europe from 1815 is in large part an account of how international change was accommodated by war or by diplomacy according to the balance of power principle. As mentioned in the Introduction to this book, and discussed further in chapters 2 and 7, a somewhat similar situation as regards the states of Western Europe and their role *vis-à-vis* the Superpowers, has existed in the period since World War II.

The operation of the balance of power principle seemed very simple in theory. Any state or combination of states intent upon expansion or aggression had to reckon with the fact that other states might, if their own interests (whether territorial, dynastic, or ideological) were sufficiently threatened, come to the aid of the intended victim. The rationale for states banding together to limit or to adjust the expansionist tendencies of other states was also simple: it was in no state's interest to allow any other single state to achieve a preponderance of power or hegemony over Europe. This has, since its intervention in World War I, also been the policy of the United States toward Europe.

In part of the nineteenth century, Britain aspired to play the role of the balancer of competing national aspirations in the international politics of Europe. The so-called Congress System stumbled irretrievably when, after 1890, two hostile coalitions were formed that eventually triggered a suicidal war in Europe from 1914 to 1918 which was resumed between 1939 and 1945.

Also, throughout the nineteenth century and until today, nationalism (or the impulse toward national self-interest which flows from nationalism) has had a profound effect on the balance of power. The process of transforming the loyalties of the various ethnic, social and economic interests within a state into a unity which would give primary allegiance to the state itself evolved in two distinct ways during the nineteenth century.

Initially, the nationalism of the various states of Europe had been aroused by the external military and ideological threat posed by the French Revolution and then by Napoleon, as well as fostered by the internal rationalization and unification of the Napoleonic Empire itself. As one scholar put it: 'Between 1789 and 1794 France changed from a country with many different outlooks and even languages to a single nation. France had created nationalism!'[1] By the latter half of the nineteenth century, the various ethnic nationalities of Central and Eastern Europe, subject minorities within the Austro-Hungarian and Turkish Ottoman Empires, espoused the cause of nationalism in order to assert their individual claims to national recognition and to an independent political existence.

The long-range effect of the dissolution of these empires as a consequence of World War I was that Central and Eastern Europe lay vulnerable to imperialistic expansionist designs. In Eastern Europe, the new states that were formed out of the Treaty of Versailles were especially weak and exposed to both Russia and to Germany. In contrast, Western Europe was not as weak, since these states, which were well-established, nationally homogeneous and relatively strong, after vacillating, perceived their direct military threat to be from a remilitarized Nazi Germany. Thus, a profound difference has existed between the nationalisms of such Western European states as France and Britain and the new or reconstituted Eastern European and Balkan states.

Nationalism in Western Europe by the twentieth century came to be identified not only with economic development due to industrialization, but also with the liberal democratic political principles that had evolved in response to the economic and social dislocations stemming from the spreading and intensifying process of this industrialization. As a result, the national states of Western Europe became the first of the modern nation-states and the leading industrial democracies. The more newly consolidated states of Germany and Italy, with differing types of industrialization, have wavered between authoritarianism and liberal democracy.

In regard to the Eastern European and Balkan states, the desire for national independence manifested itself in the struggle to obtain similar liberal democratic political reforms (such as written constitutions, controls on arbitrary governmental power, and guarantees for individual rights). But the one aspect of nationalism shared by all of these states which were created (or in the case of Poland, restored) out of the territories dominated by the Great Powers of the nineteenth century, was hostility to alien control, regardless of the forms of government which they actually came to possess. The issue of the nature and extent of the suitability for each state of various liberal democratic political reforms was still unresolved when these new states were conquered by Germany in World War II. But the force of nationalism combined with liberalism continued to assert itself after World War II in Soviet-dominated Central and Eastern Europe, as evidenced by the Berlin uprising of 1953, the Hungarian and Polish uprisings of 1956, the Czechoslovak crisis of 1968 and the Polish Solidarity crisis of the 1980s.

Looking at the question of nationalism from a slightly different perspective, we can also observe that there are some similarities between the ethnic, nationalistic unrest that resulted in the breakup of the Austro–Hungarian and Ottoman Empires and the ethnic, nationalistic unrest that lurks just beneath the political surface today in Central and Eastern Europe (and even in parts of Western Europe). (Figure 1.1 shows Europe prior to the unification of Italy and Germany and figure 1.2 shows Europe in 1871.)

### IDEOLOGY AND INTERVENTION

As described earlier, Europe in the immediate post-Napoleonic era was dominated by the Concert of Europe, which was a continuing coalition of Powers whose aims were to preserve the existence of all the members and their dynastic forms of government.[2] The English historian A. J. P. Taylor summed it up thus:

The great French revolution had left a legacy of three revolutionary causes: democracy, nationalism and socialism. In the later nineteenth century the first two of these causes ceased to be revolutionary. Democracy was the first to become respectable. . . . Germany and Italy achieved national unification. Thereafter nationalism became a right wing cause. The extreme

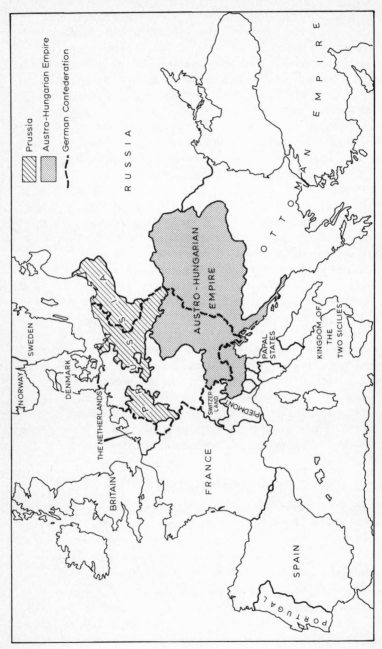

Figure 1.1 Europe prior to the unification of Italy and Germany

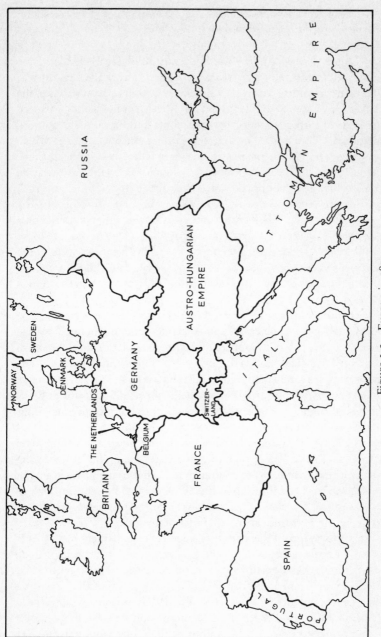

Figure 1.2  Europe in 1871

nationalists were now reactionaries and opponents of democracy. . . . Socialism was the only revolutionary cause left.[3]

The liberal democratic revolutions (outside of the Balkans) of the 1820s, 1830s and 1848 were reactions to the authoritarian regimes of the members of the Concert of Europe. Viewed retrospectively, the states of the Concert of Europe can be indicted for not having foreseen the general European trend toward ethnic nationalism and political liberalism. They were, in fact, fearful of both phenomena, which challenged political legitimacy based on heredity, and so the dynastic rulers impeded their development as much as possible. A question can also be raised about the peace-keeping ability of the Concert of Europe in view of the revolutionary outbursts throughout the remainder of the nineteenth century. On the other hand: 'For a hundred years there occurred no war of world-wide scope like those of the twenty-odd years after 1792. . . . The European wars of the nineteenth century produced shifts of power, but they were shifts within the European political system and did not upset that system as such.'[4]

It is important to recognize the distinction between the Europe dominated by a balance of power created and maintained by the states composing the Concert, and the general European political situation that had evolved during the nineteenth century. The Concert of Europe attempted to buttress its position by instituting a policy of intervention in states where liberal democratic political elements threatened autocratic, monarchical governments. This policy of intervention threatened the principle of the balance of power, as it entailed intervening in the domestic affairs of individual states. To Prince Metternich of Austria, for example, 'Rulers were the legitimate claimants to certain lands, hence to the government of peoples therein residing.'[5] It is interesting to note that the rationale of the so-called 'Brezhnev Doctrine' – the right of Soviet Communist military intervention in the member-states of the Warsaw Treaty Organization – could be paraphrased in reverse: 'Rulers [i.e., Communist Parties acceptable to the Soviet Union] are the legitimate claimants to the governments of peoples, hence to the territories of the people therein to be controlled.' The potency of the Concert's threat to the balance of power, though, had diminished when Britain declined to expand the notion of opposition to the prospect of a revolutionary France to the notion of the Concert's opposing *any* potential revolution in Europe. Performing the role of the balancer conformed more to Britain's interests. The reintegration of France into the monarchical states of Europe after the defeat of Napoleon thus weakened Britain's resolve to intervene automatically in Europe on the side of tradition and against political change.

Questions about the legitimacy of intervention for political purposes were first raised at the meeting of the Congress at Laibach in 1820, by the decision to grant Austria the right to restore order in Italy. Metternich was able to persuade Russia and Prussia to agree to his thinking, thereby creating an alignment of the conservative Central and Eastern European Powers. Britain stood opposed to intervention and France remained noncommital.[6] The situation reported immediately prior to the 1968 Soviet-led intervention might be seen in Czechoslovakia as similar. In this case, the German Democratic Republic (East Germany) and Poland strongly supported the intervention led by the Soviet Union, on ideological as well as their respective national interest grounds. Romania reportedly opposed the intervention and Hungary attempted to remain noncommital.

The failure to stabilize Europe along the lines of the *status quo* as defined in 1815 rested on the inability of the conservative states to institutionalize the political principles they shared. In contrast, in the mid-twentieth century, the two Superpowers that came to dominate Europe had effectively institutionalized the *status quo* of 1945–9, through their respective alliance systems, but both – and especially the Soviet Union – were unable to do so without a significant expenditure of national military effort. In the case of the United States, the desire to see Western Europe unified economically in such a way as to produce institutionalized forms of political co-operation has been up to now consistently frustrated. In the case of the Soviet Union, the desire to impose political conformity in Eastern Europe through direct or indirect military force has been consistently opposed by the peoples affected.

Between 1820 and 1850, Europe was subjected to the dynamic interplay of nationalism, conservatism and liberal democracy. The two multi-ethnic Austro-Hungarian and Turkish Ottoman empires had been placed under increasing stress as the various ethnic groups within these empires gave greater allegiance to themselves rather than to their respective imperial authorities. As a result, emerging ethnic nationalism came into direct conflict with those conservative forces favouring an institutionalized European *status quo*. Austria was particularly vulnerable:

All the central European revolutions threatened the Austrian Empire. Austria dominated northern Italy, and the Italian revolutionaries aimed to expel the Austrian forces. Austria was the presiding power in the German confederation, standing in the way of unification. The Emperor was also King of Hungary and extended his sway over the lesser peoples of eastern Europe. Austria represented tradition. The new order sought to combine nationalism and liberal constitutions. The European revolutionaries of 1848 aspired to achieve the French constitution of 1791.[7]

As mentioned above, equally important had been the aligning of nationalism and political liberalism. Even though the clash of nationalism and conservatism did not automatically throw nationalism into the arms of liberalism, the principles of liberalism were of themselves support for the political realization of ethnic national political independence. For example, the liberal notion of national self-determination – even though not necessarily carried out through open elections – became embodied in the revolutionary political aspirations of the various ethnic, or minority groupings.

Thus the coupling of nationalist aspirations with liberal democracy against conservative monarchical forms of government, was a crucial interaction in the mid-nineteenth century. Similarly, the coupling by the United States and its Western European allies of nationalist aspirations with liberal democratic principles against the Soviet-dominated authoritarian single-party dictatorships of the left (so-called Socialist or People's Democracies), in the latter half of the twentieth century has also been a strong force shaping European and Atlantic international politics, and will continue to be.

Two major trends emerged in the nineteenth century along with the coalescing of nationalism and liberalism in favouring an altered *status quo*. The first was geographic: Europe was split between the politically reactionary and authoritarian forces of the states of Central and of Eastern Europe, and the rising influence of the middle classes (the bourgeoisie) in the industrializing states of Western Europe. A similar distinction today can be seen between Eastern and Western Europe. A second trend was the drawing of new battle lines in the social conflict taking place. Even prior to the anti-monarchical revolutionary agitation of 1830, grievances against the entrenched aristocracy had unified the middle and working classes (the proletariat). The popular revolutions of 1830 in France, Belgium and Greece had shifted power from the aristocracy to the middle classes, leaving the working classes unsatisfied. Thus, the struggle for political power had taken on economic, class, national and hence ideological characteristics.

Nonetheless, in Western Europe – especially in Britain – many of the goals of the liberal democratic working-class revolutionaries were being realized through domestic political and economic reforms (i.e., revisionism) rather than direct revolutionary action. These states, however, were not inclined to let these liberal principles disrupt their relations with the more authoritarian and industrially backward empires of Central and Eastern Europe (including the Czarist Russian Empire). Britain could and did sympathize in the abstract with the liberal ideologues of Central and Eastern Europe, but in reality, the 'preservation of the Austrian state as a bulwark against Russian power' was of more immediate interest to Britain. Again the operation of European interstate relations emphasized the fact that the *relative* power of European states was the essential element in dictating degrees of stability and equilibrium, and not the institutionalization of a prescribed *status quo* or loyalty to a particular political ideology. With the invasion of Belgium by Germany in 1914, the diplomatic balance of power in Europe normally based on economic and military capabilities had turned into a contest of military power. A similar situation could now be emerging in Europe if the Superpowers cannot constrain their nuclear technological rivalry, which threatens to upset the relative power of both the Superpowers and their respective blocs.

### THE CONSEQUENCES OF WORLD WAR I

The consequences of World War I meant more than just the dissolution of the European system as it had existed since 1815. The action of the war itself signalled the end of two aspects of the European political tradition: the dissolution of the aristocracy as a ruling (as distinct from a reigning) class, and the beginning of the break-up of the overseas empires, bearing with it significant global consequences that have affected Europe for decades since.

World War I, which manifested the importance of Europe in world politics, also showed that European politics were no longer solely determined by Europe. The European balance of power had been destroyed, and this destruction was exemplified by more than the failure of the peace settlement to integrate a defeated Germany back into the international political system of European states. Now, non-European elements influenced the outcome of the struggle, in particular the United States.

With respect to the United States, the conception which President Woodrow Wilson held about how international politics should be pursued ran counter to the concept of the balance of power. His idea that the balance of power was to be replaced by a 'community of power' vested in a League of Nations, rested on the belief that the victorious Great Powers would pool their strength to preserve peace – i.e., collective security. The states of the world in general and Europe in particular, though, were not ready for such action. As a result, the relative balance of power of the states of Europe remained the primary determinant of national policy, but with the new consideration of the relative power of major non-European states as well.

Another aspect of what came to be called Wilsonianism was that popular sentiments favouring political liberalism and ethnic nationalism made them strong ideological as well as international political forces. Just as the emergence of weak national states in the mid-nineteenth century had affected the balance of power in Europe at that time, the desire to establish states in Eastern Europe and the Balkans on ethnic and linguistic lines in 1919 also created weak states and a weak international political system. As mentioned earlier, this ultimately paved the way for the rise of the Nazi dictatorship in Germany following on Mussolini's Fascist dictatorship in Italy that justified themselves on mixtures of political liberalism, class interest, and ethnic nationalism. (Figure 1.3 shows Europe after the peace settlements of World War I.)

The Treaty of Versailles thus proved unsatisfactory to victor and vanquished alike. The individual states of Europe had individual interests which they were convinced could best be safeguarded by putting self-interest ahead of any institutionalized collective interest as embodied in the League of Nations. The League concept that national force was only to be the *ultimate* deterrent, employed after international moral, economic, and, if necessary, military sanctions had failed to halt an aggressor, rested on the assumption that collective action would be seen as preferable to unilateral action. This assumption proved to be erroneous.

As pointed out above, the rising influence of non-European centres of national power during World War I had a profound effect on Europe during the inter-war period. In particular, the role played by the United States in the outcome of World War I inevitably meant that the United States would be a primary participant in post-war European international politics. But the subsequent absence of direct

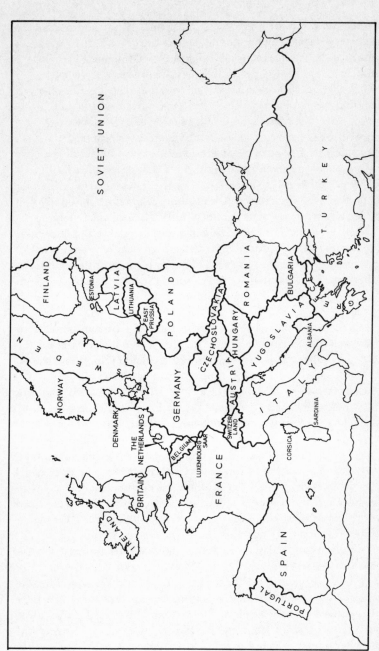

Figure 1.3 Europe after the peace settlements of World War I

United States political involvement, primarily but not exclusively because of its rejection of membership in the League, had as great an influence on the international politics of the inter-war period as a positive United States political involvement would have had.

The real question that existed in 1919 and that was not resolved according to President Wilson's conception, was: what would be the policy that the United States would form and follow toward a Europe already affected _in any case_ by its relative power? Even with the widespread popularity of President Wilson's liberal democratic political principles, and his formula for a 'just peace' as promulgated in the famous Fourteen Points, the United States failed to realize that its power was a necessary factor in a Europe in which the interaction of the relative power of its members still was, in the final analysis, the only effective means of achieving international political stability and equilibrium. This was true regardless of whether or not the interaction was expressed through the League of Nations or through some other means. Essentially, the United States did not want to recognize that it had become, among other things, a Great Power in Europe.

On the other hand, the leaders of the states of Europe had not perceived the extent to which World War I had destroyed the international political basis of Europe. As Hajo Holborn has stated: '. . . the depth of the revolutionary changes that World War I had caused in the social structure and attitude of nations was hidden from the view of the peacemakers.'[8] As in Europe after the defeat of Napoleon, an attempt, albeit half-hearted, had been made to institutionalize interstate relations. But the League of Nations was in practice, with the absence of the United States, more like an attempt to revive the coalition of European Great Powers along nineteenth-century lines than a new form of international politics to deal with the by-now global politics of the twentieth century. Being identified with the punitive or anti-German aspects of the Treaty of Versailles, in the end, of course, brought down the League.

In summary, a new worldwide international political system based on the rule of law, political liberalism and collective security thus did not emerge from the settlement of World War I. Neither the states of Europe nor the United States were prepared to sacrifice their own interests to those of an international body dedicated to the peaceful settlement of disputes. Europe was viewed during the interwar period as being in what E. H. Carr has called the 'twenty years crisis'. While some of the states of Europe may have wished to resume the pre-1914 balance of power form of international politics, their persistence in carrying on their traditional conflicts and rivalries through the League finally revealed the essential hypocrisy of their League membership. While it is true that ethnic nationalist aspirations advocated since the middle of the nineteenth century were finally recognized with the breakup of the multinational European empires, the disintegration of the old European system of monarchical states was so complete that the League was incapable of coping with the political, social and economic consequences of this breakup.

The Wilsonian dream of a Europe composed of liberal democracies thus resulted as much in international confusion as in international reconciliation. As a relatively passive participant in European affairs during the inter-war period, the United States was as much at fault in permitting this situation to occur as were the European states themselves. After a period of hesitancy, the United States finally mobilized its political will to cope with the changes in Europe which led to World War II by aligning itself against the totalitarianism of the Fascist dictatorships, and making common cause with the industrial democracies of Western Europe, and finally even with the Communist regime in the Soviet Union.

## THE FAILURE TO SETTLE THE PEACE IN EUROPE AFTER WORLD WAR II

After World War II, American persistence in continuing to base its policy toward Europe on the Wilsonian model also failed to produce a post-war reconciliation. The two major victors, the United States and the Soviet Union, soon fell to wrangling about how to arrange the political future of Central and Eastern Europe. The United States, for example, objected to what it considered were Soviet violations of an agreement reached at Yalta that the United States, the United Kingdom, and the Soviet Union ' "will jointly assist" the peoples liberated from the Axis "to form interim governmental authorities broadly representative of all democratic elements in the population and pledged to the earliest possible establishment, through free elections of governments responsive to the will of the people".[9]

The frustration of these operative principles, as evidenced by the takeover of the liberal democratic government in 1948, through a pro-Soviet Communist *coup*, of the government of Czechoslovakia produced strong anti-Soviet feelings in the United States. These feelings were due to conflicting national interests and to resentment of the nature of the totalitarian dictatorship of the Soviet Union. It was thought that the continuation of the 'natural' political evolution of Europe – i.e., a Europe composed of liberal democracies, but with political independence and territorial integrity guaranteed in this case by the Superpowers through the instrumentality of the Security Council of the United Nations rather than the discredited and defunct League – was being systematically frustrated by the Soviet Union, just as it had been nearly obliterated by the German and Italian (and also Soviet) dictatorships in the inter-war period and during World War II.

With the failure of the Superpowers to get along in the latter 1940s, each Power moved to consolidate its respective position in Eastern and Western Europe and to split Central Europe down the middle. This is discussed more fully in chapter 2. The result of this consolidation was the first effective institutionalization of an all-European *status quo* since the defeat of Napoleon. The international political system, as it affected Europe in the late 1940s, however, had undergone a major transformation since the days of Metternich and the Congress of Vienna. In the late 1940s the *European* international political system could no longer be equated with the *global* international political system.

As we have previously pointed out, the United States in the aftermath of World War I did not acknowledge its role as a European Power. In contrast, after World War II when it became clear that the Superpowers could not find a basis for mutual accommodation, there was no such abdication. The United States took the lead in opposing what appeared to be a clear threat to the European subcontinent by a single Power – the Soviet Union. Just as in the nineteenth century it had not been in Britain's interests to see Europe dominated by a single Continental Power, and so would move to counter any such threat, so likewise, briefly during its intervention in World War I but more clearly after World War II, the United States saw that no longer could it let Europe seek its own balance-of-power arrangements. Consequently, between 1945 and 1949, the United States transferred its distrust for the Fascist dictatorships to distrust of the Soviet Communist dictatorship, whose consolidation of power in Russia it had in fact earlier opposed. Thus, the deep-seated hostility between the United States and the Soviet Union became the touchstone of European international politics and the basis for a bipolarized international political system.

The United States exerted its influence and power in Western Europe to galvanize a united opposition to the threat of Soviet expansionism. From the viewpoint of the states in Western Europe, in 1945 and immediately thereafter, however, the threat to them was still perceived to come from Germany. This fear was expressed in the Dunkirk Treaty of 1947, which stipulated in article I that Britain would come to the aid of France in the event of France being threatened by Germany:

The High Contracting Parties will in the event of any threat to the security of either of them arising from the adoption by Germany of a policy of aggression or from action by Germany designed to facilitate such a policy, take . . . such agreed action . . . as is best calculated to put an end to the threat.

Building on the Dunkirk Treaty, in 1948 the Brussels Treaty was signed by Britain, France, Belgium, Luxembourg and the Netherlands (Benelux). This Treaty was also centrally concerned with Germany as well as with the Soviet Union, as indicated by article VIII:

At the request of any of the High Contracting Parties, the council shall be immediately convened in order to permit the High Contracting Parties to consult with regard to any situation which may constitute a threat to peace, in whatever area this threat should arise; with regard to the attitude to be adopted and the steps to be taken in case of a renewal by Germany of an aggressive policy, or with regard to any situation constituting a danger to economic stability.

In 1949 the United States and Canada joined with the Brussels Treaty Organization (BTO) to form the North Atlantic Treaty Organization (NATO), which also included Portugal, Iceland, Italy, Norway and Denmark. In 1951, Greece and Turkey joined; the Federal Republic of Germany (West Germany) was permitted to enter in 1955; and Spain is assuming full membership.

With the inclusion of the United States (and Canada) through NATO, the Western European coalition changed character. The preponderance of power possessed by the United States *vis-à-vis* its Western European allies changed the nature of the interaction of the relative power of the states of Western Europe. United States power, coupled with a threat perception that differed in both nature and degree from that of the Western European members, had converted the Western European coalition, concerned about Germany, into a

North Atlantic coalition conceived primarily to counter a threat from the Soviet Union.

NATO, in effect, guaranteed the states of Western Europe that the United States intended to protect them as well as itself against the hostile and apparently aggressive intentions of the Soviet Union and, by the early 1950s, a significant American military presence was restored in Europe itself to confront the Soviet Union.

NATO also affirmed that problems of national security for individual states could not be dealt with in isolation from other states. As Timothy Stanley, writing in 1965, observed:

Recent developments within the Atlantic alliance suggest that its members have been slow in adapting to the key historical trend in today's world – that the nation-state is becoming too small to accomplish its traditional purposes of military security and economic prosperity. Accordingly they have engaged in a halting search for a successor. [10]

The real question, though, was whether NATO's anti-Soviet posture, which bespoke a conventional military coalition albeit dominated by a single state, could also become an incipient form of what Mr Stanley termed a 'region-state'. [11] If so, would this region-state be primarily European – and Western European at that – or would it become an 'Atlantic' region-state? The history of NATO, viewed in terms of international politics, has provided no clear answer, partly because a Germany divided between East and West has produced an attitude among the people of the two Germanies of their being not only the point of division of Europe, but also the bridge toward a reunited Europe.

The British and the Americans, at the end of World War II, had hoped that Germany could be restored economically (but not militarily) in Central Europe, and that a liberal democratic Germany could be reintegrated into an international political system based on Soviet-American co-operation, thus avoiding the failures of the inter-war period. As the Potsdam Declaration stated:

It is not the intention of the Allies to destroy or enslave the German people. It is the intention of the Allies that the German people be given the opportunity to prepare for the eventual reconstruction of their life on a democratic and peaceful basis. If their own efforts are steadily directed to this end, it will be possible for them in due course to take their place among the free and peaceful peoples of the world.

In 1947, with a rupture appearing imminent between the United

States and the Soviet Union, partially caused by disagreement on how to treat Germany, the Truman Doctrine was conceived to oppose any Communist-led aggression, whether overt or covert, specifically in Europe but implicitly anywhere. As Robert Osgood has commented:

The Truman Doctrine, declaring that it must be the policy of the United States to support free peoples who are resisting attempted subjugation by armed minorities or by outside pressures, was the first explicit official recognition by the American government of its role as an active participant in power politics. Yet the full implications of the Doctrine were obscure because it was open-ended and provided no explicit limitations, means or priorities to indicate the extent of commitments and actions that the United States might undertake in carrying it out. Whether assistance to *free* peoples or opposition to communist aggression against *any* non-communist nation was to be emphasized, the Doctrine was an expansive definition of American security interests – a bold projection of wartime aims into the cold war.[12]

It was assumed at this time that once Soviet-inspired anti-liberal democratic tendencies could be effectively frustrated, in the first instance in Western Europe, but also to be hoped in Central and Eastern Europe, it would be possible to construct a European international political system that would restore the stability to world politics lost since 1914. This was not to be the case, however, either in Europe or elsewhere. The *de facto* dismemberment of Germany, the inability to do much about restoring the lands lost to the Poles from Soviet encroachments and lands lost to the Germans from Polish encroachments, the exclusion of liberal democratic political parties in the governments of the territories that came under the military and then political domination of the Soviet Union, and the inability of the wartime allies to agree on the implementation of the various agreements to settle the peace of Europe, led to the onset of the Cold War, which pitted the Superpowers against each other not only in Europe but throughout the world. (Figure 1.4 shows Europe and Germany at the end of World War II in 1945 and figure 1.5 shows Europe in 1984, after the consolidation of the rival political/economic and political/military blocs.)

Thus, the continuing commitment of United States power to Western Europe, which was formalized in 1949 through the North Atlantic Treaty and the subsequent creation of the North Atlantic Treaty Organization (NATO), meant that in security affairs the United States preferred to retain a direct rather than an indirect influence over the shape of Western European–Atlantic international

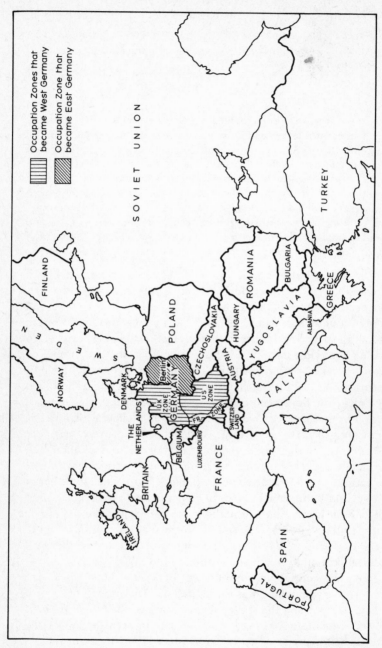

Figure 1.4 Europe in 1945

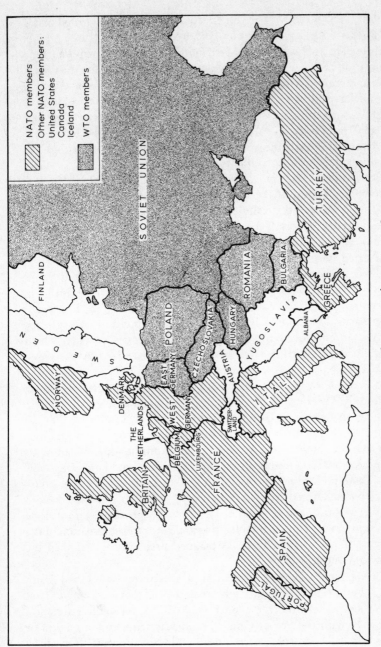

Figure I.5   NATO and WTO member states, 1984

politics, and NATO has been an effective means for the United States to do this. Even though, in the early 1950s, the United States gave its approval to the French-supported (and then rejected) proposals for a European Defence Community (EDC), as a means to integrate West Germany into the defence structure of Western Europe, and which would have created a 'European' sub-grouping of the anti-Communist Western military coalition to parallel the European Coal and Steel Community (ECSC), the United States basically preferred and welcomed the 'Atlantic' solution which finally emerged through the London and Paris Agreements of 1954–5, which made West Germany, under certain prescribed conditions, a full member of NATO. The major appeal of EDC, aside from the fact that these proposals appeared to be the only way at the time to obtain French acquiescence to West German rearmament, was that EDC could have provided the military dimension of a more broadly conceived federated Western Europe.

This leads to a second major observation about United States post-World War II policy toward Western Europe, which is that in economic affairs, the United States has followed a 'European' approach. This approach has been used for political and security goals, as evidenced by the control over West Germany which initially the ECSC has and the EDC would have exercised. As discussed in chapter 3, ECSC was welcomed as a means of placing a check on the industrial warmaking capacities of France and West Germany, along with other Western European states. If this could be paralleled by a European Economic Community (EEC) or a Common Market, so much the better as far as the United States was concerned. In other words, the movement for the creation of multinational, leading to supranational, economic arrangements which would bind the states of Western Europe indissolubly together politically, was encouraged by the United States. Even the prospect that this would create a strong political and economic 'Third Force,' bringing with it trade friction, seemed an acceptable price to pay for the elimination of the devastating warfare which has plagued first Europe and then the world in modern times.

If we see the balance of relationships between the United States and Western Europe in this light, then the fact that the United States has retained control over its nuclear forces, and has preferred to deal directly with the Soviet Union on nuclear arms limitation and/or nuclear arms control matters (meanwhile consulting with its allies) does not seem inconsistent. The nuclear aspect has all along been more clearly a deterrence against a Soviet attack on Western Europe, as well as an attack on the United States itself, rather than a means to control or to deter an outbreak of warfare (either conventional or nuclear) *among* the states of Western Europe. One of the Alliance's problems since the 1960s, in this respect, has been how to resolve the West German capacity to develop or to acquire a nuclear military capability, although West Germany has never formally voiced an interest in such weapons. This was the primary reason why there was an effort in the early 1960s to create a multilateral nuclear force (MLF) or an Atlantic nuclear force (ANF) within NATO. Both efforts foundered on their difficulty in application and on the Soviet Union's opposition, which was based on the claim that such arrangements amounted to nuclear proliferation because West Germany would be engaged directly in the management of nuclear weapons. Other states in Western Europe could also, of course, develop nuclear weapons. Dr Sigaard Elklund, Director-General of the International Atomic Energy Agency (IAEA), reported to the United Nations General Assembly in late 1969 that 70 tons of plutonium would be produced each year in the 1970s. He concluded: 'About one-third of this amount will be present in non-nuclear countries. This would correspond to some 100 atomic bombs of minimum size per week. These figures open frightening perspectives.'

There has been no lack of awareness on the part of the states of Western Europe of the character of American political and security attitudes towards them. On their part, the European member-states of NATO have used the Atlantic military relationship to ensure their own security *vis-à-vis* the Soviet Union while maintaining freedom of national action elsewhere to their maximum extent. Hence they have had the benefit of being able to concentrate their attention on economic matters which, even with all the bickering and political manoeuvring that has gone on as the European Communities (EC) has been formed, fulfils one of the major aims of United States policy toward Western Europe.

In sum, it is not inaccurate to say that the United States has achieved a high degree of success in its post-World War II policy toward Western Europe. The greatest threat to this policy has been the gradual reduction in the political cohesiveness of NATO, and hence in the strength and efficacy of the Atlantic connection. In this respect, we can see some similarities to the politics of Europe in the late nineteenth century. The weakening of the Concert of Europe resulted from changes in the ideological perceptions of the member-states, which was due in turn to economic and social developments throughout Europe. The same has been happening to NATO.

The fact is that NATO has so far ratified the *status quo* rather than acted as an agent of change, in spite of recurrent references to cultural co-operation in article II of the Treaty, and to the Harmel Report, which suggested that East–West détente as well as deterrence should be a goal of the Alliance, and the focus of attention in the 1960s and 1970s on environmental problems. This has created some dilemmas in defining NATO's mission and purpose. The same condition was true of the Concert of Europe; the individual state which felt that its interests were better served by facilitating a change in the *status quo* proved the most unreliable to the Concert, i.e. first Britain and then a unified Germany. Now the member-states of NATO have also felt at times that at least their short-run interests were better served by facilitating selected change in the *status quo*. For example, Greece and Turkey, as a consequence of their bitter rivalry in Cyprus, have waivered at times in their support of NATO.

It is noteworthy that at NATO's January 1970 meeting of Heads of State and Government, French President Georges Pompidou warmly supported West German Chancellor Willy Brandt's policies toward attempting to improve West Germany's relations with Poland and the Soviet Union, and especially with East Germany. Just a few weeks earlier, at the December 1969 Ministerial meeting of the NATO Council, the United States had emerged as the most reluctant of the member-states to explore with the Soviet Union and/or the Warsaw Treaty Organization the possibility of an all-European security conference that not only could affect such difficult matters as the status of Berlin, but also could result in the political weakening of NATO. This move, though, had a paradoxical ring. The Soviet Union apparently wanted agreements with West Germany that would render *de jure* the *de facto* post-World War II territorial *status quo*. The United States, while appearing conservative in terms of intra-NATO political manoeuvring, adhered more faithfully to the pre-Cold War objective of seeing created in Europe a multiplicity of more politically independent states, among which *might* be a reunited Germany. But as mentioned earlier and discussed later on, the signing in 1975 of the so-called Helsinki Accords, as a result of the Conference on Security and Co-operation in Europe, provided the Soviet Union with the legitimacy of the boundaries of the states of Eastern Europe that had fallen under its control.

There has been genuine concern about the diminution of NATO's cohesiveness, as the worldwide and especially the European international political situation has changed. It is difficult to know just what 'cohesiveness' means. Could it be the confidence each member-state has in the other member-states' (and particularly the United States') determination to go to the aid of one of their number if threatened or attacked in a non-nuclear fashion? Is it the measure of the willingness of the states to build up their conventional defence forces and deploy them in a concerted fashion? Is it the ability or inability of the European member-states to influence Soviet-American relations, and in particular those dealing with nuclear matters? These questions, and others implied below, all bear on the tendency of states, even in today's interdependent world, to be more concerned about their own welfare – or perceived interests – than the welfare of their neighbours or friends.

In economic affairs, the states of Western Europe are also finding it difficult to suppress their nationalistic instincts. As one commentator observed, every crisis in the EC has been characterized first by all the parties taking extreme national positions to appease their respective domestic publics, and then, at the last minute, striking a set of face-saving compromises. What is important in all this is that the influence, in terms of the power to affect national policies, of the bureaucracy of the Communities themselves, has not grown to the point where we can see a decisive shift in decision-making authority from the member-states to the institutions of the Communities.

### CHARACTERISTICS OF POST-WORLD WAR II EUROPE

In terms of power politics during the past 200 years, which is the period of the emergence of the modern state as the prime actor in international politics, Europe has consisted of four 'Great Powers' (Britain, Russia [the Soviet Union], Prussia [Germany and now the two German Republics], and France). For approximately half of this period, there were two other multinational empires which were not, by definition, states, but were Great Powers – the Austro-Hungarian Empire and the Turkish Ottoman Empire. The dissolution of these empires after World War I corresponded with the rise of two other states which have had expansionist potentialities – the United States and Japan. Politically speaking, 'Europe' has tended to be shaped according to a mix of the British and then the American geopolitical global strategy of 'defending democracy' on the one hand, and according to traditional Continental Great Power rivalries on the other.

But there are several aspects of European international politics which are unique to the post-World War II period. One is the emergence of the nuclear dimension in warfare, which has helped to place the United States and the Soviet Union in the category of global Superpowers, and gives them a dominant (although not exclusive) voice in the international politics of Europe. Another aspect which is unique is the trend toward economic integration among some of the states of Europe – mostly those that comprise the European Communities (EC). This evolution has helped to bring about a political revival of Europe – and particularly Western Europe – which has in turn enabled these states, both collectively and individually, to reassume some of the international political behaviour patterns which had characterized the pre-World War II period, even reaching back in some respects to the period before World War I.

It is generally accepted that global politics – of which, today, European international politics is but a part – is undergoing a massive shift. The Superpowers are negotiating fitfully with each other on matters of nuclear arms limitations and troop reductions; the United States is rearranging its national security priorities toward Asia and the Pacific, and this has had an impact on priorities towards Europe; the states of Europe, both to the east and to the west of the Elbe, are reaching out towards each other for new or strengthened economic ties, which may promote new or strengthened political arrangements; West Germany is increasingly becoming the economic and political 'centre' of international politics in both Eastern and Western Europe. From its location in Central Europe, West Germany is also moving toward a gradual reconciliation of the two German states, which will probably not be expressed in political and military terms, but will increasingly be expressed eventually in political and economic terms.

In Eastern Europe, organizational developments have followed somewhat similar patterns to those occurring in Western Europe. After the Soviet Union had rejected participation in the Marshall Plan for itself and prohibited all Eastern European states to share in the Plan's benefits, it was instrumental in establishing in 1949 the Council for Mutual Economic Assistance (CMEA). The original members were Bulgaria, Czechoslovakia, the German Democratic Republic (East Germany), Hungary, Poland, Romania, Albania, with Yugoslavia as an associate. The purpose of CMEA was to co-ordinate and integrate the economies of the member-states under Soviet leadership.

In the military sector the Soviet Union was the creator of an alliance known as the Warsaw Treaty Organization (WTO), or 'Warsaw Pact', which was concluded in May 1955 and whose signatories were the Soviet Union, Albania, Bulgaria, Czecho-slovakia, East Germany, Hungary, Poland, and Romania. Albania withdrew in 1968. As discussed in chapter 2, the WTO is a response to NATO, particularly after West Germany had become a fully-fledged member. As with the CMEA, the WTO has been under the virtual control of the Soviet Union, which has always provided the top military leadership.

The respective organizational frameworks that were developed in both Eastern and Western Europe between the end of World War II and the end of the 1950s are significant indicators of the evolution of distinct regional sub-systems. Other characteristics suggesting the existence of two regional sub-systems are the increasing flow of intra-regional trade within Eastern and Western Europe since the end of the war, other types of expanding economic interactions such as the increasing movement of labour within the respective regions, and the incipient co-ordination of foreign policy behaviour by the states within the two regions. These points are discussed in greater detail in chapter 5. One example is provided by studying voting patterns in United Nations fora. Particular cohesion has always been manifested by the Eastern European states, but there is also increas-ing co-ordination of voting in the General Assembly by the Western European governments.[13]

Political, socio-economic and cultural aspects also provide dis-tinguishing features for the two regional sub-systems. In Western Europe all states are basically committed to democracy, pluralism and free market forces, although governmental intervention in the economy is practised in varying degrees in most of the states. In Eastern Europe, the basic governmental form is Communist authoritarianism and the economies continue to operate under centralized planning and control, although minor variations exist from country to country. There are also religious and cultural differences between Eastern and Western Europe, with Catholicism and Protestantism prevailing in the West and the Orthodox Church predominating in the East (along with Roman Catholicism in Poland and elsewhere and Lutheranism in East Germany). Finally,

developments also show some differences, although both the people
of Eastern and Western Europe appreciate and value their respective
artistic achievements.

In summary, the struggle for power in post-Napoleonic Europe
has been multidimensional in that an average of four Great Powers,
and several more small Powers, have engaged in varying degrees of
co-operation and conflict in modern times. Since World War II,
however, the struggle must be seen as taking place on three distinct
planes, which nonetheless interact continuously. The first of these is
the nuclear plane, which involves primarily, but not exclusively, the
Superpowers and is concerned with political and security aspects.
Then there is the conventional security and the economic plane,
which is confined more to Europe, and involves primarily, but not
exclusively, the groupings in NATO militarily, and the EC economically in Western Europe; and the WTO militarily, and the CMEA
economically in Eastern Europe. The third plane is the political,
military and economic 'mix' of relationships among the states of
Europe, both Eastern and Western, among themselves.

In the following chapters we will explore further the regional
developments by examining and analysing sub-regional interdependencies in the economic, political and military sectors. These
explorations will provide us with insights as to how inter-regional
cohesion and integration has proceeded and what the prospects are
for inter-regional political and economic accommodations and for
the eventual emergence of 'one Europe' within the context of the
continuing rivalry between the Superpowers.

### NOTES

1  A. J. P. Taylor, *Revolutions and Revolutionaries* (New York: Atheneum,
   1980), p. 36.
2  Various groupings of states appeared during the tenure of the Concert of
   Europe and it is important to keep their separations in mind. The
   Quadruple Alliance was made up of the four Great Powers that had
   combined to defeat Napoleon; these were Britain, Russia, Prussia, and
   Austria. The Quadruple Alliance lasted from 1814 until 1818, when it
   became the Quintuple Alliance with the addition of France, at the
   Congress of Aix-la-Chapelle.

   The Holy Alliance, a product of Czar Alexander I's mysticism, was to
   be the spiritual embodiment of the Quadruple Alliance. It dated from
   November 1815, but in terms of governing principles this vague
   declaration contained no force. Britain opposed the idea because it had

no constitutional basis. Metternich accepted the idea because it basically suited his conservative orientation, but he did not consider it a politically viable instrument.

3 Taylor, op. cit., p. 117.
4 Hajo Holborn, *The Political Collapse of Europe* (New York: Alfred A. Knopf, 1951), p. 27.
5 René Albrecht-Carrie, *A Diplomatic History of Europe since the Congress of Vienna* (New York: Harper and Row, 1958), p. 18.
6 Frederick B. Artz, *Reaction and Revolution* (New York: Harper Torchbooks, 1934), p. 165.
7 Taylor, op. cit., p. 87.
8 Holborn, op. cit., p. 109.
9 Quoted in James F. Byrnes, *Speaking Frankly* (London: William Heinemann Ltd, 1947), p. 49.
10 Timothy Stanley, *NATO in Transition: The Future of the Atlantic Alliance* (New York: Frederick A. Praeger, 1965), p. 309.
11 Ibid.
12 Robert E. Osgood, *Alliances and American Foreign Policy* (Baltimore: Johns Hopkins Press, 1968), pp. 35–6 (Osgood's emphasis).
13 See Bruce M. Russett, *International Regions and the International System: A Study in Political Ecology* (Chicago: Rand McNally, 1967), chapters 3–6; and Werner J. Feld and Gavin Boyd, 'The Comparative Study of International Regions', in Feld and Boyd, eds., *Comparative Regional Systems* (New York: Pergamon Press, 1980), pp. 3–17.

# 2

## The Emergence of Military Alliances in Western and Eastern Europe

*If East is East and West is West,*
*Where will Europe come to rest?*
Pierre Hassner

### WESTERN NETWORKS

The military manifestation of the Truman Doctrine in Western Europe was evidenced in the early 1950s with the expansion of NATO as an allied defence structure which paralleled the Marshall Plan's economic aid programme to Western Europe. Whether the United States intended that the Truman Doctrine should have emerged, over thirty-five years, as an 'umbrella' for United States global containment of Communist expansionism through military means is a question which has yet to be resolved. In immediate terms, conjecture has it that President Truman needed the 'globalism' of his declaration to convince a Republican-dominated and budget-minded Congress to appropriate $400 million to aid Greece and Turkey. Some leading observers, such as George Kennan and Walter Lippmann, expressed their concern at that time that the open-ended nature of the Doctrine, even though emphasizing economic and financial rather than military aid, would lead to a *de facto* American expansion into political arenas where military considerations would become paramount. To quote Robert Osgood:

Given the weakness and vulnerability of most of the non-communist world in the face of Soviet and, later, Communist Chinese pressure, we can see in retrospect that it was virtually inevitable that the Truman Doctrine, backed by the theory of containment, should lead to a considerable extension of American commitments. Yet few imagined the range of these commitments at the time. Given the historic indispensability of countervailing military power as a restraint upon powerful states that, like Russia, were determined to change the political and territorial status quo, it seems to have been equally inevitable that American *military* power would be the primary element of containment.[1]

The sense of urgency of the United States for West German rearmament as a cornerstone to the military containment of the Soviet Union in Europe, arose not only from the outbreak of the Korean War in June 1950, but also from the realization that the breaking of the American nuclear monopoly by the Soviet Union made it essential that a Soviet-American war in Europe should not 'go nuclear'. To avoid this eventuality, while continuing to prepare for a nuclear war and to assert a willingness to use nuclear weapons if a war with the Soviet Union were to break out, the United States actively promoted the building-up of non-nuclear conventional forces in Western Europe.

For tactical geographic reasons as well as military, the incorporation of West Germany in the NATO alliance structure, in United States eyes, became central to the security of Western Europe. In order to facilitate rapid Western European rearmament, the United States proposed to its NATO allies in the fall of 1950 that immediate steps should be taken to rearm Western Germany.

The reaction in Western Europe, and especially in France, was one of alarm; indeed, the West German public was opposed to rearmament as well, and was not at all anxious to re-establish German military forces. There was serious disagreement as to the immediacy of the Soviet military threat, and there was some doubt about this in Western Europe, although apparently little doubt in the United States. The result, however, was a proposal to create a Western European-oriented security system. This European Defence Community (EDC) would be a parallel with the newly-formed European Coal and Steel Community (ECSC). The ECSC Treaty had been signed by the Benelux states, Italy, France and West Germany, in 1951 to pool their iron and steel industries, thus implementing the notion that a recurrence of Franco-German warfare, already having brought on three European wars, could best be prevented by integrating the two states' primary war-making industrial capabilities. (See figure 2.1 for the structure of the ECSC and chapter 3 for a detailed discussion of it.)

Debate over the EDC dragged on for nearly four years, with the United States becoming impatient over the delay in getting West German rearmament underway, and the French becoming more uncertain about whether they wanted West German rearmament at

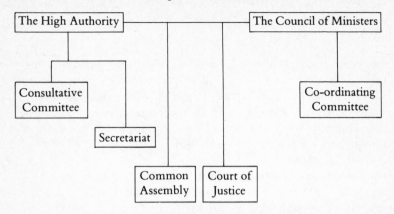

Figure 2.1    The European Coal and Steel Community, 1951

### HIGH AUTHORITY

Executive body of ECSC
9 members chosen by member-states
Decisions taken by simple majority vote
Exercise their function in complete independence in 'general interest of the Community'
Raise money by imposing levies on the industries
Deal directly with the coal and steel industries in the member-states without going through the national governments

### *Consultative Committee*

Up to 51 members representing producers, consumers, and workers
Consults with High Authority

### *Secretariat*

Administrative function

### COUNCIL OF MINISTERS

Representatives usually Ministers for Foreign Affairs
Harmonizes actions of High Authority and the governments
Can reverse decisions of High Authority
Must obtain consent of High Authority on certain matters
Can request High Authority to examine and consider proposals

Figure 2.1    *Continued*

*Co-ordinating Committee*

Assists the operations of the Council of Ministers

### COMMON ASSEMBLY

Meets to receive and consider the General Report of the High Authority
Proportional representation
Works closely with High Authority to further European integration
Power to compel Authority to resign
Influence on policy through debates and questions
Members almost identical with representatives to Consultative Assembly of
Council of Europe

### COURT OF JUSTICE

7 judges, appointed by the governments
Reviews decisions of the High Authority
Reviews resolutions of the High Authority and the Common Assembly
Can annul decisions of the High Authority
Settles disputes between members over the Treaty

all. When the French National Assembly rejected the EDC proposals
in August 1954 the incorporation of West Germany into NATO was
placed in jeopardy, requiring a new legal arrangement, which was
found in 1955 in the establishment of the Western European Union
(WEU). WEU was an extension of the Brussels Treaty Organization
and made it possible for France, along with Britain, Italy and the
Benelux states, to exercise supervision over the ban on West German
manufacture (but not necessarily acquisition) of 'ABC' weapons
(atomic, bacteriological, and chemical). (Figure 2.2 shows the
Brussels Treaty Organization in 1954 and figure 2.3 the Western
European Union in 1955.) Thus, within little more than a year after
NATO was formed, it had become involved in the problem of the
Western European states' preoccupation with their security from
Germany, and since then NATO has been as much a vehicle through
which this security can be assured as a coalition deterring a Soviet
attack against them.

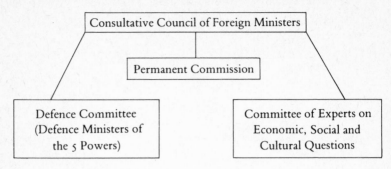

Figure 2.2    The Brussels Treaty Organization, 1954

The Brussels Treaty Organization was formed in 1948 of France, Britain and the Benelux states as a military alliance to counter the prospect of a renewal of aggression by Germany and then to cope with Soviet actions in Eastern Europe. It was an organization of regional self-defence for the defence of Western Europe under Article 51 of the United Nations Charter.

### CONSULTATIVE COUNCIL OF FOREIGN MINISTERS

Supreme organ to develop a system of automatic mutual assistance in the event of an armed attack

### *Permanent Commission*

Acts on behalf of Council when it is not in session

### *Defence Committee* (Defence Ministers of the 5 Powers)

Chief of Staff Committee
Military Supply Board
Western Union Command Organization (WUDO)
    Western Europe Commanders-in-Chief
Finance and Economic Committee

### *Committee of Experts on Economic, Social and Cultural Questions*

The Western European Union (Benelux, France, West Germany, Italy, Britain) officially came into existence in 1955 as a reconstituted Brussels Treaty Organization, which had lapsed with the development of NATO. When the French refused to ratify the EDC, a series of Protocols to the

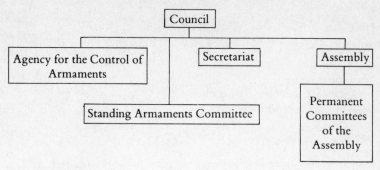

Figure 2.3    The Western European Union, 1955

Brussels Treaty were signed in October 1954 transforming the Brussels Treaty Organization into the Western European Union.

The WEU is a regional organization to defend Western Europe from attack, to help control West German rearmament, to co-operate with NATO in the defence of the Atlantic area and to promote the unity and encourage the progressive integration of Europe. In the 1980s it has also more clearly emerged as a 'European' manifestation of NATO.

COUNCIL

Formulates policy; co-ordinates defence policy and equipment
Issues directives to Secretary-General and to agencies and commissions of the organization
Ensures close co-operation with NATO

*Secretariat*

Secretary-General (Chairman of Council)
Administrative function

*Assembly*

Delegates of member-states to Consultative Assembly of the Council of Europe
Considers defence policy
Makes recommendations or transmits opinions to Council, national Parliaments, governments and international organizations
Issues Annual Report

Figure 2.3    *Continued*
*Permanent Committees of the Assembly*

Defence questions and armaments
General affairs
Space questions
Budgetary affairs and administration
Rules of procedure and privileges

AGENCY FOR THE CONTROL OF ARMAMENTS

Responsible to Council for types of armaments not to be manufactured and
    control of level of stocks of armaments held by each member-state

STANDING ARMS COMMITTEE

Responsible for co-operation between members in field of armaments

### NATO'S ORIGINS

The basic motivation for the creation of NATO was clearly the
enhancement of the security of the individual charter members and
the states that subsequently joined. Resources and capabilities of
even the most powerful of the allies, the United States, were
perceived as insufficient to forego resorting to multinational means
to meet the threat of aggression in Europe by a militarily powerful
Soviet Union.

The threat began with attempts at a Communist takeover in
Greece, increased with the Communist *coup* and seizure of governmental power in Czechoslovakia in 1948, and continued with heavy
political pressure to establish pro-Soviet influence in Norway and
Finland, with efforts by indigenous Communist parties to disrupt
the economic reconstruction of Western Europe, and in the summer
of 1948 with the blockade of Western road and rail access to Berlin.[2]

As mentioned in chapter 1, the first organizational arrangements
after the end of World War II for the enhancement of Western
European security were made by Britain and France with the signing
of the Dunkirk Treaty in March 1947. This Treaty was directed
primarily towards providing mutual aid in the event of a renewal of
German aggression. It also aimed at economic co-operation and,
therefore, a longer-range goal was to bring in the Benelux states and
perhaps later other Western European states. Alarmed by the expan-

sion and consolidation of Soviet influence in Eastern Europe and the Balkans, the British government in January 1948 called for a 'Western Union', which was followed up by preliminary negotiations with the Benelux states along with France aiming chiefly at a military alliance, but also seeking greater economic, social and cultural co-operation. A treaty to this effect was signed in Brussels on 17 March 1948. This so-called Brussels Treaty made reference to article 51 of the United Nations Charter, which authorized collective self-defence and stipulated that in the event of an armed attack on one of the signatories the other parties to the Treaty *would come to the aid* of the victim of aggression. The Treaty mentioned Germany as a potential aggressor; the Soviet Union was not named as such but was evidently very much on the minds of the Alliance partners.[3]

The principal policy organ of what came to be called the Brussels Treaty Organization (BTO) was the Consultative Council, which consisted of the foreign ministers of the five member-states and that met several times. Between meetings, policy was determined by a Permanent Commission located in London and administration matters were handled by a Secretariat, also set up in London. A unified defence force was established at Fontainebleau, France, under Field Marshal Lord Montgomery, but in fact he had very few troops to command.[4]

To the British government it soon became clear, however, that the BTO would not be sufficiently strong to deal with joint pressures, although the United States had promised to aid that organization in a way yet to be specified.[5] Ernest Bevin, British Foreign Secretary, was particularly concerned about Norway becoming so subservient to Soviet wishes that the collapse of the whole of Scandinavia might result and that 'in turn prejudiced our chance of calling any halt to the relentless advance of Russia into Western Europe'.[6]

Mr Bevin perceived two related threats: an extension of the Soviet Union's sphere of influence to the Atlantic, and a threat to destroy all the efforts made (with American approval) to build up a Western Union within BTO. He therefore strongly recommended that the United States enter into an Atlantic regional treaty arrangement in which all states directly threatened by a Soviet move to the Atlantic could participate, and these were to include the United States, Britain, Canada, Ireland, Iceland, Norway, Denmark, Portugal, France, the Benelux states and Spain when it had again a democratic form of government.[7] For the Mediterranean, he envisaged a separate system, with Italy playing a major role.

The United States response to the British proposal was given promptly by General George C. Marshall, then Secretary of State. He suggested that joint discussions on the establishment of an Atlantic security system were to be undertaken at once. The initial discussions began in Washington on 22 March 1948 and revealed a number of uncertainties in the British proposals regarding prospective membership and the geographic area to which the system was to apply. There seemed to be an increasing need to include Italy, Greece, and perhaps Turkey, in the membership list, but the acceptability of the Western zones of Germany as a member seemed at that time doubtful. Germany had been the enemy of most of the prospective members during World War II, terminated only three years earlier.[8]

For the United States to join any kind of alliance raised fundamental questions. First, although the United States had at that time potential capabilities and resources that might have been perceived by policy-makers and the public as adequate for a successful defence of its territory and people, doubt could be cast on such a judgment by the enormous advances in military, and especially nuclear weapons, technology that were being made. Second, George Washington's warning against entangling alliances was known to every American and was often reiterated in political oratory. With 1948 being an election year and the political power divided between a Democratic President and a Republican Congress, this was a most difficult time to move beyond Washington's warning into the uncharted territory of peacetime alliance politics.

The initial reaction of Secretary Marshall to the British proposal was therefore somewhat negative. He considered United States participation in a military guarantee as impossible; aid would have to be confined to supplying material assistance to the members of the BTO. Two of the most able and senior officers in the State Department supported this view.[9] On the other hand, the directors of the State Department's Office of European Affairs and the Division of West European Affairs strongly advocated a North Atlantic Treaty and alliance.

During the Spring of 1948 the State Department, reacting to the Soviet *coup* in Czechoslovakia and the continued pressure on Norway, began to commit itself to the notion of an Atlantic treaty; in April the National Security Council approved a State Department recommendation that President Truman announce that the United States was prepared to negotiate a collective defence arrangement with the BTO and also with Norway, Denmark, Sweden, Iceland and Italy. Pending the conclusion of such an agreement, the United States would regard an armed attack against any signatory of the Brussels Treaty as an armed attack against itself.[10]

Since ratification of this proposed agreement would require Senate approval and it was a Democratic President who needed consent from a Republican-controlled Senate, a bipartisan approach was essential. The means used was senatorial advice to the President in the form of a resolution introduced by Senator Arthur Vandenberg of Michigan, the Republican Chairman of the Senate Foreign Relations Committee, which was adopted by the Senate in an overwhelming vote on 11 June 1948. The so-called Vandenberg Resolution advocated the progressive development of regional and other collective arrangements for individual and collective self-defence in accordance with the Charter of the United Nations, and specifically referred to the right of collective self-defence under article 51 of the Charter. It also approved the association of the United States with such arrangements 'as are based on continuous and effective self-help and mutual aid, and as it affects national security'.[11]

The Vandenberg Resolution opened the way to the negotiation with prospective member-states by the State Department, of a North Atlantic Treaty. The negotiations included regular meetings with the Senate Foreign Relations Committee and its staff to discuss actual treaty language. These dicussions were important because there were arguments over various specific Treaty provisions, particularly those with respect to the nature of the commitment, the geographic coverage, its duration, and which other governments should be invited to become members of the prospective alliance.[12] The basic differences were due to the fact that the Western Europeans, especially the French, wanted as binding and as long a commitment as possible, and the Americans, while agreeing in principle, were constrained by what the Administration believed Senator Vandenberg would accept.[13]

Divergences of views between the United States and other prospective alliance members about the substance of the Treaty under consideration were not surprising, in view of the large gap in the capabilities and resources of the individual states involved in the negotiations. For example, France would accept membership only if the unity of command of the armed forces of the member-states were achieved at once, and United States military personnel and supplies were moved to France immediately. For Norway, the matter was also urgent because of Soviet pressure for a pact similar to the Soviet-Finnish agreements. The Soviet government tried to obtain concessions by suggesting that a rejection could trigger a Soviet attack on Norway and Sweden. Canada was another state that strongly advocated an effective treaty and was concerned that, as a result of discussions in the Senate, the draft treaty might be watered down so that it would not be much more than another ineffectual Kellogg-Briand pact. In contrast, Belgium was apprehensive about the provocative effect that such a security treaty might have on the Soviet Union. While the Belgians were anxious to obtain immediate help from the United States, they floated ideas about the armed neutrality of Western Europe as perhaps being preferable to a formal Atlantic treaty relationship.[14]

The above concerns of selected prospective alliance member-states closely reflected their urgent need for bolstering their security. Since the security of all the member-states would be enhanced regardless of the size of the contributions they were to make in the future, agreement on an acceptable balance of obligations and rights of the parties was reached by April 1948.

With respect to the prospective members' obligations, the most controversial provision was the exact nature of the commitment to respond to armed attack on a treaty member-state. The United States did not want to and could not be obliged to use its armed forces automatically to aid a victim of an attack because the Constitution stipulates that only Congress can declare war. After many negotiating sessions and consultations with the foreign ministries of the prospective members and the Senate Foreign Relations Committee, the crucial article 5 of the North Atlantic Treaty was to read as follows:

The Parties agree that an armed attack against one or more of them in Europe or North America shall be considered an attack against them all, and consequently they agree that, if such an armed attack occurs, each of them, in exercise of the right of individual or collective self-defence recognized by article 51 of the Charter of the United Nations, will assist the Party or Parties so attacked by taking forthwith, individually and in concert with the other Parties, such action as it deems necessary, including the use of armed force, to restore and maintain the security of the North Atlantic area.

Any such armed attack and all measures taken as a result thereof shall immediately be reported to the Security Council. Such measures shall be terminated when the Security Council has taken the measures necessary to restore and maintain international peace and security.[15]

In spite of the qualifying words, it was believed that Congress could be counted upon to back up the President with a declaration of war, particularly if the armed attack was not just an incident but a fully-fledged initiation of extensive hostilities.

For the southern boundary of the territorial coverage of the Treaty, the Tropic of Cancer was adopted (article 6). This avoided involving any part of Africa or any of the Latin American states as areas where an armed attack would constitute a *causus belli*. However, consultation on threats of or actual attack anywhere in the world was not restricted by the geographic parameters specified in the treaty. Indeed, consultations on possible threats is a major obligation of the member governments (article 4). Although some European governments had insisted on a treaty duration of fifty years, the final agreement reached was limited to twenty years. It was doubtful that the Senate would have accepted a longer duration.

It should be noted that the Treaty has an economic dimension as well. Article 2 emphasizes the elimination of conflict between the international economic policies of the member-states and the encouragement of economic collaboration between 'any or all of them'. However, these provisions have been used only rarely – for example, when the NATO member-states pledged contributions to an assistance programme for Turkey, which faced serious economic difficulties in the late 1970s.

In terms of rights, the member governments were given the right to be consulted, which is the other side of the coin of being obligated to consult each other in case of threats to their individual or collective security. It is noteworthy that the treaty negotiators did not spell out institutional and organizational details for the implementation of the agreement beyond stipulating the establishment of a ministerial council and committees, giving these organs the mandate to set up subsidiary bodies, including a Defence Committee. No mention was made of voting procedures, but the basic rule developed in the North Atlantic Council was that no government could be forced to take action against its will, but conversely, no government could prevent other governments from taking such collective action as they agreed upon.[16] (Figure 2.4 illustrates NATO's early structure.)

Finally, unanimous agreement is necessary to invite any state to accede to the North Atlantic Treaty. But only those states in a position to further the principles of the Treaty and to contribute to the security of the North Atlantic area may be invited (article 10). This shows that the member-states retained a maximum of

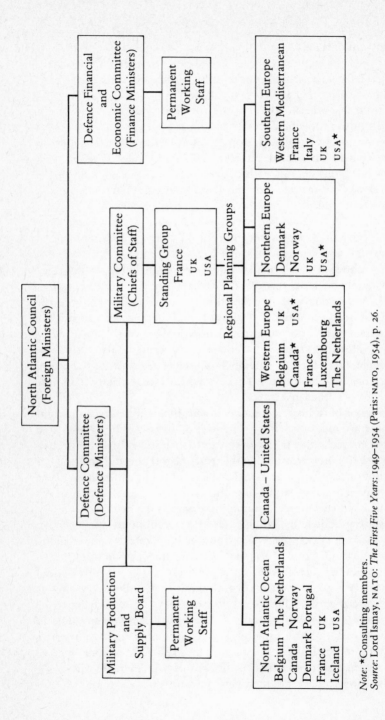

Note: ★Consulting members.
Source: Lord Ismay, NATO: The First Five Years: 1949–1954 (Paris: NATO, 1954), p. 26.

Figure 2.4   NATO's early structure, 1949

flexibility for future decision-making except for the obligations specified in article 5, and for consultation.

## THE DEFEAT OF THE EUROPEAN DEFENCE COMMUNITY (EDC)

Proponents of European unity saw in the ECSC a perfect vehicle for the achievement of their ambitions, and the progress of the so-called Schuman Plan amply fulfilled their hopes. Even before the ECSC Treaty was completed it became a model for further efforts towards Western European integration.

Immediately after the outbreak of the Korean War in 1950, the United States and its European allies sought to increase the military capabilities of the prospective members of the ECSC. One alternative was to rearm West Germany. Aware that this option might be necessary, in October 1950 René Pleven, the French Premier, suggested that the six prospective ECSC states and possibly Great Britain would pool their armed forces in Europe and place them under joint control, thereby creating a European Defence Community (EDC). The obvious purpose of this 'Pleven Plan' was to permit West German rearmament, but only under controlled conditions. Again, fear of Germany was the dominant motive for France, but for West Germany EDC could be a step on the road to full acceptance in the international community.

After arduous and complicated negotiations which lasted almost two years, the EDC Treaty was finally completed and was signed on 27 May 1952. It provided for a limited merger of the armed forces of the five member-states. The combined forces were to be placed under the control of institutions which were similar to those of the ECSC, although the EDC executive body, the Board of Commissioners, did not have as extensive powers as those of the ECSC High Authority, and the powers given to the EDC's Council of Ministers were correspondingly stronger. As a temporary measure the Common Assembly of the Coal and Steel Community was to serve as the parliamentary body for EDC, but the treaty envisaged the ultimate creation of an Assembly which would be chosen by direct election and which would serve both Communities. On the basis of this provision, plans were drafted in 1952 and 1953 for the creation of a European Political Community (EPC). (See figure 2.5 for a description of the EPC.)

While the ECSC seemed to make progress towards the long-range goal of some kind of political union, ratification of the EDC Treaty, a

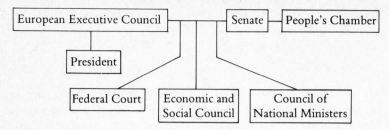

Figure 2.5    The European Political Community, 1953 (planned but not established: scheme drawn up by Ad Hoc Assembly of the ECSC)

AIMS

'Establish progressively a common market among the Member States'
Community to develop common foreign policy for its members in fields of ECSC and EDC activities
'Foster the co-ordination of the policy of Member States in monetary, credit and financial matters'
The EPC Treaty's adoption to be contingent on the ratification of the EDC Treaty

EXECUTIVE COUNCIL

Composed of delegates from member states
President chosen by majority vote of Senate
Council could be censured by Senate or censured by $\frac{3}{5}$ vote of People's Chamber

SENATE

87 members, chosen by national Parliaments

PEOPLE'S CHAMBER

268 members, elected by universal suffrage proportional representation

stepping-stone toward this objective, proved to be a difficult process, particularly in France. Successive French governments, unsure of their domestic political strength and preoccupied with other problems, refused to submit the Treaty to the National Assembly.

Meanwhile, important changes were occurring on the international scene. Soviet policy toward Western Europe became less bellicose – in part due to Stalin's death in 1953 and the consequent changes in the Soviet Union's ruling hierarchy. But it was apparent as early as the nineteenth Congress of the Communist Party of the Soviet Union in October 1952 that the Soviet Union might adopt more moderate tactics. The hard line had only provoked a firm Western response and Stalin himself had called for policy changes at that gathering. Also, in 1953 and 1954 the Korean and Indo-Chinese conflicts were settled and a general atmosphere of détente affected East-West relations. In Europe, West Germany continued its economic resurgence, while France, embroiled in a series of costly colonial wars and caught in a web of internal contradictory forces, languished. When Premier Pierre Mendès-France halfheartedly submitted the EDC Treaty to the French National Assembly in August 1954, both the atmosphere and many of the Treaty proposals were thus sharply different from what they had been when the Pleven Plan had been introduced. Even though the other five governments had ratified the Treaty, the French Assembly rejected it by a vote of 319 to 264.

With the refusal of the French Assembly to ratify the Treaty, the entire integration movement was brought into question. The plans for the European Political Community (EPC), a more ambitious undertaking towards political union, had to be shelved. The general notion was temporarily revived in 1961, called the Fouchet Plans, whereby a 'Union of States' would be created, but fears of some EC members that France would benefit most resulted in its lapse in 1962. (Figure 2.6 describes the 1961 European Political Union.)

After the collapse of the EDC, British Foreign Secretary Anthony Eden proposed that the occupation regime in West Germany be ended and that West Germany join NATO. This would be done by strengthening the Brussels Treaty and extending it into a Western European Union (WEU). These proposals, the so-called London and Paris Agreements, were embodied in a series of agreements negotiated and signed in 1954 and ratified in May 1955, at which time the WEU came into existence. (Figure 2.3 shows the structure of WEU in 1955.)

WEU was also charged with the specific task of settling the future of the Saar. Under a special Franco-German agreement, the Saar was to have a European Statute within the framework of WEU, provided that this Statute was approved by a referendum. A Commission was set up in May 1955 to supervise the referendum, which was held on 23 October 1955. The result showed that a majority in the Saar had

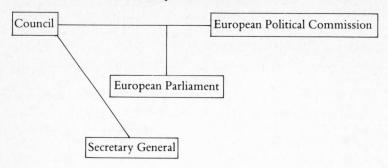

Figure 2.6   Proposed European Political Union, 1961

The EPU, only one of a number of proposals for some form of political union, was to be a limited political organization proposed by the French. Many thought of it as an alternative to a future politically-oriented EEC which would have more potential supranational controls – something de Gaulle adamantly refused to agree to.

### COUNCIL

Every four months to meet at Head of State or Government level, and at least once in intervening period at Foreign Minister level
Extraordinary sessions at request of any member
Deliberate on all questions requested to be put on agenda by any member
Decisions to be unanimous and will be binding on those who participate in adoption or who endorse it at any later time

### EUROPEAN POLITICAL COMMISSION

Senior officials of Foreign Affairs departments of each member-state meet in Paris
Set up such working bodies as it considers necessary
Assist Council in preparing deliberations and carrying out decisions
Perform any other duties that the Council entrusts to it

### EUROPEAN PARLIAMENT

Deliberate on matters concerning aims of the Union
May address oral or written questions to the Council
May submit recommendations to the Council
Council must submit report each year to the European Parliament on its activities

Figure 2.6  *Continued*

Limited sphere of powers (as Commission) *vis-à-vis* the extreme decision-making powers of the Council

SECRETARY GENERAL

Appointed by Council
Independent of Governments
Administrative function

voted against the adoption of the European Statute and furthermore had expressed a wish to be incorporated into West Germany. The Saar then became a *Land* of the Federal Republic, but remained linked economically to France. The final incorporation of the territory, now renamed Saarland, took place on 5 July 1959.

In June 1960 the activities of the four main social and cultural committees of the WEU were transferred to the Council of Europe. Later on, the Council of WEU formally approved the relaxation of the restrictions on West German arms production imposed by Protocol III of the revised Brussels Treaty that involved specified long-range and guided missiles, and the construction of certain ships and submarines.

In June 1963, following the suspension of negotiations for Britain's entry into the European Economic Community (EEC), it was agreed that the WEU Ministerial Council would meet at quarterly intervals and that the economic situation in Europe would be a regular agenda item. The Commission of the EEC would be invited to be represented during these discussions, which have continued since October 1963.

In this respect, several proposals were put forward at WEU or at NATO Council meetings held during 1968 suggesting close political and defence consultations within the framework of WEU, and specifically for discussions relating to Britain's role in Europe. These proposals were repeatedly rejected in France. Furthermore, when, at a ministerial meeting in Luxembourg in February 1969, the British proposed a meeting to discuss the Middle East situation, the proposal was approved by all the member-states except France. When the WEU Secretariat organized such a meeting in London later in the month, it was boycotted by the French, who declared that they would not attend any more ministerial meetings until further notice, because the convening of the Middle East meeting without the unanimous approval of WEU members constituted a breach of the

Treaty. These episodes were obviously manifestations of France's
desire not to see the WEU become a forum for political as well as
economic consultations among the 'inner Six' but which in addition
would formally include Britain. However, circumstances have
changed during the 1980s and efforts are being made to give the WEU
a new role in international and defence politics.


### THE EASTERN NETWORK

In May 1955, as discussed in chapter 1, the Soviet Union and its
Eastern European allies established the Warsaw Treaty Organization
(WTO). The basic legal provisions and institutions of WTO clearly
mirror those of NATO. (See appendix I for a comparison of the
treaties.) In the event of an attack on any of the WTO members,
assistance to the victim of aggression is mandatory; however, the use
of armed force as a means of aiding the attacked member-state or
states is not obligatory.

Like NATO, the WTO has a dual structure of civilian and military
institutions. The highest civilian organ is the Political Consultative
Committee that co-ordinates all activities apart from purely military
matters. It is composed of the First Secretaries of the Communist
Parties, heads of governments, and foreign and defence ministers of
member-states. In 1977 WTO established a permanent Committee of
Foreign Ministers that is subordinate to the Consultative Committee
and is concerned mainly with political consultation. Administrative
support comes from a Secretariat under a Soviet Director-General.
All decisions in these bodies are by consensus.

The military structure of WTO is headed by the Committee of
Defence Ministers. A joint command organization is required by the
WTO and the top echelon consists of a Commander-in-Chief and a
Military Council. Meeting under the chairmanship of the comman-
der, the Council includes the chiefs-of-staff and permanent represen-
tatives from each of the allied armed forces. The positions of
Commander-in-Chief and Chief-of-Staff of WTO have invariably
been Soviet officers; not surprisingly, the headquarters of WTO is in
Moscow. (See figure 2.7 for an illustration of the WTO structure.)

If France has been the maverick of NATO, the maverick of WTO has
been Romania. It refused to participate with other WTO forces in the
occupation of Czechoslovakia in 1968; it insisted during the WTO
reorganization of 1969 on the relaxation of the tight control over
WTO exercised by the Soviet government and obtained some conces-

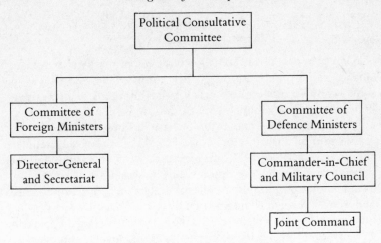

Figure 2.7   The Warsaw Treaty Organization, 1955

sions; and it advocates the concurrent dissolution of WTO and NATO.[17]

## MEMBERS

Albania (withdrew in 1968), Bulgaria, Czechoslovakia, German Democratic Republic, Hungary, Poland, Romania, Soviet Union

## POLITICAL CONSULTATIVE COMMITTEE

Co-ordinates all activities apart from purely military matters
Composed of the First Secretaries of the Communist Parties, Heads of Governments, and Foreign and Defence Ministers

## COMMITTEE OF FOREIGN MINISTERS

Subordinate to the Consultative Committee
Concerned mainly with political consultation

## DIRECTOR-GENERAL AND SECRETARIAT

Provides administrative support (all decisions are by consensus)

## COMMITTEE OF DEFENCE MINISTERS

Joint command organization
Commander-in-Chief and Military Council, which includes the chiefs-of-staff and permanent representatives from each of the allied armed forces

### THE WARSAW TREATY ORGANIZATION AS A MILITARY ALLIANCE[18]

Was the Warsaw Treaty initially conceived primarily as a military alliance and has its creation greatly enhanced the security of its signatories? To answer these questions it is important to differentiate between the Soviet Union – both then and now the hegemonial power in the region – and its junior Eastern European allies.

The four major objectives that may have motivated Stalin in aiding and abetting the Communist takeover of Eastern Europe were: firstly, denying the region to hostile Western states; secondly, ensuring that the domestic political systems in the area remained under the control of elements friendly to the Soviet Union; thirdly, utilizing the region's resources for the purpose of aiding Soviet post-war economic recovery and development; and finally, using Eastern Europe as a potential jumping-off place for a possible offensive against the West.[19] Since these objectives were formulated in the pre-nuclear age, it may be assumed that some are not as valid or relevant in the early 1980s as they were in the mid-1940s or 1950s.

While a good case can be made that the initial goals of the Soviet Union in Eastern Europe are still valid, with the possible exception of the third objective, the important point is that Eastern Europe was being viewed as a buffer zone or *cordon sanitaire* between the Soviet Union and the West. Although by the early 1950s the Soviet Union was linked by bilateral mutual defence treaties with its junior allies, there was almost a total absence of any co-ordinating institutional mechanism that could integrate the Eastern European military establishments with that of the Soviet Union.

To be sure, the absence of a unified military high command for the area was compensated for by a number of other factors. Since the end of World War II, both the Soviet Union and its Eastern European partners had sought to eradicate 'bourgeois-nationalist' influences from their armed forces. This effort took the form of large-scale purges of the officer corps, which was rapidly replaced by new, presumably more reliable, cadres. Furthermore, Soviet military advisers were placed throughout the entire military establishments in the sub-region, and in some states, notably Poland, they held the top command posts. In addition, as early as the Korean War the Eastern European states had been forced to produce Soviet-type weapons and equipment, either by expanding their existing defence industries or by creating new ones. These industries were heavily dependent on the Soviet Union for blueprints, parts and know-how, and the rate of production of various weapons was likely to be centrally co-ordinated, providing still another instrument of Soviet control.

Despite the absence of a formal multilateral defence treaty and a unified command prior to 1955, the Soviet Union exercised a high degree of control in the co-ordination of the defence systems of its Eastern European partners. Even after the signing of the Warsaw Treaty, no new elements were introduced into the bloc's military arrangements, so the need for a sub-regional collective security system in Eastern Europe cannot be easily accepted as the primary reason for the timing of the treaty, unless the signing is interpreted as simply a *de jure* recognition of the existing state of affairs.

From a purely military viewpoint, even more important than the role of Soviet military advisers was the presence of Soviet troops in four of the seven Eastern European states (East Germany, Hungary, Poland, and Romania). The only conceivable argument for linking the timing of the signing of the Warsaw Treaty to a problem of sub-regional security is the fact that the Austrian State Treaty was signed by Austria and the Big Four on 15 May 1955, one day after the signing of the Warsaw Treaty. The Austrian State Treaty terminated the agreements under which Soviet troops had been stationed in Hungary and Romania for the avowed purpose of guarding lines of communication between the Soviet Union and the Soviet occupation zone in Austria. According to some observers, the WTO, in giving the Soviet Union the right to station its forces in the territories of member-states, thus offset the nullified provisions of the Austrian Treaty.[20]

### THE WARSAW TREATY AS A REACTION TO WEST GERMAN REARMAMENT

In November 1954, a few months before the signing of the Treaty, the Conference on European Security took place in Moscow. Under the leadership of Soviet Foreign Minister Vyacheslav Molotov, the Conference strongly criticized the Western-sponsored creation of West German armed forces, and issued a warning that the Communist states would have to take steps to ensure their security jointly should West Germany enter NATO as a fully-fledged member.[21] Thus, the Moscow Conference intended to forestall further attempts at West German rearmament, which had begun soon after the

United States, Britain and France had decided in September 1950 to remove restrictions on the creation of a West German military establishment. Except in an official Note issued in March 1952, in which it appeared to have become reconciled to the re-creation of German armed forces, the Soviet Union, seconded by its Eastern European allies, periodically attacked the concept of West German rearmament. This was true both during and after Stalin's rule and remained a significant exception to the 'New Course' in Soviet foreign policy initiated by Stalin's successors, Georgi Malenkov and Nikita Krushchev.

The preamble to the Warsaw Treaty made it clear that the official reason for signing it at that particular time was the ratification of the London and Paris Agreements that brought about the entry of West Germany into NATO, discussed earlier in this chapter. As such it fitted neatly into the effort to dramatize once again the implications of any West German rearmament. This effort was directed both at the states of Eastern Europe and at NATO. The former had to be convinced that a close military alliance with the Soviet Union was necessary, whereas the emphasis on the danger to NATO of a rearmed West Germany was calculated to create dissension among NATO member-states, some of which had already expressed misgivings on the subject, France being the foremost, also discussed earlier in this chapter.

A question may be raised as to why no Soviet-sponsored military alliance was signed immediately following the creation of NATO in April 1949, or even after the initial announcement concerning West German rearmament in 1950. It may be presumed that the Soviet Union did not seriously consider NATO an aggressive alliance until West Germany was invited to join. The preamble to the Warsaw Treaty implied that a sudden transformation of NATO from a defensive to an offensive alliance took place in May 1955, the month of West Germany's entry. This particular reasoning was likely to appeal to those Eastern European states obsessed with a genuine fear of West Germany, whether alone or as part of NATO.

### OTHER DEVELOPMENTS IN EASTERN EUROPE

If neither the outside threat nor the need for a tighter mutual security system was by itself a sufficient reason for creating WTO, the combination of the two did provide an incentive for the establishment of a collective defence system. However, other developments in the sub-region most likely had a more decisive influence on the timing and the form of the Warsaw Treaty.

While an argument can be made that the Soviet Union has viewed the creation of WTO as contributing to the strengthening of the security of the Soviet Union, the same was only partly true for the other members of the Alliance. Of the seven Eastern European states, only two, or possibly three, welcomed the Treaty as safeguarding their own security. In the middle of 1955 Poland still looked at West Germany as an adversary, eager to rectify the territorial arrangements reached at Yalta and Potsdam, and hence Poland most likely appreciated a more formal military alliance with the Soviet Union that would strengthen its own position *vis-à-vis* West Germany. It also may be taken for granted that East Germany strongly favoured the Treaty, since it would reinforce its own status as a fully-fledged member of the Soviet bloc in addition to ameliorating its fear of a rearmed West Germany. Finally, Czechoslovakia was another state that had a long-standing territorial quarrel with West Germany and that presumably welcomed the Treaty for the same reason as did Poland. It is therefore not surprising that these three states became known during the next two decades as the Northern Tier, or the Iron Triangle, and thus formed the core of the Warsaw Treaty Organization.

The remaining four member-states (Hungary, Romania, Bulgaria and Albania) were clearly much less concerned about the security aspects of the Treaty. None of them viewed West Germany as a 'revanchist' state committed to altering by force the post-war territorial *status quo* in the region. Moreover, none of them was directly exposed to a threat emanating from any other member of NATO. Finally, the 'New Course', proclaimed by Georgi Malenkov shortly after Stalin's death, signalled an impending thaw in East–West relations that was bound to reduce whatever insecurity and paranoia that remained in the minds of the leaders of the respective states.

A good case, therefore, can be made that in the mid-1950s the Warsaw Treaty made some sense as a military alliance. It was perceived by at least half of its signatories as strengthening their own security *vis-à-vis* West Germany and NATO. Nonetheless, it also can be shown that this particular aspect of the Treaty has not loomed very large in the annals of the organization. There is no evidence suggesting that much progress in the direction of strengthening military co-operation among the WTO members took place until 1961, when the Berlin crisis provided the opportunity for the first display of collective action in the staging of joint military

manoeuvres. The periodic conferences of the wto's defence ministers were the only major accomplishments related to the collective
security of the area. Judging by the explicit and implicit criticism of
the wto by some of its members, the Joint Command envisaged in
the Treaty was never fully implemented and remains today essentially the monopoly of the Soviet Union.

It is impossible to say whether Soviet domination of the wto's
armed forces contributed to the military strength of the Alliance. All
that is known is that it turned out to be the major object of
dissatisfaction on the part of Romania and Czechoslovakia, which
demanded a greater voice for the smaller partners. Thus, it can be
argued that the Soviet role introduced an element of disruption into
the organization and weakened its cohesion.

The institutional changes in the Treaty's command structure
announced at the summit meeting in Budapest of the Alliance leaders
in March 1969 were partially intended to meet the criticism of Soviet
domination.[22] Nonetheless, judging by the continuing dissatisfaction, more recently articulated, for example, by Romania at another
summit meeting in Moscow in November 1978,[23] the changes have
not resulted in a radical departure from the past, which means that
for all practical purposes the unified command remains today an
appendix to the armed forces of the Soviet Union of varying quality
both militarily and politically and Romania's advocacy of the adoption of national strategies and territorial defence remains.

Insofar as joint military exercises are concerned, there have been
numerous wto manoeuvres, but whether they have contributed
significantly to the strengthening of the Alliance's military prowess
can only be conjectured. The armed intervention in Czechoslovakia
in August 1968 has provided the only example of a concerted
military action undertaken by the Treaty. Although Western
observers generally were highly impressed with the precision and
efficiency of the invasion, the participation of the troops of the
smaller partners was largely symbolic, and the major burden was
borne by the Soviet army. Consequently, the intervention in
Czechoslovakia does not seem to provide convincing proof that all
of the national armies of member-states could or would participate
effectively in a large-scale joint military operation.

### THE STRENGTH OF THE ALLIANCE

The conventional military strength of the wto was significantly diminished following a series of highly publicized troop reductions between 1955 and 1960, but since then it has been steadily increasing to the point where today it represents, at least on paper, a formidable fighting force.[24] Since there is little or no information concerning the allocation of nuclear weapons to members of the Alliance, one can only speculate that arrangements in this respect are probably not substantially different from those operating in NATO. It is known that the smaller Eastern European states have some delivery vehicles such as short-range, surface-to-surface missiles, but there is no evidence that they have direct access to nuclear warheads.

There remains the problem of the commitment to the Treaty by the member-states, which can be viewed from two different perspectives. One aspect of it concerns the willingness of a member-state to participate fully in the Treaty's activities, including joint manoeuvres, weapons standardization, and possibly combined military operations. Here the most visible maverick, as already mentioned, has been Romania, which for some time has shown its strong aversion to being involved in WTO activities. Aside from its refusal to take part in joint military exercises, Romania has initiated its own defence doctrine, patterned closely on the Yugoslav concept of the 'People's War', and has frequently called for the dissolution of military alliances in Europe.[25] On the strength of that doctrine, it may be presumed that in the event of an East–West confrontation, Romania could not be counted on as a reliable member of the WTO that would be ready and willing to shed blood in defence of Soviet interests.

The other aspect of the problem concerns the reliability of the national military establishments of the Treaty members. The emergence of new political and military elites, characterized by often virulent nationalism, as was evident in the rapid rise of the Solidarity trade union movement in Poland, has raised the question of whether the WTO forces are dependable enough. Evaluating the reliability of combat troops is at best a difficult task. A systematic attempt at estimating the reliability of the Eastern European armies in the event of an East–West confrontation concluded that the only army that could be absolutely counted upon to participate in WTO's military operations – both offensive and defensive – was that of East Germany. All the remaining military establishments were viewed as not being entirely reliable.[26] Admittedly, the evidence used in support of the above conclusion tends to be impressionistic and intuitive, yet at the same time it does correspond to a widely-held popular percep-

tion of the role played by the individual states in the overall activities
of the Alliance.

One interesting aspect of the smaller members' attitude towards
the Treaty has been their insistence that the Warsaw Treaty apply
only to Europe. Over the years there have been unconfirmed reports
that the Soviet Union has attempted to persuade its junior partners to
deploy units of their national armies outside Europe, primarily on
the Sino-Soviet border, in Vietnam, and, most recently, in
Afghanistan. These requests apparently have been consistently
turned down by the Eastern Europeans and, if true, this would
testify to a certain decline in Soviet domination of the Alliance. In
turn, this also would affect the military potential of the Alliance as a
whole.

On the other hand, certain member-states, notably Czechoslovakia and East Germany, have acted as proxies of the Soviet Union
in various parts of the Third World. Their presumed goal was to
spread Soviet influence in selected African, Asian, and Latin American states and thus improve the Soviet position *vis-à-vis* both China
and the West through the shipments of arms and advisers to states
such as Angola, Ethiopia, Zimbabwe and Afghanistan, as well as
Nicaragua and El Salvador. While all these activities have been
conducted outside the formal framework of the Treaty, they may be
viewed nonetheless as fulfilling the same objectives as those of the
WTO by strengthening Soviet security against possible Western or
other external threats.

While such threats, real or imaginary, may have existed in the
minds of the leaders of the Soviet Union in the mid-1950s, by the
early 1970s it was clearly superseded by East–West détente, which
was symbolized in the official Western recognition of East Germany;
the settlement of the Berlin issue; the 1970 treaties between West
Germany, Poland and the Soviet Union; and the bloc-to-bloc
negotiations concerning Mutual and Balanced Force Reductions
(MBFR) and European security (see chapter 8). As in the case of NATO,
the decline in the intensity of the external threat was bound to affect
the degree of military preparedness of the WTO. But in the late 1970s
East–West détente began to show signs of wearing thin and its
deterioration was accelerated in the wake of the 1979 Soviet military
intervention in Afghanistan and the events in Poland. By 1983 fears
were being expressed in both Eastern and Western Europe that the
Cold War of the 1950s was warming up. But West Germany, the
villain of the 1950s, had assumed by the 1980s the role of an

intermediary between East and West and hardly could be viewed by the WTO as a serious threat.

### CONCLUSIONS

The histories of both the WTO and NATO show striking similarities. Both alliances were established for a specific purpose. It does not matter that in both cases the reasons for their creation perhaps were more apparent than real. What mattered was that both the senior and junior partners in the respective alliances perceived the presence of an outside threat. In 1949 the United States may have anticipated Soviet pressure against the West, although a good case can be made that at that very moment Stalin already had decided to abandon any aggressive posture toward the Western defence perimeter.[27] Similarly, in 1955 the Soviet Union may have persuaded itself that as a result of West Germany joining NATO, the latter had become an aggressive organization, one that was determined to destroy the territorial and political *status quo* in Eastern Europe without seriously reflecting on the possibility that West Germany tied to NATO might be less dangerous than it would be with no military or other restraints. It may be argued that once both sides began to doubt that the threats were real, the two organizations lost their *raison d'être*, at least insofar as their security aspects were concerned.

From a purely military security standpoint, the accomplishments of WTO have not been very impressive, especially when contrasted with the initial goals of the Soviet Union, which were ultimately partly responsible for the creation of the Alliance. But as a means to ensure the political reliability of the junior members to the Soviet Union, as legitimized in 1968 by the so-called Brezhnev Doctrine, the WTO has been an effective tool of intra-Alliance military policy-making as well as an effective tool of inter-Alliance diplomacy. NATO, while not fulfilling all the goals set for it at its creation, has evolved a sophisticated system of intra-Alliance consultations, and has been an effective diplomatic tool *vis-à-vis* the Soviet Union and the WTO. This point is discussed further in chapter 8. In systemic terms, both NATO and WTO have created institutional structures and interdependencies that strengthen the existence of two regional sub-systems. The emergence of sub-regionalized interaction patterns within the military-political sphere reinforce the economic systemic arrangements initiated in the 1950s and expanded later, as is shown in the next chapter.

NOTES

1  Robert E. Osgood, *NATO: The Entangling Alliance* (Chicago: University of Chicago Press, 1962), p. 309.

2  This is drawn from Werner J. Feld and Robert S. Jordan, *International Organizations: A Comparative Approach* (New York: Praeger, 1983), pp. 56–61. For a detailed study of this period of postwar history, see Ernst H. van der Beugel, *From Marshall Aid to Atlantic Partnership* (New York: Elsevier, 1966).

3  Eric Stein and Peter Hay, *Law and Institutions in the Atlantic Area* (Indianapolis: Bobbs-Merrill, 1967), p. 1032. For a survey of the institutions of NATO as well as the conclusion of the North Atlantic Treaty, see Robert S. Jordan, *The NATO International Staff/Secretariat, 1952–1957: A Study in International Administration* (New York and London: Oxford University Press, 1967).

4  Stein and Hay, op. cit.

5  See Theodore Achilles, 'US Role in Negotiations that Led to Atlantic Alliance', Part 1, *NATO Review* 27 (August 1979): 11–14.

6  Quoted in Alexander Rendel, 'The Alliance's Anxious Birth', *NATO Review* 27 (June 1979): 15–20.

7  Ibid., p. 17.

8  For a full discussion of these problems see ibid., pp. 17–20. See also Robert Strausz-Hupé *et al.*, *Building the Atlantic World* (New York: Harper and Row, 1963).

9  Endicott Reid, 'The Miraculous Birth of the North Atlantic Alliance', *NATO Review* 28 (December 1980): 12–18.

10  Achilles, op. cit., pp. 12–13.

11  Paragraph 3 of Senate Resolution 239, 11 June, 1948, 94 *Congressional Record* 7791, 7846.

12  Achilles, op. cit., p. 14. See also Edwin H. Fedder, *NATO: The Dynamics of Alliance in the Postwar World* (New York: Dodd, Mead, 1973).

13  Achilles, op. cit.

14  For details see Reid, op. cit., pp. 14–17.

15  Quoted in Theodore C. Achilles, 'U.S. Role in Negotiations that Led to Atlantic Alliance', Part 2, *NATO Review* 27 (October 1979): 16–19.

16  *New York Times,* 15 May 1947. For a survey of how the treaty provisions were applied in the first twenty years, see Robert S. Jordan, *Political Leadership in NATO: A Study in Multinational Diplomacy* (Boulder, CO: Westview Press, 1979).

17  Drawn from Arthur S. Banks and William Overstreet, eds., *The Political Handbook of the World* (New York: McGraw-Hill, 1982), p. 45.

18  The following sections are adapted from Robert W. Clawson and Lawrence S. Kaplan, eds., *The Warsaw Pact: Political Purposes and Military*

*Means* (Wilmington, DE: Scholarly Resources, Inc., 1982), pp. 5–25.

19 Zbigniew Brzezinski, *The Soviet Bloc*, rev. and enl. edn (Cambridge, MA: Harvard University Press, 1967), pp. 4–5.

20 B. Meissner, ed., *Die Warschauer Pakt-Dokumentensammlung*, vol. 1 (Cologne: Verlag Wissenschaft and Politik, 1962), pp. 12–13. See also G. Strobel, *Der Warschauer Vertrag und die Nationale Volksarmee* (Bonn: Studiengesellschaft für Zeitprobleme, 1965), pp. 15–22.

21 Conference of European countries on Safeguarding European Peace and Security, 29 November–2 December 1954 (Moscow: New Times, 1954).

22 Lawrence T. Caldwell, 'The Warsaw Pact: Directions of Change', *Problems of Communism* 24, no. 5 (September–October 1975).

23 Charles Andras, 'A Summit with Consequences', Radio Free Europe Research, *RAD Background Report/271* (Eastern Europe), 14 December 1978.

24 For details see *The Military Balance 1980–1981* (London: IISS, 1981).

25 For an excellent discussion see Alexander Alexiev, 'Romania and the Warsaw Pact: the Defence Policy of a Reluctant Ally', *Rand Corporation, P-6270* (January 1979).

26 Dale R. Herspring and Ivan Volgyes, 'Political Reliability in the Eastern European Warsaw Pact Armies', *Armed Forces and Society* 6, no. 2 (Winter 1980):289.

27 For an interesting treatment of this question see Marshall Shulman, *Stalin's Foreign Policy Reappraised* (Cambridge, MA: Harvard University Press, 1963), chapters 1–3, 5, 6.

# 3

## The Emergence of Economic Co-operation Arrangements in Western and Eastern Europe

In 1922, the Austrian Count Coudenhove-Kalergy made the prophetic observation that Europe had the following alternatives in the future: 'either to overcome all national hostilities and consolidate in a federal union, or sooner or later succumb to a Russian conquest'.[1] In the post-World War II period, a strong trend toward the first option became apparent. The establishment of the Organization for European Economic Co-operation (OEEC) in conjunction with the implementation of the Marshall Plan, by which the United States provided extensive financial aid ($13 billion) to Western Europe from 1947 to 1951, was a first step toward Western European unification. It was an initial endeavour to transcend national barriers to sub-regional trade and to create a mechanism for facilitating the payment for imported goods. In 1960, OEEC was reconstituted as the Organization for Economic Co-operation and Development (OECD), reflecting the re-emergence of Western Europe as a major economic force in the global economy, along with the United States and Japan (See figure 3.1 for the structure of OECD.)

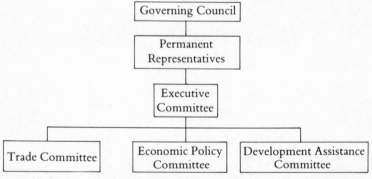

Figure 3.1   The Organization for Economic Co-operation and Development, 1960

Figure 3.1    *Continued*

In 1948 the OEEC was established to administer Marshall Aid, and by 1960 the economic recovery of Europe was completed. In December 1960 the decision was made to reconstitute the OEEC as the OECD.

The new organization reflected the change in purpose from one of restoration to one of maintaining and promoting economic growth to contribute to the development of the world economy; the aim, no longer European but world wide, is to promote economic growth and freer trade and to expand and improve Western aid to the developing countries (through the Development Assistance Committee).

The new members are: Australia, Austria, Belgium, Canada, Denmark, Finland, France, Federal Republic of Germany, Greece, Iceland, Ireland, Italy, Japan, Luxembourg, the Netherlands, New Zealand, Norway, Portugal, Spain, Sweden, Switzerland, Turkey, United Kingdom, United States. Yugoslavia and the Commission of the European Communities participate on a limited basis.

GOVERNING COUNCIL

Unanimity; country not bound if it abstains
Council decisions have force of international treaty
Passes recommendations

PERMANENT REPRESENTATIVES

Assist Governing Council

EXECUTIVE COMMITTEE

10 members, always including the 5 most important members
Assists Governing Council

ECONOMIC POLICY COMMITTEE

Chief economic advisers and policy-making officials of governments
Recommends policies to encourage economic expansion

OTHER COMMITTEES

Development Assistance Committee – co-ordinates aid programmes to
    developing states
Trade Committee – strives to resolve trade issues

Another, though modest, step was the establishment of the Council of Europe in 1949. While considered unsatisfactory by those who wanted an organization with strong 'federalist' features, the Council was set up as a pragmatic attempt at intergovernmental consultation and planning within a Western European perspective. (See figure 3.2 for the early structure of the Council of Europe.) Over the years, it has furnished the framework for the European Convention for the Protection of Human Rights and Fundamental Freedoms; become the mechanism for drafting conventions, mostly of a technical nature, for adoption by the member-states (almost all in Western Europe); and has engaged in a number of cultural projects. As Michael Curtis states, the Council 'provided a kind of

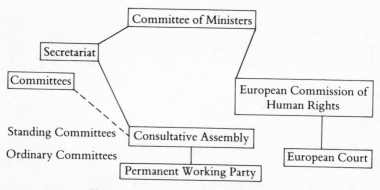

Figure 3.2　The Council of Europe, 1969

MEMBERS

Austria, Belgium, Cyprus, Denmark, France, Federal Republic of Germany, Greece, Iceland, Ireland, Italy, Luxembourg, Malta, the Netherlands, Norway, Sweden, Switzerland, Turkey, United Kingdom

COMMITTEE OF MINISTERS

Ministers for Foreign Affairs of the member-states
Decides matters of internal organization
Makes recommendations
Concludes conventions and agreements

CONSULTATIVE ASSEMBLY

Elected or appointed by national Parliaments
Submits recommendations to the Committee of Ministers
Passes resolutions
Discusses reports on any matters of common European interest

Figure 3.2    *Continued*
PERMANENT WORKING PARTY

Assists Consultative Assembly

COMMITTEES

*Standing Committee*

Represents the Assembly when it is not in session

*Ordinary Committees*

| | |
|---|---|
| Politics | Culture and Education |
| Economics | Science and Technology |
| Social and Health | Procedure |
| Legal | Agriculture |
| Regional Planning | Budget |
| Parliamentary | Public Relations |
| European non-member countries | Local Authorities |

SECRETARIAT

Administrative function

EUROPEAN COMMISSION OF HUMAN RIGHTS
EUROPEAN COURT

perpetual conscience'[2] in the development of Western European unity, but it has not made a substantial contribution to this goal.

While the Council offers a forum for debate on European unification and has also played a liaison role between different Western European international organizations (IGOs), it has had no authority to take action to initiate an effective integration process. The basis for such action was, however, laid in 1951 when the treaty setting up the European Coal and Steel Community (ECSC) was signed in April of that year in Paris and which later became known as the 'Treaty of Paris'.

## THE EUROPEAN COAL AND STEEL COMMUNITY (ECSC)

The concept of the ECSC was announced during a news conference held by French Foreign Minister Robert Schuman on a fine spring afternoon in Paris, on 8 May 1950. In his opening statement, Schuman said, 'It is no longer the moment for vain words, but for a bold act – a constructive act.'[3] This act was a proposal by the French government to place the whole of the Franco–German coal and steel output under a common High Authority, in an organization open to participation of other European states (See figure 2.1 for the structure of ECSC.) The long-term goal of this proposal was the achievement of European unity as a stabilizing factor in favour of world peace. In view of the Soviet Union's possession of the atomic bomb since 1949, Western Europe could not afford to remain fragmented and weak. Echoing the thoughts of Coudenhove-Kalergy expressed nearly thirty years earlier, Schuman intimated that if Europe was not built, war would be likely. Hence, 'the European federation . . . is indispensable to the maintenance of peace.'[4] In terms of advancing the integration process, Schuman stated:

the pooling of coal and steel would mean the immediate establishment of common bases of industrial production, which is the first step toward European Federation and will change the destiny of regions that have long been devoted to the production of war armaments of which they themselves have been the constant victims.[5]

## Motivations

While this euphoric statement was shared by many governmental leaders in the prospective member-states of the ECSC, it is important to look in greater detail at the economic and political motivations of the two main Powers involved in this integration experiment: West Germany and France. In West Germany, the direct economic benefits that might flow from a common market in the coal and steel sectors were not seen as being as persuasive as the indirect advantages of the proposed ECSC scheme. First, with the establishment of ECSC institutions, the controls upon the West German economy were lifted, especially those of the International Authority of the Ruhr[6] which, under the direction of the French, had limited the resurgence of that vital industrial region. Secondly, as already pointed out, the ECSC solution removed the Saar, which France had claimed as war reparations, from complete French administration and placed it into the hands of the ECSC authorities where West Germany would have a degree of input concerning administration and hope for eventual repatriation. Lastly, the ECSC provided domestic benefits that were clearly in the national interest since it marked an end to controls on West Germany's redevelopment of its steel industry and an end to tariff barriers against the export of West German coal – two major sources of revenue.

In terms of West German foreign policy objectives, the creation of the ECSC was also useful. Generally, it acknowledged West Germany's presence as a mimimally sovereign state within the European system, with the power to negotiate and conclude treaties. Additionally, the ECSC gave West Germany the opportunity to participate as an equal with France and superior to other Western European states, within sub-regional co-operative institutions. Thus, two important major goals of West German foreign policy were met.

For France, the direct economic benefits of the ECSC were also less important than certain political considerations. French foreign policy planners were cognizant of the fact that West Germany could not be kept under Allied control for any extended period of time. This seemed especially true in the heavy industry sector, where the Korean War placed emphasis on the renewed production of European steel. In fact, security planning dominated the French decision to propose the Schuman Plan. The genesis of the Plan came from the foreign policy planning of Jean Monnet, Etienne Hirsch, Pierre Uri and Paul Reuter who, in April 1950, presented a memorandum to Prime Minister Georges Bidault that outlined the ECSC's function to control West German industrial revitalization and eliminate the possibility of renewed Franco–German hostilities on a long-range basis.[7] As Derek Bok notes, the ECSC presented France with the solution to a serious security dilemma:

without an expanding industry, and with the growing demand for steel production occasioned by the Korean War, France could not expect the controls upon German production to be continued indefinitely. At the same time, however, the French were fearful of an unbridled development of the Ruhr into a powerful arsenal which might once more become linked with the aggressive policies of a German government. Under these circumstances, the Schuman Plan was conceived by France as a compromise whereby she would give up a part of her sovereign power to secure a degree of international control over German coal and steel.[8]

The motivations of the other prospective ECSC members – Italy and the Benelux states (Belgium, the Netherlands and Luxembourg) – towards the ECSC were less complex. They perceived that the prospects for domestic economic rehabilitation were enhanced and that political advantages were to be gained on the national as well as on the international levels.

Britain had also been invited to become a charter member of the ECSC. However, Britain declined the invitation primarily because it did not consider it beneficial to either its economic or political interests. Economically, and perhaps also politically, its relations with the Commonwealth were regarded as holding the highest priority and, in addition, it was apprehensive about the supranational powers that were to be conferred upon the institutions of the ECSC.

## Objectives and Purposes

The ECSC became operational on 1 January 1953. It is interesting to note that it included a previous experiment in economic integration undertaken by three small states – Belgium, Luxembourg and the Netherlands. In 1944, these three states had signed a customs union agreement; however, their action did not produce the economic union that had been anticipated. The principal economic objective of the new Community was to establish a single market for coal, iron and steel and to eliminate all barriers to free competitive trading, such as tariffs, quantitative restrictions, all forms of price discrimination (including those in transport) and agreements restricting trade and cartels. As discussed earlier, overarching the ECSC was the important political goal of a rapprochement between France and West Germany, which at the same time controlled the war-making potential of the latter.

## Organization and Structure

The ECSC had four major organs: the High Authority, the Special Council of Ministers, the Common Assembly and the Court of Justice. The High Authority was one of the executive agencies of the Community and had *supranational* powers. Decisions rendered by the High Authority, acting by majority vote, could bind directly enterprises in the territories of the six member-states, and these decisions could be enforced by the imposition of fines and penalties. The nine members of the High Authority were prohibited from accepting directions from the member governments and were to act only in the general interest of the Community.

The Special Council of Ministers performed two functions. It collaborated with the High Authority in the governance of the Community and, at the same time, represented the interests of the six member-states. It was authorized to issue ordinances in conjunction with the High Authority affecting directly coal and steel enterprises. It was composed of those ministers of the member-states especially interested in decisions before the Council. As a consequence, in some instances, the ministers represented the foreign ministries; in other instances, they were the economic ministers. The voting procedure in the Council varied from unanimity to two-thirds or simple majority as specified in the Treaty.

The Common Assembly had no legislative powers, but possessed a limited measure of control over the High Authority. The Assembly could force the resignation of the entire High Authority by a vote of censure and could ask the High Authority to reply to all questions put to it by individual Assembly members. The members of the Assembly were elected by their respective parliaments but were not seated in accordance with their nationality but by political alignments, that is, Christian Democrat, Socialist or Liberal.

The Court of Justice had and continues to have exclusive jurisdiction for the settlement of disputes between the member-states regarding the interpretation and application of the Treaty. In addition, private persons and enterprises are permitted to file suits with the Court under certain conditions and to obtain judgments when they have suffered damages through acts of the Community.

### Sub-Regional Integration and System Transformation

From a theoretical point of view, the creation of the ECSC was an experiment to achieve sub-regional integration of a number of sovereign states, and eventually the transformation of an existing international sub-system of several states into another one of perhaps one sovereign 'region-state' if political unification were to be successful. There are several theories attempting to explain the nature of a sub-regional integration process, but as far as the ECSC and subsequent Communities are concerned, the most appropriate theories appear to be functionalism and neofunctionalism.[9]

*Functionalism* stresses the importance of solving common problems and the building of habits of cross-national co-operation, through which the expectation of future constructive and beneficial collaboration will replace the endless quest for power as a dominant motive in international relations. International agencies will create through their work a system of mutual advantages which will assume too great a value in the eyes of their beneficiaries to be disrupted by war. Men will recognize transnational collaboration and international organization as providers of goods that their states can no longer provide by themselves. Men will no longer look apprehensively at the diminution of their state's sovereignty as a dangerous national sacrifice, but instead come to think of it as a beneficial investment in economic well-being and better services. As a result, loyalty will be increasingly divided between the state and institutions engaged in transnational collaboration. As this process progresses, people participating in as well as profiting from transnational collaboration will learn not only to accept this collaboration as useful and beneficial, but will also learn to work for further and more effective co-operation among the peoples of the world. This, in turn, will deepen the feeling of human solidarity. This line of thought is the theory of functionalism initially developed by David Mitrany in his stimulating book, *A Working Peace System*.[10] Functionalism thus was expected to shave off successive layers of sovereignty from the nation-state and eventually to produce a world thoroughly oriented to peace.

Whether this general transformation process stimulated by cross-national satisfaction of economic and social needs can in fact produce an ever-higher level of integration among states in a region or sub-region and culminate ultimately in regional states and perhaps some kind of world government eliminating all interstate conflicts, is far from certain. Functionalist theory presumes that transnational collaboration for the solution of economic and social problems is sufficiently divorced from politics to permit governments and private groups operating in transnational coalitions to pursue their common welfare interests without the troublesome conflicts of power politics. Functionalists stress the importance of learned habits of co-operation, which are presumed to be readily transferable from one sphere of activity to another. Finally, functionalists insist that special international institutions are better able than the nation-state system to attack coherently extensive economic and social problems. Artificial national barriers impair the rooting out of these problems, and only international agencies can perform this task effectively. As a consequence, these institutions were expected to become the focus of human loyalties and support.

This separation of politics from welfare may not be realistic. As we will see, the impelling forces of functionalism are often impeded by emotionally-laden and self-interested politics. Moreover, while collaboration habits can indeed be learned and socialization processes can be set in motion, they may also be placed in limbo by powerful contrary political forces. And while the transfer of functions from national governments to international institutions may result in the corresponding transfer of loyalty and support within the states making up the region or sub-region, overriding national loyalties and attachments may continue. These realities make us question the assertion that the integration process will be more or less automatic and will spread continually from economic sector to economic sector, gradually but inexorably enlarging the authority of international institutions at the expense of national governments.

To give functionalism a definitive forward thrust in a particular region or sub-region, the school of *neofunctionalism* has advocated a number of strategies:

1 Regional or sub-regional institutions must be specifically designed to further the process of integration and have a high level of authority for collective decision-making.
2 Instead of seeking transnational collaboration in matters that are not very relevant in political terms, as suggested by Mitrany, social and economic sectors must be chosen that are politically important, yet can be planned and carried out by civil servants involved in the performance of technical tasks (technocrats).
3 The tasks given to the regional or sub-regional institutions must be inherently expansive, culminating in 'spillover', or must be designed in such a way so as to cultivate 'spillover'. This term refers to a situation that is created when the attainment of an original goal within the regional integration context can be assured only by taking further actions, which in turn may create additional situations needing further action to attain regional goals. Spillover may take place from one sector of the economy to another, or from one economic sector to a political sector, or through the expansion of authority in one of the regional or sub-regional institutions, or by creating additional institutions.
4 Decisions made jointly by states in a region or sub-region and the regional or sub-regional institutions must lead to an upgrading and to the promotion of the common interests of the region.
5 Technocrats must have political 'savvy' and skills to help with spillover and to move integration processes forward. They are expected to have close links to the traditional centres of national power but, rather than make frontal attacks on national sovereignty, must move integration forward by stealth.
6 Deliberate linkages between economic and political sectors must be sought to ensure the full working of the expansive logic of

sector integration. The mix of economic and political factors may generate controversy and thereby lead to a widening of the audience interested and active in integration. The integration process may be aided by the formation of transnational groups and coalitions that perceive the upward movement of integration to be in their interest and strengthen its legitimacy.[11]

Many of these groups are likely to consist of business elites whose shared goals and common interests in integration tend to assist in the adoption of regional or sub-regional values and aid in the process of socializing the residents in states participating in integration schemes.

### Economic and Political Integration

Having discussed the functionalist theories that might explain system transformation within a geographic region or sub-region, the two central terms of economic and political integration must be defined in some detail. Both terms describe actions and processes that may have the potential of contributing and ultimately leading to the unification of separate states in a region or sub-region.

### Economic Integration

Economic integration is understood not only as the abolition of discrimination, especially tariff and non-tariff barriers, between national economic units, but also as a 'growing together' of the national economies of several states to ensure the optimal operation of the total economy in an international region or sub-region.[12]

Several levels of economic integration can be distinguished. The lowest level is the creation of a *free trade area* by several states, leading to the elimination of tariffs for goods shipped between these states. The second higher level is the establishment of a customs union, which adds a common external tariff for goods shipped from outside states into the unified market of the participating states. The creation of a *common market* raises the level of economic integration further by providing unimpeded flows of labour, capital and other economic factors between the member-states. The next higher level is *economic union*, which requires the harmonization of the economic policies of its member-states. A final step upwards would be the unification of these policies and *monetary union*. If this were accomplished, the member-states might be very close to political unification, but this final step might not really be possible without the unification of political institutions.

## Political Integration

Political integration has four sub-categories: institutional, policy, attitudinal and security integration. *Institutional integration* refers to the process of transferring decision-making powers and activities from the national units to the institutions of the regional or sub-regional IGOs. *Policy integration* is conceived as the endeavour to make policy jointly by all governments within the region or sub-region and to create a framework for the co-ordinated formulation of these policies. Because decision-making authorities and machinery require legitimization to function smoothly, support must be forthcoming by the political and other elites in the region or sub-region. This support, in turn, depends on favourable attitudes not only of the elites, although this is most important, but also of the mass public, and can become effective only if the elites and the public have a commitment to regional or sub-regional ideals, look towards the regional or sub-regional institutions for economic and other rewards, and slowly shift loyalties and expectations from the national units to the regional or sub-regional institutions. These shifts in attitudes characterize *attitudinal integration* which, in most instances, is a precondition for the first two sub-categories of political integration; but, in some instances, policy integration may engender increased attitudinal integration. In turn, progress in both attitudinal and policy integration is likely to lead to further institutional integration, which is characterized by expanded involvement of the regional or sub-regional authorities in terms of scope, level and competencies in regional or sub-regional decision and policy-making.[13]

Socialization as a process plays an important role with respect to attitudinal integration, inasmuch as it may lead to the adoption of favourable political attitudes and values for the regional integration process. Particularly important is the emergence of business elites committed to regional ideologies, inasmuch as they have the capability through cross-communications with other elites in the region or sub-region to generate support for the regional or sub-regional decision-making process and thereby to enhance its legitimacy.

The fourth category of political integration, *security integration*, refers to the expectation of non-violent relations and the concept of building a security community to assure such relations. Expectation of security through the creation of a community may pertain to peace within the region or sub-region, as well as to the prevention of aggression and defeat of outside states. How far the perception of outside threats stimulates the emergence of common goals, institutions, and identities is difficult to judge. Experiences with security IGOs such as NATO suggest that, while the common goal of protecting collectively the integrity of the member-states is regarded highly in time of major threat perceptions, its value diminishes rapidly during periods when elites and public have little concern about security. As a consequence, the processes of institutional and attitudinal integration are likely to receive little impetus, although policy integration may persist as a long-term assurance against future external threats.

### THE EUROPEAN ECONOMIC COMMUNITY (EEC) AND THE EUROPEAN ATOMIC ENERGY COMMUNITY (EURATOM)

By 1955 the ECSC was considered a success. Despite this somewhat premature assessment, it was a partial motivation for political leaders in the six member-states to begin planning for a broader European market. Another reason for moving ahead with a more extensive integration scheme was the failure of France to ratify the European Defence Community (EDC) Treaty, which would have contributed to further political unification through the creation of a partially integrated armed force of the Six. The failure to set up the EDC also made it impossible to pursue the idea of creating a European Political Community (EPC) which might have strengthened further the potential for political union of the ECSC member-states. (See chapter 2 for further discussion, including the structures, of the EDC and EPC.)

In 1956, a very important conference took place in Messina, Italy, in which Paul-Henri Spaak, a prominent Belgian statesman, played a leading role, and which produced the blueprint for the European Economic Community (EEC). (See figure 3.3 on the structure of the EEC.) The basis of this Community was a customs union with gradual elimination over a transition period of twelve years of internal tariffs and non-tariff barriers, as well as the phased establishment of a common external tariff. In addition, a 'common market' was set up in which labour and capital were to be given free movement, uniform anti-trust regulations were to be promulgated, and broad economic policy harmonization was to be attempted. In

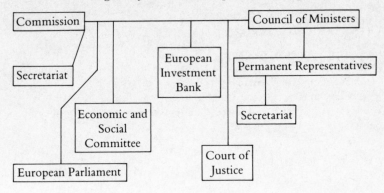

Figure 3.3   The European Economic Community, 1957

MEMBERS

France, German Federal Republic, Italy, Benelux states

COMMISSION

9 members chosen by national Governments but pledged to independence
Weekly meetings
Majority voting system, though very complex method
Applies Treaty provisions
Can bring complaints before the Court
Initiates proposals; Council cannot act without these proposals and can
   amend them only by unanimous agreement

*Secretary-General*

Administrative function

COUNCIL OF MINISTERS

One delegate from each member-state
Delegates depend on subject of meeting, thus no stable membership
Stronger role than in ECSC
Co-ordinates Community and national policies
Various voting methods, but unanimity on important issues
Qualified majority involves weighted voting

*Secretariat*

Administrative function

*Permanent Representatives*

Figure 3.3    *Continued*

EUROPEAN PARLIAMENT

Converted from ECSC Assembly
Proportional membership chosen by national Parliaments as individuals,
    not as national representatives
3 party divisions
Few powers (except censure) over Community executives
Serves ECSC, EEC, EURATOM

COURT OF JUSTICE

7 judges
Serves all 3 Communities
Court hears suits by Community members, individual firms, and private
    persons
Interprets Treaties and member-states' actions in regard to them
Developing 'community Law' code

ECONOMIC AND SOCIAL COMMITTEE

Advisory body of 101 members chosen by Council
Represents different economic and social groups in nations

*European Investment Bank*

the agriculture field, special schemes were to be instituted to assure a
higher income for farmers of the six member-states.

Besides the economic aims of increasing the standard of living of
the people living in the Community of the Six and making it possible
to employ the economies of scale in an enlarged and unified market,
political considerations also played a role in the establishment of the
EEC. It was hoped that, through the establishment of the Common
Market, the Six could gain sufficient strength to compete economically with the United States and perhaps also with the Soviet Union.
It was felt that increased economic strength would eventually give
the Six, and later the whole of Western Europe, a political position
equal to that of the two Superpowers. Moreover, as far as the
Atlantic relationship was concerned, Europe would become an equal
partner with the United States in the defence of the non-Communist
West. Finally, the problem of a divided Germany was given careful
thought, and it was anticipated that tying West Germany closely to
the West would reduce, if not eliminate, the feared possibility of

West Germany either orienting itself toward Central and Eastern Europe, as it had done after World War I, or adopting a more or less neutral attitude.

At the same time as plans for the EEC were made, favourable consideration was given to the establishment of the European Atomic Energy Community (EURATOM). The major reasons for the creation of EURATOM were apprehension that the present energy sources, mainly coal, would soon be exhausted as the main source of energy and concern over how nuclear energy would be used in due course to replace coal and other traditional energy resources. EURATOM, therefore, was to co-ordinate research and technological development for the construction of nuclear power plants, assure the availability of nuclear fuel, and seek to avoid costly duplication of effort among the six member-states. For the purpose of achieving its goal, EURATOM was to become the basis of a common market for fissionable materials and the centre of an extensive supply operation for these materials. (See figure 3.4 for the structure of EURATOM.)

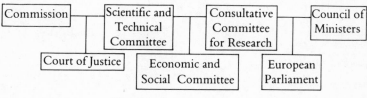

Figure 3.4   EURATOM, 1957

COMMISSION

Executive body responsible for implementing the EURATOM Treaty
Prepares proposals on which the Council takes decisions
Overlooks day-to-day operation of Community
5 members independent of national Governments

COUNCIL OF MINISTERS

Co-ordinates national policies and Community policy
Is only Community institution whose members are representative of national Governments
Makes most of the final decisions in Community affairs but can do so only on proposals from the Commission which can be modified only by unanimous vote
Most other decisions also unanimous, although there is some weighted majority voting

Figure 3.4 *Continued*

COURT OF JUSTICE

7 judges
Guardian of the Treaties of all three Communities
Their judgments binding on all individuals, firms, national Governments,
    and the executives themselves

EUROPEAN PARLIAMENT

142 members
Serves all three Communities
Exercises democratic supervision over Communities
Members appointed by and from Parliaments of member-states
Plans for direct elections
Examines budget
Can force Commission to retire through censure

SCIENTIFIC AND TECHNICAL COMMITTEE

Assists Commission and Council

ECONOMIC AND SOCIAL COMMITTEE

Assists Commission and Council

CONSULTATIVE COMMITTEE FOR RESEARCH

Assists Commission and Council

The treaties establishing both Communities were signed in Rome in March 1957 and are frequently referred to as the Treaties of Rome. Both Communities became operational in January 1958. Their institutional framework made use of some of the organs set up earlier for the ECSC as described previously. The responsibility of the Court of Justice was broadened to become the judicial arbitrator for the interpretation and application of the two new treaties. The membership of the Common Assembly was enlarged and eventually became the European Parliament. However, the new name should not convey the impression that the expanded body had been given additional legislative powers. The only new competencies added were a minimal power of debating the budget and very minor control over the executive bodies of the two new Communities.

The major executive and legislative functions were vested in a Commission for each of the two Communities and in a single Council of Ministers. In fact, this Council became the common body for all three Communities. According to both the EEC and EURATOM Treaties, a finely drawn balance was established between the powers of the two Commissions and the Council. The Commissions were given the right of proposing ordinances and decisions, but the Council was to have the last word in translating these proposals into effective Community orders. Two types of orders were to be distinguished: *regulations*, which had the force of law upon people residing in the six member-states and which were directly applicable without any assistance from the national legislatures; and *directives*, which were orders only to the governments of the member-states to translate the orders of the Community institutions into law through the normal legislative processes. Proposals were adopted by the Commission according to majority vote. In the Council, however, the initial rule was unanimity, for which a qualified majority was to be substituted in many instances after eight years. (See figure 3.5 for the structure of the combined Communities.)

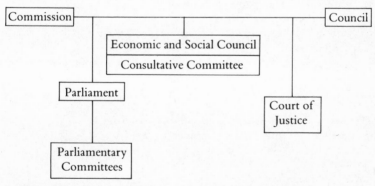

Figure 3.5   European Communities institutional chart (since 1967)

The EEC Council of Ministers agreed that the Executives of the European Community, ECSC and EURATOM should merge; accordingly, on 1 July 1967 the three Executives were merged into a single Commission.

COMMISSION

14 members
Watchdog of the Treaties

Figure 3.5 *Continued*

Rule-making functions: decisions and recommendations are binding; opinions are not

Applies and implements Treaty provisions

Participates in the preparation of acts of the Council of Ministers and the European Parliament

Collegial responsibility but with each member having responsibility for a particular sector


EUROPEAN PARLIAMENTARY ASSEMBLY

142 members

Appointed by national Parliaments from its own members

Carries out interpretations of Commission

Can compel Commissions to resign as a body if it passes closure vote

Supervises the executive organs of the three Communities

Debates annual reports of the three Communities and all other matters of interest to them

Assisted by Parliamentary Committees


COUNCIL OF MINISTERS

Representatives of governments of member-states

Co-ordinates economic policies

Makes decisions necessary for carrying out the Treaties

Conclusions usually taken by majority vote

Most decisions by unanimous vote, others by various majorities


COURT OF JUSTICE

Appointed with common consent of the Governments

Interprets the Treaties for the Communities

Full jurisdiction to settle all disputes within the Communities and to award penalties

Gives judgment on appeals

Interlocutory appeals from national Courts

Decisions becoming more closely interwoven with, and related to, municipal law of Governments


ECONOMIC AND SOCIAL COUNCIL –

Common Market and EURATOM matters

Figure 3.5 *Continued*

CONSULTATIVE COMMITTEE –

ECSC matters
Advisory bodies of representatives of various sections of economic and
  social life of members

Under the two Treaties of Rome, the Commissions were to be the
motors of the Community decision-making processes and were
expected in this particular function to promote the Communities'
interests. The Council, on the other hand, performed two functions:
together with the Commission, it managed the operations of the two
Communities and, at the same time, the Council represented the
interests of the member-states.

## THE EUROPEAN FREE TRADE ASSOCIATION (EFTA)

As already mentioned earlier in the chapter, Great Britain had been
invited to join the ECSC as one of the original members. Britain
declined this invitation, but later, in 1954, became an associate
member. Again during the 1955 and 1956 negotiations regarding the
establishment of the EEC and EURATOM, Britain was asked to join as a
charter member, but this invitation was also refused.

In July 1956, the British government suggested during a meeting
of the Council of the OEEC the appointment of a working party to
study the possibility of establishing a free trade area comprising all
the OEEC member-states and including the Common Market as one
of its members. Although scepticism and reservations about such a
plan were voiced in the prospective Common Market states, the
OEEC Council passed a resolution early in 1957 to enter into negotiations for the creation of a European Free Trade Area that would
associate, on a multilateral basis, the Common Market with other
member-states of the OEEC.

The negotiations, carried on for nearly a year and a half, were not
successful. The position of the French government, which insisted
on a common external tariff as specified for the EEC, a common
commercial policy toward third states including the Commonwealth, and the harmonization of social policies for the whole
trade area, could not be reconciled with the much more limited
objectives of the British government. Following the collapse of the
plans for a free trade area encompassing all of Western Europe,

Britain narrowed its objective and sought the establishment of a free trade area with the Scandinavian states, Austria, Switzerland, and Portugal. In November 1959, a convention establishing the European Free Trade Association was signed in Stockholm. (Figure 3.6 gives the structure of EFTA.) It called for the gradual elimination

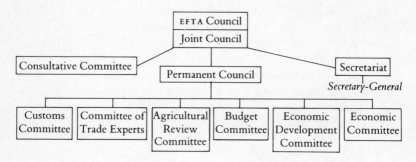

Figure 3.6    The European Free Trade Association, 1960

EFTA (comprising Austria, Denmark, Norway, Portugal, Sweden, Switzerland, UK, with Finland as an Associate Member) was a limited form of response by a number of European nations to the growing success of the EEC. It attempted to break down selective economic barriers between members while avoiding supranational controls. As the title suggests, a free trade area is a more limited arrangement than a common market.

In 1972 Denmark and Britain withdrew when they joined the EEC.

COUNCIL

Ministers or Permanent Official Heads of Delegations
One representative from each country
Unanimous voting required on important matters
No powers of compulsion

JOINT COUNCIL

EFTA members plus Finland
Met simultaneously with EFTA Council

*Consultative Committee*

Met before each Ministerial Council meeting
Reported to EFTA Council after each meeting
Discussed all matters within EFTA's sphere of activity

Figure 3.6    *Continued*

*Permanent Council*

Generally met weekly in Geneva
Composed of Permanent Heads of Delegations

*Secretariat*

Administrative function

*Functional Committees*

Customs
Trade Experts
Agricultural Review
Budget
Economic Development
Economic

of internal tariffs on industrial products but, in contrast to the EEC Treaty, no provisions were made for a common agricultural policy, although a number of bilateral and multilateral trade agreements led to a greater interchange of agricultural goods between the EFTA members. Despite objections from the Soviet Union, Finland became an associate member of EFTA in March 1961 and Iceland did the same in 1967. (See figure 3.7 for founding memberships of the EEC and EFTA.)

The institutional framework of EFTA was much more modest than that of the European Communities. It consisted of a Council of Ministers on which all member-states had one representative and which could take decisions only by unanimity, a number of committees set up by the Council, and a small Secretariat of less than 100 staff members.[14]

As soon as EFTA was established, apprehension about the unfortunate consequences of a Western Europe divided into two trade blocs prompted a number of proposals aimed at the construction of a bridge between EFTA and the Common Market. The Consultative Assembly of the Council of Europe in the fall of 1960 unanimously adopted a resolution recommending a multilateral association between the states of the two trading blocs. Another proposal advocated that the EEC, as a unit, become a member of EFTA.

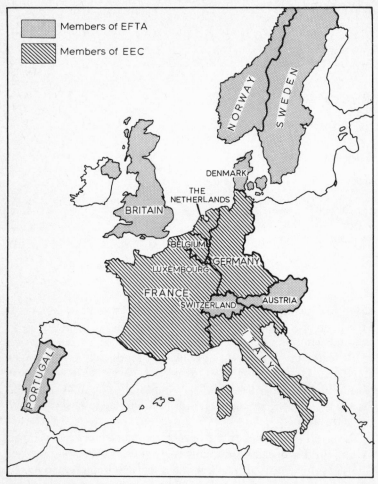

Figure 3.7   Founding Members of EEC and EFTA

In this way, it would be possible to maintain the institutional unity of the Common Market whereas, in the case of an association, the EEC 'would be dissolved like a piece of sugar in a cup of tea'.[15] A third concept advanced early in 1961 advocated the establishment of an all-European modified customs union without political character. The scheme was a cross between a free trade area and a customs union in which EFTA and the EEC would remain separate organizations but would achieve a large degree of harmonization in their tariffs toward third states.

None of these efforts succeeded in constructing the bridge between EFTA and the Common Market. The basic reason for this failure was that both trading blocs were seeking a different kind of unity in Europe and insisted on using different approaches to attain their objectives. The EEC laid out a fairly detailed master plan in advance, including the guidelines for solving (under the auspices of comprehensive Community institutions) such delicate problems as antitrust regulations, tax policy, and government subsidies. EFTA was started with a much less detailed plan, a minimum of institutions, and reliance on the member governments to work out details co-operatively as they were encountered. Moreover, Switzerland and Sweden objected to the comprehensive arrangements of the EEC Treaty as a violation of their traditional neutrality; and Austria was fearful that the unilateral declaration of East–West neutrality given in exchange for the 1955 State Treaty would bar it from becoming a full member of the EEC. Finally, and most important, Britain was reluctant to give up sovereignty to supranational institutions.

International power considerations also militated against the bridge-building process between EFTA and the EEC. France had been hostile to the expanded affiliation even before Charles de Gaulle came to power in 1958 because of the lingering suspicion that Britain was seeking to reduce France's leadership role on the Continent. West German Chancellor Konrad Adenauer was not willing to sacrifice his most important objective – Franco-German partnership – for possible trade gains and better relations with Britain. And Britain was intent on retaining its friendly ties with the Commonwealth, ties that might be impaired by a close association with the Common Market.

THE NORDIC COUNCIL

Several years before EFTA was founded, Sweden, Norway, Denmark, and Iceland set up the Nordic Council, which became operative in 1953. Finland joined in 1955. The Council's basic purpose was to serve as a forum for consultation among the member-states on matters of common interest. These matters included a Nordic labour market, efforts to increase efficiency in transport and communications, a Nordic Investment Bank (since 1976), and co-operation in social health policies. In many economic areas, the laws of the Nordic states have been almost completely harmonized; in other areas agreement has been reached on common principles and basic legal rules.[16]

The structure of the Nordic Council consisted of a Plenary Assembly with a Presidium appointed by the Assembly's members, and of a Council of Ministers in which all Nordic states are represented. The Council is not allowed to make any substantive decisions without the formal approval of the member governments. The Presidium of the Assembly and the Council of Ministers have separate secretariats; in addition, there is a Secretariat for Nordic Cultural Co-operation. Obviously, in terms of power and authority, these institutions are a far cry from those of the European Communities.

## THE COUNCIL FOR MUTUAL ECONOMIC ASSISTANCE CMEA/COMECON

The Council for Mutual Economic Assistance, best known in many Western states by an unusual abbreviation of the English title COMECON,[17] but recently more frequently referred to as CMEA, was founded in January 1949 by the Soviet Union, Bulgaria, Czechoslovakia, Hungary, Poland, and Romania. Albania joined shortly thereafter, and East Germany was accepted as a member in 1950. Initially, only European states were admitted to CMEA. Following a charter change in 1962, the Mongolian People's Republic joined CMEA in that year, Cuba became a member in 1972, and Vietnam in 1978.[18]

As pointed out in earlier chapters, the major motivation for the Soviet Union to seek the establishment of CMEA was to counter the effects of the 1947 Marshall Plan through which the United States had offered financial aid not only to Western Europe but also to the states of the Soviet bloc to overcome the ravages of World War II. However, the Soviet Union rejected this aid and compelled Czechoslovakia and Poland, which accepted the United States aid programme, to reverse their actions and to follow the Soviet example. This initiative also provided an Eastern European response to the establishment of the OEEC, although because of the fundamental difference in the Eastern and Western European economic systems, CMEA's functions differed from those of the OEEC. CMEA's major tasks are the exchange of economic experience among the members, co-ordinating foreign trade, extending technical aid to one another, and rendering mutual assistance with respect to raw materials, foodstuffs, machinery, and other items.[19]

For the Soviet Union, the underlying reasons for the creation of CMEA were both political and economic. It provided an instrument of Soviet control over the Eastern and Central European economies, aided in assuring that the Soviet model would be followed in every sphere of their political, economic, and social life, and made it possible to co-ordinate intra- and extraregional trade to the advantage of the Soviet Union by insisting on a favourable international division of labour among the CMEA member-states. For the non-Soviet member-states, economic motivations impelled them to participate in this sub-regional co-operation experiment. Of course, the disparity in military and political power between the Soviet Union and the other member-states of the organization was such that the latter hardly could reject participation at the time CMEA was formed.

It was fortunate for the other CMEA members that a policy statement made after the constituent conference in 1949, a statement that served as a substitute for a constitution for eleven years, included the principle of sovereignty.[20] This protected, at least in a legal sense, the freedom of action and independence of the Eastern European member-states, although they remained, of course, subject to Soviet political pressures. When in 1962 Nikita Khrushchev, following a Polish initiative, proposed a unified planning organ that would be empowered to compose common plans and to decide organizational matters, the proposal was rejected by Romania. Fearing that this proposal would transform CMEA into a supranational body, the Romanian government claimed that this would result in turning sovereignty 'into a notion without a content' and would restrict 'the fundamental essential and inalienable attributes of sovereignty of the socialist state'.[21]

The institutional framework of CMEA developed very slowly over about fifteen years. Up to 1956, the only body that met and discussed policy and possible actions was the Council, and it did not hold any sessions between November 1950 and March 1954. The Council is composed of the chief executives of the member-states. Although the creation of a secretariat was discussed at the constituent conference in January 1949, it was not until 1956 that a secretariat with its seat in Moscow became a reality. The task of the CMEA Secretariat is to prepare for the sessions of the Council. When, in 1962, an Executive Committee was established whose members were deputy prime ministers of the member-states, the Secretariat had the additional mission to prepare for the bimonthly meetings of the Com-

mittee. Finally, there are a number of Standing Commissions whose
number now exceeds twenty. Their fields of activity are linked to
various economic sectors and industries such as coal or electronics.
They are mainly concerned with the co-ordination of production
plans, the establishment of priorities for outputs of certain key
products, the formulation of foreign trade agreements, and the
selection of new investment projects.[22] (An organization chart is
found in figure 3.8.)

Figure 3.8   The Council for Mutual Economic Assistance
(COMECON/CMEA), 1949

MEMBERS

Bulgaria, Czechoslovakia, Hungary, Romania, Soviet Union; Albania,
Mongolian People's Republic, Mozambique, German Democratic
Republic, Cuba and Vietnam subsequently joined

COUNCIL

Composed of the chief executives of the member-states

EXECUTIVE COMMITTEE

Established in 1962, with membership composed of Deputy Prime Ministers of the member-states

SECRETARIAT

Formed in 1956, located in Moscow
Prepares for sessions of the Council and the bi-monthly meetings of the
Executive Committee

Figure 3.8 *Continued*

### STANDING COMMISSIONS

More than 20 had been created, linked to various economic sectors and
industries such as coal or electronics

Mainly concerned with the co-ordination of production plans, the establishment of priorities for outputs of certain key products, the formulation of
foreign trade agreements, and the selection of new investment projects

In accordance with the principle of sovereignty prevailing in CMEA
and also reflecting the rejection in 1962 of any conveying of supranational powers to the organization's institutions, each member-
state possesses one vote, and all decisions must be approved
unanimously. However, in principle, a state that declares itself non-
interested cannot veto an action agreed to by the other members (for
example, on specialization of production in some sector). It can only
refuse to participate.[23]

With this strong insistence on the right of maximum freedom of
action on the part of the member-states, CMEA has not made the
progress in economic integration as enjoyed by the EEC. Of course,
in view of the difference in economic systems between Eastern and
Western Europe, comparable development in integration may be
impossible anyway. Nor has it been feasible to achieve the division
of international socialist labour among the member-states that the
Soviet Union had hoped to attain and for which, according to Nikita
Khrushchev in 1962, the Soviet Union was prepared to reduce its
output of some categories of manufactures if it proved more
expedient to produce them in another CMEA state.[24] Nationalism and
economic egocentric tendencies in most Eastern European member-
states have severely curtailed the potential for such a division of
labour.[25] However, there has been increased border-crossing
economic co-operation in such fields as energy supply – for example
the Druzhba oil pipeline and an integrated electric power grid
system – rail transportation (a railroad freight car pool), and even
links in industrial production as demonstrated by the collaboration
of Czechoslovakian and Polish tractor plants.[26] An International
Bank for Economic Cooperation (IBEC) clears payments for CMEA
members.

In summary, then, some economic benefits from the CMEA
arrangements, though varying in extent and nature, have accrued to
all member-states; and it is noteworthy that 55 per cent of all exports
of the members move within CMEA. Hence, their overall capabilities

and resources have been strengthened in return for a relatively low level of obligations to the organization and the retention of a high degree of national prerogatives. For the Soviet Union, however, political control over its Eastern European satellite states through CMEA has not been bolstered materially. All of these states had by the 1970s turned to the West for financial aid for their further industrial development, both through the European Communities and bilaterally. Furthermore, while the Soviet Union may have gained certain economic benefits, the costs for these benefits may turn out to be appreciable if the Polish internal struggle of the 1980s should prove contagious in the sub-region and affect the general operations and activities of the CMEA.

### NOTES

1 Quoted by E. N. van Kleffens, 'The Case for European Integration: Political Considerations', in C. Grove Haines, *European Integration* (Baltimore: Johns Hopkins Press, 1959), p. 86. For general background information, see Werner J. Feld and Robert S. Jordan, *International Organizations: A Comparative Approach* (New York: Praeger, 1983), especially chapter 2.

2 Michael Curtis, *Western European Integration* (New York: Harper and Row, 1965), p. 47. Curtis's book contains a concise description of the structure and functions of the Council of Europe on pp. 29–47.

3 Quoted in Richard Mayne, *The Community of Europe* (New York: W. W. Norton, 1962), p. 85.

4 Ibid., p. 86.

5 Ibid., p. 88.

6 Roy F. Willis, *France, Germany, and the New Europe 1945–1967* (London: Oxford University Press, 1968), p. 105.

7 Mayne, *The Community of Europe*, pp. 88–92.

8 Derek Bok, *The First Three Years of the Schuman Plan* (Princeton, New Jersey: International Finance Section, Department of Economics and Sociology, Princeton University, 1955), p. 3.

9 For a full discussion of the various theories see Charles C. Pentland, *International Theory and European Integration* (New York: Free Press, 1973).

10 David Mitrany, *A Working Peace System* (Chicago: Quadrangle Books, 1966).

11 For a full discussion of these aspects see Leon N. Lindberg and Stuart A. Scheingold, eds., 'Regional Integration: Theory and Research', *International Organization*, vol. 24, no. 4 (Autumn 1970), which contains a number of relevant articles.

12 Cf. Bela Balassa, *The Theory of Economic Integration* (Homewood, Illinois: Richard D. Irwin, 1961), pp. 10–14, 21–5, 102–4, 118–34, 163–7. See also Jan Tinbergen, *International Economic Integration*, 2nd rev. edn (Amsterdam: Elsevier, 1965), pp. 57–62.

13 Joseph S. Nye, 'Comparative Integration: Concept and Measurement', *International Organization*, vol. 22, no. 4 (1968), pp. 885–90. See also Nye's 'Comparing Common Markets: A Revised Neo-Functionalist Mode', *International Organization*, vol. 24, no. 4 (1970), pp. 796–835.

14 For details, see Curtis, op. cit., pp. 240–2.

15 Quoted in Heinrich Siegler, *Dokumentation der Europaeischen Integration* (Bonn: Siegler, 1961), p. 383.

16 Arthur S. Banks and William Overstreet, eds., *The Political Handbook of the World 1981* (New York: McGraw-Hill, 1982), pp. 608–9.

17 COuncil of Mutual ECONomic Assistance. Finland, Iraq, and Mexico became associate CMEA members during the 1970s. Angola, Laos, and Ethiopia send observers to CMEA meetings.

18 Ibid.

19 See Michael Kaser, *COMECON* (London: Oxford University Press, 1965), pp. 10–21; and Andrzej Korbonski, *COMECON* (New York: Carnegie Endowment for International Peace, 1964), no. 549, p. 2.

20 Ibid., p. 11.

21. Ibid., p. 15. For additional details, see ibid., pp. 91–100; and Zdenek Suda, *La division internationale socialiste du travail* (Leydon: A. W. Sijthoff, 1967), pp. 42–5.

22 For details see Korbonski, op. cit., pp. 15–24.

23 Ibid., pp. 13–14.

24 Werner Feld, 'The Utility of the EEC Experience in Eastern Europe', *Journal of Common Market Studies* 8 (March 1970): 223–61, on p. 254.

25 Ibid., p. 258.

26 Ibid., p. 248, and Kaser, op. cit., pp. 133–4.

# 4

# Economic Integration and System Transformation

In the preceding chapter, we pointed out that functionalist theory assumes progressively higher levels of integration through continued transnational collaboration for the solution of economic and social problems. This progression eventually would lead to the transformation of a system of individual nation-states in a region or sub-region into the formation of a region-wide state or of a new, large federal state with a few small states. The neofunctionalists devised a number of strategies to help along this process of transformation, but whether functionalist and neofunctionalist concepts actually are confirmed in the world of reality can only be determined from actual events. This chapter examines the evolution of integration and possible unification both in the European Communities and CMEA and seeks to identify those forces tending to impel or to impede the transformation process.

What particular stimuli exist to push the process of integration to higher levels? What are the incentives of states in an international region or sub-region to integrate their economies and perhaps move towards the political unification of their separate national units? What may set into motion learning and socialization processes that could generate the needed political power for the creation of a political union and what are the counterforces seeking to prevent such a development?

## SUB-REGIONAL ASPIRATIONS AND INSTITUTIONAL SUPPORT IN WESTERN EUROPE

Among the Communities of the EC, the centrepiece of integration since 1958 has been the EEC. The common market set up by the EEC Treaty and to be implemented over a twelve-year transition period initially made spectacular progress. The internal tariffs were eliminated completely eighteen months ahead of schedule and the common external tariff was put in place at the same time. Although a few problems cropped up occasionally, the cross-national movement of labour, capital, and other economic factors was introduced successfully in accordance with the expectations of the treaties, and EEC antitrust regulations were applied Community-wide.

Intra-EEC trade grew from $7.5 billion in 1958 to $24.5 billion in 1967, an increase of 326 per cent. During this period the standard of living in the Community moved upward dramatically and the general economic posture of the six member-states* had reached impressive dimensions.

A common agricultural policy (CAP) was instituted which provided high target prices of basic agricultural commodities to be applied equally in the six member-states. To protect these target prices, the conventional machinery of customs duties and quotas was replaced by a scheme of variable import levies for a large number of important agricultural products, including grain, beef, pork, and dairy products. These levies were designed to cover the gap between world prices and the prices fixed for the internal market and to prevent low-priced imports from upsetting the high guaranteed prices of agricultural products.

To assure full success of the CAP, a European Agricultural Guidance and Guarantee Fund (EAGGF) was set up. This Fund was used to provide subsidies for restructuring inefficient farms and to finance farm exports that, because of high internal prices, were not competitive on the world market.

While the CAP did indeed increase the incomes of farmers, it has not been entirely successful because it produced large-scale surpluses of such commodities as wheat and butter primarily because no restrictions on acreage were included. Because these surpluses could not continue to pile up indefinitely without imposing a tremendous burden on storage facilities in the Community, large subsidies from the EAGGF were required to facilitate the sale of these surpluses abroad. The result was that the cost of the operation of the Fund soared to $14 billion a year by the late 1970s. These foreign sales highlighted the problems of the consumer in the EEC. On the one hand, prices were artificially raised every year and the cost of living increased appreciably; but, at the same time, some of the commodities had to be sold at bargain prices abroad. Complicating this

---

* France, West Germany, Italy, Belgium, the Netherlands and Luxembourg.

problem was the fact that some states, such as France and the Netherlands, benefited greatly from the system of high prices and subsidies because they were the largest agricultural commodity producers. On the other hand, West Germany, especially, was forced to pay a high share for the support of the Agricultural Fund and received only minor benefits from its payments. Finally, the devaluation of the French franc and the re-evaluation of the German mark in the second part of 1969 caused havoc in the smooth functioning of the CAP and required new monetary adjustments in the form of compensatory payments to assure the continued equality of farm prices in all member-states. This problem continues to plague the EC.[1]

In July 1967, a major reshuffling took place in the institutional structure of the three Communities. The High Authority of the ECSC and the two Commissions of the EEC and EURATOM were merged into one unified Commission. The result was that four major organs were now operating the three Communities, but each one was continuing to function under its own constituent treaty.

### Variations in Transformation Support

While the establishment of the unified Commission appeared to be progress on the path to integration, other developments had a negative effect on the functioning of the institutions and the manner of decision-making as laid out by the Treaties. One of these developments had its origin in Britain's application to join the EC. To the surprise of many on both sides of the Atlantic, the British government announced on 31 July 1961, that it would seek to open negotiations with the EC member-states with a view to becoming a full member of the EC. According to Prime Minister Harold Macmillan's statement in the House of Commons of 2 August, the reasons for the decision to join were primarily political: Britain would be affected by whatever happened on the Continent; there would be no security in isolation; Britain would have to play a role and should exert influence for the free development of life and thought in Europe; and Britain had to assume a place in the vanguard of the movement towards the greater unity of the so-called Free World. In the official communication of the British government to the acting president of the Council of Ministers requesting access to the EC, the Prime Minister asked that in the forthcoming negotiations Britain's special relations to the Commonwealth and the other EFTA member-states be taken into account, and that the essential interests of British agriculture be considered.[2]

Economic reasons also played a part in motivating the British decision to seek EC membership. In the Spring of 1961, Britain was in the throes of a serious balance-of-payments crisis. While exports to the Commonwealth accounted for slightly over half of total British exports in 1951, they had fallen by 1961 to only a little over 33 per cent. On the other hand, EFTA was only a moderate success as a trading group and Britain registered the lowest percentage of total exports going to the EFTA partners, namely, 12 per cent in 1962.[3]

For Denmark, which in 1961 also applied for membership – in fact, one day after Britain – economic considerations were the crucial factor for making the request for negotiations. In 1960, more than 40 per cent of Danish agricultural exports went to the EC, this constituting nearly 30 per cent of her total exports. Danish agricultural exports such as beef, pork, bacon, butter, cheese, and eggs would be affected by the EC's evolving agricultural protectionism, and, therefore, Danish farm products, especially in the important West German market, were likely to be displaced by French or Dutch goods. Admission to the EC, therefore, would be an important safeguard for the economic health of Danish agriculture. Similar considerations induced Ireland in 1961 and Norway in April 1962 to follow Denmark's lead and also to apply to the EC for admission.

The prospect of increased economic benefits would most likely also have prompted the three neutral EFTA states – Sweden, Switzerland, and Austria – to request admission if they had not feared that full membership might endanger their neutral status. All three states would have opted, if possible, for an extended free trade area between the two trade blocs, but, since the chances for such a development in 1961 were practically nonexistent, they considered associate status with the EC as the second-best solution to their problems and requested the initiation of negotiations for this purpose in December 1961. Following the example of the neutral states, Portugal also requested in the Spring of 1962 to open negotiations either as an associate or perhaps even as a full member.

After long and difficult negotiations in 1961 and 1962, the prospects for British membership seemed good. It was at that time, specifically on 14 January 1963, that French President Charles de Gaulle cast his famous veto on the entry of Britain. De Gaulle's professed reasons were grave doubts about Britain's readiness for membership because of Britain's insularity, which led towards the other shore of the Atlantic, as well as to the Commonwealth. But perhaps the most significant considerations for the veto were strategic and political. The membership of Britain was likely to threaten France's leadership in the EC and, in his view, Britain would constitute a Trojan horse for the United States, on the one hand impeding Western Europe's emergence as a unified entity under French leadership and, on the other, leading ultimately to an Atlantic Community under American 'hegemony'.[4]

The 1963 veto of British membership ushered in an at first imperceptible shift in the exercise of powers from the Commission to the Council. This became much clearer during a serious EC crisis in the Summer of 1965 when France boycotted the proceedings in the EC organs for six months. The official reason given was that France's EC partners had not fulfilled their promises with respect to the financing of the CAP, but the real reason for the boycott was de Gaulle's determined resistance to any extension of the Commission's decision-making authority and his fear that France might lose some national prerogatives.[5] Although this crisis was settled in January 1966 by the Foreign Ministers' Conference of the Six in Luxembourg, the powers of the EEC Commission did not escape unscathed. And the qualified majority voting procedure in the Council of Ministers, which, according to the EEC Treaty, was to go into effect with respect to many important issues at the beginning of that year, replacing the unanimity voting requirement, was emasculated by an ambiguous and inconclusive compromise.

Other factors were also responsible for the shift of power from the EEC Commission to the Council, upsetting the institutional balance and reducing institutional support. Nationalism began to be revived not only in France but in the other member-states, rekindled principally, but not exclusively, by Gaullist actions and philosophies. Another factor was a slowly rising opposition to the progress of political integration on the part of the basically nationalistic-oriented governmental bureaucracies in the member-states. As a consequence of all these factors, the Committee of Permanent Representatives, composed of national civil servants and subordinated to the Council as an agency responsible for the preparation of Council decisions, assumed an increasingly larger role in the decision-making process of the EC. On the other hand, the Commission was limited more and more to technical operations and to the collection of information, with its political influence cut substantially. Of course, the Commission continued to perform the functions assigned to it under the

Treaties, but with considerable reserve and a measure of passivity. By 1969 the morale of the more than 5,000 EEC civil servants plummeted, and nearly two out of three of these officials were looking for other jobs.[6]

At the end of the EEC transition period (December 1969), it became clear that not all the objectives outlined in the Treaty of Rome had been accomplished and that some policies, such as the CAP, required adjustment. To prepare the path for the Common Market's 'final' phase, a Summit Conference of the Heads of State and Government was convened in The Hague of 1 and 2 December 1969, and played a decisive role in setting the policy line and development pattern for the 1970s and beyond. The Conference addressed itself to several issues. Until the end of the transitional time, the operations of the EEC, including the support of the EAGGF, had been financed by annual contributions of the member-states with amounts determined by their size and economic strength. The conferees agreed to replace progressively the contributions of the member-states for the operation of the EAGGF by assigning independent financial resources to the Community, 'taking into account all the interests involved', and to strengthen the budgetary powers of the Parliament. This decision was one of the most important decisions made at the Conference.

Of equal significance was the agreement reached on the principle of admitting new members provided that the applicant states accepted the provisions and tenor of the EC Treaties. This meant that French opposition to the admission of Britain had finally been overcome and the EC membership could be enlarged not only by the accession of Britain, but of other qualified European states as well. A third significant agreement was to move forward on the path toward economic and monetary union and to work towards more intensive technological co-operation. Finally, the Heads of State and Government reaffirmed the will of their governments to pass from the transition period to the final stage of the Communities. In a communiqué issued at the end of the Conference, the participants expressed their desire to build a Europe which, 'assured of its internal cohesion, true to its friendly relations with outside countries, conscious of the role it has to play in promoting the relaxation of international tension . . . is indispensable if . . . world equilibrium and peace are to be preserved'.[7]

There can be no doubt that the Summit Conference at The Hague signified a change in the political direction of Europe. A new spirit, dubbed the 'Spirit of The Hague', began to pervade the EC. The emotional climate and the morale among the international civil servants took a turn for the better, and those persons in the member-states who saw in a united Europe the only hope for the future breathed easier. However, while the leaders of the six member-states agreed on many issues, many divergent interests and attitudes, as well as dissatisfied forces, remained. A close reading of the final communiqué revealed many ambiguities, although of course by their very nature communiqués are made up of compromises of various kinds. But it did not spell out what form a united Europe would take. De Gaulle's vision of a 'Europe of the Fatherlands' seemed to continue to lurk in the background as the emphasis on several occasions was on political co-operation among independent states rather than on political integration, a term that was never mentioned. On the other hand, we should note that the extent of co-operation envisaged in the communiqué goes beyond the text of the EC Treaties and as such it must be viewed as progress of sorts towards a unified Europe.

Whatever the shortcomings of the Conference may have been, one thing was clear: a new political will on the part of the member governments had emerged to intensify the integration of their economies which, by necessity, would also require a strengthening of the institutional machinery beyond the declared objective of increasing the budgetary powers of the European Parliament. In addition, the removal of all obstacles to the initiation of the negotiations with the states seeking membership in the EC opened the vista of an enlarged Western Europe moving toward unification, although it was not certain whether the increased number of EC members would produce more and deeper disparities of objectives and thereby constitute a hindrance to effective political integration.

Some of the fruits of The Hague Conference were not long in coming. On 22 December 1969, the EC was authorized to acquire its own financial resources, and the budgetary powers of the European Parliament were strengthened. For the Communities to acquire their own financial resources, a gradual approach was employed. During an interim period from 1 January 1971 to the end of 1974, all levies on agricultural imports into the Communities were to be turned over to the EC institutions immediately, while a gradual transfer to the EC institutions was put into effect for customs duties on other imported goods. Beginning in 1975, a certain percentage of the internal tax recipts of the member governments were also turned over to the Communities so that, by 1978, all expenditures of the EC, that is,

EAGGF and the operating expenses of the institutions, could be met from the above revenues.

The budgetary powers of the Parliament were increased only modestly, and again, this was done on a gradual basis. The Council, and to a lesser degree the Commission, retained much of the budgeting authority, but the parliamentary deputies were given the significant opportunity to modify the budget presented to them and in fact could increase its overall amount within certain narrow limitations.

The grant by the EC member-states of clearly defined financial resources accruing directly to the Communities and the expansion of the Parliament's budget authority were major steps on the path towards political integration. Only four years earlier, the EC had come close to collapse and passed through nine months of almost complete stagnation over the issue of autonomous financial resources and an increase in the budgetary powers of Parliament when de Gaulle strenuously objected to them. Now, new institutional and operational principles were introduced into the EC framework, which raised the position of the Parliament to that of a more important partner in the fiscal affairs of the Council and Commission. When linked to the creation of independent EC resources, it is evident that a highly political problem had been solved in favour of the common interest. This recognition of the common interest was made possible to a large degree by the convergence of national interests in the agricultural field. The need for financing the CAP and agreement on the terms for carrying out this task were important motivations to create the impetus for renewed movement toward political integration. The meeting of this need is an excellent example of the process of functional 'spillover', a vital element for the progress of integration. To accomplish the objective of financing the CAP, in which all member-states* were interested because of domestic political considerations, a broadening of the powers originally assigned to the EC institutions were regarded as necessary, and the appropriate decisions were made for this purpose.[8]

Another result of the Summit Conference at The Hague was progress in the co-ordination of the economic and monetary policies of the member-states. Motivated largely by the currency disturbances in 1968 and 1969, which were to a considerable extent the

---

* As discussed later, Britain, Denmark, and Ireland became EC members in 1973, Greece in 1981 and Spain and Portugal in 1986. Norway withdrew its application for membership when the Norwegian people expressed their opposition in a referendum.

consequences of divergent economic trends within the EC and which ultimately led to the devaluation of the French franc and the re-valuation of the German mark, the Council of Ministers recognized on 26 January 1970, that the harmonization of these trends was the only alternative to a constant repetition of these undesirable events. As a move towards common EC economic and monetary policies, the Council adopted a programme consisting of establishing defini-tive economic guideposts for the period from 1970 to 1975 and of working up an inventory of the main structural reforms to be accomplished at the national and EC levels. In addition, a joint currency float was instituted (the so-called snake arrangement) under which the currencies of the EC member-states were to fluctuate only within a 2.25 per cent margin. Some member-states (Britain, Ireland, and Italy) did not participate, however, and France moved in and out of the snake.

Of course, these were only the first, far from perfect, steps on a long political journey. While the immediate aim had to be the prevention of greater divergencies of the economic policies pursued by the member-states, the more significant task for the future was to ensure the convergence of the broad trends of national economic policies and their mutual compatibility. This means that the purely national definition of policy objectives had to give way to policy decisions arrived at in common and with strict attention to the common interest of the EC. Experience during the past decade has shown that this is not an easy undertaking, particularly since it may well involve the added delegation of normally national authority to the central institutions of the Communities and restraint on the part of the member governments in the exercise of their national preroga-tives. Even in crucial areas such as energy, full agreement on a common policy has not been possible so far, despite very compre-hensive and reasonable proposals by the Commission to the Council of Ministers.[9]

Because the economic and monetary unions need to be achieved simultaneously if they are to provide maximum benefits for the member-states as well as for the EC as a whole, the Commission elaborated a three-stage plan for their implementation. This plan, which included the creation of a unified financial market and fiscal harmonization, set 1978 as the primary target date, although the final stage could be continued to 1980. Basically, the Commission plan reflected the needs of the member-states to avoid currency disturb-ances of the kind that took place in 1968–9, because the proper functioning of the CAP is dependent upon holding currency fluctuations to a minimum. Similarly, the free movement of industrial goods was hampered by major deviations from traditional currency levels.

## The Consequences of Enlargement

The Plan for the 1970s developed by the Commission at the beginning of the period was complicated by the entry of Britain, Ireland, and Denmark. Great Britain made its second application for full membership in May 1967. Although initially de Gaulle rejected again Britain's membership, in 1969 his successor Georges Pompidou adopted a more favourable attitude, and negotiations were initiated in 1971 that culminated in the accession of the three applicants as of 1 January 1973.

To ease the economic problems for the new members caused by their entry into the EC, a five-year transitional period was worked out during which the three states were to adjust themselves to the EC system. Moreover, some concessions were made by the EC for some of the specific problems that British membership would generate for the economies of some of the Commonwealth states, especially New Zealand. To assist the Commonwealth states in Africa, the Caribbean area, and the Pacific (the 'ACP' states), an opportunity was provided for them to negotiate association agreements with the enlarged EC during the transitional period. (Similar agreements had been concluded by the EC with the former colonies of France, Italy and Belgium.)

It is important to note that while public opinion in the late 1960s was in favour of British entry, by 1970, 63 per cent of Britons queried were opposed to such a move. The main concern of many of them was an expected increase in the cost of living as a result of the CAP. There was also fear that the traditional sovereignty of the British Parliament would be undermined by the powers given to the EC institutions. As a consequence, entry into the EC aroused an intensive political battle. The Conservative government of Prime Minister Edward Health was pushing for accession, while the bulk of the Labour Party opposed membership. Nevertheless, the Parliament approved by a relatively narrow margin Britain's membership, and a constitutionally unusual referendum, held subsequently, showed that a substantial majority of the British people supported this step.

In Denmark, the proposed entry into the EC also aroused considerable opposition. However, a referendum indicated that a majority of Danes favoured membership,[10] although many Danish people continued to have reservations about their government's new relationship with the EC even after Denmark became a member in 1973. Only in Ireland did public opinion express itself strongly in favour of membership because the Irish people felt that they could gain major advantages from the CAP and were anticipating EC funds for promoting regional development schemes within Ireland.

The concerns of the British and the Danes began to generate frictions almost from the day the EC was enlarged. Although the new members had accepted the EC rules and procedures, the British government attempted to initiate changes in the CAP. In this effort it found a willing ally in the West German government. Another problem for the EC was the continued weakness of the Britsh pound, which was apt to hold back the EC plans for an economic and monetary union. Although the majority of EC members agreed on a common currency alignment, the British insisted on keeping the pound sterling out of this arrangement, and here they were joined by the Italians and the Irish. Obviously, as long as a common agreement on currency arrangements of *all* EC members could not be achieved, progress towards the economic and monetary union would be jeopardized.

Because of the anxieties described above, the 'Spirit of The Hague' and the consequent forward movement toward political integration lost some of its momentum. The surpluses generated by the CAP, which led to large accumulations of butter that had to be sold at cut-rate prices to the Soviet Union in 1973, deepened the unhappiness over the many undesirable consequences of the agricultural policy. While public opinion surveys suggested continuing support for the unification of Western Europe, few of the respondents really understood the full meaning of this process. On the other hand, important political and administrative elites in all the member-states held anxieties and reservations about the process of political integration, although they did not always express them explicitly.[11]

The anticipated favourable impact of the superior technological knowledge and political skill of the EC international civil servants on the process of integration did not materialize. On the contrary, many of the national civil servants in the member-states showed animosity and low esteem for the EC technocrats. While business and agricultural elites looked towards the EC as offering many rewards for their economic interests, their attitudes provided only limited support for the legitimacy of the EC and did not translate themselves into broad ideological acceptance of a region-state. Nationalistic tendencies, reinforced by perceptions that business and agriculture received the lion's share of the benefits flowing from the integration process, were successful in halting the 'expansive logic of integration' and have cast doubt on the adequacy and explanatory powers of functionalist and neofunctionalist theories. Despite the fact that the European Parliament received a small increase in powers, and its members are now elected by direct suffrage since 1979, it is uncertain how much these elections will aid the prestige and legitimacy of the European Parliament.[12]

In 1982 the EC was enlarged further when Greece became the tenth member-state. Greece had been an associate member of the EEC since 1961. While the Greeks were initially quite euphoric about their EC membership, the Socialist victory in the parliamentary elections of 1981, during which their leader and later Premier Andreas Papandreou fought the election campaign with the promise of withdrawing Greece from the EC, did not augur well for any substantial support to move the EC toward greater political integration.

Spain and Portugal also requested negotiations with a view to becoming EC members. Although there were some serious obstacles to be removed, especially in the area of agriculture, before the negotiations could be concluded successfully, basic agreement was reached by the Spring of 1985 for the two states to accede to the EC in 1986. This will result in a membership of twelve states with quite different political backgrounds and differing levels of economic development. Thus, the EC might become a very unwieldy organization in which progress toward political integration could be very doubtful.

Enlargement, on the other hand, could be a long-run positive factor for integration because of the tremendously increased economic power of the EC. For example, the economic strength of the EC exceeds that of the United States in certain areas. In international trade, it has become the most powerful unit in the world, and this position has been strengthened further by the free trade arrangements made with the remaining members of EFTA: Norway, Sweden, Austria, Switzerland and Portugal. This newly-found strength, applauded by the people in all EC states, has generated perceptions of pride and aroused widespread sentiments that this economic strength should be transformed into political power. Such a development, however, remains very uncertain and would require the harmonization of foreign and defence policies. In this connection we should note that efforts to develop common foreign policies by the EC have made progress, as will be discussed in the following chapter.

## SUB-REGIONAL ASPIRATIONS AND INSTITUTIONAL SUPPORT IN EASTERN EUROPE

Following the rejection of Nikita Khrushchev's proposal in 1962 to confer supranational powers on CMEA (see chapter 3), a special summit conference in April 1969 nevertheless advocated that greater emphasis should be placed on 'socialist integration and division of labour'.[13] But it was not until July 1971 that a Comprehensive Programme for socialist integration was adopted. Although this Programme included specific assurances against the creation of a supranational organization, the issue resurfaced in 1978 when the Soviet Union proposed again to make majority decisions binding on all CMEA members. However, this proposal was rejected as was done in 1962, with Romania being the most vociferous opponent, which is not surprising since the Romanian government had often shunned CMEA projects. But even the normally docile East German government complained with respect to this proposal that increasing specialization of production was leading to the transfer of certain elements of production to other CMEA states.[14] Nevertheless, Khrushchev's successor, Leonid Brezhnev, declared in 1980: 'Widening the front of specialization and co-operation demands more exact control of the integration process, adaptation of production to the requirements of growing foreign economic relations, and the creation of new raw material and production complexes on a multilateral basis.'[15]

In spite of the aspirations articulated by Brezhnev, what progress has been made in the integration process and how much institutional support has been generated? In terms of particular circumstances that might be conducive to integration, such as ethnic and cultural commonalities, uniform working conditions and social security, unrestricted movement of goods, capital, and labour within the sub-region, and harmonized economic and fiscal policies, the CMEA members remain limited in their enthusiasm in spite of a generally common culture and contemporary history (over the last thirty years), a common basic ideology (albeit enforced), and somewhat similar agricultural policies.[16] While market integration has indeed made very little progress, the integration of producing goods through specializing production processes has fared somewhat better. Measuring production integration by various means, Paul Marer and John Michael Montias tentatively found that while from 1950 to 1970 a measure of 'disintegration' occurred in CMEA because the less-developed member-states began to produce many products that previously had been the monopoly of the more industrialized members, the trend changed after 1970 and some specialization decisions were implemented.[17]

For the achievement of production integration, the principal instrument must be the co-ordination of plans. This entails a programme for the distribution of raw materials, machinery, technology, and manpower needed for the targets of the programme and the distribution of outputs. But actual integration can be attained only through joint individual production activities.

CMEA's integration plans are embodied in the 1971 Comprehensive Programme mentioned earlier. The Programme stresses improved co-ordination of plans, joint CMEA investment projects, and co-operative long-term 'target' programmes. It includes emphasis on the need of market integration mechanisms highlighted by a time-table to introduce a degree of convertibility of CMEA currencies. But, in order to lower the apprehension of most member-states about compulsory supranationalism, it introduces the principle of the 'interested party' allowing members to participate only in those CMEA projects or programmes in which they have a material interest.[18]

In spite of the Comprehensive Programme, no uniform monetary, social, or employment policies have been developed. Moreover, any extensive production integration plan would necessitate large investments in each member-state. Unless further progress can be made in production integration, however, it is unlikely that closer CMEA-wide co-operation can be achieved and a uniform industrial base can be established. Clearly, individual member-states look out for their own interests even within the framework of bilateral co-operation.[19] Only in energy supply and transportation has effective CMEA-wide transnational co-operation taken place. The reasons for this are perceptions of benefits by all CMEA members and the fact that the Soviet Union possesses nine-tenths of the crude oil and gas resources in the sub-region.[20]

What are some of the specific impediments to the lack of progress in integration and especially the lagging institutional support? Several negative factors can be identified:

1  Although the contemporary history of the CMEA member-states in Eastern Europe is similar, their historical experiences reaching back over several centuries are quite different. For example, prior to 1914, most of Czechoslovakia and Hungary were part of the Austro-Hungarian Empire, and East Germany and much of present-day Poland were lands belonging to imperial and later republican Germany. The impact of these and other historical conditions remains alive and impedes cultural and attitudinal integration.[21]

2  Many languages are spoken in Eastern Europe and it is rare to find persons who are multilingual, except for those governmental officials who are required to learn Russian. Of the various languages in the sub-region, only those persons speaking Czech or Slovak can readily understand each other. This condition also makes it more difficult to move integration forward.

3  Religious disparity is significant. Catholicism is widespread among the Poles and Slovakians, the Orthodox Church is the chief religion in the Soviet Union, Romania and Bulgaria; the majority of Hungarians adhere to the Calvinist faith; and many Czechs have their own brand of Protestantism. The diversity in religious beliefs also has had consequences for cultural development. In spite of the fact that religion is played down by the Communist ideology, it remains a social and political reality and religious diversity therefore constitutes an obstacle to integration.[22]

4  Undoubtedly, the most serious impediment to sub-regional integration is nationalism, which is found in varying degrees in all the Eastern European CMEA states. As a consequence, there is a desire to retain economic autonomy and to achieve as much industrial autarky as possible. These are very understandable aims considering that the people of Czechoslovakia and Poland were allowed only in 1918 to create their own states which they lost again temporarily from 1939 to 1945. Romania and Bulgaria achieved independent statehood somewhat earlier, in 1856 and 1878 respectively, but Hungary became independent only after World War I. The heavy-handed control exercised by the Soviet Union is also resented by many persons in the Eastern European

CMEA states, as the uprisings in East Germany (1953), Hungary (1956), Poland (1956 and 1981), and Czechoslovakia (1968), and the Polish solidarity movement, have demonstrated.

For all these reasons, there is no consensus and little enthusiasm for enhancing the integration process which might give greater power to the CMEA institutions. Therefore, support for these institutions is minimal, if it exists at all. Only when specific benefits can be attained for *national* industries or enterprises for particular CMEA actions is it likely that individual governments will support enthusiastically the institutions involved in these actions.[23]

## NOTES

1 See Werner J. Feld, 'Implementation of the European Community's Common Agricultural Policy: Expectations, Fears, Failures', *International Organization*, vol. 33, no. 3 (Summer 1979), pp. 303–34.
2 *EEC* Commission, *Fifth General Report*, Sec. 184.
3 See Randall Hinshaw, *The European Community and American Trade* (New York: Praeger, 1963), pp. 51, 52, 102–5.
4 For additional details see Werner Feld, *The European Common Market and the World* (Englewood Cliffs, NJ: Prentice-Hall, 1967), pp. 71–6.
5 For a fuller discussion of the crisis provoked by France, see John Lambert, 'The Constitutional Crisis 1965–66', *Journal of Common Market Studies*, vol. 6, no. 3 (May 1966), pp. 195–228; and John Newhouse, *Collision in Brussels: The Common Market Crisis of 30 June 1965* (New York: Norton, 1967).
6 Cf. *Le Monde*, 27–8 April 1969.
7 For the full text, see Agence Europe *Bulletin*, 3 December 1969.
8 For a more detailed discussion of the spillover hypothesis see Philip C. Schmitter, 'A Revised Theory of Regional Integration', *International Organization*, vol. 24, no. 4 (Autumn 1970), pp. 836–68, on pp. 837–46.
9 For details see Werner J. Feld, *The European Community in World Affairs* (Sherman Oaks, CA: Alfred, 1976), pp. 277–96.
10 In Norway, which had also applied for EC membership, a referendum to gauge the attitudes of the population on this application, membership was rejected.
11 See Werner J. Feld, 'The National Bureaucracies of the EEC Member States and Political Integration: A Preliminary Inquiry', in Robert S. Jordan, ed., *International Administration: Its Evolution and Contemporary Applications* (New York: Oxford University Press, 1971), pp. 228–44.
12 Werner J. Feld and John K. Wildgen, *Domestic Political Realities and European Unification* (Boulder, Colorado: Westview Press, 1977).

13 Arthur S. Banks and William Overstreet, eds., *Political Handbook of the World*, (New York, McGraw-Hill 1981), p. 590.

14 Ibid., pp. 590–1.

15 Quoted in Kalman Pecsi, *The Future of Socialist Economic Integration* (Armonk, NY: M. E. Sharpe, 1981), p. xv.

16 Details are found in Erik Boettcher, *Ostblock, EWG, und Entwickelungslaender* (Stuttgart: W. Kohlheimer Verlag, 1964), pp. 55–6.

17 Paul Marer and John Michael Montias, 'Theory and Measurement of East European Integration', in Marer and Montias, eds., *East European Integration and East–West Trade* (Bloomington, Indiana: Indiana University Press, 1980), pp. 11–16.

18 Ibid., p. 24.

19 Pecsi, op. cit., pp. 8–9.

20 Marer and Montias, op. cit., pp. 28–33.

21 See Boettcher, op. cit., for details.

22 Ibid., pp. 40–1.

23 Ibid., pp. 46–7.

# 5

# The Inter-Regional Politics of Integration

## INTRODUCTION

At the heart of the politics of integration – as in all political contests – is the struggle for power between those elites who want to retain their traditional power positions in the governments of the member-states and those who would like to shift power to the regional international institutions and thereby hope to move the unification process forward. The elites include elected or appointed politicians, national and regional (or sub-regional) civil servants, and leaders of various interest groups and large economic enterprises. In this struggle for the retention or shift of governmental power, it must be recognized that appearances have to be separated from reality and rhetoric from true intentions.

It needs also to be noted that functionalist and neofunctionalist theories may not offer adequate explanations of the regional or sub-regional process of tranformation from nation-states to a politically unified entity. Even Ernst B. Haas, the main source of inspiration for neofunctionalism, stated in the middle 1970s that the explanatory power of the functionalist and neofunctionalist theories regarding the integration process within international regions or sub-regions, especially Western Europe, has been found wanting.[1]

A new theoretical approach, therefore, is needed to explain the integrative process and to offer at least tentative predictions for its future course. For us, the most appropriate approach is a causal model, based upon the pursuit of the national interests of the chief actors in the integration process – the member nation-state in the regional or sub-regional organization. According to our 'national interest' approach, integration from its lowest form (a free-trade area) to its highest form (political union) is seen from the perspective of nation-state economic, political, and strategic interests, and of foreign policy goals. These goals largely set the scope and level of integration and define the parameters of the institutions to be created. In some sub-regional contexts, such as Western Europe, these institutions have been given a relatively high degree of independence; in other regions, for example Latin America (or sub-regions thereof), their decision-making latitude is mostly very limited. Indeed, so far, in all such arrangements, the member-states have exhibited ultimate national control, rather than permitting supranational control, of decision-making power and, despite occasional claims to the contrary, delimit for all practical purposes the role of the international bureaucracies. Thus, the member-states, as central actors in the integration process, are able to pace the forward movement of regional or sub-regional integration and, when necessary, disintegration.

Under the 'national interest' concept, the process of integration is defined by the inputs from national actors. The scope and level of authority of the integrative institutions does not reside within the calculus of international technocrats, but within the negotiated agreement of the member-states. Succinctly stated, integration is a vehicle through which member-states maximize or attempt to maximize their national interests on a long-range basis through the creation of regional or sub-regional institutions and the evolution of integrative policies. Moreover, the integrative process serves as a means through which conflicts can be resolved in a peaceful and non-coercive manner in either a pre-emptive or reactive response.

We would like to stress that it is the *national governments* rather than particular cross-national élites and interest groups, which are the effective elements in the development of integration, although governments are generally responsive to the demands of such influential constituencies. This approach assumes that governmental decision-making is rational and coherent in the sense that it serves to further the national interest and the survival of the regime, both domestically and internationally. In other words, decision-making should work towards meeting long-term goals within a coherent framework of perceived and defined national interests.

This approach requires a broad understanding of the concept of the national interest. Although the central concern of this format is the pursuit of foreign policy objectives of states which can lead to regional or sub-regional integration, domestic policies and considerations can influence greatly the evolution of planning for possible integration and the degree of national participation. Importantly, the national interest is based not only on the achievement of international power and prestige, but also on considerations of the continued social and economic health of the state itself. Thus, domestic policy objectives as shaped by domestic politics to satisfy influential constituencies, as well as foreign policy objectives, are major independent variables leading to rational decision-making which encompasses integrative international institutions.

Our approach, then, deals with the causal factors that can stimulate or can lead to regional or sub-regional integration or, alternatively, to disintegration. Rather than address only the nature of the process of integration after the threshold has been crossed, we will focus on the variables which lead up to the threshold and beyond. If these variables continue to reflect the interests and policy goals of the member-states, they are likely, especially when coupled with the additional impact of acquired learning, to stimulate growth of the integrative network within a region or sub-region. Or, this approach may well lead to an exploration of the causes of disintegration if member-states' interests and policies were perceived as being harmed rather than enhanced by the integrative process.[2] Thus, looking at the integration process from the perspective of national policies by both member- and nonmember-states of particular regional or sub-regional organizations, can provide a holistic dimension in terms of the international system that other integration theories seem to lack.

### THE SITUATION IN WESTERN EUROPE

As already indicated in the preceding chapter, progress towards a truly integrated united Western Europe has been lagging. The ambitious attempt to build an economic and monetary union by the end of the 1970s had failed, although the European Monetary System (EMS) was launched in 1979. However, not all EC member-states participate, and it has had recurrent difficulties. Currency fluctuations which EMS is supposed to control remain violent; and in March 1983 France threatened to quit the EC and collapse the whole structure unless West Germany re-valued its currency substantially, to parallel only a small devaluation of the French franc.[3] After some very tough negotiations among the EMS participants, the West German government gave in, and an adjustment of all currency rates was agreed upon. Not only West Germany but also the Netherlands, Denmark, Belgium, and Luxembourg increased the value of their currencies, while France, Italy and Ireland reduced their values.[4] The

French action reflected quite clearly the priority of *national* economic concerns over EC interests, with the French economic malaise and weak currency most likely caused by the inappropriate policies of the Mitterand regime that were to a large extent based on ideological considerations.

Earlier crises and readjustment of the EMS also had their origins in the assertion of overriding national interests by various EC member-states. Moreover, the general organizational goals of the French and other national bureaucracies also played a significant part in the EC-national government struggle. For a large number of national officials, the needs of effective Western European sub-regional integration are only a secondary choice and priority[5] and such an orientation has had a negative impact on the Western European unification process.

Strong nationalistic tendencies have also frustrated the formulation of many common EC policies, especially in the important energy field. At the same time, one 'common' policy, the CAP, which has been enormously costly and often irrational,[6] has apparently been generally impervious to attempts at adjustment and reform in spite of the fact that the CAP has crowded out other areas of needed expenditure. The reason for this 'success' is the self-interest of national ministers of agriculture who, for reasons of domestic politics, want to satisfy the demands of their influential farm constituencies at home.

Even the functioning of internal markets, the centrepiece of economic integration in Western Europe, has suffered increasing instances of national protectionism. This prompted West German Chancellor Helmut Kohl to state in March 1983 that decisions need to be taken by the European Council, the top-level periodic meeting of the EC Heads of Government, in order to maintain a 'free internal market'.[7] A variety of obstacles to the free movement of goods within the Common Market have been erected. They include campaigns to encourage the purchase of national products, preferences given to national products in the context of taxation, receiving public contracts for national products or providing preferential treatment through discriminatory technical specifications and many other measures, and erecting various frontier barriers as well as rules concerning technical safety and public health. Indeed, intra-EC trade as a percentage of total trade declined from 1973 to 1981: exports were down from 52.1 to 47.6 per cent and imports from 53.6 to 50.7 per cent. In 1982, 332 infringements of the EEC Treaty's provisions for free internal trade were reported, up from 243 in 1981 and 68 in 1977.[8] These circumstances suggest the existence of an imperfect customs union, a conglomeration of national markets, each with a continuing emphasis on its own national economic interests.

Stanley Hoffmann aptly described the political conditions underlying the EC situation in 1979 and, as he pointed out, changes in these conditions have been slow in coming:

Western Europe remains a collection of largely self-encased nation-states. The various governments of Western Europe have found it useful to establish common institutions to deal with their common problems for the following reasons: most of them are advanced industrial societies and have open economies; they are all sandwiched, so to speak, between a potential foe endowed with massive military might and the only ally that can balance and deter Russia's might . . .; and for the most part they have preserved the ties with their former colonies, whose development may now serve their own interests. But the basic unit of concern remains the nation-state, however inadequate. . . .

[T]he generation of true believers – the founding fathers of European integration, many of whom were American – has no heirs. Its successors are pragmatic. They do not doubt the advantages that cooperation, overall, brings to their nations, or the augmented influence that 'speaking as part of Europe' can give them. But they are determined to measure whether in each instance the benefits really exceed the costs; and precisely because they take the usefulness and existence of the Community for granted, they are not overly worried by temporary setbacks or general aimlessness.[9]

Hoffman goes on to say:

The future too, of course, is viewed in national terms because of the same idiosyncrasies that have kept the Western European nations from building a common state; they are partly deep residues of the past, partly distinctive features of their present political and social systems.[10]

### The Genscher–Colombo Initiative

Nevertheless, there have been repeated declarations by national leaders in the member-states that the unification process should be pressed forward. West German Foreign Minister Dietrich Genscher and his counterpart in Italy, Emilio Colombo, proposed in 1982 a 'European Act' which was to revitalize the idea of a politically united Europe through the conclusion of an appropriate treaty of unification, but later this idea was watered down. The Act originally was aimed at making certain activities currently outside the realm of the EC Treaties (for example, cultural affairs and non-military security issues) the subject of regular consultations. In addition, the powers of the European Parliament were to be strengthened. However, important EC member governments have opposed major proposals of the Act, including a sweeping extension of parliamentary powers.[11]

During the European Council meeting in March 1983, Chancellor Kohl, as presiding officer, emphasized again the need for a new *political* impetus for the integration process and for a more satisfactory performance of the Communities. He stated that the EC institutions must not be merely 'a kind of clearing house for the different national interests' although he acknowledged that these interests 'must be balanced and compromise sought'.[12]

The outcome of the Genscher–Colombo initiative for a European Act is very much in doubt and even its co-author, Signor Emilio Colombo, seemed to wonder in any case how realistic this initiative was. A West German newspaper predicted that even if parts of it were adopted, this would mean nothing more than 'changing the name of a company threatened by bankruptcy'.[13]

## The European Parliament Initiative

Another initiative for moving political unification forward has come from the European Parliament (EP). It aimed at institutional reform, more autonomous decision-making by EC institutions, and greater powers of the Parliament including a stronger voice in the budgetary process.[14] It envisaged the preparation of a draft treaty for a European Union specifying the goals and powers of the institutions. This draft treaty was to be forwarded to the governments of the member-states for possible approval and ratification by their national Parliaments prior to the June 1984 EP elections. If a number of member-states were to ratify the treaty, they could set up a union among themselves. The draft treaty was approved by the Parliament in February, 1984, by a strong majority.

Whether this initiative will have a chance to succeed depends to a large extent on the image of the EP created in the minds of the citizens of the member-states since the first direct elections in 1979 and the voter turnout during the 1984 elections, which was not strong. A high level of legitimacy of the European Parliament would be required for the plan to succeed.

In the first direct election in 1979, unlimited promises could be made, whereas in 1984 the voters asked incumbent candidates: 'What have you done in general and for us specifically during the last five years?' 'Indeed, what have the Communities done for us?' It is significant that some of the parliamentarians who were elected mainly because of their prestige and past glory never put in an appearance in the EP,[15] and many did not run again. But the above questions also motivated other parliamentarians not to be candidates again because although there have been many debates and much procedural discussion, little in fact has been done for the people in the member-states in terms of 'bread and butter issues'. This may well have been a major reason that the 1984 voter turn-out was 2 per cent lower than the 62 per cent in 1979 (with Italy showing an 84 per cent score and Britain a pathetic 32 per cent). This was a serious blow to the legitimacy of the Parliament and could furnish the death knell to the EP reform plans and any *relance* for European unification. One major reason for a lower turn-out may well have been the very large size of the constituencies of individual members of the EP, which makes it very difficult to establish a meaningful dialogue between voters and their EP representatives.

But there are other reasons to be skeptical about the success of the EP initiative. As Altiero Spinelli, a member of the EP and an astute, long-time observer of the Western European political scene, remarked in a speech to a Greek audience, 'delaying and paralysing' forces of the national structures are at work, impeding progress towards unification.

When we speak of the delaying and paralysing force of the national structures, we should be clearly aware that we are speaking essentially of the delaying and paralysing force of the national administrations, which make up the skeleton and the nervous system of the national structure, which have been created and remain in existence to hold up this structure and defend it. They are powerful because they have continuity, because they have a discreet but powerful cultural influence upon the everyday political culture of the country, because they condition to a far from insignificant extent the ideas of statesmen and parties, above all insofar as there are gaps in their heads and in their programmes.[16]

The inclination of national politicians and civil servants to hold onto their positions of power and influence is only natural; they see in any transfer of competencies to the EC institutions a political loss of these positions and therefore they utilize various political means to defeat or to delay such transfers. Often mutual distrust exists between the national and EC bureaucracies, with the former seeking to reduce the gap that exists between the higher EC and lower national salaries. In addition, both politicians and civil servants are exposed to sectoral pressures which they want to accommodate in order to retain the support of influential constituencies. Clearly, they do not want the EC institutions and civil servants placed in positions where the latter are able to offer significant rewards to these constituencies and thereby can increase or successfully solicit major support for unification.

These political constellations have not been changed with the admission of Spain and Portugal to EC membership bringing the number of EC members to twelve. On the contrary, enlargement of the Communities will tend to reinforce the determination of politicians and bureaucrats in all twelve member-states to hold onto their existing positions of power. At the same time, the number of 'Eurocrats' (as the EC international civil servants are often called) will also be increased since the workload of the 'Eurocracy' will be heavier with the addition of nearly 50 million people to the total population of the EC. Without doubt, progress towards Western European unification and transformation of the sub-regional system will not be helped by this enlargement. The disparity of objectives, views, values and cultures will be greater, making it even more difficult to reach common decisions and compromises on the operations of the Communities than it has been among the Ten.

Nevertheless, new initiatives towards reviving the political integration process were started during the European Council meetings in June 1984 (Fontainebleau) and June 1985 (Milan). In Fontainebleau, the heads of the EC governments were ready to explore how the decision-making powers of the EC institutions could be strengthened, and for this purpose established an influential *ad hoc* committee. At the same time, another *ad hoc* committee was set up to initiate steps for bringing about a 'Europe of the Citizens' which was to include the final implementation of a European passport, elimination of border checks (passports and customs), and the European flag and hymn.

At Milan, the European Council agreed by majority vote to convene an intergovernmental conference of EC members that might approve changes in the EC constituent treaties in order to prepare the path for the creation of a 'European Union'. How far all these steps towards political unification will be successful cannot be adjudged at this time. Past experiences and the realities of national political behaviour make us sceptical about the prospects.

### THE EASTERN EUROPEAN ARENA

The strong nationalist tendencies and considerations of power retention that permeate the politics of integration in Western Europe are also quite apparent in the Eastern European satellites of the Soviet Union. But the sources of concern displayed by the Eastern European CMEA members are different from those that inspire the nationalist orientations in the West.

It is not simply supranational powers *per se* to which the Eastern European governments object; they also fear the control that the Soviet Union might exercise over a supranational CMEA institution, which would reduce the economic and political autonomy retained by the other governments over their national affairs. Hence, as already pointed out in the preceding chapter, national industrial autarky and self-sufficiency remain highly desirable goals for these states in spite of the economic costs they entail and, for this reason, the flame of nationalism must be nurtured continuously. This fear of Soviet domination has also made it difficult to reach agreements on specialization of production, and there is a much greater propensity towards bilateral than multilateral agreements. However, it should be noted that the strength of nationalist impulses is not the same in all Eastern European CMEA member-states; some of them have been more willing than others to accommodate the common interest of CMEA, including that of the Soviet Union. This seems to be especially the case with East Germany and Bulgaria, whose leaders have a high ideological commitment to Marxist–Leninist doctrine.[17]

Another aspect that may have tempered the force of nationalism involves perceptions among the leaders and the more attentive public that *tangible* benefits were derived from CMEA, especially for major industries and enterprises. This may have happened occasionally in East Germany, Czechoslovakia, Bulgaria and Romania.[18] However, it is doubtful that these perceived benefits had a lasting positive impact on integrative tendencies. Rather, the basic anti-integration attitudes distrusting any kind of supranationalism were not altered significantly.

The quest for industrial autarky has created parallel industries in all CMEA states. This has encouraged those bilateral exchanges that reduce domestic surpluses and deficiencies. It has also led to asymmetries in resources and capabilities that have strengthened the dominance of the economically strongest member-state in the subregion, and increased the dependence of the other CMEA partners on the Soviet Union. This asymmetrical relationship has enabled the Soviet Union to exert a major influence on the behaviour of national political elites and on the economic decisions in the rest of CMEA in favour of Soviet needs and purposes.[19] This dependence has been an additional incentive for the Eastern European governments to oppose rather than support any further integration, even though it may be economically or politically feasible considering the natural interdependence of the CMEA member-states.

### INTERIM ASSESSMENT

In Western Europe, it is obvious that the dynamics of domestic politics militate against the transfer of further governmental powers to the EC institutions. Both elected politicians and civil servants in the member-states are generally intent on maintaining the transmission of demands and support with respect to particular interests through traditional national parties and administrators. Hence, while policy initiatives to strengthen the unification process are announced on occasion by top leaders of the national governments, as illustrated by the Genscher–Colombo proposal, there was no energetic follow-up because, except for mildly pleasing rhetoric voiced in some quarters of the two governments, there was no pressure to see these proposals implemented. On the contrary, foot-dragging and subtle sabotage were the order of the day and ultimately the initiatives came to naught. A similar fate may befall the 1984 Fontainebleau summit which agreed on instituting a 'Europe of the Citizens' with a common passport and a 'European' hymn and flag.

Although many industries and large enterprises in the member-states would benefit if all obstacles to a truly common internal market were removed and thereby their competitive position in international trade greatly improved – they could take much better advantages from the economies of scale – leaders of powerful national and cross-national economic interest groups have not been able to persuade the political and administrative elites in the member-states to give high priorities to these demands. Hence, no appropriate policies have been developed by the member governments to stop the various manifestations of protectionism which either had been in existence for many years or were introduced more recently by national authorities.

In Eastern Europe, as in the West, no transformation of the existing system of nation-states is visible. Nationalism, the quest for industrial autarky and economic self-sufficiency, the fear of Soviet domination, and the struggle to retain maximum governmental and political autonomy prevent or impede the formulation of any external policies that would move the sub-region towards enhanced integration.

## THE HARMONIZATION OF POLICIES WITHIN REGIONS OR SUB-REGIONS: ECONOMIC AND FOREIGN AFFAIRS

### The Western European Experience

The special legal basis in the EEC Treaty for the harmonization of policies is article 100, which confers a general power to harmonize 'legislative and administrative provisions of the Member States as having a direct incidence on the establishment or functioning of the Common Market'. The Council of Ministers may issue a directive for such harmonization upon an appropriate proposal by the Commission. Other articles of the Treaty deal with specific issue areas where harmonization of laws and policies should proceed. These include customs legislation, indirect taxation, exchange controls, social policies, transportation and commercial policy toward third states.[20]

There is also the possibility of the EC member-states pursuing policy harmonization through the conclusion of agreements outside the EEC Treaty framework. In such cases of intergovernmental arrangements, the Commission and other EC institutions have no guaranteed role, and whatever part they should play in the implementation of the harmonization process is specifically conferred upon them by the member-states.[21]

Some of the endeavours to harmonize policies in the EC have been generally successful. They include the CAP (although reform is badly needed), most aspects of commercial policy towards third states as far as they are specifically embodied in the EEC Treaty (such as changes in the external tariff), and tax policy where all member-states have put in place value-added tax systems but have not yet introduced fully uniform tax rates. However, even if the aspirations of the 1969 Summit meeting of the Heads of Government were to be fulfilled with respect to the achievement of an Economic and Monetary Union, major policy harmonization building-stones would still be lacking. In spite of many efforts, no truly common industrial policy has been formulated and implemented. Despite an urgent need for a common energy policy in the aftermath of the 1973 OPEC price débâcle, no agreement has been reached on an effective common approach to this issue area.[22] While the EMS represents a small (and fragile) step towards a common monetary policy, agreement on truly common economic policies regarding inflation, growth, and unemployment has not been possible, although the urgent need for such policies to overcome the general recession was expressed repeatedly by most member governments. The reason for the rhetoric on the one hand and the reality on the other is the political tendency of the governments to rely on national solutions, to claim credit if economic progress is achieved, and to blame their neighbours when things go awry.[23]

## European Political Cooperation (EPC)

Harmonizing the external policies of the EC member-states is a complex process because the formulation of such policies is not only based on the constituent treaties of the three Communities (especially the EEC Treaty) but also emanates from a policy-co-ordinating mechanism which was established by the EC member-states and evolved during the 1970s. This co-ordinating mechanism is now generally known as European Political Cooperation (EPC).

As already indicated, common commercial policies towards third states are now being formulated under the provisions of the EEC Treaty (mainly article 113) and pertain to tariff or trade agreements, trade liberalization measures, export policy, protective measures against dumping and subsidies, import and export quotas, and other similar matters related to the conduct of international trade. Association agreements affiliating foreign states with the EC in various ways and giving these states preferential trade terms also fall under the competencies of the EC institutions (article 238, EEC Treaty). However, the above activities constitute only a minor part of the foreign policy interests of the member governments and it is the EPC arrangement which serves as a co-ordinating device for many policy issues outside the EC competencies.[24]

EPC must be considered against a background of often divergent national foreign policy goals which the member governments seek to attain and the relationship of the pursuit of these goals to the formulation of EC policies towards third states. In analysing this relationship, several important factors must be kept in mind. First, the establishment of the Common Market represents in itself the realization of certain *convergent* economic foreign policy goals of the member governments. Second, in the field of external relations for which, according to the EC Treaties, the EC organs are competent, the EC represents a centralized effort of the member-states for the formulation and implementation of selected facets of their economic foreign policies, especially commercial policy. However, economic foreign policy goals cannot always be separated neatly from foreign policy goals concerned with national security or the advancement of a state's political power in general. Indeed, sometimes there is a certain degree of interdependence among the economic, political and strategic goals of a state, and the attainment of an economic policy objective may be a means for the accomplishment of a political or strategic goal. It is also possible that the attainment of economic goals may be closely intertwined with the simultaneous acquisition of political advantages or be dependent on making certain political or strategic concessions.

On the other hand, the pursuit of economic foreign policy goals may be strongly influenced by assertions of what member-states and their governments perceive as their overriding 'national interest'. Such assertions may render the formulation and execution of a co-ordinated commercial policy within the framework of the EC highly complicated or entirely impossible. Of course, in some cases, the national interest and the foreign policy goals of the member governments are compatible and could be attained through the employment of common EC policies. In fact, the use of some policy instruments, such as the conclusion of an association agreement, may be the only method available for attaining certain economic, political, and even strategic foreign policy goals and thereby enlarges the range of foreign policy instruments at the disposal of the member governments. However, significant divergent elements, some potential rather than actual, are also evident in the goals of all the member-states. Hence, it has not been and will not be unusual that a clash of wishes, wills and wiles, highly traditional in interstate relations but dysfunctional and therefore not desirable in the framework of the Communities, impedes or obviates the formulation of common external EC policies, although theoretically the member-states are not opposed to having such policies.

A third factor complicating the formulation and implementation of common policies has been the previously mentioned re-emergence of nationalism in the member-states, which has tended to accentuate what is conceived of as 'national interest'. Although

France is the obvious case of the re-emerging nationalism, flashes of strong nationalistic feelings have been observed during the last few years in all of the member-states, not the least being Britain. Beliefs that each government must serve foremost the interests of its own people before worrying about the common interest are heard frequently. Such sentiments strengthen the resolve of national governments to employ national instruments for the pursuit of their foreign policy goals rather than to submit to a joint approach under EC auspices. Since the realities of the power distribution between the central institutions and the national governments continue to favour strongly the latter, it is not surprising that the re-emergence of nationalism has severely weakened the position of the Commission as the main guardian of this interest.

Last, the views and attitudes of the national civil services in the member-states concerned with EC affairs have a significant bearing on the effectiveness of external policy-making in the EC. Sentiments of opposition against a 'takeover' of their functions by EC civil servants – the so-called Eurocrats – may express themselves in the use of subtle means to boycott the objectives of EC Treaties to turn over gradually the formulation and direction of certain economic foreign policies to the EC organs.[25]

It is important to stress that the views and attitudes of *any* civil service play a role in shaping the policies of those who wield political power in a state. These attitudes are likely to affect working papers that may become the basis for policy decisions, and tend to influence the implementation of any instructions received. Passive resistance and a lack of enthusiasm often suffice to block a policy.

The origins of EPC were in the so-called Fouchet Plan, which was elaborated in 1961 and 1962 by a committee of diplomats chaired by Christian Fouchet, then the French ambassador to Denmark. The basic idea of the Fouchet Plan – there were two somewhat different proposals made by the committee – was the creation of a Council at the level of Heads of State and Government which was to meet every four months and, acting by unanimity, was to co-ordinate foreign and defence policy. To assist the Council and to prepare policy proposals, an intergovernmental European Political Commission, perhaps in the form of a permanent secretariat, was to be established. This was to be composed of senior officials in the national foreign services and to be located in Paris.[26]

Although a chance for success seemed to exist in the early stages of the negotiations on the essentially Gaullist draft treaty for policy co-ordination, no synthesis between the divergent positions of France and the EC partners could be achieved. Therefore, the concepts of the Fouchet Plans lay dormant from 1963 to 1969. After the summit meeting of the Heads of State and Government of the Six held in The Hague in December 1969, efforts were again initiated to find new paths for the construction of some kind of European Union. One of these efforts was the creation of a committee composed of high foreign ministry officials of the Six under the chairmanship of Vicomte Etienne Davignon of the Belgian Foreign Ministry. The results of the committee's deliberations was the initiation of joint meetings of the foreign ministers of the Six every six months.

To prepare the sessions of the foreign ministers, a committee was created composed of the political directors of the Six foreign ministries, to which were added in 1973 their counterparts of the three new member-states, and in 1981 a Greek member was also included. This committee was named the Political Committee and was to meet at least four times a year, but actually has met more frequently. Subordinate to this committee are various working groups and groups of experts which have the mission to investigate particular problems and to recommend possible solutions. The locale for the sessions of the Political Committee is rotated among the member-states in accordance with whatever government chairs the EC Council of Ministers, whose presidency changes every six months. In line with the rotation of this presidency, the chairmanship of the Political Committee also changes every six months.

The major task of the periodic sessions of foreign ministers is the consideration of important questions of foreign policy. The member governments can suggest any issue for consideration that may pertain not only to general foreign policy problems but also to such matters as monetary affairs, energy, and security. Whenever the work of the Political Committee or of the foreign ministers impinges on the competence and activities of the EC, the Commission is requested to submit its own position on the matter under consideration and is invited to send a representative to the meetings.

The foreign policy co-ordination activities of the Political Committee are supplemented by periodic sessions of staff members in the embassies of the member-states, located in different capitals. Policy co-ordination meetings have also been held in the United Nations to assure the maximum cohesion in voting and policy positions of the member-states. The influence of the Commission staff in these meetings may well have been increased when the EC was granted official observer status by the United Nations.[27]

The emergence of the Political Committee as an important factor in the formulation of common foreign policies is pitting three organizational and bureaucratic groups against each other. One group consists of the officials of the foreign ministries operating through the Political Committee and perhaps in the future, through a permanent secretariat which will be concerned with the co-ordination of a wide range of foreign policy issues and, thereby, may invade the competencies of the EC. Secondly, there is the EC decision-making process, with its own group of international civil servants striving to produce and to implement external policies in accordance with the provisions of the EC Treaties. It is noteworthy that in this process, which originally was to be dominated by the international civil service of the EC, there is also an expanding control by a third group of national officials. These officials operate through the offices of the Permanent Representatives of the member-states. They have played an increasingly important role in the decision-making pro-cess of the EC through the Committee of Permanent Representatives (CPR), but have not been able to exert the same kind of influence with respect to the EPC process. Some of these national officials come from the foreign ministries of the member-states, and others are assigned by the ministries of economics, agriculture, and finance as technical experts. These experts may be called upon to give advice not only to the working groups of the CPR, but also to those of the Commission, since the major competencies of the EC are concentrated on the activities with which these technical experts are concerned. Hence, these national officials play a very salient part in formulating deci-sions for the EC and are more influential than their colleagues in the foreign ministries. We can observe, therefore, not only a subversion of the original concepts of EC decision-making in the field of foreign policy by national officials, but also we can discern competition and interpenetration between two distinct national bureaucratic groups struggling, perhaps subtly, to extend their own competencies and those of their institutions. Indeed, as Helen Wallace reports, the endeavour of different government departments in the member-states to stake out their own areas of responsibility for formulating policy has provoked tensions between foreign ministries and domestic departments, as foreign ministries have had to increase their awareness of domestic policy considerations, and ministries concerned with domestic problems have had to involve themselves more in international negotiations. At the same time, the members of the CPR have come to enjoy a special status and to acquire a certain solidarity with each other.[28]

For the foreign ministry officials, on the other hand, the Political Committee constitutes their seat of power, which they seek to expand by including within its jurisdiction every type of foreign policy issue including economic matters. It is seen as a kind of 'caucus' in which the participants 'understand each other', can engage in trade-offs on policy developments that cause few surprises, and most important, can continue to play their traditional roles without being inundated by 'innovative' proposals from the Commission experts.

The range of activities undertaken by the staff of the Political Committee that might lead to common action through the EPC process has been impressive. They include:

1  an average of some 100 communications transmitted every week over a common telex system called COREU;
2  more than a hundred sessions of common working groups composed of national diplomats to analyze important international problems;
3  meetings held twice a month to exchange information about the work and operations of the various foreign ministries that are relevant to EPC. A 'crisis procedure' is in the planning stage which will assure meetings of the Committee within forty-eight hours; and
4  representation of the EC at international conferences and in IGOs is carried out by *one* delegation.

In spite of this array of activities, the success story of the EPC process is mixed. The most significant achievement has been the coordination of policies leading to a common position during the preparatory phase of negotiations with respect to the Conference on Security and Co-operation in Europe (CSCE) that gave birth to the 1975 Helsinki Accords and the follow-up evaluation meetings in Belgrade in 1977–8, in Madrid during 1980–3 and Stockholm thereafter. The EC Commission participated vigorously and effectively in the deliberations on economic issues and contributed materially to shaping the common stand ultimately taken by the Nine and later by the Ten. EPC also became involved in the Euro-Arab Dialogue, conducted jointly with EC participants and designed to assure adequate oil supplies for Western Europe. This objective was not reached: but, in the process of negotiations, a number of declarations hostile to Israel were issued which stressed 'the legitimate rights of the Palestinian people and their need for a homeland'.[29] In 1974, the EPC apparatus was called upon to co-ordinate the policies of the Nine in the smouldering dispute between Greece and Turkey over Cyprus. While unable to find a solution to the crisis acceptable to the contending parties, the EPC effort con-tributed to limiting the conflict.

EPC also played a positive role in the democratization of Spain and Portugal during the 1970s by encouraging this process through supportive declarations, diplomatic actions, and recommendations for loans in the case of Portugal.

In Africa, opportunities also presented themselves for EPC action. Common policy stands were sought regarding the independence of Mozambique in 1975, the civil war in Angola and recognition of the MPLA regime in 1975 and 1976, the problem of Rhodesia, and the continuing difficulty of finding a solution for achieving an independent status for Namibia. Finally, a more recent and also continuing initiative is the EPC effort to evolve acceptable proposals to induce the Soviet Union to withdraw its forces from Afghanistan. So far, no proposal of the Ten has found approval by the Soviet Union, which considers the EPC suggestions as 'unrealistic'.[30]

The effectiveness of the EPC varies from international region to region (or sub-region). It has been most effective in the European–Mediterranean area; most recently, the EC foreign ministers have discussed ways of involving Spain and Portugal also in their political co-operation work, perhaps by holding talks with the foreign ministers of these states after each EPC meeting.[31] It has been less effective in the Middle East and Africa. While the problems of the Middle East have evoked a number of anti-Israeli declarations, these have not enhanced peace in the region. EPC endeavours in the southern sub-region of Africa (Mozambique, Zimbabwe, Angola, and Namibia) have not had much impact on the solutions finally reached or still outstanding in these states. With respect to policies *vis-à-vis* Asian and Latin American states, the EPC mechanism has been used only sparingly so far; on the other hand, the Commission has used its external competence to good advantage in these regions, although the scope of these relations remains fairly limited. In the relationship of the EC states to the United States and the Soviet Union, EPC has played a distinctly minor role.

In summary, the effectiveness of EPC depends on the issue area involved. As already pointed out, the EPC was and continues to be a major success in the CSCE policy co-ordination process. It has been less successful in other security issues such as Cyprus and Afghanistan. Clearly, in security matters, the EC member-states lack adequate military capabilities or resolve to employ necessary resources and, therefore, the EPC does not possess much leverage.

Regardless of how effective the EPC is as an external policy harmonizing agent for the EC member-states, it should be recognized that the EPC is basically a *national* instrument for foreign policy formulation and implementation, and its utilization is effectuated in accordance with what is perceived as best for the national interest. In addition, the EPC offers a number of special advantages to the member governments that are useful for domestic political purposes.

First, it provides an alibi when member governments are faced with hard choices such as support for Arab or Israeli positions or whether to favour Greece or Turkey in the Cyprus dispute. Under such circumstances, the EPC is a highly useful framework to divert conflicting pressures and to transfer them to an 'anonymous' body where the blame can be put on the 'group' or on other partners.

Second, the EPC can have a legitimizing effect on foreign policies of member-states *vis-à-vis* public opinion and, thereby, may give the government more freedom of action in relation to opposition political forces.

Third, the EPC is apt to increase the influence and power in international affairs of all member-states and especially of the smaller EC states. In particular, this increase of influence may be felt within NATO in relations with less-developed states outside the areas covered by EC association and preferential agreements, and in the United Nations and its specialized agencies. Clearly, the quantitative and qualitative weight of all EC states as reflected by EPC policy action is stronger than the voice of an individual member government.

How much does the EPC mechanism contribute to moving forward the political integration process? Will it become a major force in the creation of a European Union, either on a federal or confederal basis? We are rather sceptical about EPC developing into a significant stimulus to materially enhance progress towards political integration.

Without doubt, EPC has given rise to a policy co-ordination reflex in the foreign ministries of the EC. This means that most foreign policy issues requiring attention by the officials of these ministries will be evaluated in terms of their suitability for the EPC process. There is also no question that both EPC and EC channels in the external policy field are often linked very closely. But, because of the bureaucratic turf protection reasons discussed earlier, as well as concern with protecting a member-state's basic national prerogatives, any strong move towards some sort of 'communitarization' or 'federalization' would be vigorously opposed. Member governments may be interested and even willing to extend the scope of this mechanism and to rationalize its procedures and methods, but they would resist any attempt at fundamental reform which would eliminate the existing total national control over the collective EPC activities. Indeed, it is not entirely inconceivable that the establishment of the EPC mechanism was seen by some national foreign ministry officials as a counterstrategy against the prospective loss of function in their own field of action as a result of expanding involvement by the EC institutions in external policy-making.[32] Whatever some of the concealed motivations for setting up the EPC mechanism may have been, it is quite evident that at the present this mechanism and the EC external policy-making process operate side by side in a pragmatic manner.

The discussion of policy harmonization in Western Europe reveals little evidence that, with the exception of foreign policy in general, a high priority is attributed to the formulation of common policies, despite the clear rational imperative to bring about harmonization in various economic issue areas. Hence, there are no strong political demands on the member governments to step up the pace of policy harmonization. Nor does EPC stimulate such action in spite of the desire of many Europeans and of the usefulness for all the EC member governments to have Europe 'speak with one voice'. As we have seen, the basic ideological and bureaucratic dynamics of EPC are counterproductive to political integration. The preference is for EPC and EC policy-making to march together, but in different tracks.

### Eastern Europe

In Eastern Europe it is not the voluntary harmonization of the policies of the CMEA member-states that might push integration forward but joint planning and joint economic undertakings. The centrepiece for these activities during the last decade has been the Comprehensive Programme for Socialist Integration which was discussed earlier. It stresses improved planning co-ordination, joint investment projects, and co-operation in long-term target programmes.

Improved planning co-ordination must be part of each member-state's national plan and must elaborate the specific economic details of integration measures. The Comprehensive Programme lists the resources allocated for joint CMEA projects and the reciprocal commodity deliveries resulting from the project. It also specifies the resources devoted to the construction and operation of domestic industries that have bilateral or multilateral specialization agreements with other CMEA states and the reciprocal commodity deliveries resulting from these agreements.[33]

Joint CMEA investment projects, another part of the Comprehensive Programme, have been mostly carried out during the last few years in the Soviet Union. Examples are the Orenburg pipeline, asbestos mining facilities, a cellulose plant, and an electric power transmission line between the Soviet Union and Hungary. The value of these projects is $14.5 billion, about half of which is financed by the Soviet Union and the remainder by the Eastern European states.[34] The latter are not enchanted by these projects, to which they contribute labour, capital, technical know-how, and consumer goods, because the projects, located in Soviet territory, are not viewed as beneficial for their own economies and peoples. But the Eastern European governments also realize that, in return for their contributions, they are certain to receive needed raw materials from the Soviet Union. In view of the opposition to joint projects expressed by its CMEA partners, the Soviet Union has decided not to press for new joint projects in the 1980s.[35]

Co-operation in long-term target programmes is based on voluntary agreements for CMEA-wide plan co-ordination for selected sectors and key projects. It consists of joint forecasting for fifteen to twenty years of production, consumption, and trade trends to identify prospective shortages and surpluses. Medium- and long-term plans are to be co-ordinated by a sector's main branches of production and key commodities. Research and development programmes are subjected to joint planning and a continuous exchange of information is envisaged. Agreement has been reached to focus on five sectors: fuels, energy, and raw materials; machine building; industrial consumer goods; agriculture, especially food production; and transportation. In spite of Soviet insistence to move ahead with these programmes, it appears that actual co-operation has not advanced beyond a general statement of goals and intent.[36]

The reasons for the reluctance of the Eastern European governments to follow these plans have been already indicated. Some governments such as the Romanian insist on balanced, multi-sided, economic development under which no branch of industry would be sacrificed for the sake of advantages that may accrue from specialization. Even Bulgaria, normally more willing to accommodate the Soviet Union's wishes, is anxious to push its own goal of rapid industrialization. Moreover, in joint projects which have been actually initiated, such as undertakings in mining and transportation, there is much dispute among participants over who is contributing how much and how equitable the repayment arrangements are. Marer and Montias contend that for this reason joint CMEA projects will be relied on much less extensively in the 1980s.[37]

All this bodes ill for the progress of integration in CMEA. There is little incentive for the members, other than the Soviet Union, to make further integration a priority goal in their external policies. Only if the Soviet Union were to exercise brute force and compel integration in Eastern Europe would a transformation of the international system in the sub-region be possible. But the political and economic costs would be very high and, therefore, it is very doubtful if they would embark on such a course.

### INTEGRATION OR INTERGOVERNMENTALISM?

The discussion in the previous sections of this chapter suggests that few, if any, incentives exist in either Western or Eastern Europe to formulate national external or domestic policies designed to transform the current system of nation-states into a political, regional, or sub-regional unit either through a quantum jump in integration or a gradual step-by-step approach. Nationalist and bureaucratic-organizational motivations feed strong desires for the retention, and in some cases (Eastern Europe) increases in political and economic autonomy of most EC and CMEA member-states. If this is a proper characterization of current integration trends, how can the continuing operation of the EC and CMEA institutions be explained?

There is little question that these institutions satisfy important economic needs of the member-states. The officials employed by these institutions frequently possess superior expert knowledge in the economic areas in which they specialize, and may have better statistical and computer resources than are found in the ministries of the smaller member-states. Hence, their technical skills make it possible to carry out certain activities better than can be done by the national authorities. Examples in the EC are the execution of the CAP, although some of the implementation of the agricultural policies are in the hands of the national civil servants; the antitrust activities which are based on strict provisions embodied in the EEC Treaty (articles 85–7), and perhaps the politically sensitive area of sub-regional development within the territories of the Ten and the distribution of the Regional Development Fund.[38] In CMEA, the various committees and commissions provide valuable resources for the member-states in science and technology and in specific economic problems in various industrial and raw material sectors. In addition, the International Bank for Economic Cooperation (IBEC) and International Investment Bank (IIB) are useful sources of investment capital and trade credits.

The institutions may also serve as political alibis for the member governments in the event of economic failures. Since they often provide expert advice to the governments and help in the co-ordination of various economic and industrial plans, they are natural scapegoats if these plans do not work out. Indeed, the necessity to resort to national solutions may then improve the image of the national authorities in the eyes of their constituents.

These economic and political benefits which the member-states derive from the EC and CMEA institutions may reflect the integrative level which has been reached over the years and which is decidedly higher in the EC than in CMEA, but continue to be in fact the result of traditional interactions between governments which have set up IGOs to enhance the attainment of various economic, and to a lesser degree political, goals. Hence, the relationships within both sub-regional organizations, relationships which, as they increase, may presage a neo-functional all-European regionalism, are best characterized as 'intergovernmentalism' and not as integration, which denotes a process, no matter how slow, towards eventual unification of states within a particular region or sub-region. What we see going on then within both parts of Europe looks more like a giant 'co-operative enterprise'[39] rather than a purposeful march towards sub-regional political union.

So far, in our evaluation of the possibilities of system change in Western and Eastern Europe, we have focused on inter-regional forces and activities. In the next chapter we will examine economic and political factors and forces outside the two sub-regions that may have an impact on the integrative process.

NOTES

1 Ernst B. Haas, *The Obsolescence of Regional Integration Theory* (Berkeley, California: Institute for International Studies, 1975).

2 For a fuller discussion of this approach see Werner J. Feld, *West Germany and the European Community* (New York: Praeger, 1981), pp. 20–6; and Werner J. Feld and John K. Wildgen, *Domestic Political Realities* (Boulder, Colorado: Westview Press, 1977).

3 *Times-Picayune* (New Orleans), 2 March 1983.

4 Agence Europe *Bulletin*, 21/22 March 1983.

5 Ibid.; see also Agence Europe *Bulletin*, 7 April 1983.

6 See Feld, 'Implementation of the European Community's Common Agricultural Policy: Expectation, Fears, Failures', *International Organization*, vol. 33, no. 3 (summer 1979) pp. 303–4.

7 Agence Europe *Bulletin*, 21/22 March 1983, p. 5.

8 Agence Europe *Documents*, No. 1244/1245, 4 March 1983, 'Evaluation of the Working of the Internal Market' which provides extensive details.

9 Stanley Hoffmann, 'Fragments Floating in the Here and Now', *Daedalus*, vol. 108, no. 1 (Winter 1979), pp. 2–3.

10 Ibid., p. 14.

11 *Handelsblatt*, 3 March 1983.

12 Agence Europe *Bulletin*, 21/22 March 1983, p. 5.

13 *Handelsblatt*, 3 March 1983.

14 For details see Agence Europe *Documents*, No. 1214, 22 July 1983, 'Reform of Treaties and Achievement of European Union'.

15 Agence Europe *Bulletin*, 10 March 1983. See also the prophetic comments by David Marquand, written before the 1979 elections, in *Parliament for Europe* (London: Jonathan Cape, 1979), pp. 77–81.

16 Agence Europe *Documents*, no. 1246, 11 March 1983, 'Meditations on the Future of Europe', p. 6.

17 Paul Marer and John Michael Montias, eds., *East European Integration and East–West Trade* (Bloomington, Indiana: Indiana University Press, 1980), p. 26.

18 Andrzej Korbonski, 'Poland and the CMEA: Problems and Prospects', in Marer and Montias, op. cit., pp. 355–81.

19 Arpad Abonyi, Ivan J. Sylvain, and James Caporaso, 'Political Economy Perspectives on Integration', in Marer and Montias, op. cit., pp. 74–80.

20 Articles 27, 70, 75, 110, 113 and 117.

21 For a full discussion of the legal problems of policy harmonization see Alan Dashwood, 'Hastening Slowly: the Communities' Path Toward Harmonization', in Helen Wallace, William Wallace, and Carole Webb, *Policy Making in the European Communities* (New York: John Wiley and Sons, 1977), pp. 273–300.

22 See Michael Hodges, 'Industrial Policy: A Directorate-General in Search of a Role', and Robert A. Black, Jr, 'Plus ça change, plus c'est la même

chose: Nine Governments in Search of a Common Energy Policy', in Wallace *et al.*, op. cit., pp. 113–36 and 165–96, respectively.

23 For a full discussion of the status of policy harmonization, see G. Ionescu, ed., *The European Alternatives: An Inquiry into the Policies of the European Community* (Alphen aan den Rijn: Sijthoff and Noordhoff, 1979).

24 For a detailed and extensive discussion of these competencies, see Werner J. Feld, *The European Community in World Affairs* (Sherman Oaks, California: Alfred, 1976), pp. 277–96.

25 See Werner J. Feld, 'The National Bureaucracies of the EEC Member States and Political Integration: A Preliminary Inquiry' in Robert S. Jordan, ed., *International Administration: Its Evolution and Contemporary Applications*, (London and New York: Oxford University Press, 1971), pp. 228–44; and Werner J. Feld and John K. Wildgen, 'National Administrative Elites and European Integration: Saboteurs at Work?' *Journal of Common Market Studies*, vol. 13, no. 3 (March 1975), pp. 224–65.

26 For details, see Alessandro Silj, *Europe's Political Puzzle* (Cambridge, Massachusetts: Harvard University Center for International Affairs, December 1967, Occasional Papers No. 17); see also chapter 2 and figure 2.6.

27 Agence Europe *Bulletin*, 18 September 1975.

28 Helen Wallace, *National Governments and the European Communities* (London: Chatham House, PEP, 1973), p. 84.

29 *Bulletin of the European Communities* (3/1979); and Agence Europe *Bulletin*, 28 and 29 March 1979.

30 Agence Europe *Bulletin*, 13/14 July 1981.

31 For a complete listing of EPC activities see Reinhardt Rummel, *Das Europa der Zehn in der internationalen Politik* (Ebenhausen, West Germany: Stiftung Wissenschaft und Politik, 1981), pp. 233–4.

32 Ibid., pp. 136–43.

33 Marer and Montias, op. cit., p. 24. The following discussion relies heavily on the work of these two authors.

34 Ibid.

35 Ibid., p. 25.

36 Ibid.

37 Ibid., pp. 31–2.

38 For a concise discussion of this Fund, see Werner J. Feld and Robert S. Jordan, *International Organizations: A Comparative Approach* (New York: Praeger, 1983), pp. 190–6.

39 For a discussion of this notion see Werner J. Feld and Cheron Brylski, 'A North American Accord: Feasible or Futile', *Western Political Quarterly*, vol. 36, no. 2 (June 1983), pp. 286–311.

# 6

## Extra-Regional Economic and Political Relations: Sources of Conflict

### INTRODUCTION

For the study of system transformation which may be engendered by successful political integration within an international region or sub-region, extra-regional economic and political relations may be significant. A key question is the impact which external actors (i.e., non-members of regional IGOs) may have on the process of integration – whether this impact may either enhance or impede it. For an answer to this question the concept of 'externalization', developed by Philippe Schmitter in connection with neofunctionalist integration theory, is relevant. Referring to an integration scheme such as that represented by the European Communities, Schmitter advanced this hypothesis:

Once agreement is reached and made operative on a policy or set of policies pertaining to intermember or intraregional relations, participants will find themselves compelled – regardless of their original intentions – to adopt common policies *vis-à-vis* non-participant third parties. Members will be forced to hammer out a collective external position (and in the process are likely to have to rely increasingly on the new central institutions to do it).[1]

Schmitter later revised and refined his hypothesis by taking into account more systematically the role of external conditions with respect to intra-regional changes. He stated:

External conditions begin . . . as 'givens'. While the changes in national structures and values become at least partially predictable as consequences of regional decisions, the global dependence . . . of member-states and the region as a whole continue to be exogenously determined for a longer time. Nevertheless [by policy externalization, these conditions] . . . will become less exogenously determined, if integrative rather than disintegrative strategies are commonly adopted. The 'independent' role of these conditions should decline as integration proceeds until joint negotiation *vis-à-vis* outsiders has become such an integral part of the decisional process that the [global] international system accords the new unit full participant status.[2]

Schmitter suggests that the achievement of international status of the regional or sub-regional unit – in our case the European Communities – depends on the comparative performance of regional or sub-regional institutions and on the degree to which the officialdom of these institutions, that is, the Commission and its staff in particular, engage actively and deliberately in the promotion of new policies that may be acceptable to or indeed desired by national political elites.[3]

The promotion of such policies has been a major part of the struggle of the Commission to implement the provisions of the three Treaties, and in particular those of the EEC Treaty dealing with external relations competencies. Especially during recent years there have been strong efforts made to propose common commercial policies that take into account existing national policies or that would meet national policy aspirations.

Karl Kaiser looks at the role of external actors and events somewhat differently from Schmitter. He notes that external Superpower involvement may either help or hinder the development of integration.[4] Their activity may bring about regional or sub-regional integration as a response to a threat or, on the other hand, they may play an active role as catalyst, in much the same way as a chemical catalyst enhances the formation of a chemical compound. In line with this concept of open regions and regional integration, Kaiser also indicates that regional or sub-regional systems may affect the development of integration plans in other systems or sub-systems, an emulation effect.[5]

There are several kinds of inputs emanating from actions by external actors which stimulate the integration process in one direction or another. United States support for Western European unification in the 1950s was crucial for the successful initiation of this process. Continued American support in the 1960s had a lesser effect on integration, but nonetheless was important. The perceived threat of Soviet aggression during the 1950s and 1960s contributed materially to the widespread desire for a more cohesive Western Europe. Admiration by third states, large and small, for the apparently successful integration venture during the first two decades of the EC operation may also have been a positive factor.

While the examples mentioned so far were primarily political and psychological in nature, economic relations with outsiders also had, and will continue to have, a variety of effects. Outsiders, especially the United States, have been concerned with actual and potential inroads which the EEC has made on US exports worldwide as the result of the powerful economic position the EC has attained in world trade, the preferential tariff arrangements made with EFTA states, most of Africa and the Mediterranean states, and the high subsidies provided for EC agricultural exports. This has generated some economic counter-measures by third states and consequent pressure on EC decision-makers for more intensive agreement on external policy. This may lead to linkages of issue areas in the development of common external policy positions – for example, links between changes in the common external tariff, commercial policy, and general foreign policy, or the liberalization of trade, monetary policy, and international reserves.[6] All these factors have induced other states to request membership in the EC – witness the latest application for accession by Spain and Portugal – which might present challenges to the current structure of power in the EC that would most likely weaken the process of political integration while at the same time enhancing the international power position of the EC. These considerations may also have implications for CMEA as will be seen in the following discussion of extra-regional trade, agricultural, and monetary issues and friction.

### FRICTION OVER TRADE ISSUES

### *EC–United States*

The most significant extra-regional relations of the EC with Western advanced nonmember states clearly have been those with the United States. More recently, relations with Japan have also assumed a degree of importance but these relations do not have the same kind of political implications as have the EC–US relations. We will therefore concentrate in this section on the latter, which have been marked during the last twenty-five years by recurring friction but have also shown high levels of close co-operation.

The first major trade negotiations in which the EC and the United States were the main participants, were the 'Dillon Round' of negotiations in 1961. The agreements reached were modest in terms of the tariff reduction that both parties had hoped for. However, a unilateral tariff reduction of 10 per cent had already been made in 1959 by the EC when the Council of Ministers decided that the initial *internal* tariff reduction of 10 per cent for individual products as mandated by the EEC Treaty should be extended to third states benefitting from the most-favoured-nation (MFN) clause.[7]

Despite the fairly satisfactory outcome of the 'Dillon Round', especially considering the 1959 EEC tariff reduction of 10 per cent, some major economic concerns about the future impact of the CAP and about certain non-tariff barriers (NTBs) such as high domestic taxes on large automobile engines typical of imported American cars, continued to occupy United States foreign policy decision-makers. For these and other reasons, President John F. Kennedy recommended and Congress passed the Trade Expansion Act of 1962 which became the basis for an intensive round of negotiations, under the auspices of GATT, aimed at reducing tariffs and NTBs on a global level. These negotiations, which became known as the 'Kennedy Round' were to accomplish the following objectives:

1 A substantial reduction of tariffs on industrial goods, which under the Trade Expansion Act could be lowered to zero on goods produced 80 per cent in the United States and the EEC. The lower the tariffs agreed during the negotiations, the less would be the discrimination against US exports that had been institutionalized by the EEC customs union and by preferential association agreements for Africa and elsewhere.
2 Persuasion of the EEC institutions and member-states to pursue liberal 'outward-looking' trade policies.
3 Assurance that US agricultural exports to the EEC retain their 'fair share' or perhaps increase their proportion in the EEC market.[8]

The main actors in the Kennedy Round were the United States and the EEC. The negotiations were prolonged, often quite difficult, and towards the end assumed the character of an immense poker game with all the bluffs and theatrics associated with such a game. Although agreement was finally reached between all parties in the Spring of 1967, the results were not fully satisfactory to the United States. Tariffs on industrial goods were lowered by between 30 and 50 per cent, but little progress was made on eliminating or softening most NTBs. On the agricultural front, few concessions were made by the EEC to accommodate the American demands, consequently the United States was very disappointed about not obtaining an assured 'fair share' of the agricultural market in the EC. Indeed, the agricultural relations between the United States and the EC provided a continuous source of often acrimonious controversy across the Atlantic which at times led to serious friction, as we shall see later.

The adamant stance taken on some issues by the EC representatives and the general toughness of the negotiations in the Kennedy Round was a surprise to the United States. It contrasted with the climate of the Dillon Round – which was much more consensual and friendly. It became obvious in the Kennedy Round that the interests of the main negotiating parties, the United States and the EC, were diverging on a number of issues, with agriculture being the prime example. Some State Department officers in the Bureau of Economic Affairs began to wonder whether the main thrust of American policy towards Western Europe – European unification – should be sustained. Indeed, as early as 1964, questions were raised whether political integration in Western Europe was a realistic goal.[9] However, no basic policy changes were undertaken and support of Western European unification remained a primary objective in the United States.

A major strain placed upon the US–EC relationship has been the growing American realization that the EEC had become a serious competitor in international trade and investment. This has given the latter growing economic and political influence in the world, sometimes at the expense of the United States. In addition, tensions were caused by differing perceptions of the respective benefits of transatlantic trade.

A general analysis of US–EEC trade from 1958 to the beginning of 1973, when the EC was enlarged to nine members, is instructive. Table 6.1 reveals that exports of the United States during that period almost tripled, but shipments from the EEC to the United States more than quintupled. Although the United States had a surplus during the years from 1958 to 1971, it suffered its first deficit in 1972. This surplus ranged from a high of $2.3 billion in 1963 to a low of $413 million in 1968. While this continued surplus may have been a source of satisfaction to the United States, a more thorough analysis of how American exports to the EEC fared compared with those of other states presents a somewhat different picture. When the share of United States exports is compared with those of other *nonmember* states, the American portion comes out at 17.57 per cent in 1958, falling only slightly to 16.55 per cent in 1972. However, if we compare the percentage of US exports with all exports including those of EEC states to each other, the United States share dropped from 12.37 to 8 per cent. The reason for this is the tremendous increase in intra-EC trade from 1958 to 1972 – an expected result of the creation of the Common Market. During that period, this trade increased more than eight times while exports from third states into the EC increased only slightly more than three times.[10]

Table 6.1   EC–US trade relations, 1958–81 (US$ million)

|  | US exports | US imports | Surplus/ (Deficit) | Percentage of total US exports | Percentage of total US imports |
|---|---|---|---|---|---|
| 1958 | 4099.5 | 2668.5 | 1431.0 | 22.9 | 20.9 |
| 1960 | 5752.4 | 3415.7 | 2336.6 | 28.0 | 23.3 |
| 1968 | 8851.9 | 8333.8 | 518.1 | 25.6 | 25.1 |
| 1969 | 9916.5 | 8357.3 | 1559.2 | 26.1 | 23.2 |
| 1972 | 12150.6 | 12578.9 | (428.3) | 24.4 | 22.6 |
| 1973 | 17120.2 | 15697.4 | 1422.8 | 24.0 | 22.6 |
| 1974 | 22554.9 | 19363.8 | 3191.1 | 22.9 | 19.2 |
| 1975 | 23315.0 | 16483.5 | 6831.5 | 21.7 | 17.4 |
| 1976 | 25999.5 | 18213.1 | 7786.4 | 22.6 | 15.0 |
| 1977 | 27630.9 | 22678.6 | 4952.3 | 22.8 | 15.3 |
| 1978 | 32746.6 | 29597.0 | 3149.6 | 22.8 | 17.1 |
| 1979 | 43403.1 | 34070.1 | 9333.0 | 23.9 | 16.5 |
| 1980 | 54600.9 | 36742.2 | 17858.7 | 24.7 | 15.0 |
| 1981 | 52363.1 | 41647.1 | 10716.0 | 22.4 | 16.0 |

*Source*: Department of State, Bureau of Intelligence and Research, *US Trade with the European Community, 1958–1981*, Report 387–AR, 14 May 1982.

Nevertheless, from 1973 to 1981, the United States enjoyed substantial trade surpluses, which reached nearly $18 billion in 1980. However, in terms of total EC imports in 1981, the share of the United States was only 8.5 per cent, while of EC total exports 6.5 per cent went to the United States.[11]

When in 1973 Britain, Ireland, and Denmark (all former EFTA states) joined the EC, other EFTA states were given the opportunity of concluding free trade area arrangements with the EC on industrial goods. The consequence was that by the end of 1978, after a five-year transition period, most of Western Europe had become a huge trading bloc. In 1982, Greece became the tenth full member of the EC and, in spite of some current controversies, Spain and Portugal will become EC members in January 1986.

### Economic Crises and Conflicts

The increasingly serious, worldwide economic crisis during the late 1970s and early 1980s spawned national policies of the 'beggar thy neighbour' kind accompanied with growing protectionist tendencies, even *within* the EC. The upward trend in international trade reversed itself in 1981 for the first time since the end of World

War II in spite of the successful conclusion of the 'Tokyo Round' of negotiations which aimed again at tariff reductions, but concentrated more than in the Kennedy Round on the dismantlement of NTBS, setting up special codes of behaviour with respect to NTBS and safeguard clauses. These negotiations were based on the Trade Reform Act of 1974.

During the second half of the 1970s, the trade deficit of the United States assumed enormous proportions, reaching over $30 billion. How did its trade with Western Europe fare in this disastrous situation? As already pointed out and is shown in table 6.1, American exports to the ten members of the EC always exceeded imports from these states except for 1972. In 1981 although declining substantially from its record 1980 figure, the surplus was nearly $10 billion, while during that year the global trade deficit of the United States exceeded $27 billion. In terms of the share of total exports, exports to the EC accounted throughout the 1960s for more than 25 per cent, but in 1981 dropped to 22.4 per cent.

The transatlantic irritations caused by trade and monetary matters – during the first half of the 1970s the dollar was considered too weak while at the end of the 1970s it was considered too strong, as the result of very high interest rates – raises the question as to what policies should be formulated to reduce friction and to encourage greater co-operation between the United States and the EC. One possibility was the closer co-ordination of economic policies based upon studies and recommendations made by the OECD whose membership included the United States, Canada, Japan, and most other Western economically advanced states. The United States worked closely with the OECD, but the latter's excellent economic analyses and suggestions were frequently not followed and, for domestic political reasons, even within the EC, national policies were developed that ignored the OECD recommendations for policy co-ordination.

While, then, the use of the OECD as an instrument to bring about greater collaboration between the United States and the EC was considerably less than a success, another tool to achieve this purpose and to include Japan was the annual convening of the leaders of the major Western industrial democracies in so-called 'Summit' meetings. The first of these summits took place in Rambouillet, France, in 1975 and they have been held every year since then. The participants at Rambouillet were the Heads of Government of France, West Germany, Britain, Italy, Japan and the United States. Later Canada was brought into the summit process; additionally the President of the Commission of the European Communities was authorized to attend summit sessions on topics involving EC responsibilities.

Topics and effects of the summits varied from year to year. Clearly, the expectations raised among the public, sometimes almost euphoria, were often not met after the rhetoric during and after the summits had died down. Promises made during summits were or could not be kept in the face of subsequent political and economic realities. Apparent misunderstandings added to the difficulty of implementing summit objectives. A good example was the 1982 summit held at Versailles, where President Ronald Reagan believed he had obtained agreement on how the summit participants were to handle their economic and financial relations with the Soviet Union and other CMEA states. However, the imposition of American sanctions upon suppliers of materials to the construction of the Soviet gas pipe line to Western Europe following the summit highlighted the fact that full agreement had not been reached on this sensitive subject. The result was very serious acrimony among the Western industrialized states.

### The Steel Controversy

A source of major conflict for the EC–US relationship has been the importation of steel from EC member-states into the United States and this situation also may have implications for the EC integration process. During the 1970s the American steel industry had to battle increasingly stiff competition from Western European and Japanese steel producers which captured a growing share of the market. Although part of the problem were ageing steel mills and the very high hourly wages of the steel workers, the American steel industry also claimed heavy Western European subsidies were a cause of this development. Pressure from that industry through Congress and the initiation of anti-dumping suits, prompted the Administration of President Jimmy Carter to institute the so-called Trigger Price Mechanism. This device automatically imposed a countervailing duty when steel imports were sold below a predetermined price.[12]

But the Trigger Price Mechanism did not prove to be effective in halting or in slowing down steel imports into the United States. While at the time this mechanism was introduced, steel imports represented about 15 to 16 per cent of the American domestic steel market, their share rose to between 20 and 25 per cent by 1981.

Indeed, imports from Western Europe rose by 69 per cent during that period.[13] As a consequence, the trigger price system was suspended early in 1982 and a number of American steel companies filed a series of anti-dumping and anti-subsidy complaints with the Department of Commerce against EC and other foreign steel producers. Their aim was to establish a system of quantitative restrictions with respect to steel imports. Meanwhile, the United States threatened to bring to the attention of the GATT authorities for appropriate remedies the alleged dumping of steel products and illegal payments of subsidies to Western European producers.[14]

Not surprisingly, these efforts evoked strong protests by the EC institutions and member-states. Although voices were heard in Western Europe demanding retaliatory measures, the EC Commission opposed steps in that direction even after the countervailing duties on steel imports had been imposed by the United States government following the collapse of efforts for an amicable resolution of the dispute.[15] While the existence of the subsidies for Western European steel producers was acknowledged, the EC authorities pointed out that their purpose was mainly assistance for the restructuring of plants and workers' housing, and therefore was not a direct export subsidy. At the same time, the EC Council attacked the so-called DISC system in the United States as a hidden subsidy. Standing for Domestic International Sales Corporation, it allows exporters to set up such a corporation which provides the possibility for the deferral of corporate income taxes on gains made from export sales, estimated to cost the Treasury nearly $1 billion a year.[16]

Underlying this conflict was governmental apprehension with the growing number of unemployed in the steel industries on both sides of the Atlantic, with unemployment figures for steel workers standing well above the national averages. Domestic politics, in the midst of one of the most serious recessions since World War II, also played an important role. Hence, American pressures were maintained on the EC in late 1981 and 1982 to negotiate a voluntary agreement to restrict steel imports, and the EC authorities began to compile lists of American export items to the EC upon which countervailing duties could be imposed because of alleged DISC 'subsidies'. The President of the EC Commission said on 4 June 1982: 'We are only five minutes away from a trade war on steel.'[17]

Nevertheless, a solution to the conflicts on EC steel imports to the United States eventually seemed to have been found which resulted in agreements on voluntary limitations on the part of the EC member-states regarding the share of their products in the American market. In addition, a consultation procedure was set up to discuss any changes in market conditions. The United States government, in return, promised not to entertain any anti-dumping or anti-subsidy complaints until 1985.[18] The conclusion of the above agreement required protracted negotiations because the American steel industry was not satisfied with the initial accord between its government and EC negotiators.[19] Hence, this accord had to be amended and finally was accepted by all parties, but in 1983 new problems on the importation of European specialty steel have created new tensions.

In terms of its impact on the integration process, the steel trade conflict enhanced the solidarity between EC institutions and EC member governments. The institutions, including the European Parliament, stood solidly behind the European steel producers, and the EC member-states also closed ranks. The Commission's role in the EC decision-making process was strengthened by being able to negotiate on an equal footing directly with the American authorities. If there had not been a 'European' institution capable of negotiating for the totality of ten European states, the negotiations may have taken a different course and from the Western European perspective, they may have been less successful. Moreover, the subject of the negotiations, voluntary export restrictions, is not covered as an explicit external competence transferred to the EC authorities by the EC Treaties. Thus, this negotiation constitutes an extension of the Commission's powers which normally would have been reserved for the member-states. The whole episode, then, has produced at least an incremental gain to the forward movement of the integration process, but its significance in terms of system change is likely to be very minor.

## EC–Japan

While in the trade relation between the EC and the United States, it was the latter which complained about excessive imports of a particular item, namely steel, the EC authorities and member governments complained about large imports from Japan that resulted in a trade deficit for the EC of about $14 billion in 1982.[20] This deficit, caused primarily by imports of electronic consumer items such as television sets and videotape recorders, automobiles, machine tools and certain steels, has generated strong pressures for counter-measures in the member-states. In fact, at one point France instituted an oblique measure of reducing the importation of videotape recorders by mandating that all custom procedures had to take place in the city of Poitiers, hundreds of miles from the nearest port.

The EC attempted to invoke article XXIII of GATT to reverse the continuing deficits. This article provides authorization, in the event of impairment of the benefits to be derived from the GATT rules, to suspend the application of these rules by the allegedly injured GATT member-state. It is a dramatic, complex procedure and therefore the EC authorities considered it more useful to aim at the voluntary limitation by Japan of those export items which were seen as most objectionable. Since shipments of Japanese automobiles had already moderated somewhat during 1982, a limitation agreement on this item for the future may not be necessary, although Japan seems to be agreeable. However, voluntary export restriction agreements are likely on televisions and machine tools, and have been concluded on steel imports. The latter has upset the American steel industry because it fears that the EC agreement with Japan will prompt Japan to intensify its steel exports to the United States.[21]

The increasing acceptance of voluntary restrictions on selected export items by Japan and the EC reflects an erosion of the basic GATT principle of non-discrimination and of the rules on non-tariff barriers (NTBS). The agreements on voluntary export limitations, known as orderly marketing agreements (OMAS), have also been utilized in trade in textiles and footwear as well as to regulate shipping. They suggest a desire to avoid a formal breach of the GATT rules, but constitute a problem for the administration of GATT because they lack transparency. The present Director General of GATT, Arthur Dunkel, a Swiss citizen, would prefer member governments to take measures of trade restraint under the 'safeguard' provisions of GATT which would make them more legitimate under prevailing international law than the exercise of political power, as OMAS are perceived by Dunkel.[22]

In terms of power within GATT, an important, though subtle, shift has taken place in the influence exerted by the EC and the United States. While during the 1950s and 1960s the United States played the most influential role in the organization, since the decade of the 1970s this role has been assumed by the EC and its member-states.[23] This became clear during the Tokyo Round when many decisions on NTBS, especially on subsidy issues, were taken in accordance with the wishes of the EC and against the proposals submitted by the United States. This shift in power also became apparent during the GATT ministerial meeting of 24–9 November 1982, held in Geneva. A number of objectives pursued by the United States during that meeting were frustrated by the astute opposition and manoeuvring on the part of the EC. We will return to this issue later in this chapter.

## CMEA External Trade Issues

The total foreign trade of CMEA, which of course includes the Soviet Union with a GNP second only to the United States, is quite modest, amounting to $323.5 billion in 1981, or about 9 per cent of world total. CMEA exports during that year were $166.4 billion and imports $157.1 billion, showing a positive trade balance of $9.3 billion. Comparative figures with the West and the rest of the world are shown in table 6.3. Note the nearly tenfold excess of the West's trade figures over those of CMEA.

In this section we will *not* focus on the implications of trade between Eastern and Western Europe for the process of integration because this will be the main subject of the next chapter. Here we will merely outline some of the problems of trade between Socialist states committed to central planning and subject to complete government control and the free market economies of the Western states whose trade relations are governed by the rules of the GATT. In

Table 6.2  US agricultural exports to the EC (US$ million)

|  | Amount | As percentage of total exports to EC | As percentage of total agricultural exports |
|---|---|---|---|
| 1958 | 1,312.9 | 32.0 | 34.1 |
| 1960 | 1,703.8 | 29.6 | 35.3 |
| 1968 | 1,872.6 | 21.2 | 30.1 |
| 1969 | 1,736.3 | 17.5 | 29.3 |
| 1972 | 2,748.6 | 22.6 | 29.2 |
| 1973 | 4,667.7 | 27.3 | 26.4 |
| 1974 | 5,624.3 | 24.9 | 25.6 |
| 1975 | 5,705.8 | 24.5 | 26.1 |
| 1976 | 6,564.4 | 25.3 | 28.5 |
| 1977 | 6,785.0 | 24.6 | 28.7 |
| 1978 | 7,339.6 | 22.4 | 25.0 |
| 1979 | 7,847.5 | 18.1 | 22.6 |
| 1980 | 9,236.3 | 16.9 | 22.4 |
| 1981 | 9,058.8 | 17.3 | 20.9 |

*Source*: Adapted from US State Department Bureau of Intelligence and Research, *US Trade with European Community, 1958–1981*, Report 387–AR, 14 May, 1982, tables III and IV.

this connection it is important to note that four CMEA member-states are also full members of GATT. They are Czechoslovakia, Poland, Hungary, and Romania.

The main principles which underlie the GATT rules are: tariffs as protecting elements, non-discrimination, reciprocity, and consultation. Non-discrimination requires that 'any advantage, favour, privilege, or immunity granted by any contracting party to any product originating in or destined for any other country shall be accorded . . . unconditionally to the like product originating in or destined for the territory of all other contracting parties' (Article I of the GATT Treaty). There are exceptions to this rule made in GATT for free trade areas and customs unions such as the EC, and for situations involving the maintenance of security (Articles XXIV and XXI). The principle of reciprocity has also been softened in trade negotiations with developing states (Articles XXXVI to XXXVIII).

The application of the principles of non-discrimination and reciprocity only makes good sense if traditional tariffs are used as the protecting elements with the degree of protection desired depending on the cost and price of individual products determined by the forces of the free market within a state and abroad. However, in most CMEA societies selling prices and the cost of products are determined by a variety of governmental planning considerations and domestic and foreign policy objectives. This may eliminate the direct link between internal and foreign prices and therefore make the application of GATT principles to CMEA trade with Western states difficult, if not impossible. Moreover, GATT prohibits production and export subsidies and has explicit anti-dumping rules. But when price formation and cost determination are under full government control, as in most CMEA states, these rules can be easily circumvented.

Nevertheless, some of these obstacles were overcome through considerable pragmatism displayed by GATT and its Western members. This provided a reciprocity formula for GATT members Poland and Romania that was based on the exchange of tariff concessions on the part of Western GATT states against specific import concessions. In the case of Hungary, another GATT member, the Hungarian economic system was considered as sufficiently 'liberal' to accept the claim that its tariff reflected internal competitive market conditions, and therefore a normal reciprocity approach was acceptable to other GATT member-states.[24] As for non-discrimination, CMEA was not considered to fall under the exception of Article XXIV for free trade areas and customs unions. Moreover, Western European states did not eliminate all discriminatory quantitative restrictions on Eastern European exports.[25]

What were the motivations for some of the CMEA states to join GATT? Czechoslovakia was already a member in 1948 when the Communist takeover occurred. For the other CMEA members, the principal aim was economic; they wanted to increase trade with Western GATT member-states and to overcome quantitative restrictions and tariff discrimination by the latter because they did not enjoy most-favoured-nation treatment in many Western markets. The Soviet Union did not oppose their membership in GATT although for itself it looked upon it as 'second-class' membership.[26] Politically, for Poland, Romania, and Hungary, GATT membership symbolized greater independence in their foreign policy.

The results of membership for the three states was a substantial increase in both exports to GATT members and imports from these states.[27] But they have not been able to overcome all discrimination on the part of Western GATT member-states, and Poland's MFN treatment granted earlier by the United States was lifted when the Polish government imposed martial law in December 1981.

In terms of impact on the process of CMEA integration, there is no evidence of any positive effect. Indeed, the relaxation of strict political control suggested by the accession to GATT by Poland, Romania, and Hungary in the 1960s and 1970s may strengthen national impulses and aspiration rather than give greater impetus to the integration process.

### AGRICULTURAL FRICTION

The most serious frictions of EC extra-regional relations have been in the agricultural area. As for CMEA extra-regional problems, it is the import of grain into the Soviet Union, especially from the United States, which has been subject to a variety of tensions. We will first focus on the EC agricultural issues and later discuss the Soviet–US issues.

### EC–US Frictions

The export of American agricultural commodities to the member-states of the EC has produced a continuing controversy because these exports played a crucial role in view of their magnitude, as can be seen from table 6.2. This table, which includes the exports to all ten member-states, although Britain, Ireland, Denmark, and Greece joined later, shows that the share of agricultural exports of total American shipments to the EC (table 6.1) declined from 32.0 per cent in 1958 to a low of 17.5 per cent in 1969. It increased temporarily in the 1970s to between 22.4 and 27.3 per cent, the result of high world prices for grains and soybeans as well as a consequence of poor European harvests. But it started declining again in 1979, when it fell below 20.0 to 16.9 per cent in 1980 and stood in 1981 at 17.3 per cent. In terms of proportion of *total* American agricultural exports, we also see in table 6.2 that the share of exports to the then ten EC member-states stood at 35.3 per cent in 1960, but fell to 20.9 per cent in 1981.

The above figures make it clear that while the level of consumption in the EC rose steeply during the last twenty-five years, American exports were not only unable to reclaim their proper share of supplying this rising demand, but the share of total agricultural exports from the United States was nearly halved from 1960 to 1981. In other words, the EC share dropped from more than one-third of total exports to about one-fifth. It is therefore understandable that the United States is anxious to make every effort to maintain a high level of agricultural exports to the EC and that the anticipated continuous rise of living standards in Western Europe is a particularly strong incentive.

It has been a persistent objective of American policy to attack the protectionism of the CAP and to urge a modification of this policy in order to assure a 'fair share' of the EC market for American agricultural commodities. The government has argued that in view of the high level of efficiency of American farmers, its agriculture could offer its products at considerably lower cost than could Western European farmers. Therefore, increased American farm exports would benefit Western European consumers, and it was considered arbitrary to exclude such farm products from the EC markets.[28]

The United States also has contended since the early 1960s that the CAP would not only raise the cost of food for Europeans living within the confines of the EC, but would result in extraordinary surpluses. Indeed, in the Spring of 1973 pressures built up *within* the EC to modify the CAP because of the effects of high food prices on inflation in Europe. The British, especially, wanted to substitute deficiency payments to individual farmers (subsidies) for the high guaranteed prices for farm commodities, which continued to rise year after year.[29] These pressures were fueled by the emergence of enormous surpluses of some commodities, with butter as the outstanding example. When the EC Commission approved the sale to the Soviet Union of 200,000 metric tons of butter from its 400,000 ton stockpile at 20 per cent of normal EC prices, and with a loss of $362 million to be borne by the EC Agricultural Guidance and Guarantee Fund (i.e., the taxpayers), a loud chorus of criticism arose.[30] Chancellor Willy Brandt of West Germany, in a speech on 12 October 1973, insisted that the CAP must be continually re-examined as to its true benefits for producers and consumers, and room must be left for imports from other parts of the world.[31]

None of these efforts succeeded, however. Both prices for farm products and surpluses have increased. Domestic political pressures by powerful and very vocal farm groups in nearly all EC member-states have been so strong that the EC institutions and the national governments have felt obligated to raise the target prices every year. At the same time, EC farmers have sought outlets for their surpluses through expanded exports to third states, and since the exports received hefty subsidies from the EC agricultural funds, they were able in many instances to undersell the traditional suppliers of agricultural commodities. Figure 6.1 provides a graphic illustration of farm surpluses and the cost of the EC to pay for the dumping of various commodities from 1978 to 1982. Up to 1980 the EC was a net importer of cereals, but in 1982 it exported three million tons more cereals than it imported.[32]

The United States has protested the capture of its traditional agricultural export markets, but up to early 1983 did little to retaliate because it did not want to disturb American exports to the EC member-states, which were threatened by the imposition of some new tariffs on feed grains and other commodities.[33] However, in January of that year the United States did sell one million tons of wheat flour to Egypt at $25 a ton under the world price, which caused severe resentment in the EC and especially France, the traditional supplier of this item to Egypt.[34] The United States also was said to have given consideration to a subsidized sale of 20,000 tons of butter to the Soviet Union, something done previously by the EC.[35]

The EC claims that its subsidies for exports of farm products did not violate GATT rules because the world prices for the exported items were not lowered, but merely met through the subsidies. Indeed, GATT rejected an American complaint about EC export subsidies. But in view of falling export sales of agricultural commodities, the Reagan Administration has been prepared to follow

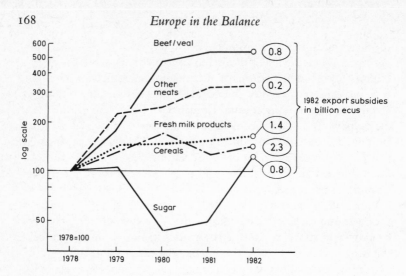

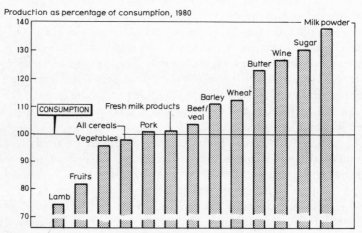

Source: *Economist*, 23 October 1982, p. 52.

Figure 6.1   European Community farm surpluses and export subsidy costs, 1979 (ECUs, value approximately US$1.00)

the subsidy route for the export of various farm products to different states, and it appeared to have the support of Congress for this policy.[36] With the EC strongly objecting to such measures and threatening retaliation, the possibility of an escalating trade war cannot be ignored as political pressures on the respective governments involved and on the EC institutions are likely to mount.[37]

## CMEA—US

As already mentioned the main agricultural issue between CMEA and the United States is the purchase of grains from the United States. Compared to this, other agricultural problems, if they existed, are insignificant.

Unknown to the United States government, in 1972 the Soviet Union experienced a catastrophic crop failure and was in desperate need of large quantities of grain. Hence, they decided to become a major buyer of grain from the United States. Contracts were concluded for the purchase of 28 million tons of this commodity, mostly from the United States. The procedure used by the Soviets for this huge purchase was very astute. It contracted separately and secretly with each of several large grain exporters such as the Continental Grain Company, and by requesting competitive bids, obtained very low prices for its purchases. In fact, as these purchases were made, grain prices advanced rapidly, subjecting Americans to higher bread and cereal costs, while the Russians benefitted from their low-cost contracts. The Soviet purchases became known as 'The Great American Grain Robbery'.

Subsequent contracts between the Soviet Union and American grain suppliers were more balanced as far as price was concerned. At the same time, the United States provided $750 million of credit to the USSR for purchases of additional agricultural products. But the grain exports to the Soviet Union suffered a major collapse when President Jimmy Carter imposed a partial embargo in order to induce the Soviet Union to withdraw its forces from Afghanistan which had been invaded in December 1979. Grain could be delivered from 'old' contracts, but new purchases were prohibited. However, the effectiveness of this embargo was questionable because other states such as Canada and Argentina were eager to fill the void left by the United States embargo. In the Spring of 1981, responding to the insistent demands of the US grain farmers, President Ronald Reagan lifted the embargo, against the strong protestation of his Secretary of State, Alexander Haig. Sales at first were to be made on an *ad hoc* basis and only for cash. When Poland imposed martial law in December 1981, an action which the Reagan Administration regarded as having been inspired by the Soviet Union, any thought of negotiating a long-term grain agreement with the Soviets was banished, at least temporarily. In 1983, however, negotiations were resumed and long-term contracts on grain purchases plus a five-year agreement for the purchase of 6 to 9 million tons of grains annually was signed in Moscow in August 1983.

What the value of American grain exports to the Soviet Union will be in the future is difficult to predict. In 1982, exports of this commodity to the USSR were $1.6 billion, but this represented a smaller volume than in 1976 when these exports reached nearly $1.8 billion but at a considerably lower price per ton.[38] Two reasons account for a somewhat bleak future for American grain exports. Other exporters have expanded and consolidated their market share, and the political climate between the two Superpowers must improve.

### FRICTION OVER MONETARY ISSUES

#### EC Problems with the United States

For a quarter century after World War II the international monetary system was based on fixed but adjustable par values of the currencies of the member-states of the International Monetary Fund (IMF), which was set up in 1944 at the Bretton Woods Conference. This system was able to cope with recurring difficulties until toward the end of the 1960s, when inflation rates began to diverge and large flows of funds – often speculative – passed through the exchange markets.

In 1971, the pressure on the dollar, whose value had been weakening in the preceding years, reached critical proportions and in August the administration of President Richard Nixon suspended dollar convertibility into gold. An immediate dollar devaluation of 10 per cent took place, followed by subsequent devaluations of an increasingly weak American currency. The result was a worldwide floating rate system, which was recognized by an amendment to the IMF Articles of Agreement that became effective 1 April 1978. As a consequence IMF member-states could select any exchange arrangement they desired, subject only to notification to the Fund and to a prohibition of pegging their currency to gold.

A substantial number of IMF members pegged their currencies either to the United States dollar or the French franc. Most of the EC states adopted in 1979 what became known as the European Monetary System (EMS) which, as described earlier, had fixed currency exchange rate limits, specified intervention points, and credits made available by the central banks when needed for maintaining the exchange limits. It was hoped that exchange rates would be modified only infrequently. These hopes were not quite fulfilled because some severe strains did develop – such as in the Spring of 1983 when France threatened to quit the EC unless West Germany increased the value of its currency by 5 per cent, which allowed France a devaluation of the franc by only half of this amount. Although the French demands were accommodated and EMS remains in force, friction is likely to recur in the future and this friction will affect the whole IMF system as much as the continuation of the EMS. In other words, this friction has its source in the extra-regional monetary relations of the EC.

Several reasons account for current and future international monetary problems, especially as far as relations with the EC are concerned. Since the late 1970s the United States, Britain, Canada, and Japan have allowed their exchange rates to float independently. Beginning in the fourth quarter of 1977, the value of the dollar depreciated significantly and the dollar came under additional heavy selling pressure in the Summer and Fall of 1979. But, as American interest rates began to rise in late 1980 and 1981 in the battle against inflation, market sentiment shifted in favour of the dollar as the result of large inflows of capital into the United States wanting to benefit from the high interest rates. In 1982 the dollar appreciated further, buoyed not only by high interest rates, but also by gloomy economic prospects in other industrial states and 'safe-haven' considerations with respect to the United States.

While the Carter Administration had resorted occasionally to heavy intervention by the Federal Reserve Bank and the central banks of some Western European states to counter excessive and, in terms of international trade, unwarranted dollar exchange rate fluctuation, the Reagan Administration suspended all intervention except for such political emergencies as the assassination attempt on the President.[39] The consequences have been a continued rise of the dollar despite a lowering of interest rates in the United States during 1982 and 1983, and increasing difficulties for American exports because of the very strong dollar and the declining competitiveness of American products. The result has been record trade deficits for the United States and a substantial account deficit as well.

Meanwhile the enormous budget deficits in the United States and the vast borrowing which the Federal government has undertaken to cover these deficits acted against an expectation that interest rates would fall. Hence, the inflow of funds from Western Europe and elsewhere continues to keep the dollar strong and has compelled other governments to maintain high interest rates in order to slow down the outflow of their funds to the United States. This has created much resentment in Western Europe and Japan, and has prompted insistent calls on the United States to bring down its budget deficits.

Prior to the Williamsburg Summit in May 1983, France voiced its strong desire to return to a fixed exchange rate system, and during the Summit French President François Mitterrand urged that an international monetary conference – a 'new Bretton Woods' – be convened to move towards such a goal. Former French President Giscard d'Estaing also expressed himself in favour of a gradual return to exchange rate stability, but in his view, France needed first a vigorous economy and a solid currency which has been sorely lacking.[40]

The EC Commission generally backed a stabilization of exchange rates, suggesting a possible move towards a system of 'zones of likelihood' for exchange rates and the use of intervention in foreign exchange markets to contain undue fluctuation of these rates. It also has criticized the United States' maintaining very high 'real' interest rates and has predicted that without a change of policy leading to a reduction of its extremely large budget deficits, no lasting recovery in the world economy would be possible.[41]

It would be, of course, naive to expect summit conferences to settle complex monetary questions. Nevertheless, every participating government has promised to aim at reducing structural budget deficits and to improve 'consultations, policy convergence, and international co-operation to help stabilize exchange markets' while studying the feasibility of exchange market intervention.[42] The French desire for a new Bretton Woods has also remained on the agenda.

From the EC point of view, the summits have emphasized how necessary it was in view of the international monetary instability to strengthen the EMS. But as long as Britain and Greece remain outside of the system, and in the face of much scepticism prevailing in the EC member-states about EMS, it is doubtful that much progress will be made. Meanwhile, during the 1984 presidential election year no reduction in the American budget deficit occurred because the Reagan Administration was anxious to provide maximum funds to fuel a robust economy. Nevertheless, in instances of severe exchange rate misalignments and extreme volatility, *ad hoc* co-ordinated intervention may be carried out by the central banks of the major industrialized states. But the long-term effectiveness of such intervention will depend on the currency market's perception of the degree of the authorities' commitment to achieve a stable outcome.[43]

## CMEA's Need for Convertible Currencies

In the extra-regional trade of the CMEA states, it is for the payment of imports that convertible currencies are needed, and it is full convertibility which poses problems. For intra-regional transactions CMEA states attempt to balance payments both in overall trade and trade by broad commodity groups, for example machinery. If complete balancing between two states is not possible, payments are made either in CMEA states' convertible currencies or in transferable rubles. Settlement takes place through the International Bank for Economic Co-operation (IBEC) in transferable rubles and through the foreign-trade bank in each CMEA state, which has accounts in the West that are used for payments in the convertible currencies of the states involved in bilateral trade.[44] It should be noted that while transferrable rubles can be used for settlement of accounts among CMEA states, they cannot be utilized by these states for payments to outside suppliers. Hence, if individual CMEA states cannot import more goods than they export, and thus have a positive trade balance with supplier states, they may have to borrow from outside, mostly Western, banks to acquire convertible currencies to pay for their purchases. IBEC will also help occasionally by providing convertible currencies for settlement purposes.[45] Finally, importing CMEA states may request long-term credits from individual suppliers or the governments of the states from which the goods are shipped.

The Soviet Union is in a much better position to pay outside suppliers than other CMEA states because it has vast natural resources, large quantities of gold, and a diversified industrial structure. It could help in making not only the ruble fully convertible, but also enhance the convertibility of other CMEA currencies. However, the Soviet government has no political interest in pursuing such a path. Progress towards currency convertibility and multilateralism within CMEA would in all likelihood lead to a large reduction of intra-CMEA trade (now about 60 per cent of total international trade) and undermine Soviet control over the organization, obviously something which is not in Moscow's interest. Thus, inconvertibility of CMEA states' currencies remains a real obstacle to extra-regional imports and to East–West economic relations. Association with the

IMF and the World Bank may offer a way out, but this too presents a political problem which seems to have been overcome only by Romania up to now.

## EC: The Lomé Convention

In the extra-regional relations of the EC with the Third World, the Lomé Convention plays a dominant role. It was first signed in Lomé, Togo, in February 1975 for a period of five years and later twice renewed for an additional five years. It links more than 250 million Europeans to over 300 million people in the Third World. More than fifty states, mostly in Africa but also in the Caribbean and the Western Pacific, are signatories. Other states in these regions may apply for membership. All are called the ACP states.

The Lomé Convention assures free access to the member-states for all industrial and 96 per cent of the agricultural products originating in the ACP states, without compelling the latter to make corresponding concessions. Thus the Convention dispenses with the need for strict reciprocity in the free trade arrangements established between the EC and the APC states. Some of the developing states wanted to eliminate the concept of reciprocity, thereby siding with a viewpoint maintained by the United States, but others wanted to maintain this principle as a symbol of their equality and independence. In the Convention the ACP states have the option to grant special trade concessions to the EC states and, equally important, are able to make such preferences available to third states. Since these provisions deviate from Article XXIV of GATT, the EC had to obtain a waiver from that organization, a stipulation that posed no difficulties. The provisions also mean that some of the ACP states currently providing reverse preferences to imported EC goods may continue to follow this practice if they so desire or are persuaded by the EC institutions to do so.

Financial aid available to the ACP in the Convention amounted to approximately $4 billion but fell far short of what the ACP wanted originally, which was more than twice that figure. About 11 per cent of the $4 billion was to be used for the establishment of an export stabilization fund to aid states heavily dependent on the export of certain raw materials and agricultural commodities susceptible to wide price and production level fluctuations. When receipts drop by a certain percentage, ACP states can request compensation. The mechanism triggering the fund operates sooner for the poorest states, which do not have to reimburse the fund.

Many ACP states had felt for many years that their progress in industrialization had been disappointing and that a systematic approach had to be taken by the EC, with proper financing not only by the European Development Fund (EDF) but also by other financial institutions in the member-states. To help these states develop and diversify their industrial capacity, an Industrial Co-operation Committee and an Industrial Development Centre have been set up to promote the exchange of industrial know-how.

The institutions of the Lomé Convention have broad powers and are divided into 'decision-making' and 'management' institutions. Prior to the conclusion of the new association agreements, Claude Cheysson, the Commission member in charge of relations with developing states at that time and later the Foreign Minister of France, made some interesting policy statements:

1 The poorest states fighting a genuine battle of survival must receive their full complement of food aid, financial aid, and technical assistance.
2 Countries that have important resources of primary commodities but need help to develop them must be given this assistance with stabilization of export earnings and the promotion of marketing of their products.
3 States that already have developed raw materials are to be aided by industrial co-operation and by the conclusion of long-term trade contracts. These states (an example would be Nigeria) should not make an appeal for financial assistance but only for different forms of industrial co-operation.
4 Agreements with the Third World states producing raw materials should include a clause assuring access to these resources by the EC in return for the aid given to them.[46]

Cheysson pointed out that the EC policy towards the affiliated states was characterized by great flexibility, enhancing the value of development aid given by Western Europe over that of other states and international organizations. Indeed, the principles developed for Lomé should also guide development assistance for Third World states outside the Convention.

Clearly, the Lomé Convention is a remarkable achievement for the European Communities. It has great economic and also substantial political significance for the EC member-states. It has reinforced the already strong ties Western Europe has with Africa and has had favourable consequences for the EC throughout the Third World.

The overall generous nature of the Convention as well as the provision dealing with promoting industrial co-operation and assistance in the industrialization of ACP economies under EC auspices will assure business firms in the EC states goodwill, which can be translated into higher exports to ACP states and favourable treatment for the establishment of local subsidiaries. Of course there is some serious doubt as to whether industrialization is the best means for all developing states to enhance their economic welfare, or whether for some of these states the highest priority should be placed on the diversification and modernization of agriculture. But given the obsession with industrialization that most Third World governmental leaders have, the Convention provisions have proved to be very attractive, although there have remained concerns about insufficient progress in industrialization and insufficient food aid.[47]

It is in the long-term implications and effects that the Lomé Convention assumes the greatest political significance for the EC member-states. The continued close relationship between the member-states and the EC is likely to give business firms not only in France but perhaps eventually also in the other member-states increased influence and control. As a consequence the EC business world is apt to be the main beneficiary if the economic level of the African affiliates eventually rises as the result of the massive infusion of financial aid. The institutionalized contacts between African and European parliamentarians and civil servants are also likely to contribute substantially to this development and, in addition, will promote political co-operation between the Lomé partners. Such co-operation may in due time lead to further extension of Western European influence in large parts of Africa and indeed in the whole Third World. For example, groups of foreign service officials of ACP states have been taken on carefully prepared and conducted tours in the EC states. The results have been co-operation and support by ACP governments for EC members' objectives in different international fora, and perhaps a subtle shift in the distribution of world power.

Third states must look at the effects of the Convention also in long-range terms. Up to now, their fears of major trade diversion do not seem to have been confirmed. Only relatively modest overall increases of EC exports to the affiliated states have been noted, and they were much smaller than the increase of total EC exports.

It is important to note that the Lomé Convention does not attempt to pre-empt the field of financial and technical assistance. Rather, the Convention complements the assistance efforts of some of the member-states, which have bilateral 'trade and aid' programmes of differing scope and emphasis. France and Britain have by far the most extensive network of bilateral agreements, but West Germany is not too far behind, followed by the Netherlands, Belgium and Italy.[48]

In spite of the many favourable implications which the Lomé Convention appears to have for both the EC and its Third World partners, the evolution of trade figures shows mixed economic results. During the decade of 1970 to 1980, for example, EC imports from the ACP partners rose from $2.7 billion to almost $27 billion, while EC exports to these states increased only from $3.5 to $22 billion. These data take into account relevant trade before and after the conclusion of the Lomé Convention in 1975. If these figures are compared with the total trade of the EC, however, they indicate a decline of the ACP share in the EC imports from 7.8 to 7.1 per cent. On the other hand, the share of EC exports rose from 6.3 per cent in 1970 to 7.2 per cent in 1980. Moreover, it should be noted that Nigerian oil exports to the EC played a major role in these data. In 1980, they represented 41 per cent of EC imports from the ACP states. After a severe contraction of all APC imports to the EC in 1981 (30 per cent), resulting in a $2 billion trade deficit for the affiliated states, their shipments to the EC rose markedly in 1982, thereby materially reducing this deficit.[49]

It is also noteworthy that the APC share in world trade has tended to diminish; it was 3.5 per cent in 1970 and 2.8 per cent in 1980. This decline in trade is especially significant when we concentrate on the export and import figures for the Third World. The APC share in total Third World exports dropped from approximately 18 per cent in 1970 to about 9 per cent in 1981. The share of APC imports of the total for the Third World fell from 16 per cent to 9 per cent. Greatly increased oil exports from the Middle East, South America, and South East Asia may offer a major explanation for the changes in exports.[50]

Although the above data suggest that the benefits received by the APC states may not have met the expectations of their leaders and indeed many complaints were voiced when the second five-year term of the Convention was negotiated, partnership with EC has nevertheless produced some important advantages. Perhaps the most significant is the impressive amount of funds spent by the EDF for a large number of infrastructure projects, training programmes, and the stabilization of prices for export crops (the STABEX programme).[51]

All in all, the Lomé Convention has turned out a definite plus for the EC, not only in economic, but especially in political terms. It has established important ties between the EC institutions, their member-states, and a major segment of the Third World with definitive implications for changes in the distribution of world power.

## The EC's Mediterranean Policy

Beginning with the early 1960s the EC embarked on extending its influence in the Mediterranean through a variety of preferential trade agreements which now cover all states rimming this body of water except Libya, Albania, and Yugoslavia. Some of these agreements were cast in the form of 'associations' authorized under the EEC Treaty (Article 238) and covered all trade; others were selective with respect to the items receiving preferential treatment.[52]

The professed rationale and objectives of the Mediterranean policy have been stated succinctly by Rolf Dahrendorf, a former member of the EC Commission, in the name of this body:

1 the quest, in relations with the Mediterranean, of a harmonious relationship between reciprocal interdependence on the one hand and the respect of mutual independence on the other;
2 the working out of a joint plan for the relations of the EC with the Mediterranean states, taking into account the characteristics of each of these;
3 the prime necessity of going beyond the purely commercial aspect of the question and of contributing to the economic development of the region.[53]

A resolution adopted by the European Parliament underlined the responsibilities and particular obligations that give the EC its economic importance in the Mediterranean basin, its situation in relation to this sub-region, and the need to develop a spirit of true solidarity. The resolution stresses the necessity for the EC to adopt a policy of development by more appropriate means than commercial measures alone.

An examination of statistics on trade relations shows the important position that the Mediterranean states have assumed in trade with the EC. Trade has expanded enormously since 1960, and the economic importance of the EC–Mediterranean relation is illustrated by the fact that apart from Libyan oil deliveries, 36.5 per cent of the exports of all the Mediterranean states go to the EC while 37.6 per cent of their total imports come from the EC. In turn, of total EC exports to third states 14.5 per cent, a hefty share, go to these Mediterranean states, while the share of total imports from the area, again omitting Libyan oil, is only 9 per cent.[54]

The EC policy towards the Mediterranean has found broad support by the elites and public opinion in the member-states. Elite surveys conducted in 1965 and 1970 have made one point clear: the over-whelming majority of the respondents (nearly 97 per cent) perceived the association agreements as useful instruments of policy; and there was almost unanimity that a preferential agreement policy in the Mediterranean was fully justified in view of the historical ties of these states to Europe.[55] What we can see, then, is a change of role in the Mediterranean basin. While historically the Mediterranean was considered by the Italians as *mare nostrum*, it is now the EC as a whole that is accepting this position.

The United States has strongly opposed the EC's efforts to create a sphere of influence in the Mediterranean. As pointed out earlier, American policy has been basically against any kind of preferential treatment by the EC outside Europe proper. During the last few years the United States government has made energetic attempts to stop the expansion of the EC's economic and political influence in the Mediterranean. In very practical terms, it was concerned about the economic effects on American exports of citrus fruits and other goods to Western Europe, but perhaps more than that, it was the increasing worldwide influence of the EC that gave rise to serious apprehension. The United States has proclaimed again and again that the preferential agreements are violations of GATT, which only permits fully-fledged customs unions and free trade areas to be exempted from the most-favoured-nation clause. The EC has admitted a possible violation but continues to claim its special responsibility for the states of the area.

Meanwhile, Greece has moved from associate to full membership, which came in force in January 1981. Spain has applied for such membership, and been admitted along with Portugal in January 1986. Thus, the influence of the EC in the Mediterranean has been solidified.

Spain's membership will have favourable strategic and political implications for the EC. Spain and its enclave of Ceuta and Melilla in North Africa (Ceuta is located opposite Gibraltar) help to control the Western part of the Mediterranean. The close relations of Spain with much of Latin America are likely to strengthen the political ties of the EC with that part of the world, and to enhance the economic intercourse between EC and Latin American states.

### CMEA and the Third World

The extra-regional relations of CMEA with the Third World as far as trade is concerned are low in comparison with those of the EC. Nevertheless, CMEA has attempted to expand these relations and has become increasingly involved in various negotiating fora within the United Nations Conference on Trade and Development (UNCTAD).

Trade between CMEA states and the Third World has increased substantially since 1960, increasing twentyfold between 1960 and 1981, as can be seen from table 6.4. In 1960 exports to the developing states amounted to about 25 per cent of total trade with non-Communist states; in 1981 it was approximately one-third. The share of imports from the Third World of total imports was somewhat smaller. Seventy-five per cent of Third World exports to CMEA consist of raw materials including tin, rubber, oil, phosphates, non-ferrous metals, fibres and wood. CMEA exports to the Third World are mostly in machinery, transportation equipment, and military goods. During the period from 1960 to 1977 CMEA trade with the developing states moved from a negative balance of payments of $145 million to a surplus of $8.346 billion, as can be seen from table 6.5. From the CMEA perspective this is a very positive development, given the general lack of convertibility of the CMEA member-states' currencies and the problems even of the ruble to constitute a truly transferable currency in the international exchange markets. Indeed, it is the aim of CMEA members to conclude the maximum number of long-term *bilateral* commercial, economic, and scientific agreements which in due time will make Third World imports a part of the CMEA states' annual economic plans.

The increased interest of CMEA in expanding its relations with the Third World is also reflected in large grants and credits for economic purposes, and even larger grants for the acquisition of military material. These grants and credits exceed $50 billion over a period beginning in 1954. To assist developing states in the utilization of

Table 6.3 East European trade with Communist and non-Communist states (US$ million)

| | | Total trade | Communist states | | | | | Non-Communist states | | |
|---|---|---|---|---|---|---|---|---|---|---|
| | | | Total | Eastern Europe | China | Other Asia | Other[1] | Total | Developed states | Less-developed states (total) |
| 1960 | Exports | 5,558 | 4,210 | 3,071 | 816 | 66 | 256 | 1,348 | 1,022 | 326 |
| | Imports | 5,623 | 3,974 | 2,792 | 847 | 98 | 237 | 1,649 | 1,120 | 529 |
| 1965 | Exports | 8,166 | 5,555 | 4,551 | 192 | 165 | 647 | 2,611 | 1,506 | 1,105 |
| | Imports | 8,050 | 5,605 | 4,668 | 225 | 120 | 592 | 2,444 | 1,647 | 797 |
| 1970 | Exports | 12,787 | 8,359 | 6,752 | 25 | 415 | 1,167 | 4,428 | 2,453 | 1,975 |
| | Imports | 11,720 | 7,630 | 6,627 | 22 | 156 | 826 | 4,090 | 2,849 | 1,241 |
| 1975 | Exports | 33,407 | 20,271 | 16,494 | 129 | 480 | 3,168 | 13,136 | 8,588 | 4,548 |
| | Imports | 37,070 | 19,415 | 15,723 | 150 | 277 | 3,265 | 17,655 | 13,566 | 4,089 |
| 1977 | Exports | 45,227 | 26,009 | 20,762 | 161 | 628 | 4,458 | 19,219 | 12,091 | 7,127 |
| | Imports | 40,926 | 23,353 | 18,839 | 177 | 400 | 3,938 | 17,573 | 13,586 | 3,987 |
| 1978 | Exports | 52,435 | 31,244 | 24,910 | 241 | 726 | 5,367 | 21,190 | 12,920 | 8,270 |
| | Imports | 50,798 | 30,494 | 24,661 | 257 | 521 | 5,055 | 20,304 | 16,244 | 4,060 |
| 1979 | Exports | 64,912 | 36,152 | 28,380 | 268 | 1,081 | 6,423 | 28,760 | 19,578 | 9,182 |
| | Imports | 57,958 | 32,810 | 26,761 | 240 | 618 | 5,191 | 25,148 | 20,405 | 4,743 |
| 1980 | Exports | 76,437 | 41,431 | 32,216 | 261 | 1,201 | 7,752 | 35,006 | 24,934 | 10,072 |
| | Imports | 68,473 | 36,420 | 29,407 | 226 | 681 | 6,106 | 32,053 | 24,386 | 7,667 |
| 1981 | Exports | 79,377 | 43,353 | 33,774 | 115 | 1,445 | 8,019 | 36,024 | 24,416 | 11,608 |
| | Imports | 73,158 | 37,172 | 29,399 | 131 | 582 | 7,060 | 35,986 | 25,356 | 10,630 |

Note: [1] Cuba, Mongolia and Yugoslavia.
Source: CIA, Handbook of Economic Statistics, 1982.

Table 6.5 Balance of payments: CMEA v. the Third World (US$ million)

|                | 1960 | 1965 | 1970  | 1975  | 1976  | 1977  | Total |
|----------------|------|------|-------|-------|-------|-------|-------|
| Bulgaria       | 6    | 10   | 49    | 287   | 178   | 361   | 891   |
| Czechoslovakia | 39   | 57   | 132   | 190   | 173   | 391   | 982   |
| GDR            | −13  | −6   | 49    | −19   | —     | —     | 11    |
| Hungary        | 15   | 2    | −38   | −39   | 9     | 78    | 27    |
| Poland         | 11   | −45  | 66    | 281   | 309   | 160   | 782   |
| Romania        | 26   | 19   | 66    | 293   | 82    | —     | 486   |
| USSR           | −229 | 298  | 937   | 37    | 1,051 | 3,073 | 5,167 |
| Total          | −145 | 335  | 1,261 | 1,030 | 1,802 | 4,063 | 8,346 |

*Source*: S. J. Noumoff, 'COMECON and the Third World,' *Economic and Political Weekly*, 23 August 1980, pp. 1443–54, table 8.

CMEA civilian and military goods, 65,330 economic technicians and 32,100 military technicians have been assigned to work in selected Third World states.[56] In addition, Technical Co-operation Offices have been established by different CMEA states in a number of developing states including India, Pakistan, Iran, Nigeria, Iraq, Ethiopia and Brazil. In other states, bilateral commissions have been set up.

CMEA has also shown an interest in participating as a unit in United Nations economic and political affairs, and especially in the negotiations which have been conducted under the auspices of UNCTAD. In these negotiations it is generally identified as Group 'D' which pertains mostly to the Eastern European members of CMEA. Of particular concern for us is the CMEA's attitude and behaviour *vis-à-vis* the negotiations regarding a broad price stabilization programme for commodities, the General System of Preferences (GSP) for Third World imports into states with advanced economies, and the transfer of technology.

The concept as developed by the Third World of stabilizing the price fluctuations of commodity prices envisaged a Common Fund which would permit the purchase of surplus stocks of commodities and thereby avoid oversupplies that would depress world prices. Although CMEA has been sympathetic to the Common Fund concept, perhaps primarily for political reasons, the absence of full currency convertibility induced CMEA negotiators initially to oppose that concept. For CMEA a system of trade bilateralism has remained imperative in international trade, which requires balancing exports and imports individually between individual trading partners. Eventually, however, in 1980 Group D agreed to commit scarce convertible currencies to the establishment of the Fund, although the Soviet Union, being among the foremost champions of state sovereignty, seemed to assume that CMEA could refuse to fulfill an obligation made toward an intergovernmental organization, such as the Common Fund would constitute, because the extent of its juridical personality may be questionable.[57]

The problem of GSP in connection with CMEA is the pricing system in Communist economies. In 1970 the member-states of CMEA declared that those states which still have tariffs were prepared to give preference for Third World imports. But they also stated that the Soviet Union had already abolished all tariffs on such imports in 1965. However, these actions had little effect, if any, because the consumption of goods in centrally planned economies does not depend on prices that are supposedly lower because tariffs are absent, but on the particular plans setting the level of imports on specific items. Although Group D has promised to increase the level of manufactured and semi-manufactured imports from the Third World, it also invokes the principles of 'mutual advantage' and 'equality of rights and obligations' in an attempt to limit the benefits Third World states may desire from GSP.[58]

On the transfer of technology to the Third World, CMEA states generally support the Third World in its efforts to create a binding code which strictly controls and *facilitates* such transfers to developing states. This includes the revision of the present patent system which would enable these states to obtain patents and technology without cost. This CMEA position is no surprise since its member-states also desire new technologies transferred mostly from Western advanced states and, therefore, would obviously be major beneficiaries of the kind of code demanded by the Third World.[59]

The foregoing discussion suggests that CMEA has expanded its trade relations with the Third World during the last two decades and has been able to do this in spite of the currency convertibility problem. In fact, as the positive balance of payments with the Third World indicates, it has benefited both economically and politically.

In its relations with the developing states in United Nations fora, CMEA has generally sided with the objectives of these states, including the establishment of a New International Economic Order as reflected in its support of the Common Fund concept, GSP, and technology transfer. By trying to accommodate Third World demands as much as possible under the constraints imposed by its planned economy system, CMEA has projected a favourable image to many Third World leaders and at the same time may have strengthened its position in the East–West struggle. But the Third World, often complaining about capitalist exploitation, may also have become exposed to a measure of manipulation by the CMEA leadership.

### CONCLUSIONS

What can we learn in terms of system change from the analysis of the extra-regional relations initiated and conducted by the EC and CMEA? Have their relations produced pressures from external governmental or non-governmental actors to push political integration of the two sub-regional organizations forward, or have they led to a diminution in the strength of the organizational ties? Or did the links between the member-states perhaps remain substantially unchanged?

As far as the EC is concerned, pressures have been exerted by the United States on the EC to change the CAP in order to enhance American agricultural exports both to the EC as well as to traditional third state markets. In addition, the United States has attempted to limit EC steel exports to the United States. These external pressures over trade, however, have not engendered any Western European desires for moving forward the pace of political integration. Rather, they are being handled by the EC and national bureaucracies in a normal intergovernmental fashion, with the national political leaderships looking after benefits for their constituencies as much as possible, or at least limiting the economic damage which external pressure may cause.

In the international monetary realm, it would not be inconceivable that the high American budget deficits, with its continuing relatively high interest rates and the very strong dollar, may be a powerful motivation to strengthen the EMS and to develop it into a viable reserve currency. But while a number of zealous supporters of Western European union have indeed clamored for such moves, the fact that Britain and Greece so far have refused to join EMS makes the prospect for this development rather bleak. Moreover, the many exchange rate adjustments within EMS and accompanying, often bitter struggles between member-states make it very unlikely that the EMS could become the standard-bearer for further progress in integration, although the ECU is slowly being accepted as an accounting unit by some central banks in the community.

The Lomé Convention and the Mediterranean policy of the EC

have received strong approval from the populace in the member-states and may in fact bolster whatever pride the Western Europeans may have in the EC. The main reason for the development of these attitudes was the extension of influence from which the individual member-states benefited much more than the common EC institutions. The EC states also have profited economically from the substantial increase in exports to the Lomé area and the Mediterranean and the institutional links established between the EC and the Lomé partners have brought certain subtle political advantages as well. But it is doubtful whether the intensification of these external EC relations have given impetus to a forward movement in the integration front. More likely it was viewed as a normal by-product of the EC operations which did not evoke a greater commitment to integration by either the member-state elites or the general public.

The EC enlargement in the Mediterranean that has already occurred with the Greek accession and is expected later to grow with the Spanish and Portuguese memberships – the latter close to the Mediterranean but not a littoral state – has not contributed to progress in integration. Greece has had second thoughts about the usefulness of EC membership, and in both Spain and Portugal there is no consensus about the advantages of EC membership. Indeed, considering these factors and combining them with the much lower economic levels prevailing in the three states compared with the prior nine member-states, the chances for both effective progress in economic integration as well as for political unification, appear to diminish. In addition, the management of the EC will become more difficult the more participant states there are. To reach compromises among twelve EC members will create many more problems than existed before 1973 when only six members made up the EC. The impact of powerful centrifugal forces could impede, if not completely halt, the march toward political unification.

Although Third World states outside the EC trading bloc, and some advanced industrial states such as the United States, have at times been critical about the Lomé Convention and Mediterranean policy, no strong pressures have developed for the dismantlement of the EC arrangements. The main reason may well be that damage to the trade of the 'outsiders' has not been serious. In fact, as shown earlier, imports into the EC members from many of the Third World outsiders have increased more rapidly than those of the Lomé affiliates, and American exports both to the latter as well as to the EC have escaped major injury from the establishment of the preferential arrangements. Moreover, all tariffs have been reduced in the Kennedy and Tokyo Rounds, narrowing differences between regular and preferential customs duties, and there is now talk by the Reagan Administration of convening another 'round'.

With respect to CMEA external relations, outside pressures that might be translated into integrative action have been minimal. The primary concern of CMEA's trading partners has been the absence of the full convertibility of the Soviet ruble and other CMEA currencies, and attempts have been made to convince the Soviet Union, which holds the key position in this matter, to remedy this unsatisfactory situation. However, accommodation to this demand has not been forthcoming to any extent and since, as we have seen, the CMEA states' balance-of-payments with most third states have been favourable because of bilateral barter and trade arrangements, there has not been a tremendous urgency on the part of CMEA to institute full convertibility.

In its relations with Third World states, CMEA has acceded as much as possible to some of UNCTAD's major demands. Combining this with the general tendency of the Eastern European (Group D) states to support Third World concepts, their mutual relations have been generally harmonious, particularly in view of the efforts of CMEA to offer grants, loans and technical assistance to a number of developing states.

Issues pertaining to the transfer of technology from East to South are complicated by the fact that the CMEA states are also anxious to obtain advanced technology from the West. Hence to transfer technology and patents to the Third World without cost, as desired by the NIEO, is likely to encounter currency and exchange rate problems that will tend to make the CMEA states shy away from NIEO demands. In any case, none of these problems can be solved any better by greater political integration of CMEA, and, therefore, whatever pressures may be exerted for CMEA policy changes will have no effect on the progress of integration or consequent system changes.[60]

NOTES

1 Philippe C. Schmitter, 'Three Neo-Functional Hypotheses about Regional Integration', *International Organization* 23 (Winter 1969), p. 165.

2 'A Revised Theory of Regional Integration', *International Organization* 24 (Autumn 1970), p. 848.

3 Philippe C. Schmitter, *Autonomy or Dependence as Regional Integration Outcomes: Central America*, Research Series, no. 17, Institute of International Studies, University of California, Berkeley, 1972, p. 7.

4 Karl Kaiser, 'The Interaction of Regional Subsystems: Some Preliminary Thoughts on Recurring Patterns and the Role of Superpowers', *World Politics* 21 (October 1968), pp. 84–5.

5 Ibid., p. 85.

6 See Joseph Nye, *Peace in Parts* (Boston: Little, Brown, 1971), p. 93 and pp. 84–5.

7 For details of the Dillon Round see Henn Fold, *The European Common Market and the World* (Englewood Cliffs, NJ: Prentice-Hall, 1967), pp. 90–3.

8 Ibid., pp. 101–3.

9 This information was gleaned from Werner J. Feld's conversation with State Department officials.

10 Werner J. Feld, *The European Community in World Affairs* (Sherman Oaks, California: Alfred Publishing Co., 1976), p. 187.

11 Department of State, Bureau of Intelligence and Research, *Trade Patterns of the West 1981*, Report 443-AR, 6 August 1982.

12 Joan Edelman Spero, *The Politics of International Economic Relations*, 2nd ed. (New York: St. Martin's Press, 1981), p. 95.

13 Agence Europe, *Bulletin*, 11/12 January 1982.

14 Agence Europe, *Bulletin*, 20 March and 16 April 1982.

15 Agence Europe, *Bulletin*, 12 June 1982.

16 Agence Europe, *Bulletin*, 24 June 1982.

17 Ibid., editorial.

18 Agence Europe, *Bulletin*, 15 September, 13 and 23 October 1982.

19 Agence Europe, *Bulletin*, 9 October 1982. See also *Business Week*, 8 November 1982, p. 42 for future us steel industry concerns.

20 Agence Europe, *Bulletin*, 27 January 1983.

21 Agence Europe, *Bulletin*, 27 January 1983 and 15 December 1982. See also *Journal of Commerce*, 24 March 1982, p. 3A.

22 David R. Francis, 'Protectionism: Pressure's Rising But the Barriers Aren't', *Christian Science Monitor*, 4 June 1981, p. 11.

23 See Robert W. Cox and Harold K. Jacobson, *The Anatomy of Influence* (New Haven: Yale University Press, 1973), p. 321; and Werner J. Feld, *GATT and Changes in the Global Economic System*, paper presented at the ISA Convention, 24–27 March 1982, p. 24.

24 M. M. Kostecki, *East–West Trade and the GATT System* (New York: St. Martin's Press, 1978), pp. 91–109.

25 Ibid., p. 109.

26 Ibid., p. 12.

27 Ibid., *passim*.

28 See Werner J. Feld, *The European Common Market and the World* (Englewood Cliffs, NJ: Prentice-Hall, 1967), pp. 96, 97.

29 *Le Figaro*, 6 July 1973.

30 *International Herald-Tribune*, 7–8 April 1973.

31 *Relay from Bonn*, 15 October 1973.

32 For details of the farm situation in the EC and its international ramifications see *The Economist* (23 October 1982), pp. 52–3. The same basic situation still exists.

33 For details see *Business Week*, 26 April 1982, p. 34.

34 Details in *New York Times*, 21 February 1983.

35 Agence Europe, *Bulletin*, 5 February 1983.

36 Agence Europe, *Bulletin*, 17 February 1983.

37 Agence Europe, *Bulletin*, 21/22 and 26 February 1983.

38 US Department of Agriculture, *U.S. Foreign Agricultural Trade Statistical Reports Fiscal Year 1980 and 1982.*

39 The Atlantic Council of the United States, *The International Monetary System: Exchange Rates and International Indebtedness* (Washington, DC, February 1983), pp. 25–6.

40 Agence Europe, *Bulletin*, 27 May 1983.

41 Europe Documents, *International Monetary Conference 1983* (No. 1259, 27 May 1983).

42 Agence Europe, *Bulletin*, 1 June 1983.

43 *The International Monetary System*, p. 28.

44 For a complete discussion of this complex settlement process see Lawrence J. Brainard, 'CMFA Financial System and Integration' in Paul Marer and John Michael Montias, eds., *East European Integration and East–West Trade* (Bloomington, Indiana: Indiana University Press, 1980), pp. 121–38.

45 Ibid., p. 126, See also Karman Pecsi, *The Future of Socialist Economic Integration* (Armonk N. J.: M. E. Sharpe, 1981), pp. 88–148.

46 Agence Europe, *Bulletin*, 30 October and 6 November 1974.

47 A detailed discussion about all problems perceived by African leaders is found in European People's Party, *European Digest: Euro-African Relations*, no. 46, June 1982.

48 See Uwe Kitzinger, *Europe's Wider Horizons* (London: Federal Trust, 1975), pp. 5 and 6.

49 Agence Europe, *Bulletin*, 27 May 1983.

50 Ibid.

51 For a list of examples see Agence Europe, *Bulletin*, 25 May 1983.

52 For details see Feld, *The European Community in World Affairs*, pp. 130–49.

53 EC, *Fifth General Report*, 1971, p. 307. In the context of this book, the Mediterranean would constitute a sub-region of an overall European regionalism.

54 Carl A. Ehrhardt, 'EEC and the Mediterranean', *Aussenpolitik*, vol. 22, no. 1 (1971), pp. 20–30.

55 Werner J. Feld, *The European Common Market and the World*, pp. 140–2;

and Feld, 'The National Bureaucracies of the EEC Member States and Political Integration: A Preliminary Inquiry', in Robert S. Jordan, ed., *International Administration: Its Evolution and Contemporary Applications* (New York: Oxford University Press, 1971), p. 241.

56  S. J. Noumoff, 'COMECON and the Third World', *Economic and Political Weekly*, 23 August 1980, pp. 1443–54.

57  For details see Robert M. Cutler, 'East–South Relations at UNCTAD: Global Political Economy and the CMEA', *International Organization*, Vol. 37, No. 1 (Winter 1983), pp. 121–42.

58  Ibid., pp. 129–30.

59  Ibid., pp. 134–5.

60  For more information, see Werner J. Feld and Robert S. Jordan, 'The Interface Between East–West Relations and the North–South Dimension', *The Atlantic Community Quarterly*, Winter 1983–4, pp. 346–55.

# 7

## Inter-Regional Political–Economic Relations

### INTRODUCTION

Systemic changes for both the Eastern and Western European regions as well as for Europe as a whole would emerge if the existing economic and political gaps between the two parts of Europe were eliminated and the Iron Curtain gradually dismantled. The 1975 Helsinki Final Act of the Conference on Security and Co-operation in Europe aimed at an improvement of European East–West relations through increased East–West trade, more border-crossing contacts, and guarantees for human rights. At the same time, the Accord ratified the territorial *status quo* and affirmed the principle of non-interference in the internal affairs of the signatories.

Follow-up conferences to the Final Act were held in Belgrade during 1977 and 1978, in Madrid from 1981 to 1983 and in Stockholm in 1984. Very little was achieved in Belgrade. The concern about human rights violations in Eastern Europe strongly expressed by the Western European states as well as the United States was ignored by the Soviet Union, which was eager to restrict activities by its own dissidents as well as those in other parts of Eastern Europe. Various Soviet proposals for agreements on 'no first use' of nuclear weapons and limiting any expansion of existing alliances (to bar Spain from entering NATO) also made no progress. The decline of US–Soviet détente was largely responsible for the failure of Belgrade; nevertheless, another follow-up conference in Madrid was agreed upon.[1]

The Madrid Conference opened just as the confrontation between the two Superpowers had intensified as the result of the Soviet invasion of Afghanistan and the deteriorating situation in Poland. On several occasions during the three years of the Madrid Conference, collapse appeared to be inevitable. Nevertheless, a compromise for a final agreement was reached in July of 1983, partly because the Reagan Administration considered it beneficial for domestic political reasons to show a more conciliatory attitude towards the Soviet Union. The negotiations on the Strategic Arms Reduction Talks (START) and on Intermediate Nuclear Weapons (INF) in Europe were entering critical stages and many Americans were in favour of some kind of summit meeting between Reagan and Soviet leader Uri Andropov to reduce the danger of nuclear war. (This is discussed fully in the following chapter.) Clearly, such a meeting, with all the television publicity accompanying it, also might have been very helpful in the re-election campaign of President Reagan.

The compromise of Madrid dealt primarily with Soviet commitments on human rights and on trade union freedoms that had been so tragically violated in Poland by the imposition of martial law in December 1981. The Soviet Union also agreed to the release of some detained dissidents. Additional follow-up meetings on East–West travel and family reunification were also promised. President Reagan, commenting on the compromise, noted that: 'It will serve as a step toward achieving . . . a more stable and constructive relationship with the Soviet Union.'

The Stockholm meeting has been focusing on measures to reduce tensions and diminish chances for surprise attacks and conflict through miscalculation. The main discussions have revolved around a passive trade between the Soviet Union's desire for a declaration on 'no first use of force', and the United States' desire for better provisions for inspections and monitoring of military exercises. The Stockholm conferees obliged to finish their work and present a report to the next formal review meeting set for 1986 in Vienna.[2]

But if a better climate for global East–West relations can be created, it is likely to benefit from and contribute to the interactions between the states of Eastern and Western Europe. These interactions are particularly important in the economic sector where significant improvements may spill over into the political sphere.

## THE IMPLICATIONS OF INTER-REGIONAL TRADE

### Background

In the trade relations between Eastern and Western Europe, the attitude of the Soviet Union towards the European Communities has played a significant role. The Soviet Union has steadfastly refused to grant formal diplomatic recognition to the EC, in contrast to the vast majority of non-Communist states which have extended such recognition. The reason for this attitude goes back to 1948, when the Soviet Union refused to participate in the Marshall Plan and prevented the states in Eastern Europe under its control from availing themselves of its benefits. Since then, it has attacked every aspect of every step that the Western European states have taken towards economic integration and perhaps political unity. However, in 1959, Soviet attitudes towards the Common Market softened as it became obviously an international economic and political reality, although gloomy Soviet predictions about the sharpening conflicts among the Western capitalist states continued. During the 22nd Congress of the Soviet Communist Party in 1962, Nikita Krushchev embarked on a sharply-worded tirade against the EEC; yet at the same time, following the theme of peaceful coexistence, the Soviet government initiated a trade offensive aimed at the conclusion of more and broader bilateral trade agreements with the West.[3] Despite the desire for greater commerce with the EC, the Soviet Minister for Trade refused in 1962 to accept a document containing EEC offers for trade concessions delivered by the Dutch ambassador in Moscow, because the Ambassador represented the EC as a whole (a unit that had not been diplomatically recognized by the Soviet Union).

The fundamental position of the Soviet government had therefore not changed at this time although it could not help but acknowledge the increasing power of the EC as an 'objective reality'. Consequently, although no ambassadors have been accredited to the EC, certain trade arrangements, especially with respect to farm prices, had already been made by the Socialist bloc with the EC, and informal contacts existed between Polish, Hungarian, and even Soviet officials and the EC personnel dealing with external relations. However, with the exception of Yugoslavia, none of the People's Democracies had yet established a diplomatic mission to the European Communities. The long and difficult negotiations in the framework of the European Security Conference dealing with economic co-operation touched on the diplomatic recognition of the EC as well as CMEA, but no tangible results emerged.[4]

However, in 1973, CMEA as an organization also made unofficial approaches to the EC to initiate a discussion on economic matters of mutual interest. The EC institutions were at first hesitant to respond affirmatively to these overtures because they considered CMEA essentially different from the EC, inasmuch as the former was seen primarily as an instrument of Soviet policy and dominated by the

USSR. However, the EC Council of Ministers later had a change of opinion and decided in May 1974 to inform the Secretary-General of CMEA through an ambassador of one of the member-states that the Commission was ready to receive any suggestions regarding CMEA–EC relations and perhaps enter into trade negotiations in a positive manner.[5] But since CMEA, in contrast to the EC, cannot make a commitment in the name of its member-states, the Commission insisted that negotiations and agreements be carried out among the national governments of the EC and CMEA states. Nevertheless, the Secretary-General of CMEA at the time, Nicolai Fadayev, extended an invitation to the then-President of the Commission, François-Xavier Ortoli of France, to visit CMEA headquarters in Moscow. The Commission expressed itself in favour of the principle of establishing contacts among leading officials, and in February 1975 an EC delegation visited Moscow and met with officials of CMEA for three days.

Although the visit to Moscow by the EC delegation established a pattern of visits and talks between EC and CMEA officials in both Brussels and Moscow, the results have been very meagre. The reasons were both organizational and political. EC officials have felt that CMEA competencies were insufficient to permit the conclusion of a viable trade agreement with the EC and they were, therefore, primarily intent on bilateral EC ties with individual CMEA member-states. Politically, the general aggravation of East–West problems in the late 1970s and early 1980s has contributed to a hardening of the differences in viewpoints held by the EC and CMEA delegations.

By 1981, CMEA continued to avoid any recognition of the EC as a legal and diplomatically independent unit and all formal communications by CMEA authorities were addressed to whoever held the Presidency of the EC Council of Ministers at a particular time and not to the Commission President. Nevertheless, attempts were made to draft a framework agreement between CMEA and the EC, but EC authorities have not considered this a preliminary step towards expanded trade relations between the two sub-regional organizations because this should be done through bilateral agreements between the EC and individual CMEA member-states.[6] For the EC, the framework agreement did not alter the competencies of the respective institutions, CMEA being much less integrated and less endowed with independent powers than the EC. Hence, the main purpose of the agreement has been the exchange of information and statistics. On the other hand, with the signature of the agreement, CMEA was to recognize the legal personality of the EC and to stop contesting its participation as an independent unit in international conventions and treaties. The fulfilment of this expectation has been doubtful in spite of a strong Soviet interest in expanding trade with Western Europe which, it is claimed, could help in the creation of hundreds of thousands of new jobs.[7] There are also indications that the new Soviet leader, Mikhail Gorbachev, is ready to recognise the ligitmacy of the EC.

Whether the existing stalemate in EC–CMEA dealings can be resolved may well depend on the future pattern of trade between the two European sub-regions and this pattern is likely to be influenced by the nature of the emerging political climate of the Superpowers. Nonetheless, an assessment of the overall trade pattern may offer insights into future developments.

## The Pattern of Trade

Despite the lack of diplomatic relations between most Eastern European states and the EC, and despite the existing ideological differences, trade between them increased more than three hundredfold from 1958 to 1981, perhaps reflecting the climate of détente and the increase in economic co-operation stipulated in the Helsinki Accords. However, it must also be noted that trade declined from 1980 to 1981, caused most likely by poor economic conditions. Table 7.1 provides detailed figures and shows that except for the

Table 7.1  Trade between the EC and Eastern European CMEA states (US$ million, exports f.o.b., imports c.i.f.)

| Destination/ origin EC(9)[1] | Year | CMEA | | |
| | | Exports | Imports | Balance |
| --- | --- | --- | --- | --- |
| | 1958 | 626 | 676 | −50 |
| | 1963 | 1,080 | 1,363 | −283 |
| | 1969 | 2,451 | 2,699 | −248 |
| | 1971 | 4,199 | 4,232 | −33 |
| | 1974 | 11,726 | 9,539 | +2,187 |
| | 1975 | 14,518 | 10,357 | +4,161 |
| | 1978 | 17,074 | 15,653 | +1,421 |
| | 1980 | 22,684 | 26,136 | −3,452 |
| | 1981 | 19,344 | 23,568 | −4,224 |

*Note:* [1] Excluding trade between the Federal Republic of Germany and the German Democratic Republic.
*Sources:* Statisches Amt der Europaischen Gemeinschaften, *Foreign Trade*, no. 2 (1973), pp. 12, 14; GATT, *International Trade 1981/1982* (Geneva, 1982), table A–18.

years from 1974 to 1978 CMEA has had a positive balance of trade. However, it must be noted that beginning with 1974, the start of the OPEC oil crunch, EC imports of fuels from CMEA states and especially the Soviet Union rose substantially from $2.56 billion in 1974 to $21.85 billion in 1981. This constituted the bulk of imports from the Soviet Union and about 25 per cent of the goods shipped from the other Eastern European CMEA states.[8]

As for the EC of Ten (including Greece), 1981 imports from European CMEA states amounted to 4.3 per cent of total imports, while the share of EC exports to that region was somewhat lower, 3.6 per cent, compared with 4.0 per cent in 1980. With respect to percentage of total trade of the EC member-states, Greek and West German exports and imports to and from CMEA held top honours: 6.8 and 8.4 per cent, respectively, for Greece and 6.2 and 5.7 per cent for West Germany.[9]

Communist Eastern European trade with the industrialized states of the West has had two major objectives. First, it serves to eliminate gaps in the economic structure and relieves temporary shortages of goods. Second, it contributes to the rapid attainment of economic development objectives. Guided by these objectives, the purchases of the Eastern European Communist states from the EEC have concentrated on industrial goods, and only 20 per cent have been devoted to raw materials and farm products. On the other hand, their exports to the Common Market have consisted mainly of agricultural commodities and raw materials, whereas industrial products have comprised only a minor part, and they have been shipped mostly by East Germany, Czechoslovakia and the Soviet Union.

In all Communist states foreign trade is handled by the state itself. The governmental agencies in charge of foreign trade possess a powerful monopoly that enables them to play the offers of one supplier against those of others in order to obtain optimum terms. At the same time, they can set export prices with little regard to cost and may engage in dumping, if, for one reason or another, they are anxious to sell certain commodities. One of these reasons may be the need for convertible currencies, which are in short supply in most East bloc states. In fact, the shortage of convertible currencies is the great dilemma of the trade with Eastern Europe. It limits the opportunity to expand exports to these states to their ability to ship in return sufficient goods for payment. The currency problem also tends to favour bilateral trade arrangements between individual EC and CMEA states because of the need for long-term credit terms, which the latter demand from their Western trading partners.

The current pattern of trade shows that during the last few years CMEA has been enjoying a healthy trade surplus with the EC which minimizes the significance of the currency problem. Natural gas deliveries from the Soviet Union to Western Europe in the new gas pipeline, much opposed by the United States, will doubtless increase hard currency receipts for Eastern Europe. But a short-lived Soviet threat to curtail gas deliveries as part of its massive propaganda campaign in 1983–4 against the introduction of new nuclear missiles in NATO didn't help to strengthen Western Europe's confidence in the Soviet Union as a reliable supplier.

### EC Problems and Concerns

Most of the trade between the EC and Eastern Europe until the middle 1980s has been governed by one-year bilateral commercial agreements of EC member-states with Eastern European states. Although up to 1974 the Commission had usually given its consent to the renewal of such agreements, a new practice was instituted in May of that year. At that time, the Commission began to insist that all negotiations for trade agreements with Eastern European states be conducted exclusively by the EC authorities, even if a temporary vacuum were created in the relations between a particular member-state and its Eastern European trading partner as a result of the non-renewal of a bilateral agreement. This new policy was confirmed by the Council of Ministers,[10] but the real effect of the new policy has been more cosmetic than real. The reason for this is that, since the early 1970s, economic relations between EC member-states and Eastern Europe have been more and more incorporated into so-called co-operation agreements. These agreements, in effect for periods of up to ten years, are designed for economic, industrial, scientific, and technical co-operation. They include the supply and construction of factories in Eastern Europe to be paid for by the export of the goods to be produced. They also relate to exchanges of patents, licences, other means of technological transfers, and co-operation in the marketing of exports to specific states.

The effect of these co-operation agreements has been a pre-emption of the common commercial policy that was to be the exclusive competence of the EC institutions. For the EC this has given rise to the risk that the classical instruments of trade policy, such as customs duties and quantitative restrictions, may well be subverted or weakened by these new forms of economic co-operation which, to a large extent, have remained in the field of national competence and national foreign policy and, therefore, have escaped EC jurisdiction.

There are other reasons why the Commission has wanted to have the co-operation agreements placed into an EC-wide system of co-ordination, namely the necessity for a uniform credit policy towards Eastern Europe and the embargo of strategic goods instituted under NATO guidelines. This credit policy was governed until 1963 by the Berne Convention, which was not a formal treaty but a kind of gentlemen's agreement to which all member governments and a number of third states, including Britain, adhered.[11] In 1960, a five-year ceiling was instituted by the participating states for credits granted for large capital equipment orders, but when Britain deviated from the five-year rule in 1963, other states, including Italy and France, followed suit. A resolution of the EEC Council of Ministers in May 1962 requiring consultation by member-states before deviating from this rule was not effective in holding the credit line, nor were discussions within NATO aiming at a five-year limitation of credits to the Socialist bloc.

Although no specific proposals on the co-ordination of credit were made by the Commission, in May 1966 the Council of Ministers instructed the Committee of Permanent Representatives to make a study of current practices. The report based on the study indicated that the longest credit terms were granted by Italy, and that West Germany led the EC in terms of the total amount and number of individual credit transactions. After long discussions, the Council eventually agreed on a five-year credit limit for deliveries to East Germany and urged that the consultation procedures be strengthened. But it was also argued that the question of credit duration could not be separated from other factors, such as volume and interest rates, and that an agreement in this field would be meaningful only if it included at least all OECD states, especially Britain, Japan and the United States. In the meantime, by the end of 1971, the total credits exceeding five years granted by firms in EC member-states (then the Six) had already surpassed $3 billion. This occurred despite hundreds of consultation meetings attended by government experts and credit insurers.[12]

In January 1973 the Commission asked the Council of Ministers for a regulation setting forth joint proposals and a management procedure to cover the duration of export credits and governmental guarantees. The anxiety of national business firms and governments to be the successful bidders in the competitive export business to Eastern Europe has made a shambles out of any well-meaning regulations agreed upon in the Council of Ministers. Indeed, the continuing strong pressure by business firms in Western Europe to sell goods to the East has contributed to the tremendous increase in trade noted earlier. The financing of this trade has required expanded and innovative banking and credit facilities which will be discussed later in greater detail.

The highly competitive nature of the export business towards the largely untapped markets of Eastern Europe has also undermined the NATO guidelines for the export of strategic goods. In view of the difficulty in finding precise definitions for the variety of goods that may fall under the embargo, there has been no complete uniformity in the interpretation of these guidelines. As a consequence, an item that one NATO state may exclude from shipment to a Communist state has been delivered by another NATO partner. For example, in view of the American promises made in the early 1970s to deliver nuclear plants and technology to Egypt and Israel for the generation of electricity, it is noteworthy that the NATO Co-ordinating Committee (COCOM) in charge of members' trade with Communist states indicated that it would be legal to sell nuclear reactors for peaceful purposes even to these states.[13]

In order to assure at least some kind of uniformity in the commercial relations between the EC and the Communist state-trading companies, the Commission has drafted a model trade agreement. With the expiration of national bilateral trade agreements at the end of 1975 (in many cases replaced by co-operation agreements, however), the EC institutions demonstrated their readiness to enter into negotiations on EC agreements with Eastern Europe as well as with other Communist states.

The contents of the model agreement were marked by the following features:

1 'Reciprocity' with assurance of an overall balance of advantages and obligations;
2 The reciprocal granting of the most-favoured-nation (MFN) clause on tariffs, but no claim on the part of the state-trading states to the tariff reductions granted by the EC to free trade or other existing preferential agreements;
3 Liberalization of current quantitative restrictions;

4 Maintenance of the principles and mechanisms of the CAP;
5 Payments and financing provisions to be worked out on an *ad hoc* basis;
6 The evolution of co-operation arrangements as far as possible under EC competencies;
7 Safeguard mechanisms to take account of the differences in economic systems between the contracting parties.[14]

Although the Council of Ministers was generally sympathetic to the contents of the model agreement, several of the Eastern European states that received a draft of this agreement reacted unfavourably, but contacts between the EC and these states were maintained on this matter. Meanwhile, the scheme of former individual bilateral agreements on quotas and tariffs has continued, but operates under the label of the EC. At the same time, long-term co-operation agreements (up to five years) between EC and Eastern European states also continue to be concluded, strengthening the resolve of the latter states to negotiate with the EC institutions.[15] The Council accepted the MFN treatment in the tariff field, which up to 1975 had not been granted by the EC states to Eastern European states except to those that were members of GATT. However, in practice this treatment had been really accorded to all Eastern European states in one form or another, although in most cases it was not reciprocated.[16]

The efforts of the EC institutions to introduce uniform rules into trade between member-states and CMEA states have yielded some successes. For example, since 1975 so-called sector agreements have been concluded with respect to steel, textiles, and fishing. Steel agreements were negotiated with Czechoslovakia, Hungary, Bulgaria and Romania; textile accords with Romania, Hungary, Czechoslovakia, Poland and Bulgaria; and fishing agreements with the Soviet Union, East Germany and Poland. The textiles accord, negotiated under the Multi-Fibres Arrangement contains quantitative restrictions on CMEA exports to the EC as well as anti-dumping and anti-fraud provisions. But undoubtedly the greatest EC achievement was the conclusion in 1979 of a full-fledged trade agreement with Romania, the only one of its kind and a likely model for similar agreements with other Eastern European CMEA members in the future.[17]

In spite of the progress made towards the objectives set by the EC in East–West trade, voices of caution were raised in the European Parliament. Major concerns expressed were:

1 *Dumping* committed by CMEA states, with respect both to industrial products and to transportation services at below-cost rates.

2 The *special status of trade between West and East Germany* according to a Protocol appended to the EEC Treaty which stipulates that trade between the two Germanies shall be considered as 'German internal trade'. The trade has been estimated at $4 billion and permits East German agricultural products entering the EC to escape the regulations of the CAP throughout the EC territory. Moreover, in view of a trade surplus in favour of West Germany, Bonn has allowed the East Germans an interest-free credit of about $400 million.

3 *Compensation operations* which are special barter transactions because of latent shortages of convertible currencies in CMEA states and which may distort normal trade relations between EC and CMEA states.

4 *Trade embargo measures* on the basis of the COCOM list prohibiting the export of strategic products. The embargo can be and has been circumvented and this tends to distort competitive capabilities of EC suppliers depending on the latter's ingenuity of finding ways around COCOM prohibition. Even the more aggressive attempts of the Reagan Administration to impede East–West trade in strategic goods, through COCOM and other bilateral as well as multilateral means, has not yielded the favourable results hoped for.

5 *The growing indebtedness of Eastern European* CMEA *member-states* which has exceeded $100 billion (if Yugoslavia is included). This situation has compelled the Eastern European states to try reducing imports from the EC while attempting vigorously to expand their exports in order to obtain hard currencies.[18] Combined with increased international tension and a growing tendency towards protectionism, the result may well be a future slowdown in the growth of inter-regional trade. More will be said about the debt problem in the next section.

## Summary

While the increase of trade between the EC and CMEA during the last two decades has been truly remarkable, with imports into the EC emphasizing raw materials, including agricultural commodities, and the flow of goods in the opposite direction concentrating on manufactured products, some problems have also cropped up. First, it has become obvious and is not surprising that this flow of trade is influenced by worldwide economic and political conditions. The better and more harmonious these conditions, the more this trade is likely to flourish. Second, currency and credit problems have a bearing on the volume and quality of this trade. Third, special concerns and situations are likely to affect trade expansion: apprehension about dumping, the effects of embargo impositions, or perceived injustices or distortions as may result from the special rules governing inter-German trade may dampen the enthusiasm for inter-regional trade.

What are the political implications of this trade in terms of system change? To enable us to make a judgment requires the examination of trade-related issues, such as the debt problem, technology transfer, and new forms of inter-regional co-operation, all of which will follow.

### LOANS AND CREDITS

CMEA imports can be financed by hard currency receipts from exports, credits by suppliers, or by funds received from hard currency loans extended to financial institutions in CMEA member-states from foreign sources. In an area with chronic currency convertibility difficulties such as Eastern Europe, credits from suppliers and hard currency loans clearly play a very significant role.

As already indicated, the level of indebtedness of Eastern European financial institutions to the West is very high. Table 7.2 provides figures for the *total* debt of the highest debtor states to banks in the West, the growth of the debt, debt service payments and their percentages of exports. The last set of figures highlights one aspect of the problem of currency convertibility. In order to make some progress in the convertibility issue, Poland and East Germany would have to double their exports to hard currency states. At the same time, these conditions are not conducive to new loan commitments by Western banks to Eastern Europe in the 1980s, especially after the very unhappy experiences in Poland, except perhaps to tide over interest payments. Nor is it likely that under these conditions the Eastern European financial institutions are very interested in or able to finance imports unless the products are urgently needed and supplier credit is not available.[19]

In spite of these dismal circumstances, the external debt-GNP ratios of the Soviet Union, East Germany and Poland remain quite low,

Table 7.2  Eastern Europe: the highest debtors

| | Debt outstanding | | Growth in bank debt[1] | | | Debt service payment 1983 | Payment as percentage of exports |
|---|---|---|---|---|---|---|---|
| | 1982 | 1975 | 1976–81 | 1976–78 | 1979–81 | | |
| German Democratic Republic[2] | 14.0 | 2.6 | 27.4 | 33.6 | 21.4 | 6.3 | 83 |
| Hungary | 7.0 | 2.2 | 24.5 | 42.8 | 8.6 | 3.5 | 55 |
| Poland | 26.0 | 3.9 | 26.7 | 44.2 | 12.3 | 7.8 | 94 |
| Romania | 9.9 | 0.9 | 33.5 | 40.6 | 26.8 | 5.5 | 61 |
| USSR[3] | 23.0 | 10.1 | 12.3 | 19.0 | 14.6 | 12.2 | 25 |

Notes: [1] Compound annual growth rates. Data of 1979–81 are adjusted for exchange rate changes.
[2] Excludes debt to banks in the Federal Republic of Germany.
[3] Includes a residual for Eastern Europe, which is mainly Council for Mutual Economic Assistance (CMEA) banks.
Source: Time, 10 January 1983, p. 45; Finance and Development, December 1972, p. 39.

while those of Hungary and Romania have moved up significantly.[20] However, regardless of clear differences in economic circumstances and management capabilities in individual CMEA states, it is the general deterioration of East–West relations, and in particular the events in Poland, which have had a major negative impact on recent Western bank attitudes towards lending to Eastern Europe, and it would take a substantial improvement of these relations before a change in these attitudes can be expected.[21]

Financial support for necessary imports can be obtained from Eurocredits, and these loans can be raised without the credit facility being linked to individual projects. In addition, Euro-bonds can be issued, but this presupposes the publication of a detailed prospectus containing comprehensive economic information. While Poland and Hungary have complied with international standards of supplying such information to Western creditors, the Soviet Union and other Eastern CMEA states have exhibited considerable reservations about this. In addition, CMEA's Moscow-based International Investment Bank (IIB) and the International Bank for Economic Cooperation (IBEC) have taken advantage of the Euro-market to raise funds.

Again, the changes in the international climate have had an impact on Eurocredits raised by Eastern European states. After having risen from $2.5 billion in 1977 to $4.7 billion in 1979 (representing at that time 6 per cent of the total of such loans in international markets), these credits fell to around $0.7 billion in 1982, hardly 0.7 per cent of the total market volume. Among individual states, only Hungary and, to a smaller extent, the Soviet Union and East Germany raised such loans during that year, and these were at conditions considerably inferior to those available in previous years.[22]

Finally, exports from the EC can be financed by credits extended by the supplier or exporter but long-term arrangements usually require some kind of insurance. For example, in West Germany, the Frankfurt-based Export Credit Company, a consortium of banks, provides favourable refinancing facilities up to 80 or 85 per cent of the invoice price involved. Large insurance companies may also furnish coverage of up to 85 per cent of an export invoice's value.

In some cases, CMEA purchasers, especially the Soviet Union, demand artificially low interest rates when EC exports are financed, for example 7 per cent on six-to-nine-year loans when the prime rate may be 12 per cent. The governments of Britain, France, and Italy have indeed subsidized interest rates for large export projects to Eastern Europe, but West Germany has generally resisted such demands for subsidies which, in fact, distort competition.[23]

As long as the ability of some of the CMEA states to repay their large loans is in jeopardy, EC–CMEA trade is likely to suffer as financing opportunities may be hard to come by. With economic conditions seeming to improve gradually on a worldwide basis and the CMEA states continuing to show a favourable trade balance, especially with natural gas deliveries expanding, the credit situation is likely to improve and to benefit inter-regional trade.

### THE EASTERN EUROPEAN QUEST FOR TECHNOLOGY

A major purpose of CMEA's expansion of trade with the EC, as with the West in general, has been the acquisition of technological know-how for the production of goods in general and for equipment of military usefulness in particular. Hence, both the technological and financial capabilities of the OECD states in general have been the magnets which have strongly motivated the Soviet Union and other Eastern European states to intensify economic co-operation with the EC member-states. In turn, the latter have been in full agreement to transfer appropriate technology to Eastern Europe because it would strengthen their export structures and create much firmer ties with the neighbouring sub-region. Conversely, the EC member governments have been generally sceptical about COCOM's lists of strategic items that were subject to embargo, claiming that the assumption that East bloc imports of technology benefited primarily the Soviet Union's military build-up often lacked empirical proof.[24]

COCOM was created in 1950. Its original members were the NATO allies except Iceland; later Japan was accepted as an additional member. COCOM's purpose was to co-ordinate the national export control programmes of the members to prevent the sale of items containing new technologies of military value to the Soviet Union and other Communist states. For this reason, the COCOM participants have compiled lists of strategic products which they pledge not to export to the Soviet bloc. In addition, COCOM supervises credit limitations on all goods shipped to the CMEA states. We mentioned earlier the five-year limit that was established in accordance with the Union of Berne for credits to these states. However, as already indicated, the credit limit has not been maintained and many Western European firms continue to be doubtful about the value of the COCOM embargo list.[25]

Nevertheless, the United States has remained committed to the

COCOM system, and, as mentioned earlier, the Reagan Administration has considered it an important instrument of its relations with the USSR and other Communist states. Hence, in 1982 and 1983, the United States was anxious to expand and update the lists of embargoed products and technologies, particularly since it did not prevail in stopping the construction of the natural gas pipeline from the Soviet Union to Western Europe. The United States has therefore wanted to strengthen the clearing house functions of COCOM and to ensure that its provisions and rules be enforced by the member-states. According to American proposals, the expanded list was to include gas turbine engines, large floating drydocks, electronic grade silicon, printed circuit board technology, robotics, and computer hardware and software.[26]

Nonetheless, in view of the somewhat negative attitudes of the Western Europeans towards the COCOM system, illegal diversion activities are likely to be a problem in Western Europe and perhaps in North America. This should not be surprising because, during the 1970s at least, respect for COCOM injunctions on embargoes and especially on credit limits had eroded. Whether the new effort in this connection can turn the situation and previous trends around cannot be adjudged at this time.

The actual transfer of technology can take two basic forms. One way to do this is to sell and ship products containing the desired technology. The shipment of advanced computers to the East bloc is an example; the installation of a sophisticated production process is another. Shipments of technology-intensive goods then become a statistic in EC foreign trade. The other form of technology transfer is through licences. It has been estimated that during the 1970s the Eastern European CMEA states purchased and received about 2,000 licences a year from the West and paid $500 million for the technologies thus obtained.[27]

There is another conceivable possibility which may transfer technology from the EC to CMEA states. This is the formation of joint ventures between Western European business firms and East bloc industrial plants. We will examine the phenomena of joint ventures and other types of transnational co-operation in the next section.

## TRANSNATIONAL FORMS OF EAST–WEST CO-OPERATION

Transnational co-operation refers to agreements between privately owned Western companies and state-owned plants and enterprises pursuing similar or complementary economic activities. These agree-ments may relate to the co-production of particular items, setting up specific production lines, the provision of markets, imparting managerial skills, and sometimes furnishing capital. The Eastern European enterprises provide labour and raw materials. In some cases, the Western firm has provided complete plants in the form of 'turnkey projects'. For example, Fiat has done this in Poland and the Soviet Union. In other cases, the agreements have involved the granting of licences and the improvement of technical know-how.

The Western firms are paid for their contributions by receiving a share of the final product which they can sell in their own markets or with shipments of raw materials. This reduces the problem of foreign exchange shortage and helps overcome the Eastern European partners' lack of marketing expertise, thereby improving the export capabilities of the Eastern European enterprises.[28]

It has been reported that by the middle of the 1970s about 1,000 transnational co-operative agreements between Western companies and their East bloc counterparts had been concluded.[29] Sub-sequently, however, the number of such agreements concluded has declined. Perhaps the anticipation of the Helsinki Final Act in 1975 was a stronger motivation for the conclusion of these agreements than the reality of the post-Helsinki era.

In several Eastern European CMEA states, legislation has made it possible for Western firms to engage in joint ventures involving Western equity participation. Hungary, Romania and Poland were the first full members of CMEA to permit direct foreign investment; they were followed in 1980 by Bulgaria. (Yugoslavia also has had appropriate legislative authority for joint ventures.) However, relatively few of these ventures have been established, and most of these were between medium and small enterprises. One other unique venture is the establishment of a bank in Hungary with Western European and Japanese capital in which the Western partici-pants hold the controlling interest.[30]

The implications of both forms of transnational co-operation go beyond the economic effects. They promote close human contacts between West and East – at least on the occupational level. Indeed, the benefits of joint ventures, which Howard Perlmutter calls 'transideological' enterprises, could also be political.[31] These enter-prises could cross not only political frontiers but also ideological lines. They may foster a pragmatic approach to collaboration between Communists and non-Communists, and the importance of ideology would gradually recede. Working together towards a shared goal, individuals of different nationalities might adopt new values; common ways of looking at problems create feelings that common interests exist. For example, even the deep-rooted psychological antipathy in Poland towards the Germans did not inhibit the Polish Communist regime from negotiating agreements with West German companies such as Krupp and Grundig.[32] Thus, the contacts established between Western Europeans and Eastern Europeans could easily be meaningful in terms of bridging the gap between East and West. In this respect, they are likely to be much more effective than contacts artificially contrived through cultural exchanges, student exchanges, or tourism.

## CONCLUSIONS

The foregoing discussion provides clear evidence that the trans-national flows between the EC and CMEA member-states in the early 1980s in terms of trade, bank loans to the East, technology transfer towards CMEA, and transnational co-operation are much more intense than they were in the 1950s. Indeed, the crescendo in these flows seems to have occurred during the 1970s, while in the early 1980s a small decline in trade was noted and the existing high indebtedness of some of the East bloc states raised caution flags regarding additional Western loans. The Afghanistan and Polish situations also put some dampers on the expansion of technology transfers in strategically sensitive areas.

What are the implications of the trends outlined earlier for change in the existing sub-regional systems? There is clear evidence of growing enmeshing between the Western and Eastern European economies which could gradually lead to social learning processes resulting eventually in economic, social, and political changes in the CMEA states and could culminate in the gradual dilution of the existing sharp political division between the two sub-regions. However, there are also indicators of impediments to such develop-ments. The current high level of indebtedness on the part of several Eastern European CMEA members makes it unlikely that sufficient additional credits and loans will be extended to the East by Western financial institutions to increase substantially the flow of trade. This applies especially to states *other* than the Soviet Union, which will earn enough hard currency from fuel sales to increase its importing capability if it so desires. The continuing transfer of technology to the East bloc, while undoubtedly a powerful incentive to increased imports, remains a sensitive and controversial issue for the West as there continues to be concern, especially in the United States, that Western Europe, by providing the advanced technology to the Soviet Union, promotes its own destruction. However, Juergen Noetzold claims that the assumption that technology imports to Eastern Europe benefit primarily Soviet military power remains unproven and that whatever technology is needed for Soviet space research and strategy can be obtained from domestic research.[33] He argues that the curtailment of technology transfers to the East would carry with it a reduction in other imports from the West and that such a development may be seen by the Soviet Union as a withdrawal of co-operation and strengthen Soviet perceptions of encirclement. Perceptions of this kind can only prompt them to accelerate their arms build-up even if this results in additional negative economic effects. Noetzold continues:

Naturally, a continued arms buildup by the USSR can hardly be in the West's interests and must lead to corresponding security efforts on the part of the West, which could very well have a destabilizing effect. There is, for instance, the problem of financing a further buildup of Western defences at the expense of social and economic projects. And, finally, the demonstration of Western economic superiority and its social welfare system in the 1960s had an effect on Eastern Europe that must not be underestimated.

The accentuation of confrontation elements in East–West relations would certainly not enlarge the scope for reforms in Eastern Europe. Instead, it would narrow it still further. If economic cooperation were to be replaced by Western sanctions, it can be taken for granted that these sanctions would not lead to the collapse of the Soviet economy, nor would they make the Soviet Union more yielding in matters of foreign policy.[34]

These arguments are not entirely persuasive. While it is correct that the accentuation of confrontation would narrow the scope of reforms in Eastern Europe, the Soviet Union has shown in 1968 in Czechoslovakia and again in 1981 in Poland that for its leadership there are definite limits to the accommodation of reforms. While the Soviet Union has tolerated economic deviations from the Communist credo in Hungary and has countenanced at times Romania's independence in foreign policy, the principles of Marxism and Soviet security have not been compromised. Hence, a high-capability Soviet military establishment and pervasive military and political control over Eastern Europe will remain very important imperatives for the Soviet leadership despite its natural desire to accept all economic benefits that may improve CMEA's economic levels. For this reason, the importation of militarily useful technology will be a high priority objective; after all, it does save enormous monetary and intellectual resources which could be spent better on other military and civilian needs. Therefore, strengthening trade flows between Western and Eastern Europe through increased technology transfers to the East bloc, regardless of its military contribution, may not necessarily be the best long-run policy for Western Europe.

Finally, the prospects for systemic changes affecting especially Eastern Europe are diminished further by the decline in transnational co-operation between Western European companies and Eastern European manufacturing and service facilities. Cross-regional socialization processes, which may lead to changes in values, the adoption of new values more congenial to pluralism and the free market, and long-term learning in this respect have shown so far only limited results in spite of vastly increased contacts between Eastern and Western Europeans. But it may be too early to make a final judgment about socialization, which is typically a very slow operation, and it is very difficult to apply empirical measures in politically sensitive areas such as encompassed by CMEA.

NOTES

1 For details see William E. Griffith, *The Superpowers and Regional Tensions* (Lexington, Massachusetts: D. C. Heath, 1982), pp. 42–4.

2 *Times-Picayune* (New Orleans, Louisiana), 16 July 1983, *New York Times*, 31 July 1985.

3 Thirty-two theses dealing with imperialist integration in Western Europe were published by *Pravda* on 26 August 1962, of which one stated that 'The extension of economic relations between States, and of peaceful co-operation is one of the most important ways of preventing war and consolidating co-operation between people.' Quoted by John P. de Gara, *Trade Relations Between the Common Market and the Eastern Bloc* (Bruges: DeTempel, 1964), p. 22.

4 See Johann Karat, 'Soviet Union and the European Communities', Aussenpolitik, English ed. 23, no. 3 (March 1972): 299–308.

5 Agence Europe, *Bulletin*, 9 and 16 May 1974.

6 Agence Europe, *Bulletin*, 16 January, 1 and 15 April 1981.

7 Agence Europe, *Bulletin*, 6/7 July 1981, 28 July 1983.

8 GATT, *International Trade 1981/82* (Geneva, 1982), table A–18.

9 For additional details, see Department of State, Bureau of Intelligence and Research, *Trade Patterns of the West 1981* (Report 443-AR, 6 August 1982), pp. 9 (table 2) and 16 (chart I).

10 Agence Europe, *Bulletin*, 18 May 1974.

11 The Berne Convention is technically the International Credit Insurers' Union, established in Berne in 1983. Its members are organizations from sixteen states including all EEC states except Italy and Luxembourg. However, in 1960 these two states accepted the five-year rule for credits.

12 Agence Europe, *Bulletin*, 11 January 1973.

13 Richard F. Staar, *The Communist Regimes in Eastern Europe*, 2nd rev. ed. (The Hoover Institution on War, Revolution, and Peace, 1971), p. 255.

14 See Agence Europe *Bulletin*, 28/29 October 1974.

15 Agence Europe, *Bulletin*, 23/24, 25 April 1975.

16 Agence Europe, *Bulletin*, 14 November 1974.

17 EC Commission, *Fourteenth General Report 1980*, pp. 242 and 297; and Agence Europe *Bulletin*, 22 January and 3 September 1982.

18 Agence Europe, *Bulletin*, 22 January 1983; and *Time*, 10 January 1983, p. 45.

19 For technical details, see Richard C. William and Peter M. Keller, 'Eastern Europe and the International Banks', *Finance and Development* (December 1982), pp. 39–41.

20 Ibid., p. 41.

21 For a broad analysis and prospects of the financial relations between Eastern European states and Western financial markets, see OECD, *Financial Market Trends* No. 24, March 1983, pp. 1–35.

22 Ibid., p. 32.

23 For details, see Axel Lebahn, 'Financing German Trade with the East', *Aussenpolitik* 33, No. 2 (1982): 123–33.

24 See Juergen Noetzold, 'East–West Economic Relations', *Aussenpolitik* 32, No. 4 (1981): 373–85, on p. 384. Japan is also a member of COCOM.

25 For a concise history of COCOM and the technology transfer to the Soviet Bloc, see Joseph C. Brada, 'Technologie-transfer zwischen West und Ost I', *Osteuropa* 31 (April 1981): 297–312.

26 US Senate, 97th Congress, 2nd Session, *Transfer of United States High Technology to the Soviet Union and Soviet Bloc Nations* (Hearings before the Senate Permanent Subcommittee on Investigation of the Committee on Governmental Affairs), pp. 536–40.

27 Joseph C. Brada, 'Technologietransfer zwischen Ost und West II', *Osteuropa* 31 (May 1981): 408–25, on p. 413.

28 Joan Edelman Spero, *The Politics of International Economic Relations*, 2nd ed. (New York: St Martin's Press, 1981), pp. 312–13; and Noetzold, 'East–West Economic Relations', pp. 378–9.

29 Noetzold, p. 378.

30 Ibid., p. 379.

31. For details see Howard V. Perlmutter, 'Emerging East–West Ventures: The Transideological Enterprise', *Columbia Journal of World Business* (September–October 1969), pp. 39–50.

32 Staar, op. cit., p. 254.

33 Noetzold, op. cit., p. 384.

34 Ibid., pp. 381–2.

# 8

## The Political–Military Dimension: East–West Asymmetry and Efforts to Avoid Regional Conflict

### INTRODUCTION

The preceding chapter has shown that if we attempt to view Europe as a potentially unified region in the future, major economic and political asymmetries would have to be overcome. But sub-regional systemic impediments in the form of alliances, especially in Eastern Europe, and inter-regional economic difficulties caused by their asymmetries, do not augur well for positive systemic changes in the region as a whole. Furthermore, the fact that the United States – a non-regional Power – has difficulty in maintaining an Atlantic political/security dimension of the East–West conflict, further complicates the possibility for a strong inter-regional evolution of the Western part of Europe towards the Eastern part (assuming the Eastern part can evolve away from Soviet hegemony).

This chapter will focus on the military–political dimension of possible systemic change and will examine how intra-sub-regional conditions within the military alliance of NATO may affect possibilities to overcome the Iron Curtain between the two parts of Europe. We will suggest what the prospects may be to move from hard bloc-to-bloc confrontation to some kind of accommodation in the military field through the complex set of negotiations that are taking place between the two opposing camps. Is there any hope for any kind of military–political co-operation between Eastern and Western Europe that can lead to bridging the existing gap and ultimately result in a politically and economically more harmonious region than Europe is at present?

Since World War II, circumstances have delineated the Elbe River as the primary point of conflict between East and West, and the determinant of ally and foe. The two global coalitions which grew up in the late 1940s and 1950s have met head-on at this point (see figure 8.1). And as we have learned earlier, as the so-called Cold War took on added dimensions in the 1960s due to changing global as well as European political conditions, new forms of conflict and co-operation have arisen both among the states located on the same side of the Elbe (i.e., in the 'Western camp' and the 'Eastern camp') and among the states lying on the opposite sides as well. Any discussion of unity and/or disunity in Western Europe must take this dual evolution into account.

As we have already seen, the growth of multinational forms of co-operation, such as the North Atlantic Treaty Organization (NATO), reflecting the Atlantic political/security dimension, and the European Communities (EEC, ECSC, EURATOM) in the West reflect the Western European political/economic dimension. They have been paralleled by the Warsaw Treaty Organization (WTO) and CMEA in the East, and by the growth of bilateral economic relations between the states of Western Europe with those in Central and Eastern Europe (see table 8.1 for the dates of establishment of Atlantic and Soviet international systems). The two Superpowers have also engaged in increasingly active trade relationships with the states located in the other's 'camp'. The liberalization of the restrictions of the Export Control Act, as regards trade with the Soviet Union and Eastern Europe, by the American Congress in 1969, over President Richard Nixon's reservations, is indicative of this trend. As then Senator Walter Mondale was quoted as saying:

The Communist countries of Eastern Europe are not hurt [by the trade limitations]. They can obtain what they need from other free world countries. Only the American businessman and the US balance of payments are substantially hurt. Basically we deny ourselves the right to compete. At a time when we worry whether our 'national interests' should allow us to trade with Russia, the Russians continue to supply us with platinum for our basic military and space industries and chrome ore which we must have to meet our needs in Vietnam.[1]

The same arguments reappeared in the 1980s, over trade restrictions against the Soviet Union advocated by the United States to 'punish' the Soviet Union for its 1979 intervention in Afghanistan, and for its successful imposition of martial law through the means of a compliant Polish military government to suppress the reforming and liberalizing tendencies of the Polish trade union, Solidarity. The major consequence, however, was to split the West, rather than to

Source: *Christian Science Monitor*, 11 October 1983, p. 54.

Figure 8.1    Where NATO and WTO face off

Table 8.1  Dates of establishment of important IGOs of the Atlantic and
Soviet International Systems

| Atlantic System | | Soviet International System | |
|---|---|---|---|
| OEEC | 1948 | Comecon | 1949 |
| Brussels Pact, | | Warsaw Treaty | 1955 |
| NATO, WEU | 1948–54 | Organization | 1955 |
| CERN (European Organization for Nuclear Research) | 1953 | Joint Institute for Nuclear Research | 1956 |
| European Investment Bank | 1957 | | |
| [Inter-American Development Bank] | [1959] | International Investment Bank | 1970 |
| ESRO and ELDO (precursors of European Space Agency) | 1964 | Intercosmos | 1969 or 1970(?) |
| INTELSAT | 1965 | Intersputnik | 1971 |

*Note*: The list provides circumstantial evidence that the creation of each of the organs of the Soviet International System was undertaken as a response to an earlier development in the West. The case for this theory is persuasively documented in Richard Szawlowski's *The System of International Organizations of the Communist Countries*. There were thirty inter-governmental bodies in the Soviet System in 1976. 'All these organizations are tightly knit together, representing a formidable combination of military and economic power. In spite of all the difficulties and shortcomings, they represent a dynamically growing potential.' Szawlowski classified the thirty IGOs into five groupings: (1) the two 'key organizations', the Warsaw Treaty Organization (WTO) and Comecon; (2) third in order of creation and alone in its class, the Joint Institute for Nuclear Research; (3) two international banks and several industrial combines; (4) international laboratories and training centres; and (5) minor bodies without international secretariats. The entire System is, according to Szawlowski, completely dominated by the USSR. The USSR supplies two-thirds of the armed forces and is twice as powerful economically as all the other Warsaw Pact nations together. Furthermore, 'no top WTO position is held by an East European.' In almost all the IGOs, Russian is the only working language.

*Source*: James R. Huntley, *Uniting the Democracies: Institutions of the Emerging Atlantic–Pacific System* (New York: New York University Press, 1980), pp. 195–6.

coerce the East. This intermingling of the politics of international economics and trade with the politics of East–West military confrontation has, at least temporarily, created an appearance of a weakening of the political resolve of NATO. We need therefore to examine the elements of NATO's capacity for political consultation and military cohesiveness.

## INTRA-REGIONAL POLITICAL COHESIVENESS IN NATO*

NATO was never intended to be, and has never been, a supranational international organization. It was not established with the notion that it would continue indefinitely, as was the case with the United Nations, or with the European Communities. NATO has been an effective coalition of states dedicated not unlike that of the Concert of Europe in the first instance to maintaining the *status quo* that emerged in Europe after World War II. Although NATO sounded as if it might intervene for ideological reasons in Central and Eastern Europe in the mid-1950s, in fact it did not. And in the 1968 Czechoslovak crisis, NATO went out of its way to reassure the Soviet Union that it did not intend to intervene on the side of the liberalizing factions in Czechoslovakia.

From 1950 to 1958, NATO helped to maintain a strong common front against the Soviet Union, while at the same time it attempted to establish effective continuing political consultative procedures and 'habits of working together' that would enable the coalition to co-ordinate its policies elsewhere in the world against the Soviet Union and international Communism, and to preclude excessive divisiveness within Western Europe itself.

These efforts, even if only marginally successful, are no mean achievements when we view the nature and extent of political–military collaboration, even in wartime, of the states of Western Europe since 1815. Thus, the independent policy of Charles de Gaulle, which began in 1958 and eventuated by the mid-1960s in the withdrawal of France from much of the NATO military organizational structure created after 1950 (but not from the political obligation of the NATO Treaty itself), may not look so deviant in nature. (The influence of de Gaulle on NATO is discussed fully in the next section of this chapter.) Essentially, de Gaulle was recognizing that NATO had by the late 1950s achieved its strictly anti-Soviet and anti-Communist Western European military deterrent function, and he assumed that the United States and the Soviet Union, once they had achieved the nuclear parity which Sputnik had presaged, would attempt to work out a *modus vivendi* in which the interests of the states of Western Europe would be only a partial consideration.

This was made evident when NATO established a special committee to consider what purposes NATO could define for itself in a

* See chapter 2 for a discussion of the WTO's intra-regional relationships.

European international world that only with difficulty could still officially affirm that NATO was essential for purely military purposes. This committee issued a report in December 1967, entitled, 'The Future Tasks of the Alliance', and which came to be known as the 'Harmel Report'. The Report states candidly:

Since the North Atlantic Treaty was signed in 1949 the international situation has changed significantly and the political tasks of the Alliance have assumed a new dimension. Amongst other developments, the Alliance has played a major part in stopping Communist expansion in Europe; the USSR has become one of the two world super powers but the Communist world is no longer monolithic; the Soviet doctrine of 'peaceful coexistence' has changed the nature of the confrontation with the West, but not the basic problems. Although the disparity between the power of the United States and that of the European states remains, Europe has recovered and is on its way towards unity. . .[2]

NATO, while maintaining as much of a military posture as it could, was also charged to pursue a policy of seeking a condition of 'détente' in Europe. As the report declared: 'Military security and a policy of détente are not contradictory but complementary.'[3] It is interesting to note that after the setback that the Soviet venture into Czechoslovakia in 1968 gave to the idea of détente, the process was resumed even before the coming to power of Georges Pompidou in France and Willy Brandt in West Germany. Essentially, the Report confirmed the situation in Europe which had already been evolving, thus making a virtue out of necessity. Even Charles de Gaulle would probably not have found fault with this statement of the Report:

As sovereign states the Allies are not obliged to subordinate their policies to collective decision. The Alliance affords an effective forum and clearing house for the exchange of information and views; thus, each Ally can decide its policy in the light of the others. To this end, the practice of frank and timely consultation needs to be deepened and improved. Each Ally should play its full part in promoting an improvement in relations with the Soviet Union and the countries of Eastern Europe, bearing in mind that the pursuit of détente must not be allowed to split the Alliance. The chances of success will clearly be greatest if the Allies remain on parallel course, especially in matters of close concern to them all; their actions will thus be all the more effective.[4]

Other changes in the international political environment have affected NATO, one of the most serious in the late 1960s being the shift to the political right of the government of Greece. A major political cleavage thus emerged, especially between Greece and the Scandinavian members of the Alliance. There had always been a difference in national outlooks between the Scandinavian member-states (Denmark and Norway) – who were suspicious of the Mediterranean members, and fearful of the Germans – and Greece and Turkey.

The Cyprus crisis pitting Greece against Turkey, for example, which has festered for so long, did not help to coalesce the northern and southern wings of NATO. Aside from the problem of Greece, Turkey at that time had been moving towards increasing political independence *vis-à-vis* the West. This was especially evident after the June 1967 Cyprus crisis when President Lyndon Johnson informed Turkish President Ismet Inonu that if Turkey did not desist from armed intervention in Cyprus (which it was threatening to do, and which would probably have brought Greek intervention), the United States might not be able to live up fully to its NATO commitment to Turkey. This warning that military aid would be cut off was bitterly resented by Turkey, and took on more weight as the Middle East crisis deepened in the early 1970s, and the Soviet Union dramatically increased its naval presence in the Eastern Mediterranean. An indication of this changing Turkish attitude was reflected in a reported statement made by the Turkish Defence Minister while he was on his way to attend a NATO planning meeting in Brussels in January 1970: 'Europe wants to build its own strategic and nuclear weapons. European countries no longer have a desire to wait for arms, including atomic weapons, which they need to defend themselves, to arrive from the United States.'[5]

With the advent to power in Greece of the military junta in 1967, inevitably a continuing political crisis arose in NATO. If NATO existed in part to forestall dictatorship, or to encourage liberalizing tendencies in states which had more authoritarian governmental systems, then how could NATO condone the illegal seizure of power in Greece by a small band of military conspirators? The question was even more difficult to resolve because the military equipment which Greece had received through NATO channels was now being used to maintain this group in office. Even though the United States held off giving the Greek military government full diplomatic support, having delayed sending an ambassador until January 1970, and had withheld military aid which would have gone to Greece if the coup had not taken place, there was, in Denmark and Norway especially, but also in other member-states such as Britain, a deep-seated hostility towards the regime.[6] To make matters worse, the military rulers justified their seizure of power in part on the necessity for the army to take control in order to ensure a strong and reliable Greece in NATO. This created some anti-NATO feelings among the general population in Greece many of whom were opposed to the junta but who had previously been anti-Communist and pro-Western. But the current Greek government, which is elected, has taken an anti-NATO posture, while ironically, the current elected Turkish government is very pro-NATO. This situation is thus a manifestation of the shifts in public attitude in Western Europe towards NATO.

Paradoxically, the military government of Greece, in its support of NATO, was not drastically out of line with the attitude towards NATO of most of the governments of the other member-states. But the reason for the anti-NATO feelings among the Greek people differed from the feelings about NATO held by the people of other member-states, which is reflective of a gradual divergence during the 1970s and into the 1980s of American and Western European perceptions of their respective interests:

The inevitability of some European entity within the alliance is increasingly recognized by the major European members of the alliance. . . . The West Germans want a stronger defense on their eastern frontier. The French, doubting the credibility of the American nuclear umbrella, believe in European cooperation, with the British and French nuclear forces as the principal elements. The Italians would favor the grouping if it contributed to European integration, but they voice the warning that if its formation gave the United States an excuse for doing less in Europe, they would be reluctant to risk it. Similar fears emerged in other capitals. To Turkey, Greece, and Portugal, the proposal for a European grouping appears part of a tendency to downgrade their interests and elevate those of the members in Western Europe. Despite the opposition, the conclusion drawn from the reports is that the European group will take shape and that the speed and scope of the process will depend upon the measures the United States takes to reduce its military commitment.[7]

But there have been some recent, and striking, successes at political consultation in NATO in the larger East–West context, even though there also have been some intra-Alliance tensions. Three forms of political consultation in particular are noteworthy. The first is the Mutual and Balanced Force Reductions (MBFR) talks that have been going on in Vienna since 1973. This decade-long negotiation between NATO and the Warsaw Treaty Organization has been very frustrating, but it can also be pointed out as a model for Alliance co-operation. The NATO members participating in the negotiations – all except France, Iceland, Portugal, and later Spain – have maintained complete unity.

The second example is the 'double-track' decision of NATO on Long-Range Theatre Nuclear Forces (LRTNF), in 1979 (now called Intermediate Range Nuclear Forces – INF), discussed further in this chapter. The commitment was to negotiate with the Soviet Union for reductions in the levels of nuclear weapons positioned in Europe, even while at the same time (the other 'track') moving ahead with the emplacement of nuclear-tipped cruise missiles in Western Europe (and the installation of Pershing II nuclear missiles). The preparations for this decision, which led to talks in Geneva between the Soviet Union and the United States, were made by two NATO committees, one dealing with the nuclear weapons 'modernization' track and the other with the arms control track. Intensive consultation took place at all levels prior to the final NATO decision against a background of continuous efforts by the Soviet Union to obstruct it. The final issue was in doubt until shortly before the decision was taken on 12 December 1979. The fact that it was taken unanimously (France did not participate) was as important from a political as from a military point of view.

The third example has been the preparation and presentation of the Western position at the 1977–8 Belgrade, 1980–3 Madrid Follow-up Meetings to the Conference on European Security and Cooperation (CSCE), which was resumed in Stockholm in 1983. Chapter 7 discusses the Helsinki Final Act and its aftermath. A special meeting was held in Ottawa in June 1985 to discuss human rights and the parties failed to agree on a definition of the subject but NATO held firm. NATO (including France) has refused to abandon the right of the first use of nuclear weapons advocated by the Soviet Union, contending that this is the best means to deter and defend against an attack from conventionally superior Soviet forces. The two Alliances now notify each other in advance of conventional military manoeuvres of 25,000 troops or more and various proposals for strengthening confidence-building measures related to monitoring and inspecting military exercises are being actively negotiated by the two blocs.

The more recent trouble spots in Alliance consultation have been overall East–West relations and what are termed 'out of area' issues. Three cases in particular have seriously troubled the Alliance. First, the Soviet invasion of Afghanistan of 27 December 1979 caught the

Alliance as a whole by surprise, although the United States, at least, had advance intelligence that the Soviet Army was massing. On a matter of this importance an immediate meeting of the NATO Council of Ministers in Brussels should have occurred, but none took place. This mistake was compounded by pressure from the United States for an early announcement of sanctions against the Soviet Union and, when the European member-states were hesitant, by the United States taking unilateral action. That the Europeans were slow, uncertain and divided did not help. They found it less easy than the United States to answer the questions: Is détente divisible and is it reversible? What should have been a serious discussion with a view to parallel action was ineffectual; what began by being an advance warning or consultation concerning possible actions became instead merely a communication of actions or decisions which already had been taken.

Later on, the Europeans accepted the full implications of Afghanistan and the need for a firm response, and the United States realized the importance of restoring Alliance unity. This was achieved by the time of the Ministerial Meeting in Ankara in June 1980. The lesson learned was applied in the Polish Solidarity crisis at the end of that year. NATO Foreign Ministers were united in their condemnation of Soviet actions and the speed with which contingency planning went ahead for sanctions in the event of military intervention by the Soviet Union in Poland provided a much-needed demonstration of Alliance cohesion.

Disunity, however, broke out again in NATO at the end of 1981 over the Alliance reaction to the Polish declaration of martial law, but the differences were patched up at a special Ministerial Meeting in January 1982. But the relief was short-lived; the subsequent problems of the Siberian gas pipeline, trade credits, technology transfers and American grain sales, as discussed in the previous chapter, bedevilled intra-Alliance relations throughout the greater part of 1982. The acrimonious disputes which arose were the result of a breakdown of effective consultation. The Heads of State and Government at the Versailles economic summit and later at the NATO summit in Bonn evidently failed to settle matters. Eventually the United States ended sanctions against firms participating in the pipeline in return for agreement on Alliance studies of various aspects of economic relations with the Soviet Union and its East European partners. Nonetheless, there still does not exist in NATO agreed formal guidelines for the conduct of East–West relations.[8]

## INTRA-REGIONAL MILITARY COHESIVENESS IN NATO[9]

Three factors sustained the Atlantic Alliance during its initial years: the atomic monopoly of the United States, the economic collapse of Western Europe after World War II, and the intransigence of Soviet policies. After the mid-1950s Europe's postwar transformation effectively undermined them all. First, American nuclear weapons no longer appeared to guarantee Western European security against Soviet attack. If their putative advances in weaponry had substance, they created a stalemate in nuclear power. By 1955 it seemed apparent to much of the world that the United States and the Soviet Union had reached a 'parity of horror' that threatened destruction not only to themselves but also to all of Western Europe. This dread of a nuclear confrontation led to the famed Geneva Summit Conference of July 1955. Second, the economic recovery of the states of Western Europe greatly diminished their dependence upon the United States. So successful were the Marshall Plan and NATO in underwriting Western Europe's recovery that it was no longer certain in the late 1950s whether the sub-region's confidence emanated from the Alliance or from the sheer energy and productivity of Western Europe itself. If these states still desired aid from the United States it was no longer a matter of life and death. As discussed in the previous chapters, the development of the European Coal and Steel Community, the Common Market, EURATOM, and the gradually increasing trade with the Soviet bloc tended to decrease allied economic dependence on the United States even further.[10]

Third, the Soviet Union weakened Western unity with its 'New Look' foreign policies. Having earlier created the image of a ruthless state, guided only by considerations of military power, the Soviets struck a new pose after 1953 designed to relieve a world living in dread of war. Because of massive American superiority the Soviets recognized that nothing could be settled by nuclear war. After 1955 they began to reveal amazing vigour, agility and pragmatism in their use of diplomacy. They moved into South Asia and the Middle East with offers of trade and economic assistance. This shift in Soviet methods and the arena of activity turned states from North Africa to Indonesia away from passive objects to arbiters in the East–West struggle. In its global contest United States policy 'outside the area' became increasingly divorced from that of its NATO allies and this aggravated the tensions within the Alliance, which still remains a problem.[11] In Europe, proposals by the Soviet Union stressed peaceful coexistence, attributing the failure of diplomatic progress to the dogmatism and rigidity of Western policy. Western revisionism gave the Soviet Union a tactical advantage. Henry A. Kissinger noted in *Foreign Affairs*:

One of the difficulties the free world has had in dealing with the Soviet bloc is that we have been clearer about the things we oppose than those we stand for. This has given much of our negotiations with the Soviet Union the quality of a stubborn rearguard action designed primarily to thwart Soviet overtures.

The rapid recovery of West Germany, with the historical fear that German political, economic, and military eminence creates throughout Europe, contributed to the opportunities confronting Soviet policy. Lester B. Pearson, Canada's noted diplomat, responded to the changing times when he wrote in 1958: 'We must take full advantage of every opportunity, even more, create opportunities through a dynamic diplomacy, to negotiate differences with those whom we now fear.'[12]

These subtle changes in the relationship between the military power of the United States and the security of Western Europe did not destroy the common interest of the NATO member-states in a system of collective defence. But NATO's acceptability rested less on the hope that the organization would bring victory in war than on the need to prevent war. NATO would fail at the moment that a nuclear war came to Europe. At the core of NATO's strength, unity, and effectiveness was the American commitment to Western defence. Without the steady conviction that the United States would fulfil its obligation to the NATO members, the Alliance would doubtless cease to exist, and therefore this essential guarantee has been continuously renewed.

For example, Secretary of State John Foster Dulles observed at a news conference in November 1957:

I think that the commitment, as far as the treaty is concerned, is as strong as it could be made. It is hard to get much further in an agreement than 'an attack upon one is an attack upon all.' That is, in turn, reinforced by the presence at the forward positions of American forces which would presumably be themselves attacked.

President Dwight Eisenhower repeated that assurance at Paris a month later.

Speaking for my own country, I assure you in the most solemn terms that the United States would come, at once and with all appropriate force, to the assistance of any NATO national subjected to armed attack. This is the resolve of the United States – of all parts and of all parties.[13]

As already pointed out, the capacity of the United States to protect Western Europe against war lay in nuclear weapons and the means of conveying them to targets in Eastern Europe and the Soviet Union. Since few assumed that a European war could be localized, the area's survival was synonymous with peace. This compelled NATO to cling to the threat of thermonuclear reprisal as the only available means of keeping aggression away from its door. But anchoring strategy to mass destruction exposed NATO to the pressures of technological change. When John Foster Dulles in 1954 announced the American reliance on massive retaliation, the defence of the United States was not at issue. Nuclear strategy would ensure the peace of Europe with reduced military forces. As long as the airplane was the only vehicle available for delivering nuclear weapons in a European confrontation, the United States required its forward NATO bases. This created a convergence of interests, for without American weapons Europe had no deterrent, and without Europe the United States had no means of reaching its prospective targets. But many Western Europeans doubted that this mutual interest would survive the replacement of aircraft with long-range guided missiles as the chief means of delivering nuclear weapons. Western Europe would no longer be essential for American strategy.

What brought the technological revolution into focus was the development by the Soviet Union of intercontinental ballistic missiles (ICBMS) that could reach targets in the continental United States. Now that the United States itself would be vulnerable to attack, would that state under all circumstances come to the rescue of Western Europe with nuclear weapons? Somehow the United States seemed more reliable when it was less vulnerable. For some Western Europeans the answer to this new challenge lay in the development of purely European nuclear deterrents. British Minister of Defence Duncan Sandys in 1957 justified the new British emphasis on nuclear armaments by citing the possible unreliability of some future American Administration. On 9 February 1959 in the London *Daily Mail*, T. F. Thompson stated the British rationale for developing its own deterrent:

Soon the United States will have its inter-continental missile bases established on its home territory. Relationships then will change. Not only between the US and Russia, but the US and Europe. For the first time in the history of modern war, America will be in a position to guarantee its own territory without having to bother with advance bases in Europe. . . . The position will then be that the United States would not dare attack Russia nor the Soviet Union the American homeland. . . . It is at this point that the British deterrent becomes important. We are in Europe. We are of Europe. . . . Britain would have to retaliate with nuclear weapons at the outset of a major attack in Europe with conventional forces. The alternative would be the end of our way of life.

The assumption that nuclear weapons assured peace rendered conventional forces almost irrelevant. British writer Alexander Bregman argued in *Western World* (October 1959) that even the strongest state would not attack a weak state as long as it faced the danger of nuclear retaliation. The British deterrent, declared one government spokesman, 'removes any danger that the Soviet Union may be tempted to invade Western Europe in the misguided belief that the United States of America, faced with the possibility of bombardment by intercontinental missiles, would shrink from saving countries which are distant from her'.[14]

By 1960 the international division of military labour was taking its toll of Allied unity. The heart of the problem was the question of nuclear control. An effective coalition requires some limitations on national sovereignty, but Western Europe's total reliance on American-controlled nuclear weapons for its peace and survival placed that Continent's destiny in the hands of a non-European Power whose global commitments often defied European interests. The greater the disproportion of military power between the United States and its NATO allies, the more obvious the centripetal force of decisions taken by the United States. That alignment of power and fear that underwrote Western Europe's defence compelled the allied governments, in any crisis, to accept Washington's conceptualization of its own and Western Europe's interests, 'The alliance is out of balance', observed James Reston, 'mainly because Europe is not doing what it could do, and it is not doing what it could do, partly because it has abdicated and partly because the United States has been willing to carry the load long after Europe was able to do much more in self-defence.'[15] Europe's survival in a crisis depended on the United States' strategy for initiating the use of nuclear weapons. That strategy created the most doubtful, yet the most essential, aspect of NATO's nuclear credibility. Europe remained hostage to United States foreign and military policy long after many Western

Europeans questioned America's reliability. It was not strange that French President Charles de Gaulle sought an escape.

De Gaulle inaugurated his assault on America's monopoly of allied leadership in 1958 when he proposed a global directorate to control NATO's decisions that would include the United States, Britain, and France. President Eisenhower rejected the plan with the argument that the United States could not designate one or two European Powers to speak for the others.[16] Nonetheless, Secretary of State Dulles recognized the need for more liberal American atomic secrecy laws to facilitate allied collaboration in the development of NATO's nuclear strategy. In 1958 a modification of the Atomic Energy Act permitted the United States to provide nuclear materials and information to any ally that had 'made substantial progress in the development of atomic weapons'. Obviously Britain was the only state that could qualify. This rebuff of de Gaulle's tripartite proposal and refusal to share atomic secrets with France reinforced the French leader's determination to build a French nuclear deterrent without American help, both to strengthen France's voice in European affairs and to increase the confidence of the French army following France's politically imposed defeat in Indo-China. As de Gaulle explained in 1958, France would attempt to 'bring together the states along the Rhine, the Alps, and the Pyrenees into a political, economic, and strategic group – to make of this organization one of the three world powers and if necessary one day the arbiter between the Soviet and Anglo-Saxon camps'. On 5 September 1960, de Gaulle issued an edict forbidding nuclear weapons on French soil unless France shared in their control. The United States then shifted its nuclear bomb-carrying aircraft from French to British and West German bases.[17]

After January 1961, President John F. Kennedy scarcely could ignore de Gaulle's direct challenge to American leadership in Europe. To counter the divisive tendencies within NATO, the Kennedy Administration, through its 'Grand Design for Europe', determined to make the West's political and economic institutions and attitudes conform to the outsized requirements of NATO. At Philadelphia on Independence Day of 1962, Kennedy declared that the United States contemplated the Western European movement towards union, as embodied especially in the Common Market, with hope and admiration. 'We do not', he said, 'regard a strong and united Europe as a rival, but a partner.' Then he continued: 'I will say here and now on this Day of Independence that the United States will be ready for a declaration of interdependence, that we will be prepared to discuss with a United Europe the ways and means of forming a concrete Atlantic partnership. . . .'[18] At his news conference that followed, President Kennedy refused to define what kind of partnership he had in mind, observing that it would be premature to do so before the European states themselves had made greater progress towards unity. Although the design was idealistic, it was rooted in the conviction that the major economic and financial concerns of the world had passed beyond the control of individual national governments.

Kennedy doubted the adequacy of Western defence. To broaden the options required to make limited war more feasible and the nuclear deterrent more credible, he stressed the need for a 'wider choice than humiliation or all-out nuclear action'.[19] The new strategy called for the creation, at least, of non-nuclear capabilities sufficient to contain limited aggressions. The purpose was not necessarily to concentrate power in conventional forces but rather to permit a 'pause' in any future fighting long enough to enable the two contestants to negotiate a cease-fire or to give the aggressor time to contemplate the consequences of further escalation.

To achieve the anticipated conventional force levels, the United States required a larger allied commitment to Europe's defence. The maintenance of 300,000 US military personnel in the European theatre had gradually destroyed the American balance of payments structure, whereas Western Europe, enjoying unprecedented prosperity, had not contributed its agreed share to either the European defence force or to the economic development of the Afro-Asian world. Western Europe by 1962 had not only closed the dollar gap but also held gold and dollar reserves that exceeded the combined holdings of the United States and Britain. This shifting economic balance motivated President Kennedy's urgent request for the Trade Expansion Act of 1962 as well as Congress' overwhelming approval of the legislation. Some Europeans admitted that Western Europe had become the special beneficiary of American insecurity. As Italian leader Altiero Spinelli observed in July 1962: 'Western Europe, thanks to American protection, has become a paradise of political, military and social irresponsibility.'[20]

To maximize Europe's contribution to conventional defence the Kennedy Administration opposed expenditures for independent nuclear deterrents, especially those of France. At Ann Arbor, Michigan, on 6 June 1962, Defence Secretary Robert McNamara declared:

'Limited nuclear capabilities, operating independently, are dangerous, expensive, prone to obsolescence, and lacking in credibility as a deterrent.' He asked the states of Western Europe to avoid conflicting and competing strategies to meet the contingency of nuclear war. 'We are convinced', he continued, 'that a general nuclear war target system is indivisible, and if, despite all our efforts, nuclear war should occur, our best hope lies in conducting a centrally controlled campaign against all of the enemy's vital nuclear capabilities, while retaining reserve forces, all centrally controlled.'[21] McNamara asked that the NATO partners leave full responsibility for nuclear warfare to the United States. In Copenhagen on 27 September, White House adviser McGeorge Bundy reminded Western Europe of the United States' commitment to Europe's defence. Writing in the October 1962 issue of *Foreign Affairs*, Bundy explained why the United States could not escape a European war:

The general nuclear war the world fears would be a disaster to the whole race, but it is the stronger members of the two great opposed alliances who would be most certainly caught in its horror. The present danger does not spare either shore of the Atlantic – or set Hamburg apart from San Francisco. . . . [W]hile our experience of the cost and burdens of genuine membership in the nuclear club makes us believe that countries which do not apply are wise, we fully recognize that this sovereign decision is not ours to make for others. But we may reasonably ask for understanding of the fact that our own place at the centre of the nuclear confrontation is inescapable.[22]

The Administration's preference for a more flexible strategy did not anticipate any curtailing of the quest for nuclear weapons systems of the highest efficiency and accuracy.

Convinced that de Gaulle would not conform to American wishes, the Kennedy Administration sought a compromise in which a European nuclear force, closely linked with that of the United States, would encompass the French deterrent as well. But this objective seemed to require the creation of an effective political and economic union in Europe that included Britain. To that end the Administration placed the full force of American influence and prestige behind the British bid for membership in the Common Market (discussed in chapters 3 and 4).

Western Europe's response to American demands for a more equitable distribution of the Western defence burden was hardly enthusiastic. Whatever its lack of military flexibility, the Atlantic-based deterrent had granted Western Europe a decade of peace without recurrent crises or prosperity-curtailing defence expenditures. Many concluded that it was precisely Europe's *inability* to fight a conventional war that had made the deterrent effective; apparently the Soviet Union understood that any NATO decision to resist even a minor Soviet attack could quickly escalate into a nuclear war. Kennedy's new emphasis on conventional weapons seemed to endanger the credibility of the nuclear deterrent and undermined further Western Europe's confidence in the American commitment to its defence. Some Europeans feared that the United States, in an effort to avoid the extremity of a nuclear exchange, might refuse to act until much of Europe again lay in ruins.[23] Not even Kennedy's success in the Cuban missile crisis of October 1962 could counter the burgeoning distrust of America's nuclear commitment. The United States and the USSR had demonstrated more vigorously than ever before their fear of nuclear war and their readiness, in a moment of peril, to reach a settlement with scarcely a nod at their respective allies. Europe emerged from the crisis thankful but was reminded dramatically of its helplessness in the face of Soviet and American decision-making.

Nowhere in his Grand Design did Kennedy resolve the question of nuclear control. The Alliance could go forward or backward; those who favoured stronger ties agreed that Atlantic unity required a sharing of responsibility for nuclear decision-making. Paris' *Le Monde* answered Kennedy's Fourth of July speech of 1962: 'The idea of interdependence could become exalting . . . only if Europeans and Americans really agreed to transform into an *equal* partnership relations that are now those of clients to protectors.' Writing in the January 1963 issue of *Foreign Affairs*, Malcolm W. Hoag observed:

We cannot simultaneously preach Atlantic community and practice unimpaired sovereignty on life-and-death matters. To try to satisfy proud and militarily vulnerable allies with vague and secretive reassurances will increase anxiety and resentment rather than produce cooperation. We must somehow reconcile the operational need for unitary nuclear control with allied political participation and partnership.[24]

Not even in his noted Nassau Agreement on a multilateral defence force did Kennedy accept the challenge. When his Administration informed the British government in November 1962 that it would cancel the Skybolt air-to-ground ballistic missile programme, it turned to the frequently discussed concept of a mixed-manned naval nuclear defence force, equipped with Polaris missiles. Still the

British–American agreement on a sea-based, mixed-manned nuclear force, announced at Nassau by the President and Prime Minister Harold Macmillan in December 1962, scarcely satisfied the NATO allies.[25] The proposal contained no arrangement for an integrated strategy; the United States gave up none of its control of the nuclear deterrent. The multilateral force (MLF) remained totally separate from American nuclear strategy.

De Gaulle, in a dramatic press conference on 14 January 1963, challenged every facet of the Grand Design. In rejecting the British application for Common Market membership, the French leader charged that Britain was not sufficiently European-minded to break its ties with the United States and the Commonwealth. He was, he said, simply furthering the emancipation of Europe. British membership in the Common Market would lead to the formation of 'a colossal Atlantic Community under American dependence and leadership'. France could accomplish little without sacrifice, he informed a French audience in April, 'but we do not wish to be protégés or satellites; we are allies among allies, defenders among the defenders.'[26] De Gaulle rejected the principle of the multilateral defence force with equal determination. 'France has taken note of the Anglo-American Nassau agreement,' he declared at the press conference. 'As it was conceived, undoubtedly no one will be surprised that we cannot subscribe to it.' De Gaulle dismissed completely the question of the integration of nuclear forces. France, he warned, would provide its own nuclear deterrent. The reason France required a nuclear strike force was made clear by French Minister of Armed Forces Pierre Messmer in the April 1963 issue of *Revue de Défense Nationale*:

For Europe to exist it must take charge of and responsibility for its own defense, and for that it must possess nuclear arms. When we reach that point it will be seen that French possession of national nuclear arms will be a key piece in the construction of Europe. . . . The decision taken by General de Gaulle to provide France with nuclear armaments is the dominant factor of our military policy. This decision is of such importance that it will orientate the destiny of our country for a long time.[27]

By no means did the French deterrent exclude the possibility of future co-operation between that force and the similar deterrents of the allies. The French leader admitted that the defence strategy of the United States covered all European targets; what he questioned, he said, was the American willingness to engage in a nuclear exchange

over issues which the United States might regard as secondary.
'[N]o one in the world, particularly no one in America,' he charged,
'can say if, where, when, how and to what extent the American
nuclear weapons would be employed to defend Europe.'[28] The
United States, involved globally as it was, might permit the Soviet
Union to blackmail Western Europe.

In a further assault on American influence in Europe, de Gaulle,
one week after his January press conference, announced the signing
of a Franco-West German treaty whereby the two governments
agreed to 'consult before any decision on all important questions of
foreign policy . . . with a view to reaching as far as possible parallel
positions'.[29] At the very least de Gaulle had placed the movement for
transatlantic partnership in temporary eclipse. His action terminated
abruptly the expansion of the European Economic Community and
administered a decisive blow to Europe's community spirit which
remains to this day.

De Gaulle's news conference evoked expressions of muffled rage
in Washington and professions of disappointment in Britain. At his
own news conference on 8 February, President Kennedy voiced
regret that France had denied Britain membership in the Common
Market. He challenged de Gaulle's assertion that the United States
did not deal with Europe as an equal partner. 'We supported
strongly', he said, 'the Common Market, EURATOM, and the other
efforts to provide for a more unified Europe, which provides for a
stronger Europe, which permits Europe to speak with a stronger
voice, to accept greater responsibilities and greater burdens, as well
as to take advantage of greater opportunities.'[30] The United States,
he added, was prepared to work with Europe to strengthen its voice
and authority.

President Kennedy selected Ambassador Livingston T. Merchant
to initiate official talks with NATO governments on the question of
participation in the multilateral defence force. Only West Germany
indicated a willingness to join and defray its share of the cost. Critics
noted immediately that the multinational force satisfied no outstanding strategic requirement and offered Western Europe no significant
political or diplomatic responsibility for nuclear deterrence. In
addition, Europeans objected to the use of highly vulnerable surface
vessels rather than submarines. To many international observers the
new defence establishment was nothing more than a small effort to
involve West Germany in a system of nuclear defence without
upsetting the delicate Cold War balance in Europe. Some charged

that the United States was more concerned with outbidding de Gaulle for West German support than with creating an effective system of nuclear sharing.[31]

To demonstrate his Administration's desire to bridge the Atlantic gap with new forms of allied co-operation, Kennedy, in late June 1963, visited West Germany, Ireland, Britain, and Italy. The trip quickly assumed the form of a ceremonial spectacle. In West Germany the President stressed the concept of partnership. At historic *Paulskirche* in Frankfurt he designated the United States and West Germany as 'partners for peace'. The greatest necessity confronting the Alliance, he stressed, was 'progress toward unity of political purpose'. In a clear thrust at de Gaulle, Kennedy declared:

Those who would separate Europe from America or split one ally from another – could only give aid and comfort to the men who make themselves our adversaries and welcome any Western disarray. The United States cannot withdraw from Europe, unless and until Europe should wish us gone. We cannot distinguish its defences from our own. We cannot diminish our contributions to Western security or abdicate the responsibility of power.[32]

At Bonn the President issued the same assurance: 'Your safety is our safety, your liberty is our liberty, and an attack on your soil is an attack on our own'.

Kennedy effectively challenged de Gaulle's assumptions of America's unreliability, but he had no measurable effect on French policy. De Gaulle's effort to defend French economic interests still determined the course of Common Market discussions. When the United States during the autumn of 1963 pressed its allies for greater defence contributions, de Gaulle replied that the American concept of 'pause' would not prevent nuclear war as effectively as reliance on instant nuclear retaliation. Nothing in the entire spectrum of Soviet behaviour disproved his contention. Late in January 1964 in another dramatic press conference the French leader defied American Far Eastern policies by announcing the French recognition of the People's Republic of China, and stressing again the need for the neutralization of South East Asia.[33] Never before had French policies clashed so directly and universally with those of the United States. During the Summer of 1965, de Gaulle announced that France would no longer tolerate its subordinate position in the Atlantic Alliance. Then in April 1966 he informed NATO that he would withdraw all French officers and troops from its integrated military system and would remove all military installations not under exclusive French control. He stated that French independence would permit nothing less.[34] Premier Georges Pompidou explained the French decision to the French Assembly.

What we criticize about the doctrine [of flexible response] is its being specifically conceived on the basis of America's geographic location, . . . limiting the atomic battlefield by sparing the territory of the Soviet Union, and therefore the territory of the United States, and thereby creating a psychological risk, that of making it believe that the war could remain localized between the Atlantic and the Polish frontier in the East, that is to say, in Europe, but a Europe doomed to destruction.

Only nuclear deterrence could guarantee the peace. 'You tell us: NATO has guaranteed peace in Europe for fifteen years,' Pompidou concluded. 'What an error if you are referring to the integrated organization! What has guaranteed peace is the Alliance, insofar as it brought to bear the threat of the US Strategic Air Command. . . .'[35] In reaction to French policy, NATO moved its headquarters from Paris to Brussels.

United States reaction to de Gaulle's repeated assertions of French independence was not unanimous. The American government denounced the French leader as being rude and malicious. For American officials there was still too much unfinished business before the Alliance to permit such contention with an obstreperous ally. Wherever the United States was in trouble, they complained, de Gaulle was sure to appear, establishing himself as an arbiter, investing little but words to reap the benefits of confusion, national rivalry, and 'big power' humiliation. For those who placed their faith in Western power and unity, de Gaulle's policies were both dishonest and disastrous. Declared the *Detroit News* early in March 1964: 'Whether it is his intent or not, Charles de Gaulle is doing a pretty effective job of wrecking the Atlantic Alliance, the most effective instrument devised so far for containing Communist expansion. . . . All de Gaulle's dreams, all this scheming, all this pontificating is possible only because of one factor – the nuclear might of the United States – which stalls the Communist drive. . . . Under that umbrella he berates the real custodian of France's security.'[36] Dean Acheson, a key architect of the NATO Alliance, termed de Gaulle's policies as 'an erosion on one side of the Grand Alliance'. French policy, he added, 'increases the difficulty of action within the alliance by opposition to joint and integrated measures to advance common interests and solve common problems'.[37]

To other analysts, conscious of the changes that fifteen years had wrought in Europe's economic and military progress, de Gaulle's challenge to American policies was both rational and predictable.[38] In an Alliance among states of unequal power, the dependence of the weaker is tolerable only as long as there exists a complete identity of interest between the weaker and the stronger. After fifteen years the Atlantic Alliance remained what President Harry Truman once described as a 'shield against aggression'. But even this common and continuing interest in mutual defence did not in itself create a body of policy. Indeed, after fifteen years of NATO the common policies required to implement the Alliance remained elusive. There was not one major European issue, political or military, on which all allies agreed, and this condition still exists. On questions outside Europe the United States often stands almost alone. Ultimately, the challenge to allied unity has rested in the sheer quality of American foreign policy. The central issue is inescapable. Can the United States establish and maintain a clear relationship between its considerable power and the objectives that it pursues?

### THE INTER-REGIONAL MILITARY BALANCE[39]

By the 1970s the military balance in Europe generally was perceived by Western experts to be shifting in favour of the WTO forces (figure 8.2 shows the overall geographical relationship of the two Alliances). The difficulties inherent in any balance of power assessment are well known, and an assessment of the NATO–WTO balance would require a comparison of many, often incomparable, quantitative and qualitative components and factors and, as a rule, unquantifiable intangible variables.[40] Also, depending on what particular assumptions underlie the comparison, it is possible to arrive at either an optimistic or pessimistic view of the balance. For example, an optimstic Western assessment of the WTO would view the hierarchical structure of the Alliance not as a source of efficiency but as an element of rigidity, inhibiting initiative and leading to distrust. An optimist would also stress the unreliability of the satellite armies. For a pessimist, the integrated hierarchical nature of the WTO would be viewed as contributing an element of strength to the WTO's decision-making ability and to its military efficiency. The optimist would not give the WTO forces the benefit of the doubt in

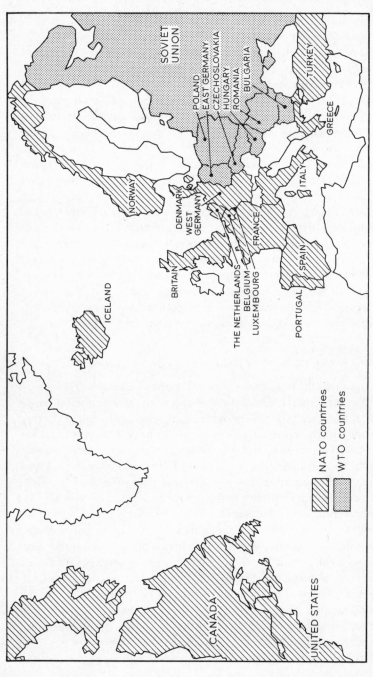

Source: *Christian Science Monitor*, 12 October 1983, p. 19.

Figure 8.2   NATO and WTO

the absence of concrete data, whereas the pessimist would rather err on the side of overestimating their strength. An optimistic assessment would consider quantitative one-to-one comparison of like items as probably misleading, whereas a pessimistic view would tend toward comparing totals of like things while excluding elements of strength that are not easy to compare. An optimist would also assume, for example, that all of the NATO territorial and reserve units as well as the French forces would be involved in the conflict and that Soviet reinforcements would be delayed, compared to a pessimist who would include only active NATO divisions and would assume rapid reinforcement of the central front by the WTO forces.[41] Subject to all these reservations and without entering into detailed comparisons, the emerging trends in the military balance between NATO and the WTO in the areas of defence expenditures and armed forces, including both nuclear weapons and conventional forces, in the Central European theatre will be summarized.[42] (Table 8.2 shows a comparison of conventional force strengths in the central region.)

As far as the comparison of NATO and WTO defence spending is concerned, there has been a sustained growth of Soviet defence outlays, at least over the past fifteen years, although, according to some estimates, not as great since the mid-1970s as the 'alarmists' would claim. There are various methods of analysing Soviet military spending and only rough estimates are possible in this area, but all analysts agree that the Soviet Union has been spending substantially more on defence than the United States.[43] It is estimated that the defence expenditures of the Soviet Union take from 10 per cent to 20 per cent of its gross national product (GNP) (or 3.4 per cent of the Net Material Product – NMP), compared to the US level of approaching 10 per cent.[44] What is important is the fact that over 50 per cent of the Soviet outlays is spent not on personnel, as in the United States and other NATO states, but on defensive investment.[45] It is significant that the Soviet allies devote much less of their respective GNP to defence spending than their leader, and with the exception of East Germany their expenditures have not increased in the past five years.[46] The Soviet Union accounts for about 85 per cent of the WTO's defence costs, whereas the US defence expenditures are about 50 per cent of the total NATO figure. As far as the NATO–WTO relationship as a whole is concerned, NATO still seems to be ahead in monetary terms, but its outlays appear to be catching up to the WTO's spending on the procurement of weapons and equipment.[47]

Table 8.2 Comparative force ratios and forces in the central region

Comparative force ratios

| | 1965 WTO/NATO | 1980 WTO/NATO |
|---|---|---|
| Tanks | 2.3 to 1 | 2.7 to 1 |
| Armoured personnel carriers/infantry fighting vehicles | 1.1 to 1 | 1.7 to 1 |
| Anti-tank guns | 0.8 to 1 | 2.6 to 1 |
| Anti-tank guided missiles | 0.6 to 1 | 1.9 to 1 |
| Artillery | 1.2 to 1 | 2.6 to 1 |
| Multiple rocket launchers | — | 7.1 to 1 |
| Tactical aircraft | 1.6 to 1 | 1.9 to 1 |
| Tons of bombs that can be delivered 100 miles away | — | 1 to 3[1] |
| Tons of bombs that can be delivered 200 miles away | — | 1 to 7[1] |
| Armoured attack helicopters | — | 1.2 to 1 |
| Air defence guns | 4.8 to 1 | 2.7 to 1 |
| Surface-to-air missiles | 0.6 to 1 | 1.5 to 1 |
| 'Armoured division equivalents' | — | 1.2 to 1[2] |
| Overall/major combatant systems | 1.5 to 1 | 2.0 to 1 |

*Notes*: [1] Carnegie Panel on US Security and the Future of Arms Control, 'Challenges for US National Security: Assessing the Balance: Defence Spending and Conventional Forces', Washington, DC, 1981.

[2] John Mearsheimer in 'Conventional Deterrence', citing US Defense Department.

Forces in the central region

| | WTO/NATO | NATO |
|---|---|---|
| Total soldiers[1] | 1,250,000 | 1,025,650 |
| Soldiers in fighting units | 720,000[2] | 580,000[2] |
| Total division equivalents | 89 | 65 |
| Division equivalents before mobilization | 57 | 26 |
| Main battle tanks | 25,000 | 9,905 |
| Artillery/mortars | 7,500[2] | 2,700[2] |
| Total fixed-wing combat aircraft | 3,105[3] | 2,516[3] |
| Fighter bombers | 1,530 | 1,866 |
| Interceptors | 1,575 | 650 |

*Notes*: [1] Another calculation of manpower, which adjusts for understrength WTO units and includes the French Army in France and 70,000 British soldiers in Britain, totals about 1,113,000 for NATO and something under 933,000 for the WTO (see Anthony Cordesman in *Armed Forces Journal*, July 1983).

[2] British Defence White Paper, 1982.

[3] These figures show less than the disparity to 1.9 to 1 reported by Karber, since the figures shown here include aircraft based not only in West Germany, Belgium, the Netherlands and Luxembourg, but also those in France, the United Kingdom, Spain and Denmark.

*Source*: *Christian Science Monitor*, 12 October 1983, p. 19, quoting from Phillip A. Karber in Uwe Neulich, ed., *Soviet Power and Western Negotiating Policies*, vol. 1, and John Collins, Congressional Research Service.

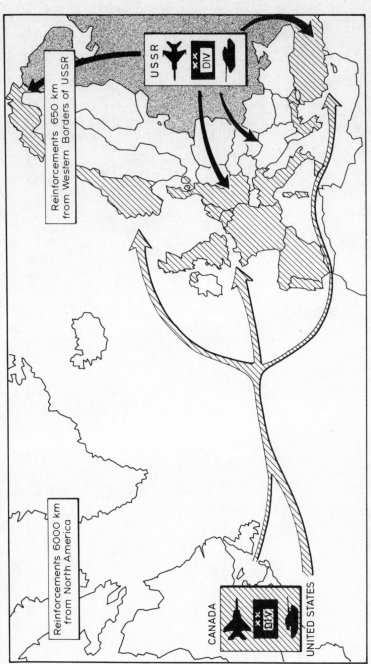

Reinforcements 650 km from Western Borders of USSR

Reinforcements 6000 km from North America

CANADA

UNITED STATES

*Source: NATO and the Warsaw Pact: Force Comparisons* (Brussels: NATO. Information Service, 1984), p. 5.

Figure 8.3 Geographical dissimilarities: a NATO Problem.

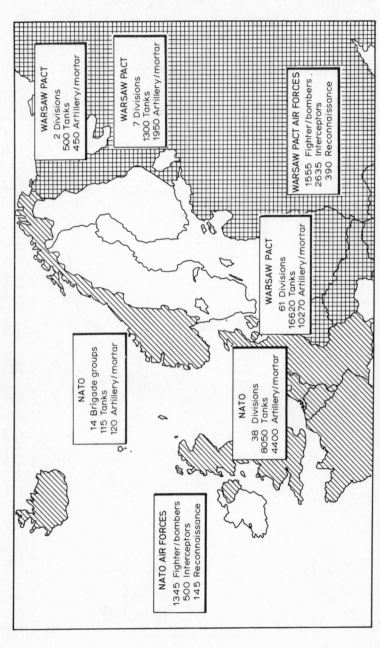

WARSAW PACT
2 Divisions
500 Tanks
450 Artillery/mortar

WARSAW PACT
7 Divisions
1300 Tanks
1950 Artillery/mortar

WARSAW PACT AIR FORCES
1555 Fighter/bombers
2635 Interceptors
390 Reconnaissance

WARSAW PACT
61 Divisions
16620 Tanks
10270 Artillery/mortar

NATO
14 Brigade groups
115 Tanks
120 Artillery/mortar

NATO
38 Divisions
8050 Tanks
4400 Artillery/mortar

NATO AIR FORCES
1345 Fighter/bombers
500 Interceptors
145 Reconnaissance

Source: NATO and the Warsaw Pact: Force Comparisons (Brussels: NATO. Information Service, 1984), p. 20.

8.1 Defence of Northern and Central Regions of NATO

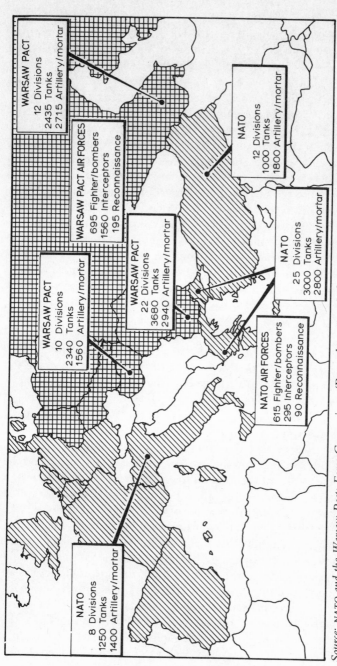

WARSAW PACT
12 Divisions
2435 Tanks
2715 Artillery/mortar

WARSAW PACT AIR FORCES
695 Fighter/bombers
1560 Interceptors
195 Reconnaissance

NATO
12 Divisions
1000 Tanks
1800 Artillery/mortar

WARSAW PACT
10 Divisions
2340 Tanks
1560 Artillery/mortar

WARSAW PACT
22 Divisions
3680 Tanks
2940 Artillery/mortar

NATO
25 Divisions
3000 Tanks
2800 Artillery/mortar

NATO AIR FORCES
615 Fighter/bombers
295 Interceptors
90 Reconnaissance

NATO
8 Divisions
1250 Tanks
1400 Artillery/mortar

*Source: NATO and the Warsaw Pact: Force Comparisons* (Brussels: NATO. Information Service, 1984), p. 22.

8.5  Defence of NATO's Southern Region

The problem of the balance of long-range strategic nuclear weapons goes far beyond the scope of this discussion. It is common knowledge that the Soviet Union over the past decade has increased and modernized its strategic forces, thus achieving at least parity with the United States. It has overtaken the United States in most measures of strength: total megatonnage, number of missiles, and weight lift. Only in the number of warheads has the United States not fallen behind, but even this advantage is disappearing with the introduction of Soviet MIRVed strategic missiles. Also, in view of the fact that a higher proportion of the United States deterrent is carried by bombers and submarine-launched missiles than in the case of the Soviet Union, the latter is ahead of the United States in the number of reliable and accurate warheads and will remain so even after the United States has deployed its new generation of highly accurate air-launched cruise missiles.[48] To this configuration must be added the so-called 'Midgetman' mobile launcher concept, the US emplacement of the MX missile, plans for high-technology space warfare (including ABM's), increased accuracy of Soviet missiles, etc., and it becomes readily apparent that de-stabilization of the nuclear balance is a very real possibility that could enhance the temptation of either Superpower to launch a first-strike pre-emptive attack.

Whereas many still believe that an approximate parity continues to exist in the strategic systems, the WTO, or strictly speaking the Soviet Union, has gained a large and growing advantage in the long-range theatre nuclear forces (LRTNF), that is, intermediate range missiles able to hit targets in Western Europe. Calculating the actual LRTNF balance in Europe depends on the criteria adopted for defining an LRTNF system, including the boundary lines *vis-à-vis* battlefield tactical nuclear forces on the one hand and strategic systems on the other; the nature of the mission (counterforce or countervalue and counterland or countermaritime); the point of mobilization at which the balance is calculated; the value of the systems (indices of survivability, reliability, and ability to penetrate defences); and, finally, their range.[49] Without the inclusion of the Poseidon missile, which in principle is a strategic system whose use in the LRTNF role would escalate the conflict to the strategic level, the Soviet Union has an advantage in arriving warheads. In any case, it has superiority both in the inventory total and in warhead counts.[50]

Of particular concern for NATO is the fact that while retaining the older LRTNF systems, the Soviet Union since 1977 has been rapidly deploying the new SS-20 and perhaps even more modern intermediate range missiles (SS-22), most of which are targeted against Western Europe. The SS-20 is a mobile missile of 5,000-kilometre range (2,700 nautical miles), carrying three independently targetable warheads with far greater accuracy – 400 metres circular error probable (CEP) – than the older Soviet missiles. The deployment of these systems has been proceeding at about 60 to 100 per year, reaching at least 250 in mid-1981, with an estimated number of up to 360 missiles in 1983. The deployment of these relatively invulnerable sophisticated missiles, more modern than any at NATO's disposal at the present time, has in NATO's view upset the LRTNF balance in Europe. Moreover, it largely has reduced the impact of NATO's 2:1 superiority in battlefield tactical nuclear weapons.

The disparity is being widened by annual deployment of Backfire supersonic bombers that can fly at low altitudes, have a range of 8,000 kilometres, and carry a three or four warhead load. In 1983 there were 210 Backfires deployed.[51] The implications of the WTO advantage in LRTNF for the strategic options of NATO will be discussed below.

In land and air forces the WTO, which already had an overall conventional superiority in the 1960s, has increased its advantage, both numerically and through a surprisingly rapid modernization of its conventional forces. For example, in Northern and Central Europe, WTO tank superiority increased in the 1970s from 2:1 to 3:1 and that of artillery from 1.5:1 to almost 4:1. Traditional NATO air power supremacy in sophisticated equipment is also being eroded as more modern Soviet aircraft are introduced not only for interception missions but also for battlefield attack.[52] In sum, even though the overall balance of conventional forces will still involve incalculable risk for the aggressor, NATO's qualitative advantages are being matched by technological advances in the WTO forces, and 'the numerical balance over the last twenty years has slowly but steadily moved in favour of the East.'[53] To complete this rather discouraging balance sheet, it is essential to consider the Soviet navy whose build-up in the past two decades, especially in submarines, means that the United States no longer has the assured control over supply lines across the North Atlantic that is so vital in the case of conflict in Europe.[54]

What has been NATO's response to the changing security balance brought about by the quantitative and qualitative expansion of the WTO's offensively oriented conventional capabilities and the LRTNF? NATO's reaction is to pursue two parallel and complementary goals:

strengthening its defence capabilities on the one hand and continuing to promote negotiations on arms control and disarmament on the other. This 'two-track' approach, described earlier in this chapter, has been repeatedly emphasized by NATO in statements and communiqués.

In restoring a satisfactory military balance, NATO's first priority was to increase the defence outlays of the Alliance. Initiated by the Administration of President Jimmy Carter, the 1977 pledge of an annual increase in defence expenditures of about 3 per cent in real terms was endorsed at the Washington summit in 1978.[55] This 'three per cent solution' was to provide guidance for the allies' defence spending in the coming years. However, primarily because of the perception gap that exists between the United States and its Western European allies in the matter of the WTO build-up and also because of ostensible budgetary difficulties, the 3 per cent target of the formula guidance has not been entirely met even though it has been repeatedly reaffirmed by NATO.[56] (The charts in figure 8.6 reveal the extent of the European contribution to NATO.)

The rather modest increase in NATO's defence spending has had to be complemented by a much stronger effort at an Alliance-wide co-ordination of national planning in order to strengthen NATO's defence capabilities by achieving a greater degree of co-operation and rationalization. The Long-Term Defence Programme adopted by NATO in May 1978 was designed to meet these challenges. The programme recommended a series of detailed actions to improve NATO's capabilities and co-operation in ten priority areas: readiness, reinforcement, reserve mobilization, maritime posture, air defence, communications, command and control, electronic warfare, logistics, and theatre nuclear modernization.[57]

Action on the modernization of LRTNF was taken in December 1979 when NATO's Foreign and Defence Ministers decided to modernize these forces by the deployment, starting in December 1983 in selected European NATO member-states of American ground-launched systems comprised of 108 Pershing II launchers (to replace the existing Pershing I) and 464 cruise missiles, all with single warheads. As an integral part of the LRTNF modernization plan it was decided to withdraw 1,000 American tactical nuclear warheads as soon as possible.[58] Although the deployment of the new systems did not start until December 1983, the withdrawal of the 1,000 older warheads was completed in 1980.[59] All of the 108 Pershing II launchers are to be deployed in West Germany. The location of the

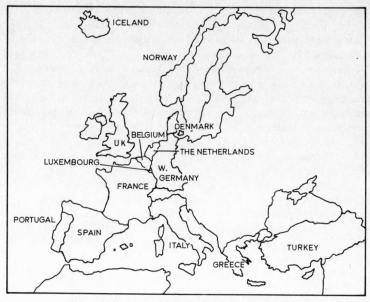

Figure 8.6　The European contribution to NATO

The population of the European Allies is over half of the NATO total.

The GDP of the European Allies is just about half of the NATO total.

Over the 1970s the European Allies *increased* their total real defence spending by over 2 per cent every year, while US real defence spending during the same period *declined* on average by a little more than 1 per cent per year.

The European Allies maintain about 3 million men and women on active duty, the US about 2 million. Including reserves, the figures are 6 million for Europe and 3 million for the USA.

The European ground forces amount to well over half of NATO's 'armoured division equivalents'.

These figures all come from a Report to Congress by Secretary of Defense Weinberger in March 1982, which explained at length how difficult it is to make exact comparisons to see just who is taking on what share of the burden of defence. But the Report did say: 'The non-US NATO Allies in aggregate appear to be shouldering roughly their fair share of the total defense effort.'

But that report was concerned with the total forces of Alliance members, including all those in the continental USA. What about ready forces in Europe, stationed there in peacetime? European Allies provide: about 90 per cent of the ground forces; about 80 per cent of the combat aircraft; about 80 per cent of the tanks; about 90 per cent of the armoured divisions.[1] At sea, in

European waters and the Atlantic, European Allies provide 70 per cent of the fighting ships.

Of course, in a time of international tension these forces would be strengthened by the addition of large numbers of reinforcements from North America. Such reinforcements would require and receive a great deal of help and assistance from European countries who have made special arrangements to provide Host Nation Support for American forces and secure lines of communication indispensable for the reception, onward transmission and support of these forces. This includes the provision of ships and aircraft for transportation. In addition, European countries would themselves be engaged in the deployment of their own reinforcements within Europe.

All this defence effort is provided by 13 independent nations. Its strength lies not just in the sheer military power it adds up to but also, as with NATO as a whole, in the fact that the forces are those of united Allies, which adds a strength of its own. So it is important to preserve that strength which comes from unity and constantly look for ways to improve it. This is what the EUROGROUP aims to do.

*Note*: [1] Figures are total standing forces for all European NATO Allies (including France, which is not a member of EUROGROUP).
*Source*: *The Defence of Europe*, US Department of State, 1983, pp. 2–3.

464 cruise missiles is projected as follows: Great Britain 160, West Germany 96, Italy 112, and the Netherlands and Belgium 48 each. (See figure 8.7 for an illustration, as of November 1983, of the comparative bloc-to-bloc distribution of new missiles.)

Even if the NATO LRTNF were completely deployed by the mid-1980s, and President Reagan had offered to spread deployment over five years as of December 1983 and if parallel arms reduction talks take on a 'serious' demeanour, the Soviet Union is still expected to be further ahead in such forces than it was when NATO's modernization plan was adopted. Moreover, the new NATO systems, although very accurate (20 metres–40 metres CEP for Pershing II and less than 80 metres for the cruise missile), would have a shorter range than that of the Soviet SS-20; 1,000 kilometres for the Pershing II and 2,000 kilometres for the cruise missile. Also, the relatively slow speed of the cruise missiles would preclude any first-strike by this particular weapon. Despite all these considerations, the Soviet Union, while in actual fact enjoying superiority in 'Eurostrategic' missiles, has reacted strongly against the NATO plan, charging the United States with attempts to upset what they allege is an approximate LRTNF parity and start another spiral of the nuclear arms race and increased military confrontation.[60] (See table 8.3 for compara-

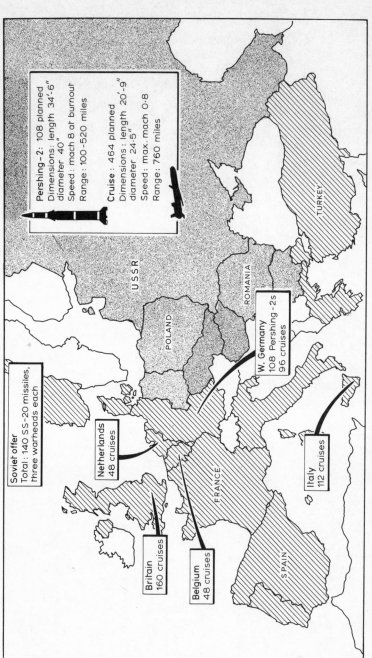

Soviet offer
Total: 140 SS-20 missiles,
three warheads each

Pershing–2: 108 planned
Dimensions: length 34'-6"
diameter 40"
Speed: mach 8 at burnout
Range: 100–520 miles

Cruise : 464 planned
Dimensions: length 20'-9"
diameter 24.5"
Speed: max. mach 0.8
Range: 760 miles

USSR

POLAND

ROMANIA

TURKEY

W. Germany
108 Pershing–2s
96 cruises

Netherlands
48 cruises

FRANCE

Italy
112 cruises

Britain
160 cruises

Belgium
48 cruises

SPAIN

8.7   Comparative bloc-to-bloc distribution of LRTNF missiles

Table 8.3 NATO/WTO nuclear war-making capacities

| Aircraft or missile launcher type | Owner/ Operator | NATO Number | NATO Number of nuclear weapons | Remarks |
|---|---|---|---|---|
| *Long-Range (over 600 miles)* | | | | |
| Poseidon/Trident SLBM | US | 40 | 400 | Committed to SACEUR for NATO targeting |
| Polaris SLBM | UK | 64 | 192 | Assumes MRVx3. New Chevaline warhead could increase RVs up to 6 |
| French SLBM | Fr. | 80 | 80 | A sixth sub will enter service in 1985, a seventh in 1990. Six subs will be retrofitted with M-4 SLBMs (MIRVx6) between 1985–92 |
| French IRBM | Fr. | 18 | 18 | Each S-3 missile has a 1 MT warhead. Work proceeding on 100 S-X mobile missiles |
| Tornado Bomber | UK, FRG, It. | 39 | 39 | 644 strike versions planned (220 for UK, 324 for FRG, 100 for Italy). Italy operational late 1983 |
| F-111 Fighter Bomber | US | 161 | 232 | 77 E models at RAF Upper Heyford, UK; 84 F models at RAF Lakenheath, UK; 127 other F-111's in US |
| Carrier Aircraft: A6 | US | 20 | 40 | Assumes 2 carriers in the Mediterranean |
| A7 | | 48 | 96 | |
| Mirage IVA | Fr. | 34 | 34 | 18 will carry ASMP medium-range (60-mile) missiles beginning in 1987–88, as will 36 new Mirage 2,000 Ns by 1988 |
| *Medium-Range (60–600 miles)* | | | | |
| Pershing Ia Missile | US, FRG | 180 | 360 | 108 to be replaced by Pershing II with US battalions |
| Lance Missile | US, Belg., FRG, It., Neth., UK | 117 | 335 | 380 more neutron shells stored in US |

| | | | | |
|---|---|---|---|---|
| Pluton Missile | Fr. | 30 | 30 | To be replaced by 180 longer-range Hades (200-mile) beginning in 1991. |
| Buccaneer Fighter Bomber | UK | 50 | 100 | Being replaced by Tornado |
| Jaguar Fighter Bomber | UK, Fr. | 80 | 80 | |
| Super Etendard Fighter Bomber | Fr. | 36 | 72 | On two carriers. 50 will eventually carry ASMP |
| Mirage III E Fighter Bomber | Fr. | 30 | 30 | Will be replaced by Mirage 2000Ns from 1988 |
| F-4 Fighter Bomber | US, Turk., | 152 | 152 | Many being replaced by F-16s and Tornados |
| F-104 Fighter Bomber | Belg., Gr., FRG, Neth., It., Turk. | 400 | 400 | |
| F-100 Fighter Bomber | Turk | 18 | 18 | Additional US and Belg. aircraft in 1984. Neth. aircraft operational in 1984 |
| F-16 Fighter Bomber | US, Belg. | 168 | 168 | |
| *Short-Range (under 60 miles)* | | | | |
| 155 mm Howitzer | Belg., FRG | 1,690 | 2,200– | Approximately 800 neutron shells for 203 mm stored in US |
| 203 mm Howitzer | Gr., It., Neth., Turk., UK, US | 390 | 2,500 | |
| *Long-Range (over 600 miles)* | | | | |
| SS-20 IRBM | USSR | 360 | 1,080 | At 40 sites, two-thirds within range of Western Europe. Each launcher may have a reload missile |
| SS-5 IRBM | USSR | 16 | 16 | Numbers are being reduced |
| SS-4 MRBM | USSR | 232 | 232 | Numbers are being reduced |
| SS-N-5 SLBM | USSR | 30 | 30 | Assumes 6 Golf II (of 13) and all of 4 Hotel II opposite Europe |
| Tu-22M Backfire Bomber | USSR | 65 | 130 | Assumes those opposite Europe. Carries one AS-4 Kitchen missile or up to 12,000 kg of bombs |

Table 8.3 continued.

| Aircraft or missile launcher type | Owner/ Operator | Number | NATO Number of nuclear weapons | Remarks |
|---|---|---|---|---|
| Tu-16 Badger Bomber | USSR | 250 | 500 | Assumes those opposite Europe. Can carry Kennel, Kelt or Kingfish air-to-surface missiles or up to 9000 kg of bombs |
| Tu-22 Blinder Bomber | USSR | 100 | 200 | Assumes those opposite Europe. Can carry one AS-4 Kitchen missile |
| Su-24 Fencer A Fighter Bomber | USSR, GDR, Hung., Pol. | 550 | 1,100 | Approximately 400 for Europe. First deployed to Poland and Hungary in August 1981 and to GDR in January 1982 |
| *Medium-Range (60–600 miles)* | | | | |
| SS-12/22 Missile | USSR | 100 | 100 | SS-22 replacing SS-12. None outside USSR. Reports that some could go to Hungary |
| FROG-7/SS-21 Missile | USSR, GDR, Pol., Bulg., Czech., Hung., Romania | 650 | 650 | SS-21 replacing FROG-7 |
| SCUD B/SS-23 Missile | USSR, GDR Pol., Czech. | 550 | 550 | SS-23 replacing SCUD B. First SS-23 to GDR in 1982 |
| Sub-17 Fitter D/H Fighter Bomber | USSR, GDR, Czech., Pol. | 650 | 650 | Less are opposite Europe |

| System | Location | | | | |
|---|---|---|---|---|---|
| Mig 27 Flogger D/J Fighter Bomber | USSR, GDR | | 550 | 550 | Less are opposite Europe |
| Mig 21 Fishbed L Fighter Bomber | USSR | | 100 | 100 | |
| *Short-Range (under 60 miles)* | | | | | |
| 152 mm Howitzer | USSR, E. Europe | | 550 | ? | |
| 203 mm Howitzer | USSR, E. Europe | 300 | | ? | Recently deployed outside USSR |
| 240 mm Mortar | USSR | | | | |

*Notes:* [1] Altogether, the US has about 6,000 nuclear weapons based in Europe, some of which would be delivered by US systems and some by allied systems.

[2] It should not be assumed that all nuclear-capable delivery systems will in fact be used to deliver nuclear weapons.

[3] The US has additional nuclear-capable aircraft that could be sent as reinforcements to Europe.

[4] There are also nuclear land mines, air-defence missiles and anti-ship and anti-submarine nuclear weapons.

*Source: Defense Monitor*, Center for Defense Information, vol. XII, no. 6, 1983, pp. 6, 7.

tive NATO–WTO nuclear war-making capacities.) The sharp Soviet reaction was prompted by a number of motivations: desire to prevent deployment of nuclear systems targeted against the Soviet homeland from the territory of Russia's historical enemy; fear of an LRTNF arms race; renewed anxiety about American forward-based systems; and, last but not least, a continuing desire to weaken NATO militarily and politically, split the Western allies, and maintain Soviet LRTNF superiority in Europe.[61] A diplomatic and propaganda offensive against NATO's LRTNF modernization plan, unprecedented in its scope and intensity, was launched and the issue has assumed a central place in the NATO–WTO confrontation, involving the two Superpowers and especially America's European allies, which naturally are the main targets of the Soviet Union's campaign.

The LRTNF confrontation shows how the Soviet Union's perception of the nuclear balance in Europe, and military security in general, differs from the way in which the same issues are perceived by NATO. The Soviet Union claims that the projected deployment of the new Western LRTNF represents a dangerous escalation of the nuclear arms race that would upset the existing balance of such forces in Europe. In the Soviet Union's view the SS-20s and the Backfires represent only a modernization of the Soviet forces necessary to counteract NATO's nuclear advantages in Europe, including American tactical battlefield nuclear weapons, the three NATO-assigned Poseidon submarines with 400 MIRV warheads, and the British and French nuclear arsenals. The Soviet Union sees in the projected American weapons a new and most dangerous threat to its homeland, since such weapons would be able to hit targets located there, including the Soviet strategic arsenal itself, with serious implications of a shift in American strategic doctrine towards a counterforce strike against the Soviet Union. The Soviet Union also alleges that the NATO plan would, in general, seriously endanger détente, especially the Soviet interpretation of this vague concept.[62]

The Western perception of the European LRTNF issue must be placed within the context of the changes in the overall strategic relationship between the United States and the Soviet Union that have occurred in the last two decades or so.[63] When the Soviet Union lagged behind the United States in its strategic intercontinental nuclear arsenal, the Soviet superiority in the otherwise less sophisticated LRTNF and its conventional strength could still be interpreted as a defensive rather than offensive posture, since any Soviet action against Western Europe would trigger an all-out response from

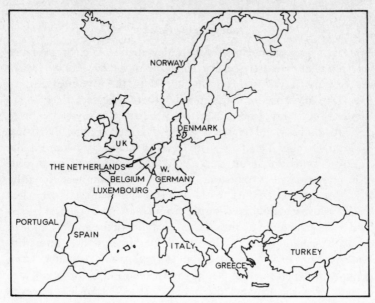

Figure 8.8   The composition of the EUROGROUP and its contribution to
NATO

The EUROGROUP is an informal grouping within NATO and is open to all
European members of the Alliance.

The basic aim of the EUROGROUP is to help strengthen the whole Alliance
by ensuring that the European contribution to the common defence is as
strong, cohesive and effective as possible.

The EUROGROUP was created in 1968, and throughout its existence it has
remained an informal body. The focus of the work is provided by meetings,
usually twice a year, of the Defence Ministers of the EUROGROUP countries;
the Chairmanship rotates each year. At these meetings, Ministers review the
practical steps that have been taken to improve defence co-operation and
direct new activity aimed at achieving a more effective and cohesive
European contribution to the Alliance. But, perhaps more important, these
meetings provide an opportunity for Ministers, in an informal setting, to
raise and discuss the important political issues of the day as they affect
defence and as they are seen from Europe.

The military contribution of EUROGROUP (in-place Forces):

| Land and air forces | | Maritime forces | |
|---|---|---|---|
| Total soldiers | 1,850,000 | Surface ships | 730 |
| Main battle tanks[1] | 10,400 | Submarines | 120 |
| Artillery[1] | 10,000 | Aircraft | 570 |
| Combat aircraft[1] | 2,300 | | |

*Notes*: [1] Figures for main battle tanks, artillery and combat aircraft include only those
assigned to NATO.

[2] France is not a EUROGROUP state, so its forces are not included.

*Source*: *The Defence of Europe*, US Department of State, 1983, pp. 2–3, 8–9.

American strategic nuclear forces under the doctrines of 'extended deterrence' and 'massive retaliation'. With the emergence by 1977 of strategic parity and the looming threat to the invulnerability of American land-based strategic missiles, there appeared, according to Western observers, to be no further need for the Soviet Union to develop sophisticated nuclear weapons targeted specifically against Western Europe. Yet, they were developed and are being rapidly deployed with the result that, under the concept of its flexible response strategy, NATO no longer has the viable option of escalating any conventional conflict to the more favourable tactical nuclear level because it would be deterred from resorting to tactical battle-field nuclear weapons by the unique capability of the Soviet Union to use its SS-20 and other modern LRTNF for strategic uses limited to Europe. The 1979 NATO decision to deploy new countervailing LRTNF is designed to close this gap in the continuum of its military options between the conventional and battlefield nuclear forces in Europe on the one hand and the strategic nuclear weapons of the United States and its Allies on the other.[64]

It soon became obvious that the Soviet deployment of new LRTNF, while securing for the Soviet Union a bargaining advantage in the escalation process of an actual armed conflict against NATO (something that NATO had hoped to achieve under its flexible response strategy), also could serve as an instrument of political pressure against the Western European allies of the United States within the range of the Soviet weapons.

### THE PERCEPTION GAP WITHIN NATO

In its campaign against the Western plan to deploy LRTNF, the Soviet Union is exploiting the growing perception gap that exists between the way the problem is seen by the NATO decision-makers, especially the American representatives, and the way it is viewed by large segments of Western European public opinion, articulated by the various anti-nuclear and peace movements. These groups and many individual Western Europeans do not seem to share NATO's anxiety over the threat posed by the Soviet LRTNF and are opposed to the deployment by NATO of missiles to counter that threat.[65] This is discussed further in Chapter 9. For West Germany, the key NATO member-state in Europe where all the 108 Pershing IIs and 96 out of 145 cruise missiles are to be located, the LRTNF issue is extremely sensitive because such deployment means that for the first time missiles capable of reaching Soviet territory will be placed on West German soil even though they will remain under American control. Caught between conflicting American and Soviet pressures, the West German government of Chancellor Helmut Schmidt, while agreeing to deployment on its territory, insisted on the precondition of concurrent acceptance of the missiles on the territory of at least one other NATO member on the continent (the 'no-singularity provision').[66] It also consistently has emphasized the need to engage in LRTNF arms control negotiations with the Soviet Union as provided by NATO's 1979 'two-track' decision: modernization plus negotiations.[67] The current CDU Chancellor, Helmut Kohl, supports this position as well.

The West German government is the main target of the Soviet anti-NATO campaign which at the same time faces a growing opposition from the left wing of the Social Democratic Party, especially dominant since the party was voted out of power in the March 1983 election, and from the spreading anti-nuclear protests. In the Netherlands, according to public opinion polls, two-thirds of the population oppose the deployment of the 48 cruise missiles there. The parliamentary election of May 1981 failed to produce the majority necessary for the approval of deployment on Dutch soil and the government, which originally had accepted NATO's modernization plan, postponed its final decision until December 1981, but it was not until the Summer of 1983 that a favourable decision was made.

The position of the Belgian government also has been ambiguous. Denmark and Noway long ago refused to accept nuclear weapons on their soil. The Italian government is committed to accept 112 missiles, but domestic political instability in Italy must be of some concern to NATO planners. In Britain, where 160 cruise missiles are to be deployed, Prime Minister Margaret Thatcher is strongly committed to the NATO plan against Labour Party opposition and a growing anti-nuclear movement. Until Mrs Thatcher's spectacular electoral victory in 1983 there was also concern in NATO that as a result of the worsening economic situation a Labour goverment might have come to power before the implementation of the modernization plan.[68]

From the very beginning the modernization decision of 1979 has been linked to a parallel NATO call for arms control negotiations with the Soviet Union to limit the deployment of LRTNF systems to mutually acceptable levels. Such talks would represent only one forum in the ongoing process of arms control negotiations between East and West. At the strategic level the SALT I agreement on limiting offensive missiles expired in 1977 and SALT II, although signed, is unacceptable to the Reagan Administration although in 1985 it pledged compliance to its rules. However, new Strategic Arms Reduction Talks (START) on strategic arms control were initiated by the Reagan Administration in Geneva in 1983; in October of that year the Administration introduced the notion of 'build-down' – gradual trimming of warheads and missiles by replacement. In 1985 when the arms control negotiations were resumed, the START talks were combined with INF and nuclear space defence (SDI), but so far no concrete progress has been made.

Since 1973, as far as forces in Central Europe are concerned, as pointed out earlier, NATO and the WTO have been engaged in negotiations in Vienna on mutual and balanced force reductions (MBFR) and in Central Europe, specifically in Belgium, the Netherlands, Luxembourg, West Germany, East Germany, Poland, and Czechoslovakia, involving the armed forces of these seven states and those of the United States, Canada, Britain, and the Soviet Union. Although consensus has been reached on a number of points, these relatively forgotten negotiations so far have failed to produce any concrete agreement.[69] Perceiving the WTO's superiority, NATO's basic objective in the MBFR talks has been to establish a more stable conventional balance in Central Europe, whereas for the WTO the main motivation has been to limit the growth of NATO's forces, especially those of West Germany.

In the course of the protracted negotiations the positions of the two sides have softened substantially from the original extreme stands. Thus, in 1978 the WTO states made a major concession on the issue of the method of calculating reductions by agreeing that the forces should be reduced to a combined ceiling of ground and air forces totalling 900,000. A compromise also was reached on the scheduling of reductions, under which they would proceed in two phases; the first was to include only the Soviet and American forces and the second to concentrate on reductions by all parties. There was also consensus on the need for 'associated measures', that is, measures to enhance confidence and facilitate verification of compliance that were to legalize the 'confidence-building measures' envisa-ged by the Final Act of the Helsinki Conference on Security and Co-operation in Europe of 1975. However, it so far has not been possible to agree on what concrete verification procedures should be adopted.

The most divisive issue of the MBFR negotiations concerns the number of troops to be taken as the starting point for reductions. Whereas NATO claims that the existing disparity of ground forces between the two Alliances amounts to 150,000, the WTO admits to only 14,000. To accept the Soviet data would mean codifying the sizeable Warsaw Pact advantage for purposes of calculating reductions. Hence, the issue remains unresolved. It re-emerged again as the fundamental impediment to agreement at the latest rounds of MBFR talks in the Winter and Summer of 1981. No progress has been made in the subsequent worsened international climate.

As mentioned earlier, protracted debates in Madrid at the 1980–3 second follow-up meeting of the 1975 Helsinki Conference considered plans for a 'Conference on Security and Disarmament in Europe', submitted by, among other participants, France on behalf of the West and Poland on behalf of the WTO. These proposals were accepted because a consensus was achieved on the nature of mandatory and verifiable confidence building measures and on the territorial scope of their applicability on the European continent. The conference took place in Stockholm in the Winter of 1984 and Spring of 1985, but its results have been very meagre.

Despite all these failures at arms control in relations between NATO and the WTO, NATO's decision on the modernization of its LRTNF was balanced by a willingness to negotiate with the Soviet Union on arms control measures concerning these weapons systems. The first round of talks opened under the Carter Administration in October 1980 and quickly ended at an impasse, having been undertaken simply to reassure domestic pro-arms control concerns without any coherent strategy or adequate preparation for the problems involved.

In view of rising popular pressures in Europe against nuclear armaments and for disarmament talks, it was a foregone conclusion that the Reagan Administration would have to resume negotiations on LRTNF with the Soviet Union.[70] However, Soviet pressure for a mutual East–West moratorium on the deployment of LRTNF was dismissed by NATO as a ploy to camouflage and stabilize Soviet superiority in LRTNF as well as to allow their continued build-up of the SS-20 force and perhaps more advanced intermediate-range missiles. Perhaps more serious consideration should have been given to Soviet fears aroused by the fact that Pershing II's can reach Soviet territory in sixteen minutes.

In the current tense climate of international politics, chances for a successful outcome of LRTNF talks appear to be even less promising than in the past. Moreover, the task of arriving at a mutually acceptable scheme of LRTNF reduction is challenging indeed when the two sides are divided by seemingly intractable differences. There is no agreement on what weapons are actually to be included in the negotiations as LRTNF, how they are to be counted (in missiles, the Soviet position, or warheads, NATO's preference), or what should be the geographical scope of the limitations.[71] Finally, as mentioned above, there remains the problem of the link between the LRTNF talks and the SALT (and START) agreements. Such a linkage can produce potentially more difficult problems of comparison and advantage. It is imperative, however, that should the LRTNF talks produce an agreement, they should be complemented by equal progress in the area of the limitation of the strategic systems of the two Superpowers.[72]

## CONCLUSIONS

Today, in the rather delicate and critical period prior to the mid-1980s deployment of NATO's new LRTNF the question remains: how can the security system of NATO adapt to the present strategic and political reality? Strategically, the NATO–WTO relationship is characterized by a military balance shifting towards the East, especially in view of the Soviet deployment of new LRTNF. NATO's long-term defence programme and LRTNF modernization can only partially reduce its inferiority. Politically, the relationship between the two Alliances must be viewed in the foreseeable future as one dimension of an intensifying confrontation that has spread beyond the traditional confines of NATO's geographical area and was precipitated by Soviet activities in Africa and Indo-China, its military intervention in Afghanistan, the Solidarity crisis in Poland, the American intervention in Grenada, and the turmoil in the Middle East. NATO needs a more determined and coherent strategy in order to deal with these realities of the 1980s.

As shown by the debate on the deployment of LRTNF, it is of crucial importance for NATO to narrow the gap that exists between public opinion in Western Europe and the NATO governments concerning their respective perception of the Soviet threat. The development of a shared perception regarding the LRTNF problem is a necessary condition for a successful implementation of the modernization decision of 1979. Parallel to this political task must be the effort to proceed to improve the military balance not only by NATO as a whole but also by the individual, especially the key European, members of the Alliance: West Germany, France, and Britain.[73] (The contributions of the so-called EUROGROUP, while significant, as shown in figure 8.5, are nonetheless inadequate.) It appears that because of decline in the credibility of the American nuclear umbrella and the growing LRTNF disparity, the French and British nuclear forces will have to complement the American systems that are to be deployed in the 1980s, even though the Soviet Union wants these forces included in assessments of the East–West balance of forces. Perhaps the time is approaching for France to rejoin the military arms of NATO in Europe; French President François Mitterrand has already reaffirmed France's strong identification with NATO's nuclear deterrence strategy. Despite the prospect of disappointment, NATO must continue to supplement its defence programmes by negotiations with the Soviet Union and the WTO for realistic, security-enhancing, and verifiable arms control agreements in order to achieve a balance at preferably the lowest level of armaments and to reduce as much as possible any incentive to use force by the potential adversaries.

The Reagan Administration's 'Star Wars' initiative, offered as a means of reducing the temptation for a pre-emptive first strike, is feared by the Soviet Union as encouraging the possibility not only of a new form of the high-technology arms race, but by supplanting 'mutual assured destruction' as the primary deterrent, lowering the threshold of nuclear threat.

Many suggestions have therefore been made in Western Europe and in the United States to strengthen the conventional weapons capabilities of NATO and thereby to raise the threshold for the necessary employment of nuclear weapons. Clearly, new and sophisticated technologies have increased the destructive potential and the accuracy of conventional weapons such as anti-tank guns and others. However, the cost of procuring these weapons is high, and this may be a serious impediment to embarking on the conventional force-modernization strategy. Moreover, it is uncertain whether the use of nuclear weapons can in fact be avoided; indeed, their employment must remain the last resort in the face of a very powerful attack by WTO forces.

The challenges faced by NATO are enormous, but to counterbalance this rather pessimistic portrayal of NATO–WTO relations, it is important to recall that the WTO and its leaders are not without their own problems and even serious dilemmas. Seen in future perspective, the Polish situation is of particular interest since it may prove to be a turning-point not only in the history of Soviet-style Communism in Europe but also of its institutionalization in the form of a military government. Equally important is the often capricious behaviour of Romania in the WTO activities and plans. Nonetheless, NATO must apply itself to rectifying the unfavourable balance in the European theatre as it stands today, concurrently pursuing the course of arms control negotiations at the conventional and nuclear levels. Such negotiations can be successful only if NATO secures for itself a stronger bargaining position than the one in which it finds itself at the present time, even though the December 1984 ministerial meeting produced a high degree of consensus that NATO should negotiate only from strength.

In systemic terms, our analysis suggests that in the political–military sector few changes in the sub-regional characteristics can be expected in the near future, precisely because of the imminence of highly complex East–West negotiations. But the last word on arms control negotiations between the two Superpowers and their respective blocs has not yet been written; we will return to this subject in chapter 10.

### NOTES

1  As quoted in *New York Times*, 23 October 1969.
2  See communiqué, NATO Ministerial meeting, December 1969.
3  Ibid.
4  Ibid.
5  As reported by Holmes Alexander, *Alexander Gazette*, 30 January 1970. He went on to comment: 'The NATO formula still reads, "An attack on one is an attack on all," but in Turkey the urgency of the 1950s has lost some tenseness as the 1970s begin. Trade is brisk between this country and the Iron Curtain bloc. Bulgarian trailer-trucks rumble through the streets of Ismir where this NATO headquarters is located. Soviet attention seems fixed in the Mid-East and Turkish sympathies are with the Arabs. The Turkish Labour Party is Marxist although Communism is outlawed. A radical minority of Turkish youth is anti-American. A screaming segment of the Turkish press is anti-NATO. 'Who needs the United States? Who can count on the USA?' Such questions, while they don't represent a consensus, are voices in a chorus of Turkish skepticism [sic] and separatism.'
6  The antipathy towards Greece stemmed in part from the publication at the Council of Europe in early 1970 of sections of a European Human Rights Council report of alleged rights violations in Greece. Subsequently, Greece withdrew from the Council. But the advent of an elected Greek government of the left in the 1980s has not resulted in any easing of Greece's relations with NATO, only changed their character.

7 *New York Times*, 30 November 1969, p. A14.

8 These points were extracted from the article by Sir Clive Rose, 'Political Consultation in the Alliance', *NATO Review*, April 1983, pp. 1–5.

9 The following section is drawn with permission from Lawrence S. Kaplan and Robert W. Clawson, eds, *NATO After Thirty Years* (Wilmington, D. E.: Scholarly, Resources, Inc. 1980), pp. 41–54.

10 Hans J. Morgenthau, 'Alliances', *Confluence* 6 (Winter 1958): 317–20; Norman A. Graebner, 'Alliances and Free World Security', *Current History* 38 (April 1960): 215.

11 Dean Acheson, 'To Meet the Shifting Soviet Offensive', *New York Times Magazine* (15 April 1956); Claude Delmas, 'How the Third World Splits NATO', *Western World* 1, No. 20 (December 1958): 43–7.

12 Henry A. Kissinger, 'Nuclear Testing and the Problem of Peace', *Foreign Affairs* 31 (October 1958): 15; Lester B. Pearson, *Diplomacy in the Nuclear Age* (Cambridge, MA: Harvard University Press, 1959), p. 88.

13 'NATO Talks on Disarmament', *Manchester Guardian* 77 (19 December 1957): 3. See also Department of State *Bulletin* 38 (6 January 1958): 7. *Guardian* writer Max Freedman regarded these verbal assurances as more important than missiles for Europe's defence.

14 Quoted in Alastair Buchan, 'Britain and the Bomb', *The Reporter* 20 (19 March 1959): 23; Alexander Bregman, 'The Nuclear Club Should be Expanded', *Western World* 2 (October 1959): 12–15.

15 James Reston, *New York Times*, 28 May 1961.

16 Henry A. Kissinger, 'The Invisionist: Why We Misread de Gaulle', *Harper's* 230 (March 1965): 74; Drew Middleton, *New York Times* 14 August 1966; editorial, *New York Times*, 28 August 1966.

17 C. Sulzberger, *New York Times*, 28 July 1966; Hanson W. Baldwin, 'NATO's Uneven Steps Toward Integration', *The Reporter* 3 (11 March 1956): 34; Malcom W. Hoag analysed the problem of European deterrents in 'What interdependence for NATO', *World Politics* 12 (April 1960): 389–90. Raymond Aron argued that de Gaulle would never permit Britain to have a privileged nuclear position. 'De Gaulle and Kennedy – the Nuclear Debate', *The Atlantic* 210 (August 1962): 36. Many other writers explained de Gaulle's determination to achieve French independence from Great Britain and the United States. Among them were Edward Ashcroft, 'Behind de Gaulle's Quarrels with His Allies', *New York Times Magazine* (September 1962): 62, 74–82; André Fontaine, 'De Gaulle's View of Europe and the Nuclear Debate', *The Reporter* 27 (19 July 1962): 33–4; Edmond Taylor, 'De Gaulle's Design for Europe', *The Reporter* 26 (7 June 1962): 15–16; and Bernard B. Fall, 'Why the French Mistrust Us', *New York Times Magazine* (6 September 1964): 6, 33–7.

18 For a detailed discussion of Kennedy's Grand Design, see Sidney Hyman, 'In Search of the Atlantic Community', *New York Times Magazine* (6 May 1962): 17, 111–14; *New York Times*, 26 May 1963; and

Kennedy's Philadelphia speech quoted in *New York Times*, 8 July 1962. Louis J. Halle criticized Kennedy's speech in 'Appraisal of Kennedy as World Leader', *New York Times Magazine* (16 June 1963): 42. Philip H. Irezise analyzed at length the rationale of Kennedy's idea of transatlantic partnership, Department of State *Bulletin* 48 (24 July 1963): 971–6.

19  US Congress, Senate, *Problems and Trends in Atlantic Partnership II: Staff Study Prepared for the Use of the Committee on Foreign Relations, June 17, 1963*, 88th Congress, 1st sess., doc. 21 (1963), pp. 11–12.

20  Washington's criticism of European defence policy was continuous in 1962. What disturbed Kennedy especially was the refusal of the allies to support the United States during the Berlin crisis of 1961. See James Reston, *New York Times*, 18 May 1962; C. Sulzberger, *New York Times*, 19 November 1962; and Drew Middleton, *New York Times*, 21 April 1962.

21  Robert McNamara's address appeared in *New York Times*, 17 June 1962. For commentary on Kennedy's nuclear policy, see Drew Middleton, *New York Times*, 25 May, 1 July 1962.

22  McGeorge Bundy, 'Friends and Allies', *Foreign Affairs* 41 (October 1962): 21.

23  US Congress, Senate, Committee on Foreign Relations, *Problems and Trends in Atlantic Partnership I: Some Comments on the European Economic Community and NATO, September 14, 1962*, 87th Congress, 2d sess., doc. 132 (1962), p. 33; Bernard Brodie, 'What Price Conventional Capabilities in Europe', *The Reporter* 27 (23 May 1963): 25–33.

24  Malcolm W. Hoag, 'Nuclear Policy and French Intransigence', *Foreign Affairs* 41 (January 1963): 294. Also on the problem of nuclear sharing is Sir John Slessor, 'Atlantic Nuclear Policy', *International Journal* 20 (Spring 1965): 143–57. American officials argued that the problem of allied partnership on matters of nuclear sharing lay in the unequal distribution of power in the Alliance. See Undersecretary of State George Ball, 6 February 1962, Department of State *Bulletin* 46 (5 March 1962): 366; Counselor W. W. Rostow, 9 May 1963, Department of State *Bulletin* 48 (3 June 1963): 858.

25  On the 'Sky Bolt' affair and the Nassau agreement, see Henry A. Kissinger, 'The Sky Bolt Affair', *The Reporter* 28 (17 January 1963): 15–18; and Ward S. Just, 'The Scrapping of Sky Bolt', Ibid., (11 April 1963): 19–21.

26  April statement in *New York Times*, 28 April 1963. For a full analysis of de Gaulle's reaction to Kennedy's Grand Design, see *Problems and Trends in Atlantic Partnership, II, June 17, 1963*, pp. 1–8. De Gaulle's press conference of 14 January 1963 appears in ibid., pp. 57–65.

27  Ibid., p. 14.

28  Ibid., p. 61.

29  For a full text of the Treaty see ibid., pp. 50–3.

30  Max Frankel discusses the American and British reaction to de Gaulle's press conference, *New York Times*, 7 April 1963. Kennedy's 8 February

statement appears in US, Department of State, *Foreign Policy Briefs* 12 (18 February 1963): 1. Secretary of State Dean Rusk made a similar appeal for European unity, 12 July 1963, Department of State *Bulletin* 49 (5 August 1963): 192.

31 Writers condemned MLF as both a political and a military venture. Among the criticisms are: *New York Times*, 23 June 1963, (editorial); a major discussion in *New York Times*, 30 June 1963; Hanson W. Baldwin, *New York Times*, 15 December 1963; Henry A. Kissinger, 'The Unsolved Problems of European Defense', *Foreign Affairs* 40 (July 1962): 535; 'Multilateral Force or Farce', *New York Times Magazine* (13 December 1964): 25, 100–7; and Ronald Steel, 'The Place of NATO', *The New Republic* 151 (14 November 1964): 19–22.

32 Kennedy's Frankfurt speech appears in US Department of State, *Foreign Policy Briefs* 12 (8 July 1963): 1; Drew Middleton, *New York Times*, 30 June 1963; and Arthur J. Olsen, *New York Times*, 7 July 1963.

33 On US pressure for larger European defence contributions, see Arthur J. Olsen, *New York Times*, 27 October 1963; and Drew Middleton, *New York Times*, 3 November 1963. De Gaulle's January 1964 press conference is analysed in *New York Times*, 26 January 1964.

34 Henry Tanner, *New York Times*, 24 April 1966. For a discussion of the NATO move to Brussels, see Robert S. Jordan, *Political Leadership in NATO: A Study in Multinational Diplomacy* (Boulder, Col: Westview Press, 1979), chapter 4.

35 Georges Pompidou quoted in *New York Times*, 24 April 1964.

36 Max Frankel, *New York Times Magazine* (5 December 1965): 54–5, 173–88; Frankel, *New York Times*, 8 March 1964; *Detroit News* quoted in *New York Times*, 8 March 1964.

37 Dean Acheson, 'Withdrawal from Europe? An Illusion', *New York Times Magazine* (15 December 1963): 67.

38 For a defence of de Gaulle, see John Grigg, 'In Defense of Charles de Gaulle', *New York Times Magazine* (23 February 1964): 66–8; Stephen R. Graubard, 'After Five Years, de Gaulle Still Towers', *New York Times Magazine* (15 December 1963): 21, 54–60.

39 The following section is drawn with permission from Robert W. Clawson and Lawrence S. Kaplan, eds., *The Warsaw Pact: Political Purpose and Military Means* (Wilmington, DE: Scholarly Resources, Inc., 1982), pp. 95–108. See also David Holloway and Jane M. O. Sharp, eds., *The Warsaw Pact: Alliance in Transition?* (Ithaca, N.Y.: Cornell University Press, 1984.)

40 The complexities of comparing elements of military power for purposes of arriving at a balance are discussed in *The Military Balance 1977–1978*, pp. 102–10, and *The Military Balance, 1983–1984*, pp. 13–14 and 137 ff.

41 For the difference that various pessimistic or optimistic assumptions can make in portraying the military balance between NATO and the WTO, see Wolfram F. Hanrieder, ed., *Arms Control and Security: Current Issues*

(Boulder, CO: Westview Press, 1979), esp. App. C: 'Nato-Warsaw Pact Military Balance: How to Make the Balance Look Good/Bad'. The military strategist, Harry E. Crow, Jr. agrees with Hanrieder's analysis.

42  For details see *The Military Balance 1983–84*.

43  Problems related to estimating Soviet defence expenditures are analysed in *The Military Balance 1973–1974*, pp. 8–9; *1975–1977*, pp. 109–10; *1980–1981*, pp. 12–13, *1983–84*, pp. 13–14. See also W. T. Lee, *The Estimation of Soviet Expenditures, 1955–75: An Unconventional Approach* (New York: Frederick A. Praeger, 1977).

44  *The Military Balance 1983–1984*, pp. 13, 150.

45  It is estimated that since 1970 the Soviet Union has out-invested the United States in military capital by at least $200 billion. See 'NATO and the Warsaw Pact', *The Economist* 276, No. 7145 (9 August 1980): 36. Soviet research and development spending amounts to 20 per cent of the Soviet defence budget, whereas the United States is only about 10 per cent. Robert Komer, 'Looking Ahead', *International Security* 4, No. 1 (Summer 1979): 108, 110. See also *The Military Balance, 1984–1985*, p. 125.

46  The defence expenditures of the Soviet union combined with its allies averaged 4–6 per cent. *The Military Balance 1983–1984*, pp. 124–5 and 150.

47  Ibid.

48  For data on the strategic forces of the Superpowers, Britain, and France, see *The Military Balance 1983–1984*. pp. 21, 25.

49  Ibid., pp. 116–17. See also Lawrence Freedman, 'The Dilemma of Nuclear Arms Control', *Survival* 23, No. 1 (January–February 1981): 2, 5–6. The 160-kilometre range is a rough separation of short-range battlefield from long-range theatre nuclear weapons.

50  *The Military Balance 1983–1984*, pp. 118–20.

51  Ibid., pp. 15 and 121.

52  See details in the essays by Bill Sweetman and Robert W. Clawson in the Kaplan–Clawson book cited above.

53  *The Military Balance 1983–1984*, p. 137.

54  In the Baltic the WTO has a 3 to 1 advantage. In the Mediterranean NATO still enjoys an advantage but can no longer be assured of exercising necessary overall sea control. Bernard W. Rogers, 'Increasing Threats to NATO's Security Call for Sustained Response', *NATO Review* 29, No. 3 (June 1981):1.

55  North Atlantic Council, Final Communiqué, *NATO Review* 26, No. 4 (August 1978): 28, 29.

56  See Elizabeth Pond, 'US Gets NATO Allies' Commitment on Defense Spending', *Christian Science Monitor*, 14 May 1981.

57  See North Atlantic Council, Final Communiqué, 'The Long-Term Defence Programme: A Summary', *NATO Review* 26, No. 4 (August 1978): 29–31.

58  Communiqué of the Special Meeting of NATO Foreign and Defence Ministers, *NATO Review* 28, No. 1 (February 1980): 25.

59 North Atlantic Council, Final Communiqué, meeting of 11–12 December 1980, *NATO Review* 29, No. 1 (February 1981): 25–7.

60 For a typical Soviet perception of the NATO plan see Boris Ponomarev, 'A Pact for Peace and a Pact for Aggression', *World Marxist Review* 23, No. 8 (August 1980): 3, 6.

61 See the discussion in Stephen M. Millett, 'Soviet Perceptions of the Theater Nuclear Balance in Europe and Reactions to American LRTNFs', *Naval War College Review* 34, No. 2 (1981): 3–17.

62 Ibid.

63 For example, see, Stephen Hammer, Jr, 'NATO's Long-Range Theatre Nuclear Forces: Modernization in Parallel with Arms Control', *NATO Review* 28, No. 1 (February 1980): 1–6; and Paul Buteux, 'Theatre Nuclear Forces: Modernization Plan and Arms Control Initiative', *NATO Review* 28, No. 6 (December 1980): 1–6. See also the analysis in Stanley Hoffmann, 'New Variations on Old Themes', *International Security* 4, No. 1 (Summer 1979): 88–107. For a popular overall review see Elizabeth Pond, 'The State of the Alliance: The Missile Watch', *Christian Science Monitor*, 19 June 1981.

64 This gap was emphasized by West German Chancellor Helmut Schmidt in his now famous address at the International Institute for Strategic Studies in London in the Fall of 1977, in which he called upon the United States to counter the Soviet deployment of the LRTNF systems. Initially, President Jimmy Carter (but not the Pentagon) was reluctant to do so in adherence to the concept of mutual assured destruction (MAD), and the principle of joining Europe with America for defence purposes. See Elizabeth Pond, 'The State of the Alliance', op. cit. and Pond, 'Can NATO Lessen Its Nuclear Tilt?' *Christian Science Monitor*, 14 October 1983.

65 On the same day that a WTO Conference was held at Kent State University a conference on nuclear war reflecting this opposition was taking place in Groningen, the Netherlands. See Elizabeth Pond. 'US, European Antinuclear Groups Join in Peace Quest', *Christian Science Monitor*, 28 April 1981.

66 During the discussions leading to the two-track decision to proceed with the deployment of LRTNF and to engage in arms control negotiations with the Soviet Union, West Germany urged that the NATO LRTNF missiles be based on ships at sea. See interview with Chancellor Schmidt in *Frankfurter Rundschau*, 30 June 1981, translated by the German Information Center, New York, *Release from Bonn – Statements and Speeches* 4, No. 11 (6 July 1981).

67 For example, see the statement by Chancellor Schmidt, ibid. See also his statement before the *Bundestag* on 9 April 1981, translated by the German Information Center, New York, *Release from Bonn – Statements and Speeches* 4, No. 6 (10 April 1981); and his statement before the *Bundestag* on 26 May 1981, translated in ibid., No. 29 (27 May 1981). See also the

statement by the West German Minister for Foreign Affairs in a *Deutschlandfunk* interview, 13 April 1981, translated in ibid., No. 7 (13 April 1981).

68 For a review of the position of the European NATO members on the issue of deploying LRTNF, see Gary Yerkey, 'Europe's Antiwar Movement of '60s Turns to Antinuclear Protest for '80s', *Christian Science Monitor*, 28 April 1981; Elizabeth Pond, 'Dutch Election Results Reflect Antinuclear Mood', ibid., 28 May 1981; and David K. Willis, 'Europe Blows Hot and Cold over New NATO Missiles', ibid., 29 June 1981. It is perhaps ironic that the new Socialist government of France under President Mitterrand is among one of the strongest opponents of the Soviet missile build-up and staunchly supports NATO's LRTNF modernization plan with concurrent pursuance of arms control talks with the Soviet Union. See Mitterrand's interview with the *New York Times*, 3 June 1981, reprinted in excerpts in French embassy, *Statements from . . . FRANCE*, No. 81 60.

69 For a detailed study of MBFR talks see John G. Keliher, *The Negotiations on Mutual and Balanced Force Reductions: The Search for Arms Control in Central Europe* (New York: Pergamon Press, 1980). See also *Third German–American Roundtable on NATO: The MBFR Negotiations* (1980; Co-sponsored by the Konrad Adenauer Stiftung and the Institute for Foreign Policy Analysis, Inc.); and Ernst Jung, 'The Vienna MBFR Negotiations after Seven Years', *NATO Review* 29, No. 3 (June 1981): 6–9. For a study of the relationship between détente and MBFR, see 'Détente and the European Force Reduction Negotiations' (Unpublished paper by P. Terrence Hopmann, prepared for delivery at the 22nd Annual Convention of the International Studies Association, Philadelphia, Pennsylvania, 18–21 March 1981).

70 In June 1981 the United States and the Soviet Union agreed to resume talks on the limitation of LRTNF. See the *New York Times*, 6 June 1981. The talks began in November 1981, but were suspended in November 1983 by the Soviet Union in protest against the emplacement of Pershing II's and cruise missiles in Europe.

71 For the difficulties inherent in LRTNF arms control negotiations, see Freedman, 'The Dilemma of Nuclear Arms Control'. See also James A. Schaer, 'European Arms Control: Right but Risky', *Christian Science Monitor*, 23 June 1981. For a more detailed analysis see Robert Metzger and Paul Doty, 'Arms Control Enters the Gray Area', *International Security* 3, No. 3 (Winter 1978/79): 17–52.

72 This is emphasized by Freedman, 'The Dilemma of Nuclear Arms Control'.

73 For some thoughts on this theme see Pierre Lellouche, 'Europe and Her Defense', *Foreign Affairs* 59, No. 4 (Spring 1981): 813–34.

# 9

## Perceptions of European Politics and Projections for the Future

### INTRODUCTION

If regional or sub-regional integration is to make progress, the mass publics and especially the elites residing in the various sub-systems must adopt favourable attitudes towards such a goal. Such attitudes may lead to commitments to regional or sub-regional ideals, look towards regional or sub-regional institutions for economic and other rewards, with the possible result that loyalties and expectations are gradually shifted from the states in the region or sub-region to central regional or sub-regional institutions. This kind of attitude is called 'attitudinal integration' by Joseph Nye[1] and may lead to 'policy integration' which is conceived as the endeavour of national governments to make policy jointly and to create a framework for the co-ordinated formulation of these policies. While in most instances attitudinal integration is a precondition of policy integration and later integration of institutions, characterized by expanded involvement of the regional or sub-regional authorities in terms of scope, level, and competencies in policy-making, it should be noted that progress made in policy integration may engender or strengthen attitudinal integration.

Perceptions and attitudes of different publics in Europe may offer some clues not only about integration within the two sub-regional systems but also about East–West relations. The latter attitudes may be significant with respect to the relationship between Eastern and Western Europe and, beyond that, the possible improvement or deterioration of conditions between the two Superpower blocs. However, it must be firmly kept in mind that, while the attitudes of the public may indeed have an influence on relationships between governments – obviously much more in pluralistic democratic systems than in the Socialist bloc dictatorships – other factors such as domestic politics and governmental perceptions of the distribution of international power are likely to be much more decisive in policy-making, as we have already pointed out on several occasions.

The availability of relevant survey data on mass public and elite attitudes in Europe is uneven. It is quite good in the Western part in terms of both 'West–West' attitudes and perceptions of some aspects of Eastern Europe, especially the military threat. Not surprisingly, survey data in Eastern Europe are scarce and not up-to-date. As a consequence, we will begin with the presentation of Western data and commence with views on economic and political integration within the EC.

### WESTERN EUROPE: ECONOMIC AND POLITICAL FACTORS

#### Integration

Since 1973, the Commission of the European Communities has undertaken semiannual surveys of the population of the EC member-states to determine a variety of attitudes. Most importantly, these surveys were to probe every six months whether respondents were for or against efforts to unify Western Europe. But even before 1973, similar questions were asked and table 9.1 shows the responses separately for the six original members (France, West Germany, Italy and the Benelux states) and the three member-states which joined in 1973 (Great Britain, Ireland and Denmark). An initial inspection of this table shows that the aim or ideal of a united Western Europe continues to enjoy a wide measure of support. However, as for the individual member-states, figure 9.1 clearly indicates this support has been declining in all member-states since 1973, with the exception of Britain where the intial commitment to unification was relatively low. Also noteworthy is the very low support in Denmark and the somewhat erratic attitudes in Greece, the EC's latest member.

Finally, a possibly significant change compared to previous polls is a decline in support for European unification in West Germany. In 1973, strong support was expressed by 49 per cent of the West German respondents; the figure fell to 28 per cent in October 1982. Support 'to some extent' increased during that period from 29 to 42 per cent and opposition rose from 6 to 16 per cent. The decline was particularly strong among elites (opinion leaders).[2] One explanation for this change might be the continued strong desire for German reunification although this is generally viewed as an unrealistic goal.[3]

Table 9.1 Attitudes towards the unification of Western Europe (%)

| Date of survey | For | | Against | | No reply | Total % | Total no. |
|---|---|---|---|---|---|---|---|
| | Very much | To some extent | To some extent | Very much | | | |
| *The Six* | | | | | | | |
| 1962 Jan.–Mar. | 40 | 32 | 4 | 1 | 23 | 100 | 6,334 |
| 1970 Feb.–Mar. | 34 | 40 | 4 | 2 | 20 | 100 | 8,752 |
| 1973 Sept. | 35 | 36 | 3 | 2 | 24 | 100 | 9,153 |
| 1975 May | 39 | 37 | 3 | 1 | 20 | 100 | 6,149 |
| 1975 Nov. | 33 | 41 | 2 | 2 | 22 | 100 | 5,691 |
| 1978 Oct. | 33 | 47 | 4 | 2 | 14 | 100 | 5,442 |
| 1979 Apr. | 34 | 47 | 6 | 1 | 12 | 100 | 5,589 |
| 1979 Oct. | 34 | 46 | 6 | 1 | 12 | 100 | 5,583 |
| 1980 Apr. | 30 | 49 | 6 | 2 | 13 | 100 | 5,426 |
| 1980 Oct. | 32 | 44 | 7 | 2 | 15 | 100 | 5,538 |
| 1981 Apr. | 27 | 47 | 9 | 3 | 14 | 100 | 5,518 |
| 1981 Oct. | 34 | 44 | 8 | 2 | 12 | 100 | 5,522 |
| 1982 Apr. | 29 | 49 | 7 | 2 | 13 | 100 | 6,665 |
| 1982 Oct. | 28 | 47 | 8 | 3 | 14 | 100 | 5,352 |
| *Great Britain, Ireland, Denmark* | | | | | | | |
| 1973 Sept. | 30 | 33 | 6 | 5 | 26 | 100 | 13,484 |
| 1975 May | 35 | 34 | 5 | 4 | 22 | 100 | 9,550 |
| 1975 Nov. | 31 | 38 | 5 | 4 | 22 | 100 | 9,150 |
| 1978 Oct. | 30 | 45 | 8 | 3 | 14 | 100 | 8,788 |
| 1979 Apr. | 30 | 45 | 6 | 4 | 15 | 100 | 8,976 |
| 1979 Oct. | 30 | 45 | 8 | 4 | 13 | 100 | 9,021 |
| 1980 Apr. | 27 | 46 | 9 | 4 | 14 | 100 | 8,882 |
| 1980 Oct. | 29 | 43 | 9 | 4 | 15 | 100 | 9,001 |
| 1981 Apr. | 26 | 43 | 10 | 6 | 15 | 100 | 9,878 |
| 1981 Oct. | 31 | 43 | 9 | 4 | 13 | 100 | 9,911 |
| 1982 Apr. | 26 | 45 | 10 | 5 | 14 | 100 | 11,676 |
| 1982 Oct. | 26 | 44 | 10 | 4 | 16 | 100 | 9,689 |

*Source:* Adapted from *Eurobarometer*, no. 18, December 1982, table 8 (Appendix).

Figure 9.1  Attitudes towards the unification of Western Europe in individual EEC states

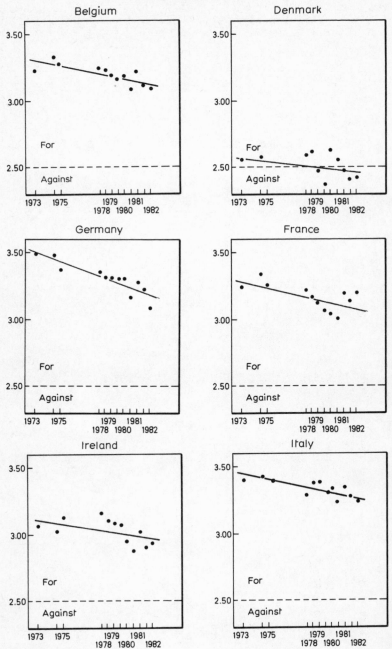

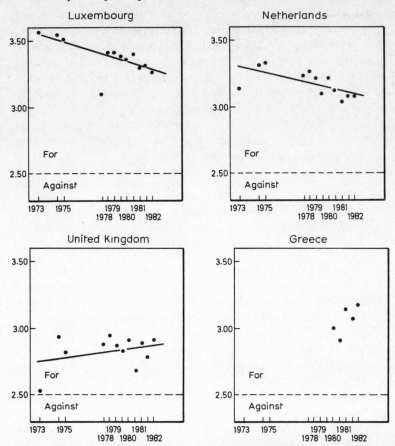

*Note*: The index is formed by dividing the percentage of the negative responses into those of the positive responses, but only 'very much for' and 'very much against' are considered.

*Source*: *Euro-Barometer*, no. 18, December 1982, graph 10.

Another reason may be the recognition that the realistic prospects for a united Europe – some kind of new fatherland – may have further and further diminished and, therefore, many West Germans are again seeking a more definitive national identity. We will return to this issue later in this chapter.

### Interdependence

It is not unreasonable to assume that the greater the awareness of regional interdependence among people residing in the various states of a sub-region, the greater is the incentive to seek unified policy-making mechanisms. Indeed, if the actual degree of interdependence is so high that no state in Western Europe is strong enough to solve on its own the manifold problems it faces, the rational solution would be increased solidarity in joint decision-making and the appropriate sub-regional institutions to achieve this task. To test then the awareness as well as the realization of interdependence, the Fall 1982 public opinion survey of the European Commission included the following questions:

How much effect do you think that political decisions made by other countries (in Western Europe) have on your life in (country) these days? A lot, a fair amount, very little, or none at all?

In the future, do you think that the effect of other countries' decisions on our lives will increase, decrease, or remain the same?

About 70 per cent of the respondents expressed awareness of the interdependence; a few more in Denmark and a smaller percentage in West Germany. Respondents in Luxembourg, Denmark, Britain and Ireland tended to think more that this situation will increase. The West Germans believed it would remain the same in the future, but overall, few think it will diminish. For whatever reason, one Greek in three did not answer the second question. Details of the data are found in table 9.2.

An interesting aspect of this table is the significance of nationality in the responses given to the above questions. They show a clear correlation between the number of people in particular states who consider their lives strongly influenced by decisions taken in states other than their own and those who believe that this interdependence will increase in the future. Indeed, this parallelism can be discerned also on an individual basis. Moreover, as can be seen in table 9.3, elites recognize both interdependence and the increase of inter-dependence between governmental decisions in the various Western European states more than the mass publics. But, in spite of this recognition of not only interdependence but most likely growing interdependence, the *Euro-Barometer* does not find any favourable evidence which would link these responses to a positive view of strengthening the EC institutions and of moving forward on the unification of Western Europe.[4] Thus, the two issues are kept apart in the minds of many Western Europeans and the awareness of sub-regional interdependence does not produce a strong stimulus for the

Table 9.2  Dependence on other states (%)

'How much effect do political decisions made by other countries have on life in your country?'

|  | A lot | A fair amount | Very little | Not at all | Don't know | Total | Index[2] |
|---|---|---|---|---|---|---|---|
| Belgium | 25 | 33 | 15 | 4 | 23 | 100 | 3.04 |
| Denmark | 37 | 46 | 8 | 1 | 8 | 100 | 3.29 |
| France | 26 | 44 | 14 | 5 | 11 | 100 | 3.04 |
| Germany | 12 | 50 | 26 | 2 | 10 | 100 | 2.78 |
| Greece | 29 | 35 | 10 | 4 | 22 | 100 | 3.13 |
| Ireland | 32 | 36 | 16 | 7 | 9 | 100 | 3.01 |
| Italy | 31 | 33 | 13 | 6 | 17 | 100 | 3.08 |
| Luxembourg | 34 | 42 | 15 | 4 | 4 | 100 | 3.11 |
| Netherlands | 22 | 51 | 16 | 3 | 8 | 100 | 2.99 |
| United Kingdom | 37 | 42 | 12 | 3 | 6 | 100 | 3.20 |
| EC[1] | 26 | 43 | 16 | 4 | 11 | 100 | 3.03 |

'The effect on our lives of decisions in other countries will:'

|  | Increase | Remain the same | Decrease | Don't know | Total | Index[3] |
|---|---|---|---|---|---|---|
| Belgium | 34 | 34 | 8 | 24 | 100 | 3.02 |
| Denmark | 55 | 26 | 8 | 11 | 100 | 3.31 |
| France | 36 | 46 | 4 | 14 | 100 | 3.05 |
| Germany | 27 | 50 | 12 | 11 | 100 | 2.77 |
| Greece | 29 | 28 | 12 | 31 | 100 | 2.85 |
| Ireland | 52 | 29 | 5 | 14 | 100 | 3.32 |
| Italy | 40 | 28 | 8 | 24 | 100 | 3.13 |
| Luxembourg | 61 | 32 | 3 | 4 | 100 | 3.40 |
| Netherlands | 48 | 39 | 4 | 9 | 100 | 3.23 |
| United Kingdom | 53 | 33 | 6 | 8 | 100 | 3.28 |
| EC[1] | 39 | 39 | 7 | 15 | 100 | 3.06 |

*Notes*: [1] Weighted average.
[2] 'A lot' = 4, 'Not at all' = 1; 'Don't knows' excluded.
[3] 'Increase' = 4, 'Remain the same' = 2.5, 'Decrease' = 1; 'Don't knows' excluded.
*Source*: *Eurobarometer*, no. 18, December 1982, table 18.

construction of a regional 'Europe'. Perhaps the questions were not sufficiently concrete and too long-term oriented to elicit not only cognitive, but also strong affective responses.

## Benefits and Costs

In order to tap the more utilitarian views of respondents in the EC states, the Commission included in the questionnaires over the last

Table 9.3 Dependence on other states by leadership rating
(Community as a whole, %)

'How much effect do political decisions made by other countries have on life in this country?'

| | Leadership rating | | | | |
|---|---|---|---|---|---|
| | Non-opinion (−−) | leaders (−) | Opinion (+) | leaders (++) | Percentage of respondents |
| A lot | 18 | 23 | 31 | 43 | 26 |
| A fair amount | 34 | 45 | 47 | 41 | 43 |
| Very little | 16 | 19 | 15 | 11 | 16 |
| Not at all | 7 | 3 | 2 | 3 | 4 |
| Don't know | 25 | 10 | 5 | 2 | 11 |
| Total | 100 | 100 | 100 | 100 | 100 |
| Index | 2.84 | 2.98 | 3.11 | 3.27 | 3.03 |

This dependence will:

| | | | | | |
|---|---|---|---|---|---|
| Increase | 26 | 37 | 47 | 58 | 39 |
| Remain the same | 39 | 41 | 38 | 31 | 39 |
| Decrease | 6 | 9 | 7 | 6 | 7 |
| Don't know | 29 | 13 | 8 | 5 | 15 |
| Total | 100 | 100 | 100 | 100 | 100 |
| Index | 2.92 | 2.97 | 3.15 | 3.32 | 3.06 |
| **Base** | 2414 | 3384 | 2833 | 1058 | 9689 |

*Source: Eurobarometer*, no. 18, December 1982, table 19.

ten years such items as EC membership benefits for the respondents' states, the desirability of a joint battle against unemployment, the acceptance of personal sacrifices for the sake of greater solidarity in the EC, and the achievement of better understanding between the member-states.

Perhaps it was a reflection of the poor economic conditions, but while in 1978 30 per cent perceived benefits less for their own state than for other EC states, the percentage rose to 40 per cent in 1982. In 1978 only four states had positive responses (Belgium, Luxembourg, Ireland and Italy); in 1982 negative responses dominated in all member-states with three out of four British respondents saying that their state had benefited less than the others. See table 9.4 for details. But, in spite of the envy implied in these data, majorities on average in the EC as a whole have indicated over a period of ten years that they considered EC membership 'a good thing'. Only in Britain did a plurality perceive membership 'a bad thing' from 1973 to 1982 while

Table 9.4 Perceptions of comparative benefits for own and other Community states

| | October–November 1978 | | | | | October 1982 | | | | |
| | More | Less | Neither[1] | Don't know | Total | More | Less | Niether[1] | Don't know | Total |
|---|---|---|---|---|---|---|---|---|---|---|
| Belgium | 20 | 13 | 32 | 35 | 100 | 10 | 20 | 36 | 34 | 100 |
| Denmark | 17 | 26 | 34 | 23 | 100 | 19 | 24 | 38 | 19 | 100 |
| France | 13 | 22 | 30 | 35 | 100 | 13 | 26 | 35 | 26 | 100 |
| Germany | 20 | 31 | 32 | 17 | 100 | 18 | 45 | 17 | 20 | 100 |
| Greece | — | — | — | — | — | 15 | 40 | 23 | 22 | 100 |
| Ireland | 39 | 28 | 14 | 19 | 100 | 31 | 40 | 14 | 15 | 100 |
| Italy | 27 | 21 | 24 | 28 | 100 | 18 | 26 | 28 | 28 | 100 |
| Luxembourg | 18 | 16 | 51 | 15 | 100 | 22 | 33 | 32 | 26 | 100 |
| Netherlands | 15 | 24 | 33 | 28 | 100 | 20 | 22 | 32 | 26 | 100 |
| United Kingdom | 14 | 49 | 17 | 20 | 100 | 5 | 75 | 9 | 11 | 100 |
| EC[2] | 19 | 30 | 26 | 25 | 100 | 15 | 40 | 23 | 22 | 100 |

*Notes:* [1] Volunteered.
[2] Weighted average.
*Source: Eurobarometer*, no. 18, December 1982, table 23.

in Denmark such a plurality showed up only in April 1981 and during the remaining years the responses, including a neutral option, were pretty evenly distributed. There appears to be a very slight downward trend on this issue in most EC states, especially in Britain, but in Luxembourg and the Netherlands the trend is upward. Opinion leaders are slightly more positive than the general public.[5]

For the battle against unemployment, a majority of respondents in the EC (54 per cent) would prefer joint action. As for the individual member-states, all show majorities except Britain, Ireland and Luxembourg where the results are virtual ties. No significant differences exist between the responses of elites and the public. Support of joint action against unemployment correlates positively with support for the unification of Western Europe; indeed, the more individuals favour joint action, the greater their zeal for unification. This holds true for all ten member-states.

Willingness to sacrifice, however, to aid another EC member-state experiencing economic difficulties by paying a few more taxes, for example, is another matter. Although in slightly different form, this question was included in the surveys in 1978, 1981 and 1982. The results are found in table 9.5.

Perhaps reflecting human nature, the table shows that negative responses are in the majority, especially in 1982 when only the majority of Italians were prepared for the sacrifices suggested. Indeed, only Italy supported sacrifices during all three surveys, and the Netherlands did so in 1978 and 1981. In terms of a trend, it appears that the responses in support of the principle of solidarity tend to be on the decline.

If, then, support for sacrifices to help another EC state is in the minority, have the existing interdependency and co-operation among the EC member-states that are part of the EC system increased the general understanding between the EC states during the preceding twelve months? This question has been included in the questionnaire since 1977 and was answered during that year and in 1978 generally in a positive manner, with the exception of Denmark. However, in both 1981 and 1982 surveys, the assessment has been negative in all member-states except Ireland and Greece, perhaps because it is the most recent EC member. Opinion leaders are more positive in their responses than the general public and the percentage of 'don't knows' is high, ranging from 14 to 22 per cent during the years this question was asked. Not surprisingly, these responses correlate with the views of the respondents on the unification of

Table 9.5 Willingness to make sacrifices to help another state (%)

| | October–November 1978 | | | | April 1981 | | | | October 1982 | | | |
|---|---|---|---|---|---|---|---|---|---|---|---|---|
| | Yes | No | Don't know | Total | Yes | No | Don't know | Total | Yes | No | Don't know | Total |
| Belgium | 28 | 53 | 19 | 100 | 20 | 62 | 18 | 100 | 20 | 61 | 19 | 100 |
| Denmark | 42 | 40 | 18 | 100 | 42 | 46 | 12 | 100 | 30 | 48 | 22 | 100 |
| France | 37 | 52 | 11 | 100 | 28 | 58 | 14 | 100 | 31 | 59 | 10 | 100 |
| Germany | 26 | 47 | 27 | 100 | 28 | 47 | 25 | 100 | 30 | 48 | 22 | 100 |
| Greece | — | — | — | — | 57 | 37 | 7 | 100 | 40 | 48 | 12 | 100 |
| Ireland | 39 | 48 | 13 | 100 | 42 | 48 | 10 | 100 | 23 | 63 | 14 | 100 |
| Italy | 64 | 24 | 12 | 100 | 69 | 24 | 7 | 100 | 48 | 38 | 14 | 100 |
| Luxembourg | 34 | 47 | 19 | 100 | 54 | 36 | 16 | 100 | 37 | 57 | 6 | 100 |
| Netherlands | 60 | 28 | 12 | 100 | 48 | 36 | 16 | 100 | 41 | 47 | 12 | 100 |
| United Kingdom | 35 | 53 | 12 | 100 | 36 | 57 | 7 | 100 | 22 | 71 | 7 | 100 |
| EC[1] | 41 | 43 | 16 | 100 | 40 | 46 | 14 | 100 | 33 | 54 | 13 | 100 |

Note: [1] Weighted average.
Source: Eurobarometer, no. 18, December 1982, table 22.

Western Europe. Those favouring unification as a rule express the opinion that understanding has increased.[6]

## The European Parliament

As mentioned in a preceding chapter, the direct election of the European Parliament (EP), which began in 1979, offered hope to many adherents of European unification that the 'new' parliament would become the political motor for the political integration process. This did not quite happen and with the 1984 elections in the offing, it was considered important to test the populace as to its awareness of the activities of the EC. Obviously, to assure that the EP is a significant actor in the political arena of the combined EC member-states requires a high turn-out at the 1984 elections and this turn-out was likely to depend on how widespread this awareness is. For this reason, the following questions were included in the Fall 1982 survey:

Have you in recent times read or heard anything about the Assembly of the European Community, that is to say the European Parliament? If so, has what you read or heard given you a generally favourable or unfavourable impression of the European Parliament?

As can be seen from table 9.6, Community-wide 54 per cent of the respondents stated to have read or heard something about the EP, which is slightly more than in the Fall of 1978 (50 per cent). This is far less than at the time of the election in 1979 (65 per cent in April 1979)

Table 9.6  Public awareness of the European Parliament (%)

|  | 1977 April–May | 1978 Oct.–Nov. | 1979 April | 1979 October | 1982 October |
|---|---|---|---|---|---|
| Belgium | 46 | 49 | 65 | 45 | 56 |
| Denmark | 49 | 60 | 76 | 65 | 42 |
| France | 57 | 57 | 65 | 67 | 40 |
| Germany | 33 | 51 | 60 | 77 | 70 |
| Greece | — | — | — | — | 57 |
| Ireland | 47 | 48 | 73 | 67 | 60 |
| Italy | 52 | 49 | 77 | 66 | 52 |
| Luxembourg | 62 | 49 | 76 | 76 | 62 |
| Netherlands | 40 | 48 | 76 | 76 | 62 |
| United Kingdom | 58 | 44 | 55 | 55 | 50 |
| EC | 49 | 50 | 65 | 66 | 54 |

*Source: Eurobarometer*, no. 18, December 1982, table 26.

and therefore the degree of awareness of the public had to be strengthened if a good voter turn-out in June 1984 was to be expected.

It is interesting to note that awareness of the EP between the Fall of 1978 and 1982 had gone up substantially in West Germany, the Netherlands, Luxembourg and Ireland (12 to 19 per cent) and moderately in Belgium and Britain (6 to 7 per cent). It fell materially, however, in France and Denmark (17 to 18 per cent).

Equally noteworthy were the responses to the second part of the question, which can be gleaned from table 9.7. Opinions about the EP of those who have read or heard something (and can remember it) suggested more of a 'bad' impression (18 per cent) than a 'good' impression (15 per cent), but 21 per cent did not have any specific opinion or did not know. Looking at the results in the various member-states, we find that 'good' impressions are considerably more widespread than the 'bad' impressions, which predominate only in Italy and Greece. But, it is perhaps even more significant that in five states (Belgium, France, West Germany, Greece and Ireland) it is the 'neither good nor bad' impressions and the 'don't knows' which have plurality.

These figures did not augur well for the voter turn-out in the EP elections. Indeed, the result was lower than in 1979. Unfortunately, the election campaigns did not have a positive effect on turn-out. Viable links need to be established between constituents and EP members or candidates, even though this is admittedly a very difficult and perhaps impossible task. Obviously, if the campaign issues in future elections are able to deal with concrete pocketbook items, the percentage of voters going to the polls might well rise over those of 1979 and 1984.

## WESTERN EUROPEAN SECURITY PERCEPTIONS

### *West–West Relations*

For most citizens of the United States, NATO has been and continues to be the centrepiece of the common defence of Western Europe and the United States.[7] Many Western Europeans have a lower commitment to NATO; they often resent the power and influence of the United States in this organization and they frown about the near-monopoly of the United States in Alliance nuclear decision-making while, at the same time, being apprehensive about the certainty of

Table 9.7 Impressions of the European Parliament (%)

| | Per 100 respondents | | | Per 100 respondents having read or heard something | | | |
|---|---|---|---|---|---|---|---|
| | Good impression | Bad impression | No impression or don't know | Total having read or head something | Good impression | Bad impression | No impression or don't know |
| Belgium | 11 | 12 | 33 | 56 | 19 | 22 | 59 |
| Denmark | 11 | 17 | 14 | 42 | 26 | 40 | 34 |
| France | 11 | 10 | 19 | 40 | 27 | 25 | 48 |
| Germany | 17 | 20 | 33 | 70 | 24 | 29 | 47 |
| Greece | 23 | 7 | 27 | 57 | 40 | 13 | 47 |
| Ireland | 18 | 20 | 22 | 60 | 29 | 33 | 38 |
| Italy | 23 | 12 | 17 | 52 | 44 | 22 | 34 |
| Luxembourg | 14 | 26 | 22 | 62 | 23 | 42 | 35 |
| Netherlands | 12 | 28 | 26 | 66 | 17 | 42 | 41 |
| United Kingdom | 9 | 30 | 11 | 50 | 18 | 59 | 23 |
| EC[1] | 15 | 18 | 21 | 54 | 27 | 33 | 40 |

Note: [1] Weighted average.
Source: Eurobarometer, no. 18, December 1982, table 27.

American retaliation with strategic nuclear weapons in case of a Soviet attack on Europe. (This situation was discussed fully in the preceding chapter.) In fact, the confidence of Western Europeans in the ability of NATO to defend their sub-region is frayed, as can be seen by responses in Britain, France, West Germany, Italy and Belgium as shown in table 9.8.

Table 9.8  Confidence in NATO's ability to defend Western Europe against attack (%)

'In general, how much confidence do you have in the ability of NATO to defend Western Europe against attack?'

|  | United Kingdom | France | West Germany | Italy | Belgium |
|---|---|---|---|---|---|
| Very much | 12 | 5 | 16 | 16 | 7 |
| Fair | 44 | 34 | 45 | 33 | 36 |
| Not very much | 25 | 29 | 29 | 19 | 24 |
| Not at all | 10 | 9 | 6 | 9 | 9 |
| No opinion | 9 | 23 | 4 | 23 | 24 |

*Source*: *Newsweek* (international edition), 15 March 1982.

With large minorities in all fives states surveyed showing little confidence in NATO (from 35 per cent in Britain and West Germany to 28 per cent in Italy), it is not surprising that consideration is being given to other defence arrangements. They include the establishment within NATO of a unified Western European defence force under European command, but allied to the United States; the withdrawal of national military forces from NATO but remaining in the organization for policy consultation and logistical co-ordination; the creation of an independent Western European defence force under European command and *not* allied with the United States; or relying exclusively on national defence establishments without any alliance. The percentages of responses favouring one or the other arrangement or preferring accommodation with the Soviet Union are displayed in table 9.9. While there is a majority or substantial plurality in all four states surveyed which wish to continue the NATO Alliance, a unified Western European command is arousing considerable interest, either within NATO or completely independent from the United States. This desire for such a Western European command has also been expressed and debated in the European Parliament and involvement in security affairs has been suggested

Table 9.9  Preferred policies for protection (%)

'What are the best arrangements for protection from outside attack?'

| | United Kingdom | West Germany | Belgium | Denmark |
|---|---|---|---|---|
| Continue in the NATO alliance among the countries of Western Europe and the United States and Canada | 37 | 53 | 25 | 49 |
| Establish within NATO a unified West European defence force under European command but allied to the United States | 20 | 22 | 18 | 10 |
| Withdraw our military forces from NATO, but otherwise remain in NATO for things such as policy consultation | 5 | 7 | 8 | 4 |
| Establish an independent West European defence force under European command, but not allied to the United States | 10 | 8 | 7 | 5 |
| Rely on our own nation's defence forces without belonging to any military alliance | 11 | 2 | 5 | 8 |
| Reduce our emphasis on military defence and rely on greater accommodation with Russia | 5 | 4 | 2 | 4 |
| Don't know | 12 | 4 | 35 | 20 |

*Source*: Elizabeth Hamm Hastings and Philip K. Hastings, eds., *Index to International Public Opinion, 1981–1982*, p. 609.

for the EC. If the EC were to play a significant role in such an endeavour, it could mean a return visit to the efforts in the 1950s to establish integrated Western European armed forces *à la* EDC venture. This may well raise the question whether such a force should be equipped with nuclear weapons or be denuclearized, a highly complex and politically sensitive issue.[8]

It is not only the nature of the defensive arrangements which concern the Western Europeans, but also the kind of co-ordinated or joint foreign policy the Western European states should pursue.

If a truly common Atlantic foreign policy could be formed across most issues facing the NATO member-states, the problem of policy coordination would be solved. However, in spite of a comprehensive mechanism in place to co-ordinate the foreign policies of the member governments of the EC, the so-called European Political Co-operation (EPC) scheme, the results have not been overwhelming as we discussed earlier. Still, some successes have been recorded; for example, the common policies developed with respect to the negotiations leading to the signing of the CSCE Final Act in Helsinki and policy towards the Israeli-Arab conflict.

Interestingly, as table 9.10 shows, the publics in most major NATO states do not favour a common Atlantic foreign policy. West Germany is the exception. The British prefer an independent foreign policy, while the remainder opt for a common EC policy. It should be noted that the EC constituent treaties also provide selected instruments for foreign economic policies which, however, have not always been fully used by the EC member-states.[9]

Part of the reluctance to seek a common Atlantic foreign policy may stem from perceptions that the United States does not always deal wisely with world problems. This is evident from the responses shown in table 9.11. With the exception of West Germany and Belgium, confidence in American policy efficacy is on the lower end of the continuum.

The doubts expressed by many Western Europeans about the wisdom of American foreign policy actions carry over into the nuclear weapons field. When asked about the effect of the deployment of American intermediate range nuclear weapons (Pershing II and cruise missiles) in Europe, a majority of respondents in Britain and substantial pluralities in other Western European states felt that deployment would increase the chances of a Soviet attack, but others believed that it would provide greater protection. Details are found in table 9.12. Similar disparities of opinions seem to exist with respect to the US troops stationed in Europe. As can be seen from the same table, only many West Germans appear to think that these troops do provide greater protection, which is not astonishing since the bulk of these forces are stationed in West Germany.

We mentioned earlier the doubt Western Europeans have about the American resolve to retaliate massively with nuclear weapons in the event of a Soviet attack on Europe because it would expose cities in North America to nuclear holocausts, and some of the preceding polls attempted to explore the degree of confidence which the Western Europeans have in NATO and American foreign policy capabilities. But what about the confidence of Europeans in the support which the Western European allies would furnish the

Table 9.10 Preferred policy arrangement by state (%)

'Which of the following statements comes closest to your views of how (survey country) should conduct its foreign policy?'

| | Belgium | West Germany | France | Italy | United Kingdom | Netherlands | Weighted average[1] |
|---|---|---|---|---|---|---|---|
| Make its own foreign policy decisions independent of other nations | 16 | 12 | 27 | 16 | 35 | 22 | 22 |
| Join with the other EC member-states to develop a common European Community foreign policy toward the rest of the world | 33 | 25 | 38 | 40 | 20 | 33 | 30 |
| Join with the other EC member-states and with the United States to develop a common Atlantic foreign policy | 19 | 37 | 11 | 25 | 28 | 25 | 25 |
| Join with the other EC member-states and with Eastern Europe and the Soviet Union to develop an all-European policy | 5 | 10 | 8 | 6 | 6 | 8 | 8 |
| Don't know | 26 | 16 | 16 | 13 | 11 | 12 | 15 |
| Total | 100 | 100 | 100 | 100 | 100 | 100 | 100 |

Note: [1] Six-state average weighted to reflect population size.
Source: USICA, Research Memorandum, 13 November 1980, table 3.

Table 9.11  Confidence in US foreign policy (%)

'In general, how much confidence do you have in the United States to deal wisely with world problems – a great deal, a fair amount, not very much, or none at all?'

|  | United Kingdom | France | West Germany | Belgium | Switzerland | Denmark |
|---|---|---|---|---|---|---|
| A great deal | 6 | 4 | 16 | 7 | 4 | 5 |
| A fair amount | 29 | 36 | 41 | 38 | 29 | 33 |
| Not very much | 39 | 35 | 33 | 20 | 51 | 30 |
| None at all | 21 | 12 | 7 | 10 | 12 | 18 |
| Don't know | 5 | 13 | 3 | 25 | 4 | 14 |

*Source*: Elizabeth Hamm Hastings and Philip K. Hastings, eds., *Index to International Public Opinion 1981–1982*, pp. 608–9.

Table 9.12  Effects of nuclear missile deployment and the stationing of American troops in Europe (%)

'Do you think that having American nuclear missiles stationed in (name country) increases the chance of an attack on this country, provides greater protection against such an attack, or has no effect?'

|  | United Kingdom | France | West Germany | Belgium | Denmark |
|---|---|---|---|---|---|
| Increases chance of an attack | 42 | 24 | 27 | 24 | 21 |
| Provides greater protection | 29 | 31 | 41 | 25 | 29 |
| No effect | 24 | 23 | 28 | 21 | 24 |
| Don't know | 5 | 22 | 4 | 30 | 26 |

'Do you think that having American troops stationed in (name country) increases the chances of an attack on this country, provides greater protection against such an attack, or has no effect?'

|  | United Kingdom | West Germany | Belgium | Denmark |
|---|---|---|---|---|
| Increases chances of an attack | 25 | 15 | 22 | 16 |
| Provides greater protection | 24 | 48 | 25 | 33 |
| No effect | 46 | 33 | 27 | 26 |
| Don't know | 5 | 4 | 26 | 25 |

*Source*: Elizabeth Hamm Hastings and Philip K. Hastings, eds., *Index to International Public Opinion, 1981–1982*, pp. 610–11.

United States in its policies *vis-à-vis* the Soviet Union? Table 9.13 paints a somewhat dismal picture, with a majority of 2,748 European respondents having little or no confidence at all that such support is or would be forthcoming.

These responses may well reflect a widespread desire in Western Europe to focus on arms control rather than to strengthen NATO. This orientation has been especially strong in Italy (60 vs 22 per cent) and in West Germany (50 vs 18 per cent), while it is less pronounced in France (35 vs 21 per cent) and in Britain (40 vs 31 per cent).[10] It may be bolstered by strong Western European concern about the Reagan Administration military build-up and 'US aggressive policies towards the USSR' that became evident during extensive public opinion surveys conducted by the *International Herald-Tribune* and the Atlantic Institute in Paris. This survey also indicated that 'inadequate defence' was the *least* important source of concern in the seven Western European states surveyed – Britain, France, Italy, the Netherlands, Norway, Spain and West Germany.[11]

Finally, both in political and security terms, it is interesting to note that the close relationship between the two core states of Western Europe, France and West Germany, which was constructed initially by President Charles de Gaulle and Chancellor Konrad Adenauer, has remained firm through a number of French presidents and West German chancellors. Indeed, public opinion polls taken in the Spring of 1983 show that the majority of Frenchmen consider the Germans as their best friends, and for the Germans, their neighbours to the west are perceived as the second-best friends, after the Americans. A strong majority (69–70 per cent) of both French respondents (1,000 interviews) and German interviewees (1,237) favour a political union of the two states and a common defence (63

Table 9.13  Confidence in Western Europe's support for the
United States (%)

'How much confidence do you have in general that our allies in Western Europe support the USA in its policies against the Soviet Union?'

| | | |
|---|---|---|
| Very much | 6 | |
| Fairly much | 34 | |
| Not very much | 37 | 52 |
| Not at all | 15 | |
| No opinion | 8 | |

*Source: Newsweek* (international edition), 15 March 1982.

per cent in France and 61 per cent in West Germany), with both states united in case of a Soviet attack. As for moving the EC towards political integration, both the French and West German respondents regarded their two states as the most ardent champions of a united Europe.[12] The rather startling results of this part of the survey are shown in table 9.14.

Table 9.14 The two true Europeans (%)

'Within the European Community, which do you consider the two countries most attached to European unification?'

|  | Results in France[1] | Results in West Germany[1] |
| --- | --- | --- |
| Great Britain | 7 | 9 |
| France | 53 | 36 |
| Denmark | 2 | 4 |
| West Germany | 56 | 79 |
| Italy | 5 | 5 |
| Belgium | 10 | 7 |
| Luxembourg | 6 | 9 |
| Ireland | 1 | 0 |
| The Netherlands | 5 | 19 |
| No opinion | 24 | 10 |

*Note*: [1] More than one response was allowed and therefore totals exceed 100.
*Source*: *Figaro Magazine*, 9 July 1983, p. 47.

What the long-range implications of such a French–West German development may be for integration or security is difficult to judge at this time, but there is no doubt that some kind of intra-Western European interest in these issue areas exists.

### West–East Relations

Since the 1960s the nature of the relationship between Western and Eastern Europe has been a function of the degree with which the policy of détente has been pursued. In turn, depending on the state of détente, Western European economic intercourse with the East has flourished or languished. An important stimulus for détente has been and remains the magnitude of the threat perception of a Soviet attack on Western Europe and, as can be seen in table 9.15, a vast majority of respondents in Britain, West Germany, Belgium, Switzerland and Denmark regard such a threat as 'not so likely' or 'not at all likely'. In spite of the low threat perception, this table also shows

Table 9.15  Perceptions of the Soviet threat to attack Western Europe (%)

'How likely do you think it is that Russia will attack Western Europe within the next five years – very likely, fairly likely, not so likely, or not at all likely?'

|  | Great Britain | West Germany | Belgium | Switzerland | Denmark |
|---|---|---|---|---|---|
| Very likely | 6 | 4 | 4 | 4 | 2 |
| Fairly likely | 15 | 11 | 19 | 21 | 13 |
| Not so likely | 24 | 57 | 28 | 40 | 42 |
| Not at all likely | 48 | 24 | 25 | 31 | 25 |
| Don't know | 7 | 4 | 24 | 4 | 18 |

'What about Russia? Do you have a very favourable, somewhat favourable, somewhat unfavourable, or very unfavourable opinion of Russia?'

|  | Great Britain | France | West Germany | Belgium | Switzerland | Denmark |
|---|---|---|---|---|---|---|
| Very favourable | 2 | 2 | 1 | 1 | 1 | 1 |
| Somewhat favourable | 12 | 11 | 19 | 10 | 12 | 9 |
| Somewhat unfavourable | 32 | 41 | 54 | 30 | 48 | 40 |
| Very unfavourable | 42 | 32 | 23 | 31 | 35 | 34 |
| Don't know | 12 | 14 | 3 | 28 | 4 | 16 |

'How much influence do you think Russia has on what is going on in Poland at the present time – a great deal, a fair amount, not very much, or none at all?'

|  | Great Britain | West Germany | Belgium | Switzerland |
|---|---|---|---|---|
| A great deal | 67 | 48 | 47 | 51 |
| A fair amount | 23 | 37 | 24 | 36 |
| Not very much | 4 | 10 | 5 | 7 |
| None at all | 1 | 2 | 3 | 1 |
| Don't know | 5 | 3 | 21 | 5 |

*Source*: Elizabeth Hamm Hastings and Philip K. Hastings, eds., *Index to International Public Opinion 1981–1982*. pp. 608, 610, 611.

that most Western Europeans have a generally unfavourable opinion of the Soviet Union – most likely made even worse since this poll was taken (1982) by the shooting down of a South Korean civilian airliner on 1 September 1983 – and that they blame the Soviet Union for much of the suffering to which the Polish population has been exposed through its own repressive government.

Another somewhat puzzling paradox is that, despite the low Soviet threat perception, a survey conducted in Britain, West Germany, France and Italy regarding the goals of Soviet foreign policy suggests that a strong majority considers 'expansion' one of the main Soviet objectives (between 77 and 84 per cent). In addition, sizeable minorities believe that Soviet foreign policy is motivated by ideological drives towards world domination and the overthrow of capitalism as well as by nationalistic drives to expand borders and to enlarge its sphere of influence. Defensive motives are also seen by many as determining Soviet foreign policy goals: the empire must be consolidated and the allies defended. Few regard détente and arms control to be significant objectives. Details are found in table 9.16.

What we see, then, based on the data presented so far, are perceptions in which the recognition of hard facts competes with hopes based on past Soviet behaviour with respect to Western Europe. There has been no military aggression and one can think of various reasons which would induce the Soviet Union *not* to engage in military action. There is, of course, the ever-present threat of political pressure, but again so far this has not been utilized. In addition, deep hope continues to burn in the chests of Western Europeans (as well as Americans) that conditions in Eastern Europe will change, the Soviet Union will be forced or find it advantageous

Table 9.16  Perceptions of Soviet foreign policy goals (%)

'What would you say are the main goals of Soviet foreign policy?'

|  | Great Britain | West Germany | France | Italy |
|---|---|---|---|---|
| Expansion | 77 | 84 | 75 | 77 |
| Ideological answers implying world domination, global hegemony, to hasten decline of capitalism, etc. | 49 | 36 | 33 | 33 |
| Nationalistic answers: expand borders, gain territory, enlarge sphere of influence, etc. | 41 | 54 | 33 | 52 |
| Maintain or consolidate empire: defend itself and its allies | 59 | 57 | 33 | 29 |
| Détente, arms control, avoid arms race | 3 | 4 | 6 | 1 |

*Note*: More than one response was allowed and therefore totals exceed 100.
*Source*: Kane, Parsons & Associates, Inc., 'A Study of Leadership Attitudes in Western Europe and Japan Regarding Key Foreign and Defense Issues,' New York, June 1981.

to relax its controls somewhat, and will adopt a more accommoda-
tive stance in its relations with the West. These may all be reasons to
explain why Western Europeans seem to tend towards the espousal
of neutralism, as can be discovered in table 9.17. More will be said
about this in chapter 10.

Table 9.17  Growing Neutralism (%)

'Some have said that Western Europe would be safer if it moved toward neutralism in
the East–West conflict. Others argue that such a move would be dangerous. Would
you, yourself, favour or oppose a move toward neutralism in Western Europe?'

|                | Favour | Oppose |
|----------------|--------|--------|
| West Germany   | 57     | 43     |
| Netherlands    | 53     | 32     |
| Great Britain  | 45     | 42     |
| France         | 43     | 41     |

*Source*: William Schneider, 'Elite and Public Opinion: The Alliance's New Fissure',
*Public Opinion*, February/March 1983, p. 6.

### EASTERN EUROPEAN PERCEPTIONS

Public opinion surveys as conducted in the West of course do not
exist in Eastern Europe. Yet, data on opinions are being collected
anonymously for Radio Free Europe Audience and Opinion
Research (RFEAOR) by Western European polling organizations from
Eastern Europeans visiting the West. Numerous Poles, Hungarians,
Czechs and Slovaks have been interviewed and the mix of travellers,
large in numbers, consists of blue-collar workers as well as managers
and professionals. Radio Free Europe is not identified as the sponsor
of any interviews and respondent anonymity is strictly observed.
Because of the proximity of Poland, Hungary and Czechoslovakia
to the West, people from these states have become the focus of
survey attention. They are 'historic' states, having existed prior to
World War II. East Germany is equally close to the West, but
because of the uncertainties and various implications of the German
– German relationship, West Germans have been excluded from
systematic surveys.

    If we try to determine the prospects for political integration in
Eastern Europe, one indicator may be the preferences which respondents have for governmental systems. In 1975 and 1976[13] respondents were asked about their personal assessment of the 'basic idea of

Table 9.18  Preferences for governmental systems (%)

'Would you say that the basic idea of Communism is good, a mixture of good and bad, or bad?'

|  | Czechoslovakia | Hungary | Poland |
|---|---|---|---|
| Good | 28 | 26 | 17 |
| Mixture of good and bad | 38 | 44 | 38 |
| Bad | 34 | 29 | 42 |
| No answer | 4 | 1 | 3 |

'Would you say there is more good or bad in this mixture?'

|  | Czechoslovakia | Hungary | Poland |
|---|---|---|---|
| More good than bad | 4 | 7 | 4 |
| Good and bad balanced | 17 | 15 | 17 |
| More bad than good | 17 | 22 | 17 |

'Here is a list with different kinds of systems of government practices on it – which is the one you consider best?'

|  | Czechoslovakia | Hungary | Poland |
|---|---|---|---|
| As in Sweden | 22 | 16 | 28 |
| As in Austria | 22 | 23 | 12 |
| As before the war (own country) | 20 | 8 | 13 |
| As in the USA | 13 | 16 | 24 |
| As in Yugoslavia | 8 | 14 | 6 |
| As Marx describes it | 4 | 8 | 3 |
| As exists now (own country) | 3 | 12 | 7 |
| Don't know | 8 | 3 | 7 |

Source: *World Opinion Update*, vol. 1, no. 1, September 1977, p. 6.

Communism'. As can be seen from table 9.18, the responses were quite negative, even after an additional probing question was added. A third question was to elicit their actual preference in government and the table suggests that the highest preference is a democratic-socialist form of government as found in Austria and Sweden, followed by a more classical democracy such as the United States.

Considering that any progress in Eastern European sub-regional integration must include the Soviet Union, it is interesting to see which image the Russians project to some of the Eastern European nationalities. Table 9.19 provides data as to the different characteristics by which not only the Russians' image is measured, but also

Table 9.19 East European images of Americans and Russians
(% selecting given characteristic)

| Characteristic | Poles | | Hungarians | | Czechs/Slovaks | |
|---|---|---|---|---|---|---|
| | USA | USSR | USA | USSR | USA | USSR |
| Hard-working | 64 | 52 | 53 | 23 | 59 | 44 |
| Intelligent | 66 | 37 | 51 | 13 | 68 | 30 |
| Practical | 63 | 27 | 71 | 26 | 74 | 19 |
| Brave | 46 | 56 | 29 | 27 | 36 | 63 |
| Peace-loving | 61 | 41 | 41 | 28 | 58 | 47 |
| Generous | 60 | 29 | 63 | 8 | 66 | 30 |
| Advanced | 76 | 22 | 52 | 17 | 72 | 32 |
| Backward | 5 | 53 | 1 | 49 | 1 | 49 |
| Conceited | 42 | 59 | 32 | 44 | — | — |
| Domineering | 21 | 59 | 11 | 58 | 22 | 39 |
| Cruel | 9 | 46 | 6 | 49 | 3 | 32 |

*Source*: RFEAOR, 1969, 1970.

that of the Americans. Clearly, the Russians show up worse than the Americans, who score higher on most positive features (except bravery) while the Russians score high on such negative characteristics as backwardness, conceit and domineering behaviour. Although this survey stems from the period of 1965–9, it remains valid, especially when taking into account the 1968 events in Czechoslovakia and the happenings in Poland since 1980. These data offer no encouragement for progress in sub-regional integration.

Finally, some survey data have been developed on desires and projections regarding the course of East–West relations that may have a bearing on the overall European regional integration process and the overcoming of the gap between Eastern and Western Europe. Those data are derived from 1970, but at least the desires may not have changed much. The responses on projections and predictions are broken down by respondents in general and those below the age of twenty-five. Only Poles and Hungarians were interviewed and the results can be found in table 9.20.

Both Poles and Hungarians have as their highest goal the achievement of genuine rapprochement between East and West, and a plurality in both states consider it likely, with the young more optimistic than the older generation. Apart from that development, they wish and foresee greater Western influence, again with the younger respondents somewhat more optimistic. Growing crises are anticipated by people in both states, and the young are less pessimistic. East–West war is really not expected and has not

Table 9.20  Desires and predictions on East–West relations (%)

| Development | Poles Desire | Poles Likely Overall | Poles Likely −25 | Hungarians Desire | Hungarians Likely Overall | Hungarians Likely −25 |
|---|---|---|---|---|---|---|
| Genuine rapprochement | 65 | 36 | 40 | 74 | 31 | 45 |
| Greater Western influence | 31 | 28 | 29 | 24 | 18 | 22 |
| Greater Eastern influence | 2 | 10 | 12 | 2 | 16 | 12 |
| Growing crises | 0 | 21 | 15 | 0 | 31 | 19 |
| East–West war | —[1] | 2 | 1 | 0 | 3 | 0 |

*Note*: [1] Less than 0.5%.
*Source*: RFEAOR, 1971, 1972.

| Bilateral treaties between . . . and: | USSR | Poland | Czecho-slovakia | Hungary | Bulgaria | Soviet Occupied Zone of Germany |
|---|---|---|---|---|---|---|
| Poland | (1945) 1965 | — | | | | |
| Czechoslovakia | (1943) 1963/70 | (1947) 1967 | — | | | |
| Hungary | (1948) 1967 | (1948) 1968 | (1949) 1968 | — | | |
| Bulgaria | (1948) 1967 | (1948) 1967 | (1948) 1967 | (1948) 1969[1] | — | |
| GDR | 1964 | (1950) 1967[1] | (1950) 1967[1] | (1950) 1967[1] | (1950) 1967[1] | — |
| Romania | (1948) 1970 | (1949) | (1948) 1968 | (1948) | (1948) | 1950[1] |

*Note*: [1] Cultural, technical, financial, economic and/or agricultural agreements.

occurred, but the crises have occurred and with increasing recurrence. Moreover, the optimism in Eastern Europe which was generated when the Helsinki Final Act of the European Conference on Security and Cooperation was signed nearly vanished after the Belgrade Review Conference concluded in 1978. A survey of 6,000 visitors to West Germany from Poland, Hungary, East Germany and Romania revealed that only 12 per cent of the Poles and 20 per cent of the Romanians believed that the Belgrade meeting would improve their situations. The remainder were pessimistic about the outlook.[14] Obviously, an effective rapprochement between East and West is not viewed as 'around the corner'.

NOTES

1 Joseph S. Nye, 'Comparative Integration: Concept and Measurement', *International Organization* 22 (4) (1968): 855–80, esp. pp. 874–7.
2 Commission of the European Communities, *Euro-Barometer* (No. 18, December 1982), p. 56.
3 Werner, J. Feld, *West Germany and the European Community* (New York: Praeger, 1981), pp. 109–22.
4 *Euro-Barometer* (No. 18, December 1982), p. 51.
5 Ibid., pp. 76–82.
6 Ibid., pp. 73–5, table 9 in Appendix.
7 Werner J. Feld and John K. Wildgen, *NATO and the Atlantic Defense* (New York: Praeger, 1982), ch. 4.
8 In this respect, see the cogent comments by Simon Serfaty in *Fading Partnership* (New York: Praeger, 1979), pp. 36–42.
9 Werner J. Feld, *The European Community in World Affairs* (Sherman Oaks, California: Alfred Publishing, 1976), chapter 2.
10 These are 1981 figures and come from Kenneth Adler and Douglas Worman, 'Is NATO in Trouble?' *Public Opinion* (August/September 1981).
11 *International Herald Tribune*, 10 October 1982.
12 *Figaro Magazine* (9 July 1983).
13 Attitudes of people in Eastern Europe change slowly and therefore data have a much more enduring value than in the West.
14 *L'Express*, 12 December 1977.

# IO

# Whither Europe?

*The formation of the national State is therefore a stage in history and nationality has become something given in the European reality which any proposal for the reorganization of Europe has to take into account.*[1]

## DIFFERING CONCEPTIONS OF NATIONALISM

As we pointed out in the beginning of this book, the evolution of the nation-state in Western Europe was quite different from the evolution that occurred in Central and Eastern Europe. The intriguing question which is with us today is whether the cognitive and emotional differences created by nationalisms in the Western and in the Eastern European states can be overcome sufficiently to produce a measure of sub-regional and eventual regional political unity in Europe. In theoretical terms, can system transformation be achieved? The enforced dependence of the Eastern European states on the Soviet Union, and the dilemma as to whether the East and West Germans should be reunited in a unitary, loosely federal, or confederal relationship, if at all, are bound to keep the international politics of Europe volatile.[2] What, then, is the prospect for European unity and stability that is presented by possible multinational arrangements and the continued implementation of existing multinational obligations? How is the conception of state sovereignty being altered in practice (if not in theory)?

Interdependencies created purposely or by the satisfaction of social, economic and military needs have been the main sources of the change. For example, even though West Germany has acceded to a 'territorial' *status quo* in regard to East Germany, it has done so only by affirming that the 'political' *status quo* is not frozen. The so-called 'humanitarian' provisions of the Helsinki Accords provided for this. In other words, in our judgment the movement of people, and the degree and nature of political and economic contact of East and West Germany, and Eastern and Western Europe, will probably continue and, selectively at least, expand. It also seems apparent, however, that all the states of Europe will seek to resist as much as possible outside interference or obligations unless they might be helpful to their national interests. In Western Europe, the French resentment over the American economic presence in Europe can be weighed against the French desire for greater American investment in France. Likewise, the British desire to partake of the advantages afforded by the EC can be weighed against the British desire to renegotiate the terms of the Common Agricultural Policy to which Britain and West Germany have contributed more than they have received.[3]

In Eastern Europe, the Romanians' desire to pursue an independent trade policy *vis-à-vis* the Soviet Union can be balanced against the Romanians' desire to continue a governmental system in consonance with that of the Soviet Union, even if it should result in a lessening of Western enthusiasm to build up the Romanian economy. Poland, more than any other Eastern European state, is caught in a duality which requires political loyalty to the Soviet Union partly as a reassurance against a resurgent Germany, while at the same time the Poles would like to become more 'European' in their economic and trade patterns, and their cultural life.

The Nordic states, even while drawing increasingly closer together into sub-regional arrangements, such as the 'Nordek' customs union, cannot break away completely from their respective national aspirations – Denmark's and Norway's desire to retain a NATO connection out of an earlier fear of the Germans as well as a continuing fear of the Russians; Sweden's desire to behave as a neutral in the context of the Soviet–American rivalry; and Finland's desire to remain politically reliable to the Soviet Union even while establishing economic and trade ties with the West, including the EC.

If any criticism can be made of American policy towards Western Europe in the post-World War II period, it might be that the United States has had a too-mechanistic attitude towards how Western Europe should be organized in order to attain the goal of Western European political union. Given its previous history, since the end of World War II Western Europe has shown a surprising ability to organize functionally. What remains questionable is the extent to which such multinational functional arrangements will result in lasting political achievements that can contribute to political stability. If not, then we must ask ourselves if perhaps there have been set into motion international organizational interactions which are becoming ends in themselves rather than contributing to larger, more multinational or even supranational goals. Hence sub-systemic transformation towards a new unit is likely to remain a distant vista.

The United States has recently been criticized for claiming that NATO is its own justification for existence. If the critics are correct, the United States might be placed in the position of supporting a military coalition whose sense of cohesiveness could become more apparent than real. On the other hand, as one observer commented only half in jest, what would the foreign policies of most of the NATO member-states be if it were not for NATO?[4]

The frequent use of the word 'organized' by the United States in explaining its long-term political aspirations for the Western Europeans implies a condition which has not really been capable of realization. Western Europe has not been a unit which can be 'organized' – only the special conditions that existed immediately after World War II conveyed the contrary impression. As soon as the United States stirred up longstanding European nationalistic tensions, which first occurred in 1950 over the question of West German rearmament – only five years after the end of World War II – then the necessity of 'organizing' Western Europe became even more apparent and, for the United States, highly desirable for Cold War purposes. But we must remember that the Atlantic Alliance, one of the means by which the United States might have encouraged Western Europe to submerge its nationalism, has nearly foundered at times over controversial policies such as the rearmament of West Germany or East–West trade. Moreover, NATO has continually been beset with the divisiveness which comes from differing conceptions of national interests, and this tendency is likely to become greater rather than less in the future.

In other words, the United States must accept the fact that its ability to 'organize' Western Europe is limited. The great disparity in power between the United States and the states of Western Europe obviously gives the United States considerable influence over European international politics. But this simply means that, as in the case of nineteenth-century European international politics, the shape of the future will be determined more by the various combinations and permutations of the relative power of particular states than by supranational evolutions encouraged by either the United States for

Western Europe or, for that matter, by the Soviet Union in Eastern Europe. As regards Central Europe, the manner in which the two Germanies may eventually reconcile themselves to each other is not likely to be within a supranational framework of either an Eastern or a Western variety.

Looking at the question of nationalism from a different perspective, we can observe that there are some similarities between the ethnic nationalistic unrest which is accelerating in Eastern Europe and the ethnic nationalistic unrest that resulted in the break-up of the Austro-Hungarian and Turkish Ottoman Empires. Taking a long view, we should acknowledge that the Soviet Union has borne the brunt of controlling the tendency for conflict in this area, even while imposing an unattractive form of authoritarian control over these restless national minority populations. American resentment over the means by which this control has been exercised, and hostility towards the ideological backdrop which has served as a justification for these means, should not blind us to the realization that, with the demise of the League of Nations system of collective security and with the inability of the Soviet Union and the United States to work together in a permanent coalition through the medium of the United Nations Security Council, no effective international system other than Soviet Russian hegemony now exists to forestall a resurgence of the internecine warfare which is so much a history of Central Europe and the Balkans, and which has drawn in armed forces from outside the area in war after war. The fact that the United States has not chosen to intervene on the side of these minority populations against the Soviet Union, when the opportunities presented themselves, does not weaken this observation. And, very likely, the United States may have to accept at least tacitly some version of the so-called Brezhnev Doctrine of limited sovereignty for Eastern Europe if an all-European political settlement is to be arrived at. The problem is to create politically tolerable circumstances in which the rivalries endemic in this area can be limited or 'dampened down' without introducing brute force to impose settlements or to preclude changes which might be beneficial. In other words, we must ask the question: what kind of an all-European security system can be devised which can accommodate itself to the nationalistic yearnings and hostilities of these populations without being so unstable as to bring on more warfare in Europe?

## THE CENTRAL PLACE OF WEST GERMANY IN EUROPEAN
## INTERNATIONAL POLITICS

It is important to place the politics of Europe into both a short-term and a long-term perspective. In the short-term consideration, the bifurcation of Europe into two sub-regions after World War II remains the prime political reality. The consequent pluralism of the Western European and the Atlantic area and the more hegemonial nature of the Eastern European area does not detract from their essential regional 'Europeanness' and, in fact, leads to the long-term consideration that the nationalistic particularisms of the various states of both Eastern and Western Europe will form the nature of the associations of each with their respective Superpower and will continue to have an impact on the degree of unity and/or disunity within each sub-region and between the sub-regions. This is especially true as regards West Germany and its relationship with East Germany, with the states of Eastern Europe, and with the Soviet Union. As one observer commented:

The broad alternatives for German security are not much different now than a decade ago, or even two. They amount to a more neutral stance, a role within a truly independent European defense arrangement, or a more independent, assertive position. None of these contingencies is likely, yet none is out of the question.[5]

The central point is that the future of West Germany will be determined essentially according to the character of its relationship to the United States. As discussed in chapter 2, the continuing commitment of American military power to Western Europe, which was formalized through the North Atlantic Treaty, brought its direct intervention into the heart of Europe. We believe that this Atlantic regionalism has been and will continue to be an effective means by which the United States can influence the political–military situation in Western Europe in general and in West Germany in particular, even though periods of NATO 'disarray' will undoubtedly continue to occur. It is significant, for example, that the Christian Democratic Chancellor Helmut Kohl in office argues as strongly for a strong NATO–US nuclear 'presence' in West Germany as did his Social Democratic predecessor Helmut Schmidt.

Although the United States supported the EDC proposals of the 1950s, which would have created a Western European subgrouping within NATO, the Atlantic solution of integrating West Germany directly into the Alliance which finally emerged was consistent with the geopolitical outlook of the United States *vis-à-vis* the Soviet Union. The major appeal of EDC, aside from the fact that these proposals appeared at the time to be the only way to obtain French acquiescence to the rearmament of West Germany, was that EDC could have provided the military dimension of a more broadly conceived Western European sub-regional structure. In the 1980s, such a sub-regional military dimension probably would not be entirely unwelcome to the United States if it were linked firmly to NATO and to the political decision-making organs of the EC, and perhaps through the WEU which, although largely moribund during the last decade, may become a future framework for a European defence build-up.

A variety of other proposals have been put forward over the years to rearrange the Atlantic connection, including a dumbbell configuration of linked but equal partners; a multilateral force (MLF) to share United States nuclear military power with its allies in NATO; the withdrawal of American troops to force the Western European allies to do more (in the 1960s this idea was expressed through the periodic submittal in the Senate of the so-called Mansfield Resolution and more recently (1984) by a resolution introduced by Senator Sam Nunn); the decoupling of American strategic power from Europe in the context of a US–Western European theatre deterrent; and a strengthened conventional defence which would reduce NATO's dependence on nuclear weapons for Western Europe's defence (currently being advocated by General Bernard Rogers, the NATO Supreme Allied Commander Europe – SACEUR).[6]

This leads us to a second major observation about American post-World War II policy towards Western Europe, which is that in economic affairs an indirect approach has been used in order to encourage the Western European states to develop multinational institutions of economic co-operation that would deter any revival of Franco–German hostilities and that would deter or ameliorate various forms of economic conflict. The economic power of West Germany has so far been sublimated primarily to the need for West Germany to remain a reliable partner with both the United States and France. It might become very difficult, however, to continue to separate the promotion of Western European – and particularly West German – sub-regional economic interests from the West German commitment to preserve an Atlantic political-military solidarity.

Although not probable at present, further strengthening of the European Monetary Sytem (EMS) even taking on in the foreseeable future the responsibilities of a reserve currency with likely periodic revaluations of the DM, and therefore become less dependent on the US trade dollar. Overall East–West trade relations, as discussed in chapters 3 and 4, are also important factors when weighing the economic role of West Germany between East and West.

It is not inaccurate to say that, although the United States has achieved a high degree of success in its post-World War II policy towards Western Europe, centred on a strong identification with West Germany, the greatest threat to this policy has been the gradual reduction in the political cohesiveness of NATO, and hence in the strength and efficacy of the Atlantic connection. In this respect, we can see some similarities to the politics of Europe in the late nineteenth century. The weakening of the Concert of Europe had resulted from changes in the perceptions of national interest (and perhaps national purpose) of the members, which was due in turn to economic and social developments throughout Europe. The same has been happening in NATO. Examples are: widespread popular resistance to the introduction in 1983 and 1984 by the United States of nuclear weapons in Western Europe and an increasing trend toward neutralism among West European publics; the British opposition to the American 'rescue mission' in Grenada in 1983; the French opposition to American policy in Central America in 1982; general opposition of Western Europe (and particularly France) to American policy in South-East Asia in the 1960s and 1970s; the persistent Greek-Turkish hostility over Cyprus; and conflicting attitudes towards East–West trade (both 'strategic' and otherwise).

Furthermore, the cementing of a common ideology – either the political one of defending and promoting liberal democracy, or the economic one of unifying Western Europe through functional integration – no longer carries much force as a determinant of national policy in the West. As former West German Chancellor Helmut Schmidt put it:

We're afraid of strategy guided by ideology. We're looking for strategy guided by experience and competence. . . . You might think of Germany as being a very small territory – say, the territory of Louisiana and Mississippi combined – but you have 60 million people living in that little territory and seven armies in that territory – and 5,000 nuclear weapons.[7]

By the same token, the preservation of Marxist–Leninist solidarity in the Socialist bloc of Eastern Europe no longer serves as a universally accepted guide for national action.

The fact that NATO has so far ratified the *status quo* rather than acted as an agent of change has created some dilemmas in defining NATO's mission and purpose. This has produced contradictory strains in West Germany's self-image, because the desire for eventual unification can lead to a weakening of the ties with the United States and with the EC. This may be so even though in the Bonn Conventions concluded in 1952 with the United States, Britain and France, the three Western Powers assumed responsibility for Germany as a whole as follows: 'A unified Germany enjoying a liberal-democratic constitution, like that of the Federal Republic, and integrated within the European Community'. However, with the signing of the Helsinki Accords in 1975, the post-World War II territorial *status quo* was affirmed. Treaties already had been concluded in 1972 with the Soviet Union, Poland and Czechoslovakia which had the effect of removing West German irredentist claims from the diplomatic agenda of West Germany and these neighbouring states. However, it should be noted that the anticipation of a unified Germany expressed in the Bonn Conventions reflects the Preamble and other provisions of the Basic Law (constitution) of the Federal Republic looking forward to the eventual reunification of the two Germanies. Indeed, there has always been a strong current in West German public opinion that the goal of German unity must be pursued although the expectation of realizing this goal has been quite low.[8]

Nevertheless, the desire for German reunification has been an important incentive to improve the relationship between West Germany and East Germany and was a major motivation for the formulation of former Chancellor Willy Brandt's *Ostpolitik*. The basic sources for this policy, whose broad goals have been adopted by Brandt's successors in the West German chancellorship, remain operative in the 1980s and fuel the temptation to keep alive the prospect of closer political as well as trade and social ties between the two Germanies. Hence, a constant source of uncertainty is injected into Western European alliance politics which can have a potential weakening effect in NATO cohesiveness. Put in other terms, although West Germany wants a firm American deterrent force to confront the Soviet Union in Central Europe, it does not want a bellicose United States threatening to initiate a devastating conflict that would engulf West Germany or drive apart the two Germanies. Anxieties therefore are bound to exist in the American–West German relationship which the Soviet Union will do everything to foster.

In summary, there has been genuine concern about the possibility that a politically weakened NATO would result in a relaxation of the Atlantic political-military connection. In fact, it is difficult today to know just what 'cohesiveness' means. Could it be the confidence each NATO member-state has in the other member-states' (and particularly the United States') determination to come to the aid of one of their number if threatened or attacked? Is it the measure of the willingness of the states to build up their conventional defence forces and to deploy them in a concerted fashion? Is it the ability or inability of the Western European member-states to influence Soviet–US relations, and in particular those dealing with nuclear matters? These questions, and others discussed in chapter 8, all bear on the tendency of states, even in today's interdependent world, to be more concerned about their own welfare – or perceived interests – than about the welfare of their neighbours or friends.

### THE POLITICAL–MILITARY DIMENSION

Through its participation in the short-lived Strategic Arms Reduction Talks (START) with the Soviet Union, the United States manifested its desire to pursue the possibilities of strategic détente (i.e., nuclear arms limitation and/or control) with the Soviet Union. Ironically, if revived in any significant way, START, or some variation thereof may appear to weaken the resolve of the United States to protect the interests of its Western European allies against Soviet blandishments. Consequently, another problem facing the immediate future is the need for the United States to contain or control its arms race with the Soviet Union, while at the same time reassuring its Western European (and presumably equally anti-Soviet) allies that it still harbours intentions of destroying the USSR if the peace and security of Western Europe are endangered.

But there is little likelihood that any East–West negotiations will succeed in the foreseeable future, even though preliminary negotiations take place in 1985. Two reasons lend credence to this bleak prognosis: first, the Soviet Union seems to be intent on retaining its superiority in land-based strategic launchers because this is perceived as providing an important military advantage gained since the early 1960s in the competition with the United States. Clearly, the Soviet Union has not been able to realize Nikita Khrushchev's boast to 'bury' the United States economically; in fact, its economic performance during the last decade has been extremely weak and is faltering badly. Second, the climate for the negotiations has been deteriorating, mostly because of the sharp anti-Soviet and anti-Communist rhetoric that emanated from the first Reagan Administration and especially from the President himself. Accusing the Soviet leadership again and again of cheating and immorality, and labelling the Soviet Union as the centre of all evil may make useful domestic political headlines in the United States, but it is poor diplomacy and has dismayed most allied governments and peoples. This rhetoric was even stronger in the aftermath of the downing of the Korean passenger plane KAL-007 by Soviet interceptors. Regardless of how we may judge the Soviet government as such, it speaks as a Superpower and such attacks tend to push the Soviet Union into a diplomatic and propaganda corner which has produced many negative reactions such as compounding arms control discussions, already highly complex.

As far as the INF negotiations are concerned, they have already fallen victim to the circumstances outlined in the preceding paragraph. Following a favourable vote in the West German Bundestag in November 1983, the United States began deploying the first Pershing II missiles and this became the trigger for the Soviet delegation to the INF talks to walk out, and the START talks were also suspended. (Cruise missiles had begun to arrive in Great Britain a few days earlier.) On the heels of the walkout, Soviet leader Yuri Andropov announced retaliatory measures 'to ensure the security of the USSR' and its allies.[9] These measures consisted of the deployment of additional SS-20 missiles, nuclear weapons in Czechoslovakia and East Germany and possibly Bulgaria, and additional submarine-launched missiles near the coastline of the United States. Further actions were discussed at a later meeting of WTO defence ministers in Sofia, Bulgaria. Without doubt, the extremely short flight time of the Pershing II from launch to target in the USSR has greatly increased the already existing security anxieties of the Soviet leaders. Clearly, the break-off of the INF negotiations by the Soviet-Union, the deployment of the new American missiles in Western Europe, and the additional deployment of Soviet nuclear weapons have constituted a serious escalation of tensions in Europe and have increased the danger of 'hair-triggering' and unforeseen disasters.[10] The death of Yuri Andropov and the succession of Constantin Chernenko to the top leadership of the Soviet Union did not in itself lead to a significant amelioration of the US–Soviet relationship. New developments, however, are unfolding under the leadership of Mikhail Gorbachev.

While Western officials were busy attributing the blame for the situation to the Soviet Union and were urging the Soviet negotiators to return to the bargaining table, which later they did, the peace movements in various Western European states (West Germany, Britain and the Netherlands) had been unable to persuade their governments and the United States to delay or to cancel deployment of the cruise and Pershing II missiles. Hence, Soviet desires for retaining its perceived nuclear advantages over the West could not be fulfilled by 'piggy-backing' on the peace movements and positive action had to be taken, to maintain its 'superiority'. From the Western perspective, the same logic prevailed to 'catch up', although a number of arms experts and scholars have argued that additional nuclear missiles delivered by NATO aircraft and submarines would have been sufficient to restore the nuclear balance in Europe.[11]

Indeed, the question has been raised whether the famous 'double-track' decision made by NATO in 1970 – negotiations on INF control or, in the event of failure, deployment of missiles – was prudent or in fact necessary.[12] Obviously, it put the Superpowers and their allies in a bind and, moreover, it spawned the peace movements with their domestic and international political consequences. But the decision *was* taken and the likely implications are continuing with more severe confrontation between East and West, possible further build-up of conventional weapons in which WTO already has a substantial and real edge over NATO, and increased difficulties and lower prospects for an eventual bridging of the gap between Western and Eastern Europe, East–West summitry and gesture, concerning nuclear weapons testing to the contrary notwithstanding.[13]

Although public opinion in the United States and in Europe strongly favours the success of these negotiations, their prospects are far from certain given the various political and bureaucratic interests at play in the governments of both Superpowers. Hence, it is not unlikely that the arms build-up and protracted confrontation between East and West will continue. The consequences of pursuing such objectives , including moving ahead with the Strategic Defence Initiative (SDI) or 'Star Wars' could threaten whatever détente is left between Western and Eastern Europe and erode the economic co-operation and the long-range exchanges upon which the Soviet Union depends for improving its declining economic performance, without which it may not be able to sustain the arms race. On the other hand, some confidence in mutually beneficial arms control could be built if future US–Soviet negotiations were to encompass all categories of nuclear weapons testing, and if France and Great Britain were invited and agreed to participate in these talks. Some progress should also be sought in the MBFR negotiations which saw a modest revival in the Spring of 1984.[14]

## THE POLITICAL–ECONOMIC DIMENSION

A major sub-regional change in Western Europe depends on the process of economic and political integration, as we have discussed in chapter 3 and especially in chapters 4 and 5. In spite of recurring rhetoric by governmental leaders and politicians in the EC member-states favouring European union, and despite a variety of plans aiming at the same goal, progress has not been made to any degree. This lack of progress is due in part to different conceptions of the meaning of European union – should it be a federation, confederation or merely a symbol? – and in part of the realities of powerful political and economic interests preferring the benefits of national-istic particularism and the familiarities of traditional political chan-nels to new patterns of influence and rewards. The result has been traditional intergovernmental co-operation with the institutions mostly of the EC, but also with the OECD and other economic organizations providing important and needed services which, however, have furnished little organic input into the integration process. Indeed, integration reached low ebb in December of 1983 when the European Council meeting in Athens could not even agree on the words of a formal communiqué. It seemed to be somewhat rejuvenated by the European Council meetings at Fontainebleau in June 1984, and Milan in June 1984 but the prospects for unification remain bleak as explained in chapters 4 and 5.

This does not mean that common policies and actions within and outside of the EC have not been formulated and implemented, in some cases completely, in others incrementally. The CAP, various aspects of EC commercial policy towards third-states, and the EMS are examples. But with the exception of the CAP, which is supported by the political power of the national farm constituencies and seems to persist generally in spite of vigorous attacks by some governmental elites especially in Britain and West Germany, other co-ordinated policies manifest a substantial degree of fragility. And in fact, this fragility extends to the Common Market itself. On an increasing number of occasions, the basic provisions of free circulation of goods within the EC have been violated, leading to complaints by the disadvantaged member-states to the Commission and the Court of Justice. Although eventually most of these violations were rectified, they are clear evidence that the EC enterprise has changed character and has lost much of the esprit which in the 1950s and early 1960s offered hope to many Europeans and to the United States that the day of sub-regional unity had dawned in Western Europe and a true sub-systemic change was in the process of taking place on the old continent.

National interests have reasserted themselves with a vengeance in both Western and Eastern Europe. Economic and political trade-offs have become the order of the day in intra-EC relations. France's ability to delay the implementation of the truly integrative aspects of the EC, especially as regards agricultural commodity support prices, has been qualified by France's need to obtain concessions from its market partners as it struggles to regain control over its declining economic situation. West Germany, by the same token, while talking strongly of integration and multinational co-operation rather than unilateral action, has at times taken unilateral steps to protect its own economic interests. The persistent demands of Britain for relaxations of commitments will make any progress towards economic unity more difficult to attain although the issue of its budget contribution seems to have been settled in June 1984. Finally, the enlargement of the EC to include Spain and Portugal was held up by France because French farmers feared the competition of their Iberian counterparts.

In identifying the major problem areas of Western European integration, we should ask ourselves: why have the smaller states permitted themselves to be drawn into new and in some cases ambiguous political relationships? The strongest motivation has been the traditional one of weak states – by involving themselves with the strongest friendly state(s) they can influence it (them) both to their benefit and/or to the disadvantage of their chief prospective enemy(ies). Does this principle of international politics apply to post-World War II Western Europe?

Since the 1860s, the major threat to the Netherlands, Belgium, Luxembourg and Italy, as well as to France and Britain, has been Germany. Before then, however, the chief threat to Western Europe, as well as to Britain, had been France. And the chief rival to France often had been Britain. These longstanding national political–security predilections still occupy a place in the national calculations of the states of Western Europe. For example, as pointed out earlier in this book, the purpose of the European Coal and Steel Community was to foreclose the resurgence of German industrial militarism, which would likely be directed against France and the Benelux states. The strong desire of the Benelux states – and especially the Netherlands – to see Britain remain in the Common Market in part goes back to their desire not to be dominated by France. Britain's reluctance, first to commit troops formally in Western Europe in advance of hostilities and then to sign the Treaty of Rome, is consistent with its desire not to become too committed to any one state or group of states in Europe in advance of a clear threat to its and/or their political existence.

### SYSTEMIC CHANGE OR STATUS QUO?

In the Introduction we stated that for an international system to be altered on the global, regional or sub-regional levels, a major if not dramatic change is required. For example, if the existing system of states in sub-regional Western Europe were merged, through integration such as that which the EC process might produce, into a large state covering either all or most of Western Europe, this sub-regional international system would have been radically altered. Or, if the basically confrontational nature of the interrelationship between Eastern and Western Europe were replaced by broad economic and political co-operation with a drastic dismantlement of opposing military forces, the international politics of Europe would be changed dramatically. In both cases, the effects of these changes would reach far beyond regional or sub-regional boundaries and would affect the economic and political relations with both allies, mostly the United States, and adversaries. A very serious systemic change would also follow the outbreak of war between the two Superpowers and their respective allies: given the incredible and unforeseeable consequences of such a disaster, the nature of the resulting system cannot be predicted.

If the discussion in this book has indicated anything, it is that peaceful systemic changes in either the Western or the Eastern European sub-regions are unlikely in the remaining years of this century. This does not mean the complete absence of forces at work that could eventually bring about at least incremental changes. We have noted such forces in both Western and Eastern Europe. In Western Europe, strong aspirations are expressed again and again to see 'Europe speak with one voice'. However, nationalistic egoism and particularistic concerns as well as the political safety of traditional political and administrative channels remain too powerful to permit the unifying or integrative forces to take hold and expand. Nevertheless, the deterioration of the 'Community' threatened in 1983 may have been halted in 1984 at the Fontainebleau 'Summit'. Moreover, appeals to regenerate public support for European Union were being made by eminent intellectuals in full-page newspaper advertisements and in the EP, which in February 1984 adopted a draft for a European Union with increased powers vested in the EC institutions.

The situation is somewhat different in Eastern Europe. There, nationalism serves as a protective shield against Soviet control and Communist uniformism of thought and action. If nationalism could prevail, the current economic and political pattern might well be altered and the states of the sub-region, with the exception of the Soviet Union, could adopt new economic and governmental forms and procedures which, while perhaps not liberal democracies, may be social democratic politically and a mixture of socialist central planning with a private or market orientation economically.

In summary, then, systemic change of the regional and sub-regional economic and political patterns in Europe is unlikely in the foreseeable future. The *status quo* is apt to prevail, although the application of a more skilful diplomacy by all parties involved to overcome the existing serious cleavages and misunderstandings, and drastic improvements in the nature of the rhetoric could set the stage very gradually for incremental amelioration and change.

Eventual systemic transformation may also be aided by social pressures. Students especially have been restive in France and the Netherlands. This student unrest, recently felt in West Germany and most acutely in West Berlin, takes a generalized anti-NATO, anti-American political form. It can also be seen as rising from certain common tensions of industrial societies which cannot help but affect European international politics in the future. We need only recall how the *de facto* alliance of the workers and the students in France in 1968 almost brought down what before then was thought to be the most stable regime among the larger states in Western Europe, and how the sudden rise of West German 'Greenies' in the early 1980s caused the Social Democratic Party to shift leftward.

It is easy to overlook the fact that liberal democratic parliamentary forms of government can be as fragile in Western Europe as elsewhere in the world. The nature and extent of political liberalization varies from time to time in any one state and between states. The hostility of the EC in the 1960s towards Greece under the military dictatorship mentioned earlier shows the disunity which can be brought on from the supplanting of parliamentary democracy through a military coup. Similar hostility resulting in disunity could develop (especially so on the part of the United States) if there emerged an authoritarian regime in Western Europe of the extreme left. Social tensions which are permitted to fester and to sow seeds of internal dissension, as the period between the two world wars showed only too well, can result in political extremism. The consequences could be a greater trend towards nationalistic particularism than has been true recently, and hence a trend which could bring disunity rather than unity.

### TRENDS IN EUROPE WHICH WILL AFFECT EUROPEAN INTERNATIONAL POLITICS IN THE 1980S

1 There may be greater cognizance by the United States and the Soviet Union that they share 'parallel' interests as regards such matters as nuclear weaponry, arms limitation, East–West trade, and continuing political influence over the two Germanies. The current Geneva talks might in time reveal this parallelism. This does not imply that the Superpowers would act in concert, or that they would diminish their efforts to weaken the respective alliance blocs, but rather that there might be some areas of US–Soviet political interaction which would not be limited to considerations of Western European or Eastern European bloc arrangements, or which would necessarily serve the changing perceived political–security interests of particular states in either Western Europe or Eastern Europe. The SDI negotiations possibly could, for example, undermine European confidence in NATO's 'forward strategy' based on mutral assured destruction, but serve the Superpowers' interest in reducing the overall level of threat.

2 There could be increased overt international political manoeuvring among the states of Western and Eastern Europe according to the relative power of the individual states involved that would

encourage sub-regional disunity, taking into account their relationship to one or the other, or both, Superpowers.

3 More evidence of traditional nation-state nationalism in Western Europe and ethnic minority nationalism in Eastern Europe might appear which would have the aspect of weakening, or at least altering, the two-bloc political configuration of Europe. One indication of this is the more openly anti-American expressions and actions based on national political considerations among America's European allies, and the anti-Soviet expressions and actions based on national political considerations among the Soviet Union's European allies.

4 Increasingly direct (or bilateral) diplomatic intercourse might take place between the Soviet Union and the states of Western Europe. On the other hand, there might not be much increase in direct (or bilateral) intercourse between the United States and the Socialist bloc partly because of internal anti-Soviet political pressures in the United States including ideological reasons, and partly because of continuing Soviet political pressures on its allies. There could very likely be increasingly direct (or bilateral) economic and political intercourse between the states of Western Europe with their Eastern European counterparts, all of them seeking to decrease their dependence on their respective Superpower.

5 A gradual trend might emerge which would reveal a continuing Soviet inclination to ensure the political reliability of its Eastern European allies by compelling subservience in national party affairs to the Soviet Union, yet permitting some latitude in economic developmental needs by increasing trade relationships with the West.

6 A gradual trend could emerge which would reveal a distinction on the part of the United States *vis-à-vis* its Western European allies between attempting to maintain their political reliability (i.e., adherence to NATO) and acknowledging their inclinations to engage in proliferating East–West trade relations. The ultimate resolution of the Soviet gas pipeline arrangement with Western Europe is an example.

7 The continuation of the evolution of Western European political–economic unity remains uncertain and co-operation is likely to follow more intergovernmental lines than organic integration, although this does not exclude closer collaboration.

8 The perception of the Soviet threat to Western Europe could

change even more in the 1980s than in the 1970s, with a general consensus emerging that a Soviet conventional military attack would not be mounted unless East Germany were to become much more accommodating to West German overtures and incentives for closer economic and eventually political association. The new deployment of Soviet nuclear medium-range missiles in East Germany may be a signal to both East and West Germany about Soviet security concerns.

9 Within the Atlantic Alliance, there might be a greater trend towards visualizing the *raison d'être* of the Alliance in terms of extra-military activities, while at the same time NATO will probably remain the prime vehicle for the co-ordination of nuclear military affairs among the member-states. New forms of 'nuclear sharing' may well be studied, especially in the context of SDI, but their political implementation could prove as difficult in the future as they have in the past, the current Geneva talks notwithstanding. In spite of demands in the European Parliament and elsewhere that a 'European' military organization be established with a certain degree of autonomy within the Alliance, these efforts are likely to fall short of success.

10 Events outside Europe, and especially in the Middle East, the Mediterranean and in Central America, can affect the international politics of the states of Europe, not necessarily along bloc lines.

11 There will be widespread international political acknowledgement of the existence of two German states; at the same time, the two might draw closer together in economic and trade affairs but not militarily. Both states could become more politically volatile domestically, which would affect their behaviour in international politics. The West German habit of granting trade concessions and loans to East Germany in order to widen areas of all-German humanitarian concerns will continue but may upset West Germany's EC partners. At the same time, the East Germans have granted an increasing number of exit visas to citizens wishing to emigrate to West Germany. Although most of these persons are elderly, a few younger East Germans have also received visas. Whether these developments will continue and constitute a trend for the future is difficult to predict; temporary interruptions of this trend, if it emerges, are likely and the whole pattern is likely to depend on both the future of East–West relations and the interactions within Eastern Europe.

NOTES

1 Max Beloff, *Europe and the Europeans* (London: Chatto and Windus, 1957), p. 49.
2 The notion of a reunited neutralized Germany keeps reappearing. See, for example, Norman Birnbaum, 'Consider a Neutral, Reunified Germany', *New York Times*, 1 December 1983.
3 The most recent attempt to bring about a successful renegotiation, at the Athens 'Summit' meeting of the ten EC member-states in December 1983, ended in an impasse, but the Brussels and Fontainebleau 'Summits' in March and June 1984 made progress.
4 A book which discusses the notion that there is an increasing erosion of consensus among the states of Western Europe and North America that threatens the future of NATO is Frans A. M. Alting von Geusau, ed., *Allies in a Turbulent World: Challenges to U.S. and Western European Cooperation* (Lexington, Mass., Lexington Books, 1982).
5 Peter H. Merkl, ed., *West German Foreign Policy: Dilemmas and Directions* (Chicago: The Chicago Council on Foreign Relations, 1982), p. 29.
6 These points are discussed further in the Atlantic Council Policy Paper, *Arms Control, East–West Relations and the Atlantic Alliance: Closing the Gaps* (Washington, DC: The Atlantic Council, 1983). See also *Strengthening Conventional Deterrence in Europe: Proposals for the 1980s*, Report of the European Security Study, The American Academy of Arts and Sciences (New York: St Martin's Press, 1983), Part I.
7 'Schmidt Raps U.S. Policy in 3rd World', *The Times–Picayune/The States–Item* (New Orleans), 20 October 1983, p. 10.
8 For details see Werner J. Feld, *West Germany and the European Community* (New York; Praeger, 1981), chapters 5 and 6.
9 *Times–Picayune* (New Orleans), 25 November 1983.
10 See Mark A. Uhlig, 'Before High Noon', *New York Times*, 6 December 1983, for a discussion of ways to avoid a 'hairtrigger world'.
11 *Defense Monitor*; David Holloway, 'The View from the Kremlin', *The Wilson Quarterly* (Vol. VII, No. 5, Winter 1983), pp. 102–11.
12 Graeme Paxton, 'INF and Perceptions of the Atlantic Security: A Time for Change?' Paper presented to the Annual Meeting of the Committee on Atlantic Studies, September 23–25, 1983, Racine, Wisconsin.
13 The build-up of conventional weapons was, in fact, emphasized at the NATO Ministerial Meeting of December 1983. See also *Strengthening Conventional Deterrence in Europe*, op. cit.
14 For details, see Agence Europe, *Bulletin*, 9 February 1984.

# The North Atlantic Treaty and the Warsaw Treaty: A Comparison*

| **THE NORTH ATLANTIC TREATY** | **THE TREATY OF FRIENDSHIP, CO-OPERATION AND MUTUAL ASSISTANCE** (Warsaw Pact) |
|---|---|
| *Place and date of signature* <br> Washington, DC, 4 April 1949 | *Place and date of signature* <br> Warsaw, 14 May 1955 |
| *Membership* | *Membership* |
| Sixteen countries: Belgium, Canada, Denmark, France, Federal Republic of Germany, Greece, Iceland, Italy, Luxembourg, the Netherlands, Norway, Portugal, Turkey, United Kingdom, United States. (Greece and Turkey acceded to the Treaty in 1952; the Federal Republic of Germany in 1955; Spain in 1982.) | Eight countries: USSR, Poland, the GDR, Czechoslovakia, Rumania, Bulgaria, Hungary and Albania. (On 3 December 1961 diplomatic relations between the USSR and Albania lapsed. Since then Albania has not in practice participated in any Warsaw Pact activities. On 12 September 1968 Albania denounced the Treaty.) |
| *Duration* | *Duration* |
| Indefinite duration. After the Treaty has been in force twenty years, any Party may cease to be a Party one year after deposit of its notice of denunciation. | Twenty years, with automatic prolongation for another ten years for those members who have not served notice of denunciation one year before the twenty-year period expired. |

* *Source*: NATO Information Service, reprinted 1976.

The Warsaw Pact and the North Atlantic Treaty have often been compared and contrasted. In reality, the two are very different, especially as regards their origins and the structures of their organizations, as will be clear from the following brief analysis of both systems.*

## THE ALLIANCES IN THEIR HISTORICAL CONTEXT

The North Atlantic Treaty was signed in Washington on 4 April 1949, following an intiative by a number of European countries and Canada. It was prompted by fear of the possible use of force in Europe, as in the Communist *coup d'état* in Prague (1948) and the Berlin Blockade (1948–9). It was ratified (on 24 August 1949) after extensive parliamentary debate in member countries.

The creation of the Warsaw Pact began at a conference of Communist bloc leaders in December 1954, called by the Soviet Union. On 11 May 1955 (six days after the Federal German Republic joined NATO as a result of the Paris Agreements of October 1954) the USSR organized at Warsaw a 'Conference of European Countries for the Protection of Peace and Security of Europe'. On 14 May the Pact was signed between the USSR, Albania, Bulgaria, Czechoslovakia, Hungary, Poland, Rumania and the GDR.†

### Motives for the Warsaw Pact

The signatories of the Warsaw Pact have always claimed that their initiative was a response to the signing of the Paris Agreements of October 1954. As regards the motives which may have caused the USSR to propose this Pact, it may be recalled that following the death of Stalin in 1953, the USSR intensified its nuclear programme. But since the Eastern bloc was still behind the United States in the nuclear field, it had to rely on its superior conventional military strength. Consequently, a large military force was kept in a high state of readiness, which in turn required a unified command.*

The North Atlantic Treaty constitutes a freely established political Alliance of sovereign and independent member nations. Its organization is subordinated to the political authority of the governments, all of which

* The Warsaw Pact's secrecy about its organizational structure accounts for the vague nature of some of the comparisons.

† The full texts of both Treaties are given on pp. 317–27.

‡ Under the Peace Treaties with Hungary and Romania (1947), the USSR had the right to maintain military forces in these two countries in order to safeguard its lines of communication with its base in Austria. With the signing of the Austrian State Treaty in May 1955, this right lapsed. However, in the meantime, the Warsaw Pact had provided a new basis for stationing Soviet troops in both countries.

are represented on the North Atlantic Council. It should be added that no Allied forces or weapons can be stationed on the territory of a member country of NATO without its agreement.

The Warsaw Pact brings together countries whose governments are controlled by Communist parties in a way which serves to mask the control which the most powerful of them, the Soviet Union, exercises over its allies. The Pact provides primarily for a military system enabling the armed forces of the member states to be placed under Soviet command.

## Duplication of Defence Agreements

The North Atlantic Treaty is the sole defence agreement between Canada and the United States on the one hand and the Western European countries on the other.

The Warsaw Pact, on the contrary, is superimposed upon a series of bilateral mutual aid treaties linking the members to one another. The USSR also concluded status-of-forces agreements with Poland, Hungary, Rumania, and the GDR between December 1956 and May 1957; all these remain in effect, except the one with Romania, which lapsed in June 1958 when Soviet troops left that country. (A status-of-forces agreement was concluded with Czechoslovakia following the 1968 invasion.)

## COMPARATIVE ANALYSIS OF NATO AND WARSAW PACT STRUCTURES

### Differences in Civil Organization

#### Supreme Authority

In the Warsaw Pact Organization the body most nearly corresponding to the North Atlantic Council at ministerial level is the Political Consultative Committee. It is usually composed of Heads of Governments and Chiefs of National Communist Parties, accompanied by Ministers of Foreign Affairs and/or Ministers of Defence.

Although this Committee should, in theory, meet twice a year, it held only about a dozen meetings between 1956 and mid-1970. There is no equivalent to the NATO Council of Permanent Representatives (composed of representatives of member governments meeting at least once a week) or to NATO's numerous specialized committees on military or non-military matters. The Joint Secretariat and the Joint Armed Forces Command of the Warsaw Pact have both been headed normally by Soviet officials.

#### Secretariat

The Secretary General of NATO is also Chairman of the North Atlantic

Council. He is a statesman or diplomat from one of the member countries; there is no prerequisite as to his nationality.

As regards the Warsaw Pact, one of the several Soviet Deputy Foreign Ministers fills the nominal position of Warsaw Pact 'Secretary General', but this title appears to be a minor adjunct to his regular Ministry responsibilities.

## Political Consultation

Political consultation in NATO has become a major function of the North Atlantic Council, assisted by the Political Committee, which also meets at least weekly.

In the Warsaw Pact Organization there has been a 'Permanent Commission' responsible for making recommendations in the field of foreign policy, but it is not clear that this organization still exists. The Foreign Ministers of the Warsaw Pact hold joint meetings once or twice a year.

## Differences in Military Organization

### Military Structure

In NATO the highest military authority, the Military Committee, which is composed of the Chiefs of Staff of the member countries, is subordinate to the political authority, the North Atlantic Council. The Chairman of the Military Committee is elected by the Chiefs of Staff for a two- or three-year period. NATO Supreme Allied Commanders receive their directives from the Military Committee, not directly from any member country.

In the military organization of the Warsaw Pact all key positions are held by Russians. At its head is the Soviet Commander-in-Chief of the Joint Armed Forces of the Warsaw Pact, whose deputies are the Defence Ministers, or other designated military leaders, of the member countries. The Chief of the Soviet Air Defence is also in charge of the air defence system of the Pact. Normally non-Russian senior officers receive extensive political indoctrination in the USSR before appointment. In March 1969 a Committee of Warsaw Pact Defence Ministers was set up, one of a number of changes intended to give the East Europeans a greater voice in the Organization's affairs.*

### Comparative Strengths

Within the Atlantic Alliance the quantitative strength of the armed forces of the United States is about equal to that of the other member countries

---

* The Committee meets rarely. Its functions are not clear.

taken together. Besides the United States, the United Kingdom and France possess nuclear arms.

On the other hand, the position of the Soviet Union in the Warsaw Pact is much more preponderant. Compared with those of the other member countries, the numerical strength of the Soviet Union is in the ratio of approximately 3:1. The USSR is the only country among all Warsaw Pact nations possessing nuclear weapons.

## THE IMPLICATIONS OF THE ABOLITION OF THE ATLANTIC ALLIANCE AND THE WARSAW PACT

If NATO were to be dissolved, its members would lose their principal organization for political and military consultation and co-operation. The West would be deprived of an effective allied defence system, which is of vital importance to its security. The collective military framework provide by the Alliance for the stationing of North American troops in Europe would be removed. If these forces left the European continent, the European member countries of NATO would be separated from their North American allies and thereby be placed in a most unfavourable military position. Their individual national efforts would be no equivalent for the conventional and nuclear forces which the Soviet Union had stationed in Europe.

If the Warsaw Pact were to be abolished, the USSR would be able to maintain the present disposition of its military strength. Moreover, there would remain a network of bilateral treaties in Eastern Europe. The military and political hold over the other member countries of the Pact would not be weakened.* For example, all those provisions of the agreement on the stationing of Soviet forces in Czechoslovakia (October 1968) which are known – as well as the other status-of-forces agreements between the USSR and its Pact allies – are sufficient by themselves to assure continued Soviet military presence.

A withdrawal of Soviet forces from the Warsaw Pact countries in exchange for the departure of United States and other Allied forces from European NATO countries would also change the military balance considerably in favour of the USSR. The Soviet Union, for instance, could return its units quickly to Eastern Europe, while the role of its medium-range missiles targeted on Western Europe would be unaffected, since they are, in any case, stationed within the Soviet Union.

In conclusion, it may be observed that the dissolution of the two Pacts would seriously upset the existing military balance in Europe, unless

---

* Many of these bilateral pacts have recently been strengthened, according to Soviet publications. On 18 May 1968 the Soviet Government newspaper, *Izvestiya*, described the bilateral treaties as supplementing the Warsaw Pact and as 'an organic part of the whole system of agreements uniting the Socialist States of Europe'.

other measures were to be taken contemporaneously – measures which would require fundamental changes in political relations between East and West.

## TEXTS OF NORTH ATLANTIC TREATY AND TREATY OF FRIENDSHIP, CO-OPERATION AND MUTUAL ASSISTANCE

### NORTH ATLANTIC TREATY

(Washington, 4 April 1949)

#### Preamble

The Parties to this Treaty reaffirm their faith in the purposes and principles of the Charter of the United Nations and their desire to live in peace with all peoples and all Governments.

They are determined to safeguard the freedom, common heritage and civilization of their people, founded on the principles of democracy, individual liberty and the rule of law.

They seek to promote stability and well-being in the North Atlantic area.

They are resolved to unite their efforts for collective defence and for the preservation of peace and security.

They therefore agree to this North Atlantic Treaty:

### TREATY OF FRIENDSHIP, CO-OPERATION AND MUTUAL ASSISTANCE*

(Warsaw, 14 May 1955)

#### Preamble

The Contracting Parties, reaffirming their desire for the establishment of a system of European collective security based on the participation of all European States irrespective of their social and political systems, which would make it possible to unite their efforts in safeguarding the peace of Europe:

mindful, at the same time, of the situation created in Europe by the ratification of the Paris Agreements, which envisage the formation of a new military alignment in the shape of 'Western European Union', with the participation of a remilitarized Western Germany and the integration of the latter in the North Atlantic bloc, which increases the danger of another war and constitutes a threat to the national security of peaceable states;

* Translation published in *New Times*, no. 21, 21 May 1955 (Moscow).

*The Articles of the Warsaw Pact are arranged for comparison with corresponding Articles of the NATO Treaty and are not in numerical order.*

being persuaded that in these circumstances the peaceable European States must take the necessary measures to safeguard their security and in the interests of preserving peace in Europe;

guided by the objects and principles of the Charter of the United Nations Organization;

being desirous of further promoting and developing friendship, co-operation and mutual assistance in accordance with the principles of respect for the independence and sovereignty of States and of non-interference in their internal affairs;

have decided to conclude the present Treaty of Friendship, Co-operation and Mutual Assistance and have for that purpose appointed as their plenipotentiaries; (follow the names of the plenipotentiaries of Albania, Bulgaria, Hungary, East Germany, Poland, Romania, the Soviet Union and Czechoslovakia), who, having presented their full powers, found in good and due form, have agreed as follows:

### Article 1

The Parties undertake, as set forth in the Charter of the United Nations, to settle any international dispute in which they may be involved by peaceful means in such a manner that international peace and security and justice are not

### Article 1

The Contracting Parties undertake, in accordance with the Charter of the United Nations Organization, to refrain in their international relations from the threat or use of force, and to settle their international disputes peacefully endangered, and to refrain in their international relations from the threat or use of force in any manner inconsistent with the purposes of the United Nations.

and in such manner as will not jeopardize international peace and security.

*Article 2*

The Contracting Parties declare their readiness to participate in a spirit of sincere co-operation in all international actions designed to safeguard international peace and security, and will fully devote their energies to the attainment of this end.

The Contracting Parties will furthermore strive for the adoption, in agreement with other States which may desire to co-operate in this, of effective measures for universal reduction of armaments and prohibition of atomic, hydrogen and other weapons of mass destruction.

*Article 2*

The Parties will contribute toward the further development of peaceful and friendly international relations by strengthening their free institutions, by bringing about a better understanding of the principles upon which these institutions are founded and by promoting conditions of stability and well-being. They will seek to eliminate conflict in their international economic policies and will encourage economic collaboration between any or all of them.

*Article 8*

The Contracting Parties declare that they will act in a spirit of friendship and co-operation with a view to further developing and fostering economic and cultural relations with one another, each adhering to the principle of respect for the independence and sovereignty of the others and non-interference in their internal affairs.

### Article 3

In order more effectively to achieve the objectives of this Treaty, the Parties, separately and jointly, by means of continuous and effective self-help and mutual aid, will maintain and develop their individual and collective capacity to resist armed attack.

(Also see NAT Article 9.)

### Article 4

The Parties will consult together whenever, in the opinion of any of them, the territorial integrity, political independence or security of any of the Parties is threatened.

### Article 5

The Parties agree that an armed attack against one or more of them in Europe or North America shall be considered an attack against them all, and consequently they

### Article 5

The Contracting Parties have agreed to establish a Joint Command of the armed forces that by agreement among the Parties shall be assigned to the Command, which shall function on the basis of jointly established principles. They shall likewise adopt other agreed measures necessary to strengthen their defensive power, in order to protect the peaceful labours of their peoples, guarantee the inviolability of their frontiers and territories and provide defence against possible aggression.

### Article 3

The Contracting Parties shall consult with one another on all important international issues affecting their common interests, guided by the desire to strengthen international peace and security.

They shall immediately consult with one another whenever, in the opinion of any one of them, a threat of armed attack on one or more of the Parties to the Treaty has arisen, in order to ensure joint defence and the maintenance of peace and security.

### Article 4

In the event of armed attack in Europe on one or more of the Parties to the Treaty by any State or group of States, each of the Parties to the Treaty, in the agree that, if such an armed attack occurs, each of them, in exercise of the right of individual or collective self-defence recognized by Article 51 of the Charter of the United Nations, will assist the Party of Parties so attacked by taking forthwith, individually and in concert with the other Parties, such action as it deems necessary, including the use of armed force, to restore and maintain the security of the North Atlantic area.

Any such armed attack and all measures taken as a result thereof shall immediately be reported to the Security Council. Such measures shall be terminated when the Security Council has taken the measures necessary to restore and maintain international peace and security.

exercise of its right to individual or collective self-defence, in accordance with Article 51 of the Charter of the United Nations Organization, shall immediately, either individually or in agreement with other Parties to the Treaty, come to the assistance of the State or States attacked with all such means as it deems necessary, including armed force. The Parties to the Treaty shall immediately consult concerning the necessary measures to be taken by them jointly in order to restore and maintain international peace and security.

Measures taken on the basis of this Article shall be reported to the Security Council in conformity with the provisions of the Charter of the United Nations Organization. These measures shall be discontinued immediately the Security Council adopts the necessary measures to restore and maintain international peace and security.

### Article 6

For the purpose of Article 5, an armed attack on one or more of the Parties is deemed to include an armed attack:

on the territory of any of the Parties in Europe or North America, on the Algerian Departments of France,* on the

* On 16 January 1963 the French Representative made a statement to the North Atlantic Council on the effects of the independence of Algeria on certain aspects of the North Atlantic Treaty. The Council noted that in so far as the former Algerian Departments of France were concerned, the relevant clauses of this Treaty had become inapplicable as from 3 July 1962.

territory of Turkey or on the islands under the jurisdiction of any of the Parties in the North Atlantic area north of the Tropic of Cancer;

on the forces, vessels, or aircraft of any of the Parties, when in or over these territories or any other area in Europe in which occupation forces of any of the Parties were stationed on the date when the Treaty entered into force or the Mediterranean Sea or the North Atlantic area north of the Tropic of Cancer.

### Article 7

This Treaty does not affect, and shall not be interpreted as affecting, in any way the rights and obligations under the Charter of the Parties which are members of the United Nations, or the primary responsibility of the Security Council for the maintenance of international peace and security.

### Article 8

Each Party declares that none of the international engagements now in force between it and any other of the Parties or any third State is in conflict with the provisions of this Treaty, and undertakes not to enter into any international engagement in conflict with this Treaty.

### Article 7

The Contracting Parties undertake not to participate in any coalitions or alliances and not to conclude any agreements whose objects conflict with the objects of the present Treaty.

The Contracting Parties declare that their commitments under existing international treaties do not conflict with the provisions of the present Treaty.

## Article 9

The Parties hereby establish a Council, on which each of them shall be represented to consider matters concerning the implementation of this Treaty. The Council shall be so organized as to be able to meet promptly at any time. The Council shall set up such subsidiary bodies as may be necessary; in particular it shall establish immediately a Defence Committee which shall recommend measures for the implementation of Articles 3 and 5.

## Article 6

For the purpose of the consultations among the Parties envisaged in the present Treaty, and also for the purpose of examining questions which may arise in the operation of the Treaty, a Political Consultative Committee shall be set up, in which each of the Parties to the Treaty shall be represented by a member of its Government or by another specifically appointed representative.

The Committee may set up such auxiliary bodies as may prove necessary.
(Also see WP Article 5.)

## Article 10

The Parties may, by unanimous agreement, invite any other European State in a position to further the principles of this Treaty and to contribute to the security of the North Atlantic area to accede to this Treaty. Any State so invited may become a Party to the Treaty by depositing its instrument of accession with the Government of the United States of America. The Government of the United States of America will inform each of the Parties of the deposit of each such instrument of accession.

## Article 9

The present Treaty is open to the accession of other States irrespective of their social and political systems, which express their readiness by participation in the present Treaty to assist in uniting the efforts of the peaceable States in safeguarding the peace and security of the peoples. Such accession shall enter into force with the agreement of the Parties to the Treaty after the declaration of accession has been deposited with the Government of the Polish People's Republic.

## Article 11

This Treaty shall be ratified and its provisions carried out by the Parties in accordance with their

## Article 10

The present Treaty is subject to ratification, and the instruments of ratification shall be deposited with respective constitutional processes. The instruments of ratification shall be deposited as soon as possible with the Government of the United States of America, which will notify all the other signatories of each deposit. The Treaty shall enter into force between the States which have ratified it as soon as the ratifications of the majority of the signatories, including the ratifications of Belgium, Canada, France, Luxembourg, the Netherlands, the United Kingdom and the United States, have been deposited and shall come into effect with respect to other States on the date of the deposit of their ratifications.

the Government of the Polish People's Republic.

The Treaty shall enter into force on the day the last instrument of ratification has been deposited. The Government of the Polish People's Republic shall notify the other Parties to the Treaty as each instrument of ratification is deposited.

### Article 12

After the Treaty has been in force for ten years, or at any time thereafter, the Parties shall, if any of them so requests, consult together for the purpose of reviewing the Treaty, having regard for the factors then affecting peace and security in the North Atlantic area, including the development of universal as well as regional arrangements under the Charter of the United Nations for the maintenance of international peace and security.

### Article 11, 2nd paragraph

Should a system of collective security be established in Europe, and a General European Treaty of Collective Security concluded for this purpose, for which the Contracting Parties will unswervingly strive, the present Treaty shall cease to be operative from the day the General European Treaty enters into force.

### Article 13

After the Treaty has been in force for twenty years, any Party may cease to be a Party one year after its

### Article 11, 1st paragraph

The present Treaty shall remain in force for twenty years. For such Contracting Parties as do not one notice of denunciation has been given to the Government of the United States of America, which will inform the Governments of other Parties of the deposit of each notice of denunciation.

### Article 14

This Treaty, of which the English and French texts are equally authentic, shall be deposited in the archives of the Government of the United States of America. Duly certified copies will be transmitted by that Government to the Governments of the other signatories.

year before the expiration of this period present to the Government of the Polish People's Republic a statement of denunciation of the Treaty, it shall remain in force for the next ten years.

### Article 11, 3rd and 4th paragraphs

Done in Warsaw on 14 May 1955, in one copy each in the Russian, Polish, Czech and German languages, all texts being equally authentic. Certified copies of the present Treaty shall be sent by the Government of the Polish People's Republic to all the Parties to the Treaty.

In witness thereof the plenipotentiaries have signed the present Treaty and affixed their seals.

### Communiqué on the ESTABLISHMENTS OF A JOINT COMMAND
of the Armed Forces of the Signatories to the Treaty of Friendship, Co-operation and Mutual Assistance
(Warsaw, 14 May 1955)

In pursuance of the Treaty of Friendship, Co-operation and Mutual Assistance between the People's Republic of Albania, the People's Republic of Bulgaria, the Hungarian People's Republic, the German Democratic Republic, the Polish People's Republic, the Rumanian People's Republic, the Union of Soviet Socialist Republics and the Czechoslovak Republic, the signatory States have decided to establish a Joint Command of their armed forces.

The decision provides that general questions relating to the strengthening of the defensive power and the organization of the Joint Armed Forces of the signatory States shall be subject to examination by the Political Consultative Committee, which shall adopt the necessary decisions.

Marshal of the Soviet Union I. S. Koniev has been appointed Commander-in-Chief of the Joint Armed Forces to be assigned by the signatory States.

The Ministers of Defence or other military leaders of the signatory States are to serve as Deputy Commanders-in-Chief of the Joint Armed Forces, and shall command the armed forces assigned by their respective States to the Joint Armed Forces.

The question of the participation of the German Democratic Republic in measures concerning the armed forces of the Joint Command will be examined at a later date. A Staff of the Joint armed Forces of the signatory States will be set up under the Commander-in-Chief of the Joint Armed Forces, and will include permanent representatives of the General Staffs of the signatory States.

The Staff will have its headquarters in Moscow.

The disposition of the Joint Armed Forces in the territories of the signatory States will be

> effected, by agreement among the
> States, in accordance with the
> requirements of their mutual
> defence.

## BILATERAL TREATIES OF FRIENDSHIP, CO-OPERATION AND MUTUAL ASSISTANCE SIGNED BY WARSAW PACT MEMBERS

The treaties are valid for a period of twenty years and, unless indicated differently, commit the co-signatories to immediate mutual assistance – including military assistance – in case of armed aggression. They were signed in the years indicated in the table below, just before expiration of slightly different treaties signed some twenty years earlier. These original treaties (indicated in brackets) were aimed in particular at mutual defence against aggression by a re-armed German state (with the exception of the treaties concluded with the Soviet-Occupied Zone of Germany in 1950; the latter concerned cultural, technical, economic and financial but no defence co-operation).

# Index